Shattered Illusions

H. L. Chandler

A Wings ePress, Inc.
Mystery/Suspense Novel

Wings ePress, Inc.

Edited by: Jeanne Smith
Copy Edited by: Joan C. Powell
Executive Editor: Jeanne Smith
Cover Artist: Trisha FitzGerald-Jung
Image: Pixabay

All rights reserved

Names, characters and incidents depicted in this book are products of the author's imagination or are used fictitiously. Any resemblance to actual events, locales, organizations, or persons, living or dead, is entirely coincidental and beyond the intent of the author or the publisher.

No part of this book may be reproduced or transmitted in any form or by any means, electronic or mechanical, including photocopying, recording, or by any information storage and retrieval system, without permission in writing from the publisher.

Wings ePress Books
www.wingsepress.com

Copyright © 2021 by: Louise Chandler Guffy
ISBN 13: 978-1-61309-557-7

Published In the United States Of America

Wings ePress Inc.
3000 N. Rock Road
Newton, KS 67114

What They Are Saying About

Shattered Illusions

Shattered Illusions by H. L. Chandler grabs your interest immediately with the murder of Kate's brother, Henry, and a phone call threatening her own life if she does not do as they say.

We feel inside Kate's mind and follow her fears as she struggles to find Henry's killer. But the killer is one step ahead of her and it may end up being Kate who is in danger.

Shattered Illusions is an action-packed thriller that will leave you turning pages into the night.

H.L. Chandler has the rare ability to be interesting and provocative. My admiration is complete. I give this story a five-star rating.

—Marcia Marlow, Reading Specialist
Missouri Southern University.

Dedication

To readers, who make writing worthwhile. What would authors do without you? Thanks for spending time with this story.

* * *

One

Henry Shore had met with Leland Webern on a Monday. By Tuesday afternoon, Henry was dead and Leland had disappeared. Henry and his sister, Kate, had moved to Greenfield six months before the tragedy. When Leland Webern had arrived in town on Monday, he had gone straight to the Shore home. Now Leland was missing, and the police suspected him of shooting Henry.

"I simply do not understand," said Kate. "Why would Leland kill Henry? I don't think Henry knew him very well. I certainly didn't know him. Why would Henry invite him to stay overnight with us if he was some sort of threat?"

"There, there," said Ronda, "try not to think about it. Besides, there is no proof Leland killed him."

"Where is he then? The police certainly believe he did it, or that I've made him up to cover my guilt."

"I'm just sorry I didn't meet him...I'd vouch for you and they'd have to believe you," Ronda said, her dangling earrings swaying.

Kate and Ronda were sitting on the swing in the side porch of Ronda's house. *The Daily News*, Greenfield's newspaper, lay on the floor at Ronda's feet. In the two weeks immediately after the death and disappearance, the story made bold headlines. In the following days, when there was nothing new to report, it slipped to a back page, soon making no appearance at all. Forgotten by most of Greenfield's twenty thousand residents.

Ronda was Kate's only friend in Greenfield. She was a widow who lived nearby and, having time on her hands, had called on Kate. Otherwise, they probably would not have met because Kate was too reserved to make the first move. Besides, Kate thought Ronda had shown more than a passing interest in Henry. She was near Henry's age of forty. She had moved to Greenfield a few months before the Shores, so she too was relatively new in town.

Kate was slightly taller than average and had always been slender, but now she bordered on thin. She had tied her shoulder-length auburn hair in a ponytail revealing what her mother, Grace, had called a strong-featured face. She wore no makeup and preferred tailored clothes because, as Grace had also pointed out, she wasn't the type for frills, so Kate tried to soften her appearance with a gentle manner. Since Henry's death, the grass-green eyes she normally saw in the mirror had turned dark with worry.

In contrast, Ronda was shorter, heavier, and what some would call voluptuous. She kept her short hair colored a pinkish/orange shade nature never intended, while deep red lipstick adorned her round face. Kate didn't wear much jewelry, but she thought the many rings on Ronda's fingers were pretty. She agreed with the old saying about not judging a book by its cover. Ronda looked worldly wise, but she'd been helpful and comforting when Kate had no one else. Ronda lived off her husband's life insurance, which would keep her afloat until, as she put it, *some nice man comes along.*

Henry had been dead for two months; Kate was a nervous wreck and spent more and more time at Ronda's house. She needed the company, but it was also a way to hide from the police. Of course, they could find her if they searched long enough. Kate's overly generous mouth drew up in a knot and her broad forehead wrinkled.

"I don't know how many times I can tell the police I didn't know Mr. Webern before he arrived here."

Ronda fiddled with the string of silver beads at her neck. "You took a shine to him though, didn't you?"

"Who? Oh, you mean Webern. Of course not. I barely knew him."

Kate was thirty-five and her hopes of marriage had grown dim, although there was a spark, enough to stir some interest in Leland when he'd arrived on their doorstep. For the couple of days he was in their home, he'd given Kate the sense he was interested in her, too.

"Just why did he come to see Henry?" Ronda asked.

"I don't know."

"But he stayed overnight in your house. Surely you heard them talking. He and Henry must have said something."

"Do stop, Ronda. You're as bad as the police."

Ronda shrugged. "I'm sorry. It is such a mystery. You can understand people being suspicious."

"Are you suspicious of me? How can you even use the word? I've heard the rumors. How people look when I'm out. I've stayed home because of it. They don't know me. What right do they have to judge me?"

Ronda reached to pat her arm, but Kate jumped up and began to pace.

"One of the detectives pounced on me about Mr. Webern when I made the mistake of referring to him as *Leland*. Asked if I'd known him before. Did he come here at my invitation? Oh, I know where he was heading. Thinking I had him kill Henry."

Kate stopped pacing, placed her hands on the porch railing, lowered her head, and sobbed. Ronda went to her side, putting an arm around her shoulders.

"I'm so sorry, dear. I can't imagine how hard this is for you. Grieving for your brother, wanting justice for his death, and those awful policemen throwing suspicion on you."

Kate clamped her lips and swallowed the last sob. She swiped the tears from her cheeks. No matter how much she talked about what had happened, it did not seem real. She was completely alone. Maybe she should go back to Chicago. Somewhere along the way from college to mid-thirties, she'd lost all close friends. Most of the girls she knew had married, putting distance between them. By the time children arrived, their communication had dwindled to Christmas cards. Male friends had either married or taken off for parts unknown. Kate pasted on a smile and turned from the railing.

"I'm sorry, Ronda. I'm tired. I can't seem to get enough sleep. I'll see you tomorrow."

As Kate headed for the wide steps, Ronda hurried along at her side.

"What will you do for supper? I'll fix something here. Or we can eat out if you like."

Kate started down the steps. "No. I have to fend for myself. I can't go on like this."

Ronda remained on the porch and when Kate reached the sidewalk, she turned and waved. Ronda waved back, and went inside.

It was late afternoon and the mid October sun sent shafts of pale gold slanting through the brown leaves of the oak trees. A slight breeze shook loose a few more dead leaves which fluttered to the sidewalk. Kate took long strides, head down, barely noticing where she stepped. Her boots crunched the dry leaves. She crossed her arms about her waist, holding a thick sweater tight against her body. The day wasn't cold, just cool. Still, Kate shivered and hurried along, eager to reach home. She lived two blocks south and one block east of Ronda. She doubted they would have met if Ronda hadn't brought a small basket of muffins to welcome her and Henry. Ronda had said she knew the house was for sale and when the sold sign went up, she had watched for the new owners.

Before coming to Greenfield, the Shores had lived in Chicago. There the family had for two generations owned Shore Import/ Export Company. When a heart attack killed their father, Henry ran the company alone. Three years ago, they lost their mother, Grace, to cancer. Since Henry and his sister were unmarried, they were the last of that branch of the Shore family. Henry had been married for ten years, but the childless marriage had ended in divorce. His ex, Alisha, had remarried. When Henry had decided to sell Shore Import/Export, Kate had agreed. Henry's reasons seemed sensible, and due to the sale, they did not want for money. Henry had been good with investments. What he'd not been good about was sharing information.

Kate left financial matters to Henry and she ran the domestic side of their lives. In her heart of hearts, she longed for a home of her own to manage. Yet, she was no beauty and the young men who did show an interest had been discouraged by her father, and yes, Henry as well. It wasn't voiced, but always in subtle ways suggested, that the suitors were fortune hunters. Before any meaningful relationship could form, each man drifted away, leaving Kate with the family's condolences like, *He wasn't worth much, you're better off without him.*

As she hurried along, the brisk air helped to clear her mind. Earlier, on Ronda's porch, she'd almost lost control. She rarely cried, and never in front of anyone. It was embarrassing. People thought she was shy, but she really wasn't. If the need arose, she could speak out as well as anyone. For most of her life, there simply had been no reason to assert herself. She had all she needed. Life, if not perfect, had been satisfactory. She was practical enough to know no one has everything she wants.

When Henry had sold their business, he had taken the Greenfield house as part payment. He'd mentioned something about a tax advantage. The houses in the small subdivision on the edge of town were newer than the ones closer to the center of Greenfield. Henry had also said he was ready for a quiet life in a peaceful setting. Kate didn't object. She liked the semi-rural area, the rolling fields making pleasant views in all directions. She had hoped to join some ladies' groups, maybe volunteering at the public library.

When she rounded the corner of Meadow and Vine streets, her house came into view on the far corner of Vine. The house was a two-story country style with a wrap-around porch and a gable roof. Although the exterior design was from a time past, the interior was completely modern. It was large for two people, but Henry had to have an office, and Kate enjoyed the sunroom. Now, the rooms seemed to grow larger and emptier by the day.

Kate did know the next-door neighbors, Mr. and Mrs. Shelden, an elderly couple whose outdoor activities consisted of gardening for her and golfing for him. Before the murder, Alice Shelden had smiled and waved when their paths crossed, but with a crime next door, the Sheldens grew distant. It was just as well. Kate didn't feel like entertaining. To say nothing of the endless questions they might ask.

She checked the mailbox on the street, found nothing but several advertisements. She folded them and briskly went along the brick walkway to the porch, where she picked up a copy of the newspaper. As the door closed behind her, she stepped into a heavy silence, put the papers on a side table in the foyer, and hurried to the kitchen. She needed a cup of hot tea. Pale sunlight streamed through the kitchen windows, giving the room a dusky glow.

While the water heated, Kate removed her sweater and put it over the back of a kitchen chair. The house was comfortably warm; still Kate felt cool. The spells of shivering chill came and went, having nothing to do with the actual temperature. It was strictly emotional, but so far, she had little control over it. When the teakettle sang, she poured the boiling water over the tea bag in a china cup.

Sitting at the table, Kate stared into the cup before her. Small tendrils of steam twisted and swirled into the air above the tea. What was she going to do? Loneliness settled in the pit of her stomach. One by one, she had lost her family members. When Henry Senior passed away, there was her mother, Grace, to care for. Actually, caring for Grace wasn't a new task. Grace had been a beautiful woman, full of life, always giving parties, making everyone laugh. Grace Shore was the center of their social world, but as a homemaker, she was a disaster. From the time Kate could walk and talk, she had been a small utility for her mother. Used for everything from carrying messages to the two Henrys to finding a lost hairbrush or earring. Kate had been happy in Grace's service. Grace had been like a fragile, beautiful butterfly. Something to be sheltered and cherished.

When Kate was small, Grace had often hugged her and said what a good girl she was. Grace had named her Katherine; she said it sounded strong and trustworthy, but she'd ended up being Kate to everyone else. She had felt like a tiny star circling a shining sun, glad to be in its orbit. In her teenage years, when friends told Kate her family was using her, she had laughed. Different people have different talents, she told them. Mother's is to make people happy, and I'm happy to help her. Kate had grieved when her father died, but the loss of her mother still hurt. She missed Grace's smile and her laughter.

Kate took a sip of tea, her thoughts filled with the past. She wished Grace were still alive. She wouldn't help in a practical way, but with Grace to care for, Kate wouldn't have to decide what to do. She supposed this would not be a problem for other people. To most, it would mean freedom instead of the empty future she envisioned.

She missed Henry, but he'd been gone so short a time she still expected him to walk into the kitchen, or call to her from his office. Even the funeral had not settled as a reliable memory. She had to concentrate, and go over the events to see them clearly. Otherwise, those days were a misty blur. The funeral had been simple. She had Henry's body flown back to Chicago and buried him in the same cemetery as their parents. Years before, Henry Senior had purchased an entire row of gravesites for the family. Standing beside Henry's grave, Kate had imagined occupying the next plot. She had no idea who would arrange for her.

She recalled looking at the people surrounding the grave. Uncle Byron Shore, her father's brother, his wife Elaine and their two grown sons, Michael and Thomas. Both of them married with children of their own. Neither Michael nor Thomas's family attended. Byron and Elaine lived in New York. Before Kate was born, something had split the family. The only times Kate saw her uncle, aunt, or cousins was when someone died. She hadn't expected much support from them, being a bit surprised they had done more than simply send flowers. Even though they had attended her father's funeral, and even Grace's, their showing up to bury Henry made her wonder why they were there. More surprising was finding Henry's ex-wife there along with her husband, Jared. Although, considering Jared Roth was now part owner of Shore I/E, maybe they were there to represent the company.

She had expected Aunt Iris and Uncle Bert to come. Aunt Iris was her mother's sister. Although Iris was as pretty as Grace, she had chosen to be prim rather than flashy. Where Grace would wear bright colors in the latest styles, Iris wore tans, grays, and navy. She even allowed her well-shaped body extra pounds to give herself a solid motherly appearance. Iris was practical and strict; if she had ever broken a rule of any kind, no one knew about it. They were as different as two sisters could be. Kate remembered her mother joking about Iris. *She is a saint!* Grace would laughingly say. *But, she will do anything for you. Remember that, Katherine.* Kate did remember and after the funeral, Aunt Iris proved her sister right. Iris had stopped Kate as they headed for the cars after Henry's burial. She had tucked a lace handkerchief into her black purse, squared her shoulders, and frowned at Kate.

"What will you do now, my girl? You must come live with us. We don't have much excitement in our lives, but we are comfortable in our community. There is always room for a willing worker. Your mother depended upon you; I can see why. You will fit in just fine. This is best for you, Kate."

Kate took another sip of her now cool tea, and tried to remember how she'd answered Aunt Iris. The exact words were lost, but she remembered wanting to run. Iris would capture her; pull her into her world where church and civic service took up every day. Kate had no idea what to make of her life, but she wanted it to be her choice. She had been happy assisting her mother and caring for Henry, at least she thought she had. Now, without a purpose, she was adrift and wondering what was ahead.

The fall sun sank lower in the pale sky, extinguishing the dusky gold shimmer in the kitchen windows. Kate stood and took the half-empty cup to the sink. She should make something for dinner. The refrigerator held plenty of fresh fruit and vegetables, and frozen food filled the freezer. She hadn't been able to curb the habit of sensible grocery shopping; there had been too many years of doing it for the family. Her parents had employed a cook and a housekeeper and Kate had worked closely with them, leaving Grace free for her activities. When it was only she and Henry, Kate had cut back on household help. It had seemed extravagant to pay for work she could do.

Kate stood in front of the kitchen sink and stared out the window. She felt stuck in time and space, no reason to move. There was no one to care for, no task before her. If she were of no use to anyone, she couldn't justify her existence. Somewhere along the line, she had identified so strongly with family members that when they were gone, so was her identity. She wondered if perhaps widows felt the same. A lifetime of caring for a husband and raising children, only to end alone. Those women learned how to cope. Kate knew older women who had started new lives. If they were to go on living, they had to. She knew time helped. Perhaps it would help her.

As lavender shadows lengthened beneath the hedge along the sidewalk and dusk gathered under the eaves of the porch, Kate shuffled her feet, proving she could still move. Even if her mind wasn't ready to function, maybe her body could lead the way. She'd make supper, clean the kitchen afterward, and spent the evening watching some television show. Then a warm bath and to bed...it was the sensible thing to do. She remembered dozens of people at Henry's funeral saying *take care of yourself*. They meant it kindly, but at the same time, it was clear she was her own responsibility. Except for Aunt Iris, and Kate suspected Iris was speaking out of duty and a hope of gaining another pair of working hands. As Kate tore apart some lettuce for a salad, she wondered if Aunt Iris might be her only option. That would be the easy way. If not, she'd have to find some other purpose, a reason to live.

For several weeks, an idea had lurked in the back of her mind. A half-formed thought. A thought she tried hard to reject. It had something to do with an obligation, a duty to her family. It was ridiculous to think there was anything she owed her family at this stage. They were gone. Nothing she could do about it. She had been a faithful, loving daughter and sister, no one could expect more. Yet, as she argued against the nagging feeling, the stronger it became. It offered a reason to go on, a piece of work left undone. One last thing she could do for the family. Still, each time it bubbled to the surface, she turned away from it. If the police hadn't found Leland Webern, or discovered the reason for Henry's death, she certainly couldn't.

When the kitchen phone rang, Kate jumped, her hand knocking over the salad bowl on the counter. Since Henry's murder, the slightest thing startled her. She grabbed a kitchen towel and dried her hands as she rushed to the wall phone.

"Hello?"

"Is this Kate Shore?" asked a harsh male voice.

"Yes?"

"We know your brother told you where it is. If you don't hand it over, you'll end up like Henry. Don't go to the police. Someone will contact you."

"I, I, who is this? What do you want?"

The phone line went silent, an empty dead void.

"Hello. Who is this?" Kate punched the phone connection button. She again cried *hello*, but this time into a dial tone.

Trembling, she hung up and going to the kitchen table dropped onto a chair. She must call the police; tell them someone was threatening her. Maybe they could trace the call. She put a hand over her eyes, bowed her head, and tried to think. The thought that came was, *take care of yourself.* The people at the funeral surely hadn't dreamed their advice would have meaning in a situation such as this. She stood, quickly checked the back door, and found it secure. Making her way through the dining room and on to the front foyer, she checked the alarm system, which seemed to be working. She made the rounds of the windows on the ground floor, closing drapes and looking through the rooms for anything out of place. Henry's office was dark; she hadn't been in there for days. Running up the stairs, she checked the bedrooms and bathrooms. As her heartbeat slowed, she made her way back to the kitchen.

The shutters above the sink were still open. The early night was dark; Kate saw her reflection in the window glass. She crossed to the counter and peered out at the empty porch, while a streetlight on the corner of Vine spread a yellow circle onto the sidewalk. She quickly closed the wooden shutters. She leaned against the counter and tried to think. She had understood the caller's words, but they made no sense. Henry had not told her anything. He had rarely told her anything of real importance. The phone call was more than alarming. The caller had threatened to kill her.

She opened an upper cabinet, took out a glass, and filled it with water. She drank slowly and waited for her hands to stop shaking, and her legs to stop trembling. Yes, she should call the police, but maybe they wouldn't believe her. They'd think it was a trick to throw suspicion away from her. What real protection could they provide; they couldn't put a policeman at her door night and day. Still, she had to let them know of the threat. Kate set the empty glass on the counter, and went to the telephone to dial the Greenfield police. Detective Simpson was not in; she hadn't expected he would be. She didn't remember the names of the other officers who had come after Henry's death, but Simpson had left her his card.

"This is Kate Shore. I want to report a threatening phone call."

"Do you know the caller?"

"No. It has something to do with my brother's death."

"What was said?"

"He wanted to know about something Henry told me, but he hadn't told me anything."

"Did the man threaten to come to your house?"

"No. He said someone would contact me. What are you going to do?" Kate heard the quiver in her voice.

"If you feel in danger, I can send a patrol car to make sure the house is secure. Do you want that?"

Kate pulled a kitchen chair closer and sat. She had suspected they couldn't do much, and she didn't see what a couple of policemen chatting with her would accomplish.

"That's not necessary. I've checked the house. I'm alone. But I thought I should report the call."

"Yes, and I'll make a note in your file."

The woman gave instructions on how to respond to harassing phone calls, about not engaging the caller. Rather, to hang up and record the date and time of the call and the caller's gender along with what he said. Kate thanked the woman for the information and ended the call. She still trembled, but reporting the call had given a small sense of fighting back.

She stood and stepped to the counter, set the overturned salad bowl upright and gathered the spilled lettuce back into it. The little appetite she had had was gone. Still, she hadn't eaten since a bowl of cereal that morning. She needed a decent meal. In the past, she had stayed strong for her family; you can't help others if you are weak. As if from habit, Kate took a chicken breast and some broccoli from the freezer. She finished preparing the salad and set the table...the normal tasks helped settle her.

After setting the oven's timer for the chicken, Kate left the kitchen. A feeling other than fear was growing in her. At first fear had enveloped her, but as the fear faded, something else was taking over. It was a strange feeling, hard to recognize. Yet, slowly she was becoming angry. The anger mingled with the idea that she could still do something for Henry. In the past, she was seldom angry, and never for long. She was more inclined to be hurt rather than angry. When people weren't feeling well, they said sharp things. There were misunderstandings among family members. By the time Kate rationalized the situations, her hurt feelings were resolved. Therefore, the hot flush that made her heart race and her lips tighten was an unfamiliar feeling of wanting to fight back.

She crossed the foyer and entered Henry's office. Since his death, she hadn't used the room. She had gone through the desk, found all the necessary financial records, and using his various passwords, closed his online accounts. Their attorney, Jim Burton, took care of finishing the legal end of Henry's life. Jim was an old man, ready to retire. He'd been the personal attorney for the Shore family for as long as Kate could remember. He had not been involved in the sale of the company...Shore I/E's attorneys had handled it. Touching the switch beside the door, she turned on the overhead light.

Kate reached the desk that faced the door, stepped behind it, pulled back the swivel chair, and sat. The desktop was bare except for a small lamp which she turned on, shedding a glow over the leather insets. She had cleaned out and organized the drawers; she knew what was in each one: stationery, envelopes, nothing important. Yet, she wondered if she had missed something. She drummed her fingers on the desk, her back was rigid and her lips tight. Now the anger was turning to frustration. She had relied upon the police to solve the mystery, but the phone call changed the situation. Maybe Henry had been involved in something that caused his death. She had never questioned anything he did. The business ran smoothly. During the years of Henry's control, the company grew. The growth and profitability made it easy to sell. The buyers and their attorneys had studied the operation in detail. It had taken over a year to put the deal together.

It didn't seem reasonable to connect Henry's death to the sale of the business. If anyone was unhappy with the arrangements, the deal would not have gone through. Kate didn't know all the people involved, but she was sure she'd never heard Leland Webern mentioned. Perhaps his connection was to what Henry was doing after the sale. Kate leaned back in the chair. Henry hadn't been doing much of anything in the last six months of his life. He'd been playing golf more. He managed the investments. He had seemed happy. Still, there was a reason someone had killed him. He must have been up to something, and he had kept it secret. Another small wave of anger surfaced, because neither Henry nor her parents had included her in their decisions, or even asked for her opinion.

She hadn't really expected them to consult with her, and she never supposed they had anything to hide. Now the lack of knowledge seemed dangerous. Henry should have told her if there were things she needed to know. Although he didn't know he was going to die, did he? Kate stared into space, the surrounding room becoming a hazy blur. Until the telephone call, she was dealing only with grief and a longing for justice; now there was fear mixed with anger. If the caller wasn't some absolute crank, she was in danger and didn't know why. Bringing some logic to bear, she tried to think of what she *did* know.

The caller the same as admitted killing Henry, or at least knowing why he was killed. He didn't want police involved, so it must be something illegal. Kate tried to form an image of the man based on his voice, but gave up because all that came to mind was rough, ugly, and despicable. If she could find him, she'd kill him. The jarring thought jerked her out of a daze. She'd never been capable of violence. The man said Henry had told her something, but he hadn't. Surely, this man would not kill her while being convinced she had something he wanted. For the moment, it was a welcome realization. He spoke of '*we.*' He might have been trying to make her think he wasn't alone in his threat. She hoped it was a bluff; it would be easier dealing with one man.

When the odor of baked chicken reached Henry's office, Kate quickly hurried to the kitchen. She was only slightly less confused over the situation, but a few things seemed clear. She could leave everything to the police, or try to investigate on her own. As she removed the chicken, the stove's timer sounded. The beeping so startled her she almost dropped the pan she was holding. She'd set the timer because lately she had made mistakes, such as boiling things over, not taking mail out of the mailbox, and once leaving the bathroom shower running. When there were others to care for, she had been confident and capable. Alone, she felt inept and insecure. She didn't understand how this could be, but somehow Henry's death had changed her.

With the broccoli done, she prepared the rest of the meal and poured a water glass full of white wine. Maybe a large amount would make it easier to sleep.

As she finished eating and stood to clear the table, the telephone rang. Kate froze, then slowly put the plate back on the table, and took a second to gather her thoughts. The ringing continued. She tried to remember the policewoman's instructions, but nothing came to mind. All she could think was that there was no sense in hiding. Better to face whatever came.

"Hello?"

"Kate? Are you okay? You sound funny."

Kate pulled a chair closer and slumped onto it.

"Ronda. I'm fine. Just surprised at you calling."

'I'm worried. This afternoon you were upset."

"Well, I'm better now."

Ronda was silent for a few seconds. "You don't sound better. Has something happened?"

Kate hesitated to tell Ronda of the threatening telephone call. She would want all the details.

"Kate? Are you still there? I know something must be wrong. I can come right over. I'll stay the night if you are scared. Did something frighten you?"

"No." she said with a slight laugh. "Not at all. I've just finished dinner. I'm perfectly fine."

"Okay. If you are sure. I'm alone, too; I understand how it can get to a person."

Kate pressed the phone to her ear, tempted to plead for Ronda to come stay with her. Still, she wasn't ready to confide in anyone. If her family had kept secrets, maybe she should, too.

"Thanks for the offer, Ronda. I'll be fine. I had a big glass of wine with dinner and I'm ready to fall asleep," Kate added a laugh to cover her nervousness.

Ronda chuckled. "Sounds like something I'd do. Just remember, if you need to talk, I'm here. Rest well."

Ronda hung up; Kate slowly replaced the telephone receiver and remained seated. When the phone had rung, it had sent a shock through her. She had feared it was the previous caller. If it had been, she didn't know what she would have said. Ronda's call made her realize how unprepared she was. She couldn't keep stammering, asking questions they wouldn't answer. She didn't even know if the next encounter would be by telephone. The man hadn't said how or who would contact her.

Her head was spinning with thoughts of how to handle this threat, or maybe it was the wine clouding her mind. She quickly cleared the table, rinsed the dishes, and put them into the dishwasher. When the dishwasher started, it sounded overly loud, the water swishing and slapping inside the machine. The noise made it hard to hear anything else. It might even drown out the security alarm. She almost stopped the dishwasher. Ronda had asked if something had frightened her. The truth was it had terrorized her. Time after time, she had to push the fear away. Her mother had called her Katherine, a strong name. Maybe it was time to live up to the name. She turned off the kitchen lights, checked the house once again, and climbed the stairs to her bedroom.

She wanted to sleep, to be unconscious, for the nagging thoughts to stop. The only way that would happen was to make a plan, something to settle her mind. The first thing was to stop being afraid. The next was to go on the offence, find out what the threat was, and end it. Both tasks seemed nearly impossible, but the sketchy plan helped to satisfy her tumbling brain, and sleep came.

Two

The next morning Kate was stiff and sore, as if she'd been mountain climbing instead of sleeping. It had not been a relaxed, restful sleep. She'd been tense even while unconscious. She swung her legs over the edge of the bed and shoved her feet into house slippers. As she dressed, she tried to think of what to say if, or when, someone contacted her. They might call again, or maybe send a letter, or email, or even a face-to-face encounter. She wished it would be the latter. Seeing a person behind the voice would help. There would be someone to plead with. If they could see her, they'd have to know she was telling the truth. She washed her face and combed her hair, tying it back with a scarf.

In the kitchen, she opened the window shutters and a flood of bright sunlight poured into the room. Automatically, she made coffee and put a bowl of oatmeal into the microwave. All the while, her mind whirled with possible scenarios. No matter how last night's caller next contacted her, she would have nothing to tell them. If this went on over a long enough time, they would give up. Maybe they would finally believe she didn't know anything. Still, she had no idea what kind of people they were. If they were convinced she couldn't help, they might become angry enough to kill her. Obviously, they didn't get what they wanted from Henry. If they had, they wouldn't still be looking for it.

As Kate buttered a piece of toast, a thought struck her. If they killed Henry because he wouldn't give them the information, they were stupid. Whatever they wanted had died with him. Since only she and Leland had been in the house that day, it was no wonder the police suspected them. Unless someone else had been there. Her mind buzzed with the details, as it had for the past two months.

She had made breakfast for the three of them. Afterward, Henry and Leland went to Henry's office and closed the door. Kate had straightened the kitchen, gone upstairs, made three beds, cleaned the bathrooms, and dressed to go shopping. It had been late August, the heat and humidity were high, so she wore cotton slacks and a thin blue tee shirt. Coming downstairs, she stopped at the office door and hesitated before opening it. Inside she heard Henry and Leland earnestly discussing something, but the only words she made out were Henry saying, *I can't do that.* What Leland answered, she didn't hear and when she opened the door, they quit talking.

"Ronda and I are going shopping, then lunch and maybe a movie," she told them.

Leland stood, crossed the room, and took her hand. "This is probably goodbye, Kate. I'll be gone by the time you return."

"Oh, I am sorry. It was nice meeting you. I hope you will visit us again," she said, withdrawing her hand and backing away.

His leaving was surprising and, she had to admit, disappointing. She had hoped to become better acquainted.

She closed the office door, went to the kitchen, and into the connecting two-car garage. She backed her Acura out, being careful to miss Leland's black Lincoln in the driveway. As she drove away, she had held a small hope Leland might still be there when she returned. She and Ronda had lunch and shopped for a couple of hours. As they put the bags into the car, Ronda said, "I've had enough walking around in this heat. The movie theater will be a cool treat."

Kate had hesitated; it was only mid-afternoon. Maybe Leland hadn't left yet.

"Would you be too disappointed if we didn't go? I'm ready to go home."

Ronda had frowned. "Don't you feel well? Henry won't expect you back this soon, will he?"

"I doubt Henry remembers I'm gone," Kate had laughed. "I guess I'm a bit tired."

Arriving home, Kate had found the driveway empty and supposed Leland had left. He hadn't offered any chance of return; she shrugged and carried her purchases into the kitchen. She paused to put away the grocery items before taking the dress she'd bought to her bedroom. She didn't stop at Henry's office because his car hadn't been in the garage; she supposed he had gone somewhere. Henry often went out alone to play golf. Sometimes when asked where he was going, he'd reply *sightseeing.* In other words, mind your own business. Still, she did wonder where he spent his time. However, part of their successful living arrangement was an agreed upon privacy.

The day Leland had shown up, Henry introduced him as a business associate.

"Kate, this is Leland Webern. We worked together on a trade deal when I was still at the company. He is asking my advice on a new business venture."

Leland had a nice smile; it went with his friendly brown eyes. He was tall, which made Kate feel dainty. While not quite handsome, he was certainly pleasant looking.

"Welcome, Mr. Webern. Henry's friends are always welcome," she'd said.

"Please, call me Leland. I'll try not to be a bother."

The house was large and Kate had no problem with overnight guests. It was a treat. On Monday evening she had made dinner for the three of them and afterward they had sat talking.

"Did you know many of the people at Shore when Henry was there?" she asked.

"Kate, Leland doesn't want to talk business. That's all we've done today," Henry chided.

"Well, business bores me anyway," she laughed. "If it isn't too personal, Leland, do you have a family."

For a few seconds, Leland had focused on his coffee cup. Then looked up and smiled at her. "I never married...too busy, I guess. No brothers or sisters, and my parents have passed away."

"Oh, I am so sorry," she said. "I shouldn't have asked you such a question."

His being alone had made Kate sympathetic toward him. It was part of the reason she couldn't believe he had killed Henry. In her opinion, a third person had come to the house. Whoever it was must have found Henry alone because Leland probably left right after she did. When Kate had given the police this version of events, they had discounted it. They found no evidence of anyone else being in the house. Not even Leland. At first, it surprised her, but that morning she had cleaned his bedroom and the bath. She had also noticed how extremely neat he was. Perhaps he had a reason.

Kate's breakfast sat half-eaten. The coffee was cold, so she refilled the half-empty cup and put it in the microwave. When the microwave beeped, she took the hot coffee and again sat at the table. As she slowly sipped coffee, she recalled the worst part of that day two months earlier.

~ * ~

After putting the new dress on a hanger, Kate had gone downstairs, intending to put out something to thaw for dinner. Passing Henry's closed office door, she had decided to do a bit of cleaning while he was out. Henry smoked and the desk was always messy. She never touched his papers, only straightened them enough to dust. When Kate opened the door, she had stopped just inside the room. She had frowned, and even leaned forward. She couldn't believe her eyes. Henry should not be home. She hadn't heard him come in, but there he was, slumped over the desk, his arms across the top, his head face down. She had thought he was asleep, yet it seemed so absurd she had called out to him: *Henry, sit up, you can't be asleep.*

She had continued to cross the room, her pulse quickening. She had rushed to the desk, and reached out to touch him, that was when she saw the blood soaking the back of his shirt. Kate had gasped and hurried around behind Henry to take him by the shoulders, trying to set him upright. In the process, her slacks and the bottom of her tee shirt pressed against his back. She had not noticed the blood stains on her clothing until the police pointed them out. They didn't find the gun used to shoot Henry, but the bullet that went through him had lodged in the wood paneling behind him. It was determined he must have been standing when shot, and fallen onto the chair and forward across the desk.

The rest of the day had passed in a blur. After two patrolmen and a detective had left, Ronda had taken Kate home with her until the house was no longer considered a crime scene. She didn't know what she would have done without Ronda in those first days. The only thing keeping the police from arresting Kate was that she'd been with Ronda most of the day. Shopkeepers could attest to it, along with date and time stamps on her sales slips.

A month later, they had found Henry's car stripped in a rundown part of St. Louis. Kate had tried to tell the police Leland could not have taken Henry's car; he had one of his own. He couldn't drive two cars away. There must be someone else involved, maybe the killer. She was certain this proved a third person had been there. The police couldn't find any evidence that even Leland had been in the house, the only fingerprints belonging to Henry and Kate. She had explained the absence of fingerprints. She was a good housekeeper. Kate had trouble thinking Leland would harm Henry. She had never heard a cross word between them.

~ * ~

Kate finished her coffee and went to the kitchen sink to rinse the cup. She had gone over the events dozens of times. She never left anything out; she always remembered it the same way. The day was slipping away, and she had not formed a plan. She was a bit worried the caller might learn she had told the police. She wished there were something she could do other than wait, because her frayed nerves would not allow that. She would take some action, even if it was wrong. Maybe find someone to give her advice. It wouldn't be fair to involve Ronda. Perhaps a private detective...they were supposed to keep confidences, the same as between a lawyer and his client. A *lawyer*, of course, *Jim Burton*. The Shore family attorney. She should have thought of him before.

She hurried from the kitchen to the office. Henry's phonebook was in a desk drawer. Her cell phone was in her purse, but it was upstairs, and Henry's cell phone was missing. The police suspected the killer had taken it. If he had, it must not have the information he was after. Henry had insisted on landlines in the house. He believed they provided more privacy. Sitting at the desk, Kate found Jim's Chicago office number. Just thinking of talking with him provided relief. Jim had taken care of everything for her. He and Henry had plans in place, making it easy to transfer the bank accounts and the property. Henry might have had his secrets, but he had always taken care of her. She put aside the memory of her brother's kindness. It didn't matter now. Her hand shook as she dialed Jim's office. He would help.

"Burton Law, Mrs. Farber speaking," said Mary, Jim's long-time secretary.

"Mrs. Farber, this is Kate Shore. I need to speak with Mr. Burton. I'll make an appointment. I want to talk with him in person. I'll drive in today, and be available anytime tomorrow."

There was a pause before Mary Farber answered.

"Oh, Kate. I've been meaning to contact you. I am so sorry, things have been unsettled here. I hate to tell you, but Jim, Mr. Burton, passed away four days ago." Mrs. Farber stopped; there was a catch in her voice.

Kate was stunned into silence.

Mrs. Farber continued. "The funeral was yesterday. I've been trying to clear up some of the work. Jim's son is an attorney. He will be coming in tomorrow to decide how to settle things here at the office. I'm sure some of our clients might go with James, even though his office is in St. Louis." Mrs. Farber waited for Kate's reply.

"I don't know what to say. What happened to Mr. Burton?"

"A heart attack. He'd been struggling with heart disease for a while. We all had hoped he'd have some restful years in retirement.

This must be a shock for you, coming so soon after losing Henry. Still, Mr. Burton did settle most everything."

"Oh, yes. He did a wonderful job, as always. I'm not calling about the estate."

"I see. Would you like to talk with his son? I'm sure he'd be glad to help. Or perhaps suggest another attorney if it isn't in his area of expertise."

"No. Well, maybe later. I'll think about it. I am very sorry about Mr. Burton. Give the family my condolences, and for you, too. I know you will miss him. Goodbye."

Before Kate could hang up, Mrs. Farber caught her.

"Wait, do wait. Just a minute. There are a couple of things I can tell you."

Kate heard the sound of rustling papers.

"Here we are," said Mrs. Farber. "Jim had talked with the insurance company; the policy on Henry's life is due to be settled shortly. They have all the necessary information. He arranged for the payment to go directly into your savings account. He wanted to give you the option of where it should go from there."

The last thing Kate cared about was Henry's life insurance. "Thank you so much. Whatever he did is fine—"

"One more thing, Kate. There is a box here. It contains some things from your mother. Henry brought it to us when you moved from the Chicago house."

"What? Why didn't Henry give it to me?"

"I imagine it is a surprise, but don't blame Henry for not telling you. Grace had left strict instructions. Henry was carrying out your mother's wishes, and Mr. Burton respected them."

"What is in this box?"

"None of us knows. You are the only one who can open it. And if, unfortunately, you were deceased, it was to be destroyed."

"Why wasn't it given to me before?"

"Another stipulation. You were to receive it *only* if you were completely alone. Grace told Henry that, after her death, he was to deliver the box to us."

"So as long as Henry was alive I wouldn't get it?"

"Correct."

"What if I were married?"

"I believe the same restriction applies. Mr. Burton was about to contact you. He would have done so sooner, but Henry hasn't been gone long. Jim didn't want to mention your mother quite yet. We knew how hard her passing was for you. He wanted to give you a bit more time to get over losing Henry. What shall I do? I can ship it to you."

"Let me think a minute."

Mrs. Farber was patient.

"Don't ship it, Mrs. Farber. I'll be there tomorrow, the next day at the latest. Will I need to give you a definite time?"

"No. Any time during regular office hours will be fine."

After a few more words of sympathy, the call ended. There was too much sorrow in the world. At least in Kate's world. Thoughts of her mother came rushing back. Such a mystery. All she could imagine was that Grace must have had some things she wanted Kate to have. Still, after Grace died, Kate had taken the items that meant anything to her. Before her death, Grace had given Kate all her valuable jewelry. It had been a sad, yet precious time.

Kate sat at the desk in Henry's office, the silent telephone receiver still in her hand, not even a dial tone sounding. Jim Burton's death was a shock. As she slowly returned the receiver to its cradle, a heaviness settled over her. Mr. Burton was probably in his late seventies. He was always a hard worker; she too wished he could have had some leisure years. Maybe she would use his son if she needed legal advice. Although she doubted she would. The way Henry and Mr. Burton had attended to things, she was financially secure. As for the box, it probably held things important to Grace. The only mystery was why Kate couldn't have it unless she were alone. Yet, it was impossible to know what was in another person's mind. Some days toward the end, Grace hadn't made complete sense. By the time it was over, she was almost glad for her mother's release.

Now Kate slightly regretted deciding to pick up the package in person. She should have let Mrs. Farber mail it. It had waited this long; a week or more wouldn't matter. She could call back and tell Mrs. Farber to send the box after all. Still, Kate got to her feet and left the room, starting for the foyer stairs. She climbed to the second floor to pack an overnight bag; she was far too restless to wait for delivery of the box. Not because she was eager to see the contents, but because if she didn't take some action, she might explode. It was unbearable to wait around for a killer to contact her. She wouldn't make it easy for him. Maybe after stopping at the law offices, she'd go on to see Aunt Iris. She and Uncle Bert lived in Pinecrest, around eighty-five miles from Chicago. However, she'd have to make it plain it was only a short visit.

Considering a couple of days with Iris, she packed a few more clothes. It didn't take long to gather bathroom items and the meager makeup she used. There was no need to stop the mail or newspaper, Ronda could collect them. No sense advertising she was gone. She set the suitcase in the kitchen by the garage door and made one last round of the house. Everything seemed in order. She would stop at Ronda's house on the way out of town. If Ronda wasn't home, Kate would call her later, but it would be better to talk in person because Ronda worried about her. It was comforting to have one person who cared. Kate loaded her bag into the Acura, backed out of the garage, and headed toward Ronda's house.

When she pulled into the driveway, she parked behind Ronda's sedan. As she stepped out of her car, Ronda opened her front door and stood waiting.

"Kate, you drove over. Are you giving up on walking for the exercise?" she called.

"No, I'm on my way out of town."

Ronda straightened the strands of gold beads around her neck as she held open the door. Kate entered the front room, and Ronda took her arm, guiding her to the sofa.

"Sit down and tell me what this is all about."

Kate sat, and tried to decide how much to tell her.

"I'm going to Chicago."

"But that's at least a four-hour drive. Why are you going?"

"I wanted to see our attorney, but he's passed away. So many people dying lately."

"Are you going to his funeral?"

"No, it was yesterday."

"Then why?"

Kate's original reason was to get Jim's advice about the threatening phone call, now it was to pick up an old, probably unimportant box. She had already decided to keep the phone call from Ronda, but it might be okay to tell her about the box.

"This may sound silly, but I'm going to pick up a box. They could mail it, but I decided to get it instead. Henry had left it with our attorney who was to give it to me if ever I was alone."

Ronda put a hand to her chest, her blue eyes wide.

"Henry left it? What is in this box?"

"I don't know. Probably things my mother wanted me to have. Nothing makes much sense."

"Well, that settles it. I'm coming with you." Ronda stood and rushed to the dining room where her purse sat on the table. She opened it and took out her cell phone. "I had a hair appointment, need a touch up you know, but I'm canceling right now!"

As she started to dial, Kate hurried to her side.

"Don't do that! Please. I can go alone. Besides, after stopping in Chicago I might want to drive on to see my aunt and uncle. I don't know how long I'll be gone. Oh, not long. Still, my plans aren't settled. Not that I wouldn't enjoy your company."

Ronda slowly put the cell phone back into her large handbag. "If you are sure."

"I am, but thanks. I would like you to keep an eye on my house, though. Maybe pick up the paper and mail for a few days?"

Kate started walking to the front door, Ronda beside her.

"Of course, I'll pick them up. Glad to, but what do you think is in this mysterious box? You did say it is in the attorney's office, didn't you?"

Kate nodded. "Yes."

"I don't remember you saying who the attorney is, or was. My, you have had a time of losing people close to you. I guess you'll know who to see since he is gone. Is the office easy to find? If you have trouble, you can always use your GPS. I'd be lost without mine."

Kate laughed. "I won't have any trouble. Jim Burton's office has been in the Stoner Building for years."

As they stood beside Kate's car, Ronda gave her a hug. "Keep in touch. Call me if you need anything."

Backing onto the street and driving away, Kate saw Ronda standing near the porch as she waved goodbye.

Leaving Greenfield behind, heading northwest toward Chicago, Kate wondered why she was taking off on a four-hour drive in the middle of the afternoon. Still, she had nothing else to do. Besides, she felt safer on the road, with no one knowing where she was. It was better than being a sitting duck in the house. As the miles slipped by, she relaxed. Maybe she *would* go to Pinecrest to see Aunt Iris. She should call and find out if it would be convenient, but she'd wait until she had picked up the box. Plenty of time afterward to call, and if they were not at home, maybe she would find something else to do. Realizing she was free to do whatever she wanted was a pleasant thought.

Instead of focusing on the losses, she needed to count her blessings. Kate's lips lifted in a half smile. That was her mother talking; counting blessings was her way of staying happy. Although sometimes there wasn't much happiness in Grace's life. Henry Senior was a driven man, too busy to spend time with his wife and two children. However, it was hard to fault him because he had built a business and provided well for them. It didn't leave her brother, Henry, many challenges. He only had to pick up where his father had left off. As far as Kate knew, Henry had continued their father's method of business. Yet, when he saw an opportunity for their future security, he took it. Kate was satisfied with the sale; for one thing, it had taken a burden off Henry. Over all, Henry's life hadn't been easy. His dedication to work had cost him his wife, Alisha.

The late afternoon sun put a blinding glare on the pavement; Kate reached for her purse and took out sunglasses. Thinking of Henry's life and the family's past brought back a bit of tension. Things were not always peaceful…still most families had good and bad times. She had sometimes wondered how Alisha felt about her new husband buying into the business. Maybe Jared Roth wouldn't devote as much time to the company as Henry had, and it would keep Alisha satisfied. Although she didn't remember Alisha complaining about the many things Henry's income bought her. Kate tried to remember the name of Jared's partner, but it escaped her. It wasn't important. Shore I/E was no longer her concern. The truth was it had never been of much concern to her.

Her father had said he didn't like bringing business home, and her mother seemed happy with the arrangement. Kate stiffened her jaw; it didn't do to think of the past. No one could change the past; only the future mattered. Still, the past did have a hold on her. She couldn't go forward without knowing why Henry died, and why someone was threatening her. If Henry's death went unsolved, maybe in time she could adjust to it, but not if someone wouldn't let her. Beside all that, she needed to make a life for herself. She could sell the house and move back to Chicago. She didn't need to work, but for health and sanity reasons, perhaps she should find a job. Nothing too demanding, simply something to keep her occupied. Thinking of the future made her feel hollow and useless, because there was no one in that future to share her life.

Kate gripped the steering wheel; self-pity was sneaking up on her. She could not let that happen. She must be optimistic. The future was an adventure. Yet, her emotions were too unsettled to think of finding a new life when the one behind was a mystery. She had not yet adjusted to Henry being gone. Time after time, she wanted to turn to him and ask his opinion. She had never realized how dependent she was upon her brother's direction. It was sad to think of going ahead alone. Thoughts of Henry brought back the nagging feeling of owing him something. She tried to brush it away; she wouldn't know where to start looking for his killer.

The sun sank lower and the west side of the interstate glowed with its last rays, while the east side turned lavender and gray with shadows racing along beside the vehicles. Kate reached Chicago a bit after seven. The evening traffic was still heavy as she made her way across town to the Marriott Hotel. It was midweek and unless some convention was in town, she would find a room there. Perhaps this trip was unnecessary, but it served one purpose: Kate felt safer and more relaxed. The sadness and uncertainty remained, but she doubted anyone could harm her while in the car or hotel room. No one knew where she was, and it brought a smile of satisfaction. Control did that for a person.

Kate checked into a room with a beautiful lake view. After a room service dinner, she stood and watched the brick, stone, and cement city below sparkle like a dazzling bejeweled kingdom. The lake shimmering with smeared color from streetlights and neon signs. It was a place alive, a place to hide. Maybe not forever, yet for one night it was a sanctuary. Kate took a shower, watched some late news, and fell instantly asleep.

~ * ~

The next morning Kate was in no hurry to reach Jim Burton's office. As it was only the second day after his funeral, she didn't relish facing the grieving. It would be painful to see Lila, Jim's widow, but she would surely be at their home. Mary Farber was a different matter. She was always professional and she undoubtedly felt sorrow but wouldn't be obvious about it. Kate was sympathetic, but weary with the emotional pain suffered by the survivors. It had been too short a time between the losses.

As far as she knew, Mrs. Farber still had Mr. Farber. How the woman had married, raised two daughters, and served the law office for around thirty years was a mystery. It had to be like managing two different lives. She should be an inspiration to all women. Considering Mary's accomplishment left Kate disappointed with her own. However, there was still hope. She was probably half Mrs. Farber's age; perhaps there was still time to make something of her life.

Kate had packed a navy-blue dress with a matching jacket. A string of her mother's pearls and low-heeled pumps completed the outfit. She had a light breakfast and didn't check out until noon. She planned to reach the office close to one o'clock. She'd miss the morning rush, and give the staff time to have lunch. Although office procedure was likely disrupted. Mrs. Farber had mentioned Jim Burton's son coming to help either reorganize or perhaps close the office. None of which should affect Kate's situation. She would pick up the box, and leave them to it. She drove along the lake and considered visiting her family's old neighborhood. Wondering if the new owners of their home had changed things. Probably not, as they hadn't lived there long. Besides, there was no benefit in revisiting the past...it was better to forget.

She pulled into the parking lot next to the Stoner Building and took a ticket from the attendant. Her suitcase was in the trunk, but from long habit, she checked the car to make sure there was nothing to tempt a thief. The lot was secure; still it didn't hurt to be careful. The buildings along the street were all two and three stories, most built of stone, some with brick trim. It was an old area, yet still well maintained. Jim Burton's offices were on the top floor. A small elevator was available, but Kate took the stairs. The staircase curved upward out of the lobby to a landing on the second floor, then on up to the reception area of the third floor. There was a pleasant looking blonde at the reception desk.

"May I help you?" she asked.

"I'm Kate Shore, here to see Mrs. Farber."

"Please have a seat. I'll let her know you are here."

Kate stepped back to an overstuffed chair and sat. In minutes, Mrs. Farber came to greet her. She was tall, with thick gray hair cut short to frame a surprisingly wrinkle-free face. She smiled and reached out to shake Kate's hand. Kate stood and met her halfway.

"I see you made it," Mary said.

"Yes. It was good to get away for a bit. But I am so sorry for the loss everyone must be feeling."

Mary Farber stopped smiling, and Kate was sorry she'd mentioned a painful subject. The receptionist ducked her head and began typing. Mrs. Farber put her arm around Kate and said, "Please, come into my office."

In the office suite, boxes sat on the floor and papers covered the desk and a small end table. Across the room was an open door leading to another office. Mrs. Farber led her into the adjoining room. It too seemed in disarray. It had been Mr. Burton's office. Kate looked around, wondering if they were getting ready to move or close the offices.

Behind them, a young woman Kate took to be a secretary came into Mrs. Farber's office and stood in Burton's doorway.

"Sorry to bother you," she said. "But the detective is back. Will you see him, or should I call James?"

"Bring him in."

The secretary left and Mrs. Farber cleared some papers from a desk chair and pointed Kate to it.

"Please, sit here. Listen while I speak with this man and it will help you understand what has happened."

A middle-aged man with thinning brown hair entered the room. Mrs. Farber gave him a slight smile.

"Is there something else?" she asked.

"Just wanted to make sure you'll get the list to us as soon as you can. It will help with insurance claims, too." He shrugged and lifted an eyebrow. "I suspect you know that."

"Yes. Mrs. Burton came yesterday and removed Mr. Burton's personal items. We haven't missed any large office equipment, but we will do our best to give you a complete list."

The detective thanked her and left. Kate stood and faced the woman.

"What happened? Why are the police here?"

Mrs. Farber sighed and leaned against the desk.

"It is hard to believe the trouble we've had over the past week. First Jim passing away. His wife, Lila, of course is too upset to make any quick decisions. At this point, she doesn't much care. I suspect his son, James, will close the office. I'll stay on to help with what I can. We hardly know what to do."

The efficient Mrs. Farber look around the room...her thoughts seemed to be wandering. Kate waved at the messy room.

"I still don't understand. What happened?"

"A robbery. We were robbed last night."

"How awful. I hope you didn't lose anything irreplaceable."

Mrs. Farber closed her eyes, then opened them and grimaced. "I'm not sure, we haven't been through everything, but the box your mother entrusted to us is gone, and it is certainly irreplaceable."

Kate opened her mouth to speak, and then shut it. She turned around, surveying the room as if she could discover the box.

"I...I don't believe it. Why would they take it? Did it look expensive?"

"No. It was a square cardboard box about twelve inches by twelve inches. Sealed with clear packing tape. Grace had put a handwritten note on the top, it just said, *For Katherine*. Henry said Grace made him promise to deliver it."

Kate walked in a small circle, returned to the cleared chair, and sat again. She stared in disbelief. "This is terrible."

"I know. I wish there were something I could do. Maybe the thief was hoping it was something of value, or he opened it and saw something he wanted. Oh, Kate. I am sorry."

Kate's dismay and outrage grew, but Mary's sense of failure touched her. Kate stood and went to her side.

"It's okay. You couldn't have known this would happen. Maybe the police will find the crook and recover what he took."

Mrs. Farber looked doubtful. "I wouldn't depend on it. I'm afraid it is lost forever. I don't want to be vengeful, but I hope something terrible happens to him. We suspect it is a man, but who knows?"

Kate started to speak, but the phone on the desk rang and Mrs. Farber answered it. Kate barely listened to the conversation. She was too dazed and lost in her own thoughts. She had never believed the box contained anything other than something of sentiment. Some personal reminder of her mother. Because Grace wanted her to have the box only if she were alone in the world, it must contain something to comfort or encourage her. Despite thinking the box held little monetary value, Kate felt enormously cheated. She had lost the last bit of communication from her mother. It was an emotional violation.

This in turn stirred her building anger, much like the anger she had felt after receiving the threatening telephone call.

When Mrs. Farber hung up, Kate tried to smile.

"Are you absolutely sure the box is gone?"

"We've been through every office, every desk, and cabinet. I knew you were coming today and I had placed the box on the top shelf of my closet. Jim had kept it in the office safe."

"Did they open the safe?

"Yes. There was some money. Of course, they took it. Also some bonds."

"Well, they would have found the box anyway."

"I feel we have failed you. Grace and Henry, too. I remember him saying we should tell you to bear in mind that it was special."

"I'm sure it was, but don't worry. It wasn't your fault."

Kate and Mrs. Farber walked to the lobby, sat in two armchairs and talked, while the receptionist went on with her work. James Burton came from one of the other offices and stopped to speak with Mrs. Farber.

"James, this is Kate Shore. I've told her about losing the box."

He shook Kate's hand, his eyes filled with sadness. "Miss Shore, I am sorry. We were shocked by the robbery."

Kate stood. "Please don't apologize. And accept my condolences. Your father was such a help to our family. Forget the box; you have enough to worry about."

James spread his hands. "You can see we are in a mess. We may close this office. I doubt I could maintain a second location."

Mrs. Farber patted his arm. "Whatever James decides, I will be retiring. I had intended to anyway."

After a few more words, James returned to his office and Kate said goodbye to Mrs. Farber.

From what Kate knew about Mrs. Farber, she deserved some years of peaceful retirement. Lives everywhere changing. Still, none of them had any bearing upon the direction of her new life. A new life—she contemplated the idea. However, it all came back to the same thing. Until someone solved Henry's murder, or she became resigned to never finding the answer, she couldn't start over. Especially if the threat to her life continued.

When Kate left the Stoner Building, she looked in both directions. It was near four o'clock and the street was moderately busy. No one paid attention to her, but she remained on guard. She had come to retrieve a piece of her past, only to find it stolen. She had a growing suspicion that the loss of the box in the break-in was no accident. As Kate neared the parking attendant's booth, she took the parking ticket out of her purse, and realized her thoughtlessness. She'd forgotten to ask the law firm to validate it. Still, under the circumstances, the parking fee was the least of her problems! Instead, now there were more questions.

Three

Kate put the car key in the ignition, but didn't turn it. She was lost in thought. She had no idea what might be in the box; it probably wasn't important. Particularly since there was the possibility that she would never have known about it. Yet, now that she did know, a strange sort of loss settled over her. Even stranger was a thief taking it. Unless he had been in a hurry and grabbed it, thinking it held something of value. She laughed softly. He was in for a surprise because it surely held only personal family items. For a second she considered the notion that the box had been the thief's target. Then dismissed it. Her problems caused her to think events centered around her, when obviously they didn't. Henry had carried out his mother's wishes by not telling Kate about the box. That would have been easy for him; Henry had always been able to keep a secret.

A glance in the rearview mirror told her the parking attendant was wondering why she hadn't driven away. Kate started the car, no sense risk paying for another hour. As she turned out onto the street, she wondered where to go. Aunt Iris was still an option, but she doubted she'd get many answers to the situation from her. Maybe she could stop by Shore. The office help would be leaving in a short while, but workers would still be in the warehouse and shoreline sheds. Their hours depended upon when deliveries arrived. Jared Roth might be in his office. Maybe he was using her father's old office, or perhaps he'd taken Henry's. Since Jared had a partner, they would be using both. When Henry sold the business, she hadn't cared who Jared's partner was. Maybe she'd heard his name, but as with other business matters, she hadn't paid much attention. It was becoming clear that she had been naïve, or maybe a more accurate word was foolish.

She had to change, stop assuming someone else would take care of things. It was down to her; there was no one else. The sooner she got used to it, the sooner she could get on with life. Heading toward the Cooper Industrial Park on the lakefront, Kate thought of questions she wanted answered, questions that might lead to Henry's killer. Who was Jared's partner, how was business, were they happy with the deal they had made? However, her nerve failed. She couldn't walk in and start questioning Jared. She should have talked to him at Henry's funeral, established some connection so she would feel free to see him. Besides, she didn't know the right questions to ask. The closer she got to the industrial park, the greater her doubts. Kate slowed the car and when another driver honked at her, she pressed on the gas and missed the turnoff to Shore Import/Export.

It was just as well; it probably saved her an embarrassing situation. If she left the city right now, she could reach Pinecrest that evening by six or seven at the latest. On the way, she'd call Aunt Iris. It was short notice, but if they weren't home, she'd find a motel. In the morning, she'd call again, and even if they were out of town, it didn't matter. She didn't need to be anywhere. As she neared the north side of Chicago, it brought back memories of where Henry and Alisha had lived when they were married. Six years ago, they had divorced and Alisha had kept the house. Henry had moved home where Kate was caring for Grace. Out of habit, Kate turned toward the wealthy, older neighborhood.

The winding streets with beautifully landscaped lawns, mature bushes and trees, gave the area a sense of graciousness apart from the bustle of the city. Alisha had found it easy to give up Henry, but not her dream home. She had acquired a new husband within a year, and four years later Jared Roth started negotiations to purchase Shore. It was mildly amusing how Alisha arranged things in her life. She had obviously enjoyed being the wife of a successful businessman, and loved the home he provided. In the ten years of their marriage, she had redecorated the house about as many times. Perhaps in seeing no way to redecorate Henry, she had exchanged him for Jared. However, like her home, there was another thing Alisha was not willing to do without. Kate had suspected Alisha had been behind Jared's bid for Shore. The goose that laid Alisha's golden eggs.

As Kate turned on Forest Lane, she only intended to drive past the house Henry had bought, just to see how it looked after six years. Henry had certainly been clever at making money; still, their father had built a firm foundation. She drove slowly past the sweeping lawns, some of the large brick or stone houses were hidden by fences, others by billowing trees. Yet no brown or orange leaves accumulated on these well-maintained driveways. Approaching the house, Kate saw a black Lincoln parked at the top of the curved U-shaped driveway. Maybe Alisha was home. Kate passed the drive's first entrance, but on impulse she turned into the second one. As she neared the house, a man came out of the front door. Kate stopped halfway up the right-hand side of the drive to watch.

Alisha patted the tall man on the shoulder, and turned to reenter the house. The man, carrying a thin briefcase, hurried down the steps to his car. He seemed in a rush. He had brown hair, and the same physical build as Leland Webern. Kate stared, her mouth open. It couldn't be. Yet, when he lifted his head, opened the Lincoln's door, and climbed in, Kate caught a glimpse of his face. The likeness was amazing, it had to be him! As the man started his car and pulled away toward the street, he didn't seem to notice the car down the drive behind him. If she were not so shocked, she'd follow, run him down, and demand answers. Instead, she continued the curve toward the front of the house and watched as the Lincoln turned onto Forest

Lane. She hadn't intended to drop in on Alisha, but seeing the man she took to be Leland leave, there was nothing else she could do.

Kate parked, and ran up the front steps. Her hand shook when she pushed the doorbell. The chimes echoed behind the carved wooden door with its large cut-glass window. Kate saw Alisha enter the foyer and head toward the door. She was her usual well-groomed self. Her blonde hair hung long, loose, and shiny. When she opened the door, her blue eyes widened.

"Kate!" she exclaimed.

Kate tried to smile, wondering how to explain her visit. They had once been sisters-in-law, admittedly not close, but they had never shared harsh words.

"Yes. Sorry to show up without calling. I was in town and thought I'd drive by."

Alisha reached for Kate's arm and pulled her forward.

"Come in. How are you? Are you doing okay?"

Kate nodded as Alisha led her toward the living room across the foyer from the winding staircase. The room was much as Kate remembered. A brick fireplace with a wooden mantel and large gilt-edged mirror above it. There were tall narrow windows on either side of the fireplace; their dark green velvet drapes were new to Kate. As were the two, matching forest-green club chairs on either side of a marble-topped end table. Alisha took Kate to a curved sofa across the room.

"Sit down. Would you like something to drink? Warm cider? Not quite winter yet, but still cool enough for a hot drink."

Kate sat and held her purse in her lap. The house around them was quiet, only the faint ticking of the large grandfather clock in the foyer.

"Nothing, thank you. I really don't know why I stopped." Kate hadn't decided how to approach Alisha about the man that just left her house. Slowly seemed the best course.

Alisha sat on the other end of the sofa and smiled. "I bet you're lonesome. Have you met anyone in, where is it now, Greenfield? You must get out, Kate. Try to make new friends."

"I know, but it isn't easy. I'm still trying to get over Henry's death."

Alisha shook her head, her golden hair falling across her forehead. She raised her hand, the long nails glossy with white polish, and brushed the hair aside.

"I'm sure it is awful for you. I saw how stunned you seemed at the funeral. I would have stopped to talk, but what could I have said? Besides, Jared was in a hurry to get back to the business." Alisha gave a half laugh. "Men. They are all alike when it comes to work. Jared is almost as bad as Henry was."

Kate didn't know what to say. This was most often how it was with her. She sat there looking at Alisha who seemed to glow with life. A person who said something even if it was the wrong thing. Alisha reached out and grabbed the life she wanted. Kate felt like a mud hen sitting beside a flamingo.

Alisha leaned forward. "Oh, I'm sorry to talk of Henry that way, but you know how it got with us. Whatever spark was there to begin with, well, it simply died. I really think Henry was happier when he moved back home with you and your mother."

Kate nodded. She never thought of Henry as being happy. Contented seemed to fit him better. "I hope so...perhaps he was."

Alisha straightened her back and pushed the thin gold bracelets a bit higher on her left arm.

"At least we parted friends," she asserted. "Listen, Kate, if you'd like to stay a few days, I have plenty of room. I'm having a party tomorrow night. Many of the office workers from Shore will be here. I bet you know some of them. You might even find some handsome guy interesting. How about it?"

Kate smiled. "Thank you, but no. I'm on my way to visit Aunt Iris in Pinecrest."

Alisha made a bitter face. "That doesn't sound like much fun. I've seen your aunt."

Kate had to laugh. "I know. Still, she is a good soul. She means well."

"Really, Kate. I don't mean to push, but you need to do some socializing or you'll never find a man."

"You're right. Still, it doesn't seem to be my style."

"You mean you don't find men attractive?"

"Oh, nothing like that. Many men have caught my attention. Like the one who left here just before I came. I saw him from a distance, but what I saw was attractive. Dark hair, tall, nice build. Who is he?"

A slight frown rippled across Alisha's smooth forehead. "You must mean John Holden."

"Not Leland Webern?"

Alisha's satiny lips trembled slightly before bursting into a smile. "Well, you have excellent taste, but poor eyesight." Alisha laughed. "I don't know this Mr. Webern you mentioned, but John would be a fantastic catch. He is single and very well off. He's Jared's partner."

Kate tried to put the information in order. No matter what Alisha said, she was very sure she'd seen Leland. She had to see him again, whatever he was calling himself.

"I guess I'd heard his name before, but I'd forgotten. I was never very interested in the business. What was he doing here?"

"Jared forgot some important papers this morning. He went straight to the airport for a business trip to Mexico and when John needed the papers, he came here to get them. They work well together."

"So Mr. Holden is in the office while Jared is away?"

"Yes. It works out well. They trade off, not so much travel for one person."

"How long is Jared going to be gone?"

"He'll be back tomorrow around noon. He had better be. He knows we're having the party tomorrow evening. Please say you'll stay. John will be at the party. I'll introduce you." Alisha tilted her head and smirked. "You can't say no."

Kate stood. "I am sorry, Alisha. I'm not in the mood for a party. I do hope it will be a success and everyone will have a great time."

Kate started toward the living room door, Alisha close behind her.

"I wish I could help, Kate. Maybe in time you'll want a more social life. Come visit me any time."

At the front door, Kate turned and gave Alisha a hug. "Thank you. That means a lot to me. I might sell the house in Greenfield and come back here."

"Don't do anything hasty, Kate. Maybe a small town is what you need, and your new house is beautiful."

"The house is fine, but I don't need much room."

"You never know. There must be a few single men around there. Give it time."

Starting down the steps, Kate said, "We'll see. Bye now."

She couldn't be sure, but she thought Alisha, standing on the step, waving goodbye, looked relieved.

As Kate drove away and turned onto Forest Lane, she was trembling from head to foot. She had seen Leland, she was as sure of it as of her own name. Besides, there was something off with Alisha. Granted, Kate had surprised her by dropping in unexpectedly, but there was something. She had never been *that* nice. Acting as if they were close friends, caring about Kate's social life. Even inviting her to a party, asking her to visit any time. Yet, advising against moving back to the city. The trembling had subsided, but Kate's mouth was dry and her mind whirled with unsettled thoughts. However, she knew one thing: she wasn't leaving the city until she had confronted Leland, or John if that was his real name. She wasn't going to wait until tomorrow night to see him at some party. She needed to face him alone.

The bright fall day was fading. To the west, the blue denim sky held streaks of apricot-colored clouds. A mild breeze tossed the tops of trees, shaking off a shower of brown or gold leaves. Kate headed toward the lake, and turned south. The streets were busy with after-work traffic. Shore's front office would not be open; however, Gladys, the head of the accounting department, often worked late. At least she had when the family owned the business. If Ralph, the gatekeeper, was on duty, she'd have a chance of getting into the building. She didn't know for sure if either of those employees had stayed on after the sale. Besides, maybe Leland hadn't gone back to the office. Perhaps tracking him down wasn't wise, but she had to find the man. If he'd gone home, she'd get his address and confront him there.

Along the lakefront, the wind was stronger, tossing up short white-topped waves. A few people wearing hoodies or hats and scarves hurried along the sidewalks. The weather was never certain, especially in the fall. Kate remembered times in Chicago when she had left home without a jacket and in a short while wished she had one. The big shining lake was like living near an ocean. Her father had situated Shore I/E with docks on one side and railroads on the other. At first, there were only a couple of warehouses in the area. Kate had been too young to have seen them, but in time, Cooper Industrial Park developed around them. Now even the ground under Shore I/E was an asset. Before selling to Jared and his partner (Kate squinted at the thought of who the partner was), Henry had offers from buyers wanting to buy simply for the location.

Entering the industrial park, Kate was careful to avoid large trucks and forklifts still at work. They might call New York 'the city that never sleeps,' but Chicago seemed to run a close second. If Kate remembered right, a filmmaker took the nickname and applied it to a movie about Chicago. Some lights atop tall poles came on as dusk descended. Kate had rarely gone to Shore's offices and warehouses, but she knew the way. Some of the buildings had new names on large signs above their roofs, or painted on their sides. Although she did see some familiar businesses. Shore Import was near the center of the park. As she drew close to the yard, enclosed by a ten-foot, barbed wire topped fence, she saw a light on in the guardhouse.

Kate pulled up in front of the gate and powered down her window. A tall, thin, gray-haired man stepped out of the narrow shed. She peered at him. He looked like Ralph; it had been at least four years since she had been to Shore. It was the year before Grace had died.

He squinted through black-rimmed glasses. His gaze questioning, he straightened and cocked his head.

"Is this who I think it is?" He chuckled.

"Ralph," she cried. "Yes, it is me. Kate Shore."

Ralph stepped closer and bent down to face her. "What the blazes you doing here, girl?"

"Is Mr. Holden here? I've come to see him."

Ralph nodded. "I haven't seen him leave, leastways not out this gate." Ralph's narrow face grew somber. "Listen, I can't say how sorry I am about Mr. Shore Junior passing. How are you getting along?"

"Oh, I'm doing fine. I do miss him. Hard not having a big brother to look out for me."

"He did. Took the whole burden of this business when Senior passed. Not that you wouldn't have helped if he'd wanted. Course, there at the end you had your ma to care for."

"How are things here, Ralph? Since the sale, I mean. I know it hasn't been long."

"Well, we all knew it was coming. Leastwise for a year. Most everyone stayed. A couple of the youngsters in the warehouse took off. There's always high turnover there. No, I'd say things are about the same. Mr. Roth came in saying he didn't want to make any kind of big changes."

"How about Mr. Holden?"

"Don't see a great deal of him. I gathered he was more the money-man behind the deal."

Kate remembered Alisha saying John Holden was rich. She had thought she meant he had money because of a good income from Shore. Maybe Jared Roth had a partner because he couldn't have swung the deal alone.

"But you think he is here now?"

"I couldn't swear to it, but I imagine he is."

"I'm glad you were here, Ralph. I wondered how I'd get in."

"Another hour and I wouldn't be. The night man will come on then. Want me to call ahead for you? I'm supposed to announce visitors, but since it's you—"

"I'd rather surprise Mr. Holden. If it's okay."

Ralph narrowed his eyes behind his black rimmed glasses. "You aren't here to cause trouble, are you?"

"Look at me, Ralph. Can you imagine my ever making a fuss of any kind?"

Ralph laughed, showing a mouth full of false teeth. "No mum, I sure can't."

As Ralph stepped back to the guardhouse to open the gate, he called, "Good to see you, Miss Shore. You take care, now."

Kate smiled and nodded as she drove into the yard. In front of the long two-story brick-fronted building, there was parking for guests and employees. Between the sidewalk and the building grew a neatly trimmed yew hedge. On either side of the glass double doors were carriage lamps. Henry Shore Senior had wanted an attractive entrance for what could be a messy business. A warehouse formed the back half of the building, both floors there used for smaller imports that are more valuable. Behind the warehouse was a large asphalt yard with parking for trucks and other equipment. Along the lakeshore stood another type of warehouse, more of a large open shed, meant for merchandise in wooden crates and plastic containers.

Kate ignored the guest parking and drove around the building to the yard behind. There was a long loading platform, with stairs up the right side, and three overhead doors, two of them closed. The first overhead door was open, but there was no one in sight. She parked at the end of the building near the platform. As she sat for a minute to gather her thoughts, she looked around the yard. Across the pavement, there were a couple of men in the waterfront shed, loading crates into the back of a pickup. They might be bringing merchandise to the loading dock with the open door. Kate put her purse into the glove compartment, quickly got out of the car, locked it, and shoved the key into her dress pocket. She ran to the side stairs, gained the platform, and entered the building before anyone could stop her.

Going through the warehouse, she saw it was nearly full, the shelves and items clearly labeled and clean. Even if Jared Roth weren't as controlling an operator as Henry had been, it would take a while for standards to slip. The well-trained employees could probably run the business, except for the buying and selling and making decisions about the narrow profit margin. Still, she shouldn't judge, and it wasn't her concern. Nothing happening at Shore could make a difference in her life. At least not financially. If there were some other unsettled matter, she needed to know what it was. If John Holden had used another name when he met with Henry, did Henry know, and had they both deceived her? Making her way along the center aisle, Kate remembered the few words she'd heard Henry say, 'I can't do that.' He and Leland seemed friendly toward each other; it didn't appear to be an argument.

She took a back staircase to the second floor where her father and Henry had offices. Accounting and the reception area were on the first floor in the front half of the building. The wide second floor central hallway had a dark green carpet with a gray leaf pattern. The carpet looked new; perhaps Alisha had been at work. Kate's father had used the larger office, its windows overlooking the front parking lot. Facing the hall, on either side of the door, were two windows. Anyone passing would see Henry Senior working at the large walnut desk. The office was dark except for the late afternoon light coming through the front windows. Farther along the hallway, a faint glow showed beneath the door to the second executive office.

Kate slowly walked toward Henry's old office. Its hallway walls were solid, the only window in the upper half of the door. The outside windows in this office faced the loading docks. Trying to stay hidden, she had entered the back of the building. If Holden were in that office, she hoped he'd have been studying something on his desk, and not looking out the back windows. Her earlier trembling returned, and she tried to relax. There was nothing wrong with her being in the building. Not really, or maybe only a little wrong. For an instant, she hoped Holden wasn't there. Still, thinking of Henry's murder and the phone call, she had no choice. If she didn't face him, she couldn't go on. She was nervous, but not afraid. Maybe Leland had a good reason for staying hidden. She hoped he could clear up the mystery of why he'd not returned.

She slowly moved to the door and peered through the window before quickly ducking back out of sight. He was there. Sitting at the desk, papers in front of him. She was inclined to knock, but instead took a step forward and grasped the doorknob. She opened it before she could lose her nerve. She stepped into the doorway.

John Holden looked up. There was shock in his eyes and his forehead wrinkled in a frown. Clearly startled, he started to rise. Kate threw out her hand, palm toward him, in a stopping motion.

"No. Don't get up. No need to be formal with me."

From his half-risen position, he said, "Who are you?"

The questioning look on his face made Kate falter. He truly looked as if he didn't know her. Maybe she had made a mistake. Then her resolve returned. He could not put her off so easily.

"You know who I am."

Holden shook his head. "No, I don't." He stood and started around the side of the desk. "You must have the wrong office. Who are you looking for?"

"Leland Webern."

"Who?"

His reply was astounding; she hardly knew what to say. This man had been in their home, he had talked with Henry. She didn't think he had killed Henry. Still, she was certain he knew something about it.

"Leland, you visited Henry. I know you did."

He held out his hand. "I'm sorry, I don't know either of those men. Why did you think Mr. Webern was here?"

"I saw you at Alisha's house. The police in Greenfield are looking for you."

"Do you mean Alisha Roth? I do know her. She is my partner's wife."

Kate felt a sneer creep across her face. She couldn't believe how Leland was denying everything.

"Yes, I know. Jared Roth bought this business from my brother, Henry Shore. I'm sure you know Henry is dead. I am also sure you know who I am."

"Katherine Shore," he said it as if it were the first time he'd said her name.

"In Greenfield you called me Kate."

"Please, Miss Shore. I do know your brother is dead. Jared and Alisha attended the funeral. I would have gone but I really didn't know him. I saw him a few times during the purchase of the business. You must know I've never met you."

Kate stood staring at him. This was unbelievable. He gestured toward an armchair beside his desk.

"Come, sit down. Something has badly upset you. Maybe I can help."

He was lying. Still, if she were to learn anything, she'd need to stay, to talk with him. She crossed the room and sat. She vaguely noticed the chair's tan and beige swirl design upholstery was new. When Henry worked in this office, the side chairs were maroon leather. Alisha's touch was all over the place, as if she wanted to erase every trace of the Shores. Maybe she had something to do with permanently getting rid of Henry, too. Kate couldn't think straight. It was like being on a tilt-a-whirl at the fair. She watched as Leland/John returned to his seat behind the desk.

"May I get you something to drink? Water or something stronger?"

Kate glared at him.

"Well, now," he said. "Tell me what this is about."

"You are the most accomplished liar I've ever seen. Why did you come to Greenfield to talk with Henry?"

He smiled, held up his hand, and started to speak. Kate stopped him.

"No, don't bother to deny it. I was there, as you well know. It is something held over from this business, or it wouldn't involve both you and Henry. It is something bad enough to get him killed. Maybe something illegal you want hidden. Or is it just Henry's murder?"

John stared at her, tapping his fingers on the desktop. This time Kate waited for him to speak.

"Quite a story," he said. "If I recall, Henry has been gone for a bit over two months. Why are you here now? If you think his death is connected with this business, why not tell the police?"

"I tried to. Except I knew you as Leland Webern and Henry said he knew you from before, connected with some other dealings, and you'd come to get advice from him about starting some business. Nothing to do with Shore."

"And you thought you'd find this Mr. Webern here? Even if your brother said he knew him in some other connection?"

"I'll not go round and round about this. You disappeared. I had no idea how to find you until I saw you at Alisha's."

"I am so sorry, but you have made a mistake. The shock of Henry's death. How could you recall what this Webern looks like? Perhaps I resemble him. Maybe the same build and coloring. I'm a common looking person. I've been mistaken for others before. Please, Miss Shore, if the police are looking for this man, they can handle it."

"Then you won't mind me telling them about you. Let the police sort out your identity."

John reached into the breast pocket of his suit jacket. He took out a thin brown billfold and slid it across the desk.

"Please, look for yourself. You'll find a driver's license, an insurance card. I think my voter I.D. is there."

Kate rose, leaned forward, and picked up the billfold. She couldn't stop herself. She opened it and examined the items in the card slots. They were as he said. All the identification of John Holden. Of course, it would be. Obviously, he had carefully thought out his impersonation of Leland Webern. Still, might not he be Leland Webern masquerading as John Holden? However, it didn't make any difference what he called himself, or even who he truly was; he had been at her home. She closed the billfold and slung it back across the desk; he picked it up and returned it to his breast pocket. He took a business card from the holder on the desk and standing, held it out to Kate. She took it and put it into her dress pocket.

"Keep my card, Miss Shore. Call me if you have more questions. You've seen my identification, does that satisfy you?"

"No. It only means you go by two names. I don't know which one is accurate but I know you were there when Henry died."

John's jaw tightened and his lips narrowed. "I was not. You must come to your senses. I am not who you think I am."

Kate gave a harsh laugh. "I agree with you. You are not who I think you are, because when you were at the house you had me fooled. I thought you were Henry's friend. I thought the two of you had some problem in common."

John stood silent; she could almost read the thoughts passing behind his eyes. While he was clearly deciding how to handle her, she also was making plans. If she got out of this office in one piece, she'd get back to Greenfield and tell the police what she had found. She could phone them, but because the man was more than prepared to defend his current identification, it would be better to make her case in person. When the silence stretched on, Kate broke it.

"If you think I'm afraid, you are mistaken. Nothing will stop me from going to the police."

The corner of his mouth lifted in a half smile. "Have I tried to stop you?"

"Not since I've been here, but maybe you or someone connected with you has."

"Someone tried to stop you from going to the police?"

"Yes. A rough sounding man on the phone. Demanding I tell him about Henry's business. Do you know who the caller was?"

John abruptly came to her side, grabbed her upper arm, and tried to lift her to her feet.

"I've had enough of this game, Miss Shore. I will give you the benefit of the doubt. Maybe you believe I'm this other person, no doubt the death of your brother has unsettled your mind. For this, I am sorry, but I can't help you. Please go. Go back to Greenfield, talk to the police. If you are receiving threatening calls, ask them for protection."

He pulled Kate to her feet. She was so close she caught the faint spicy scent of his aftershave, the same one Leland used. Kate pulled away.

"You can throw me out, but I'll get to the bottom of this. I have nothing else to do. If you intend to stop me, you should do it now."

John stopped and held up his hands.

"You are free to leave. But, please take my advice. Let the police do their job. You look like a nice person, take care of yourself."

When she stepped into the hallway, John firmly closed the door behind her. She had confronted him, and it had come to nothing.

Kate's face grew warm, a bit of the trembling returned. She slowly walked along the green carpeting toward the back stairs. She would go to the police, especially now that she had found the man who had stayed in their home. Descending the wooden steps, she recalled how strongly he had denied being there when Henry died. Maybe he wasn't. She had no way of knowing when he had left. If he was gone before the murder, he should have come forward. His denial of knowing her said it all. John Holden had a lot to hide. She was more certain than ever a third person had been there. Maybe John dropped the killer at the house and he escaped in Henry's car.

Kate went out the side door and it locked behind her. Standing on the loading dock, she could see all three overhead doors were down and tall security lights had come on in the yard. As she descended the few stairs, she took the car key from her dress pocket. John's card slipped out and fell on the step. She picked it up. In the car, she retrieved her purse from the glove compartment and put the card into it. Sitting behind the steering wheel, a weakness settled over her as she backed the car out into the lot. She looked up at the back of the building. The windows in John's office reflected the yard light's glare; maybe he was standing behind them watching her leave.

She didn't feel strong enough for a long drive; however, she should go home immediately and report what she had found to the police. If she stopped for something to eat, rested a bit, she could reach Greenfield by midnight. She could sleep a few hours, and go to the police station early in the morning. She no longer thought of the man who had visited Henry as Leland. The John Holden she had confronted clearly had a convincing identity. John it was, then.

As she left the lakefront and headed toward I-94, she had a small feeling of accomplishment. She had discovered the man who had been with Henry the day he died. Although she'd found him by accident, it was still a step forward. As evening deepened, colored neon lights came on advertising open businesses. Traffic picked up in mid-city, but rather than stressing her, the activity brought renewed energy. It was the vibrant beat of life, people busy living, doing what was necessary to sustain them. The odors and the colors flowed together like the city's lifeblood; the sounds were its heartbeat. There were millions of people with problems, but the strong ones didn't give up, and neither would she. The idea of visiting Aunt Iris was gone. Perhaps when this was over and she was out of danger, she'd visit. For an instant, a tiny tinge of discouragement tainted her enthusiasm. She had no plans beyond finding Henry's killer. If she escaped the current danger, a lifetime stretched before her. It could be a long empty time.

Turning into the parking lot of a Burger King near the interstate, Kate decided, like Scarlett, she'd think about that tomorrow.

Four

After a short stop for food, and time in the restroom where she washed her face, Kate was ready for the trip back to Greenfield. In parts of the city, the interstates mingled then divided, giant rivers of asphalt branching to the south and to the east. She found I-65 and settled down for the long drive. While she had stopped to eat, night had fully claimed the sky. Following the red taillights of the traffic heading south, it seemed one long train of individual cars. Strangers with only one thing in common: their direction. Whenever a vehicle veered toward an exit, she felt a small loss, as if they were deserting this caravan of the night. She made up reasons for their departure. Perhaps they'd reached home, were arriving for a family visit, or had business in the area. She had never paid attention to strangers; she was involved with her family even as it had dwindled. With Henry gone, every passing day confirmed how alone she was. Uncle Bryon and Aunt Elaine living in New York might welcome her. The distance between the brothers had formed before she was born. They couldn't hold that against her.

Kate brushed the thought away. If she formed a connection with any side of the extended family, it must be with her mother's sister. She believed what Grace had said: you could count on Iris. As the miles passed, her mind wandered until she jerked it back to reality. She straightened in the driver's seat, and put more attention on the bright, white path the headlights cast upon the pavement ahead. The stop at Burger King had refreshed her, but her situation was like carrying a heavy burden. She had been willing to leave finding Henry's killer to the police, even though the urge to do this one last thing nagged at her, but the threatening phone call had changed things. It had made her reach out to Jim Burton hoping for advice. His death and the office break-in added to her sorrow and confusion.

She had heard of crooks who read the obituaries and when families were at the funeral, used the time to rob the house. Maybe it happened to Mr. Burton's office, but breaking into a law office seemed a stretch. More naturally, it would have been his home, and if it had been, she wouldn't have lost the box Grace left for her. Kate rolled her shoulders and relaxed her grip on the steering wheel. She didn't fear falling asleep while driving; the thoughts thrashing about in her mind prevented it. If she didn't find some answers, she might never rest well again.

As it had turned out, the trip to the law office was unnecessary, yet finding John Holden had made it very worthwhile. Alisha had been friendly; it could have been out of pity, although she didn't think of Alisha as being compassionate. Moreover, when Kate had mentioned the possibility of returning to Chicago to live, there might have been alarm in Alisha's eyes. She'd said how nice the house in Greenfield was and that Kate should try to make friends there. To Kate's knowledge, Alisha had never seen the house. Maybe she had seen a picture; the house had been part of the purchase price.

The dashboard clock read nine o'clock, at least two or more hours to Greenfield. Any rest stops would make it longer. The interior of the Acura was like a space capsule, a place suspended. It felt secure and safe, a haven where ideas could come together. She concentrated, trying to use the uninterrupted time wisely. When she reached home, she would sleep, even if it meant a sleeping pill. She needed to be strong for tomorrow, to be convincing when telling the police about Mr. Holden. She would talk with Detective Simpson about the telephone call, too. He probably knew of her reporting it. Now she could add Holden's use of the phony name. Both undoubtedly connected to Henry's murder, as well as what she'd overheard Henry saying to Leland. At the time, the few words, *'I can't do that.'* hadn't seemed important, just Henry objecting to something Leland wanted to do, if only she knew what it was.

It was hard to stop thinking of John Holden as Leland, but seeing as he had abandoned the name, she'd have to. No matter what his name, he and Henry had shared some secret. In the telephone call, the thug had threatened her with death if she went to the police. Maybe John and Henry had faced the same threat. However, John seemed willing to involve the police. He must be confident in his new identity. It came back to one thing...someone wanted something and was willing to kill for it. Her life had turned into a giant tangle of twine with no way to untangle it. If she could find one string to pull, this mess might start to unravel.

So far, she had only told the police and John about the telephone threat. Perhaps there wouldn't be another call. It was wishful thinking, especially when the caller had said someone would contact her.

It was about an hour to Greenfield; the exit was coming up shortly. Leaving the interstate for the less traveled highway brought a small jolt of fear. It put her closer to the scene of Henry's death and the site of her problems. It was tempting to keep driving. Find another town, figure out how to become someone else, as John had done. It would be a relief to leave these problems behind, but it wasn't possible. She couldn't step aside from an obligation. There must be justice for Henry; it would also provide the peace she needed. Every day brought more questions, and doubts about how Henry had conducted business. Something had put Henry, and now her, in this situation. Henry Sr. had never spoken well of his brother, Bryon, criticizing him for past deeds. She had always taken it to mean her father held the moral high ground in the estrangement...now she wondered. If her father had problems, maybe Henry had inherited them as well as the business. Still, as the last of their side of the family, she had a duty to make a tidy end of it.

Several miles from Greenfield, Kate stopped at a Conoco station for gasoline. Filling the tank, she stood under the dark, starless sky more lost and alone than ever. There was no one left to need her help, no one alive, except herself. She gave a harsh laugh. Perhaps she had a duty to take care of herself. A night breeze strengthened, further chilling the air, and she turned up her collar. It seemed a long time ago when she'd put on the blue dress with its jacket. The people at Henry's funeral told her to take care of herself. Even John had used those words, meaning there'd be no help from him. It angered her; he shouldn't express concern if he wasn't willing to help. Back in the car, Kate pulled away from the filling station and drove out of the surrounding light. The two-lane highway ahead was almost deserted. The farmhouses along the road were dark, with a yard light near an out building brightening small areas. She passed one slow-moving pickup, and two cars sped by going in the opposite direction.

By the time she reached Greenfield, only an all-night laundromat, a couple of gasoline stations, and the mini-mart were open. Yet, it didn't matter as she intended to drive straight to the house, not even stopping to let Ronda know she was back, although Ronda might still be awake. Sometimes, Ronda had an overnight guest. She never discussed her visitors, and Kate had never asked. Still, one afternoon when she arrived to visit Ronda, one of her male friends was leaving. Ronda had acted flustered and didn't introduce him, just quickly shut his car door, and hustled Kate into the house. Kate didn't get a good look at him, but wasn't really interested.

Kate drove through an older neighborhood, and turned on Meadow Street, which took her past Ronda's house. It was after midnight, and a glance showed it was completely dark. A couple of blocks farther on, she turned left on Vine and seeing her house on the far corner brought a surge of relief. 'Be it ever so humble,' she thought. The Greenfield house was a quarter the size of the big family home in Chicago, but now even it seemed too large. She turned in the driveway, and hit the garage door opener. As the overhead door raised revealing both empty spaces, it emphasized Henry's loss. As long as she lived here, there would be only one car in the garage. She turned off the ignition and closed the garage door. Weary and stiff from the long drive, Kate opened the car door, grabbed her purse, and stepped out. The overhead light dimly illuminated the area.

Moving to the car's rear door, she opened it to take out the suitcase. She set it on the cement floor, closed the car door, and retrieved the house key from her purse. The garage led to a mudroom and laundry. She would drop her suitcase there and unload any dirty clothes in the morning. She expected to be in bed within minutes...she wasn't hungry, and far too tired to stop for anything else. She unlocked the door, pushed it open, set the bag inside, and entered the utility room to turn off the security alarm. She did all this by the garage light. When she switched on the inside light, Kate blinked, gasped, and took a step back.

The cabinet above the washer and dryer was open, detergent and other washing liquids were setting out, some of them spilled. A tall storage closet was also open, brooms and other items tossed about. Kate stepped around her luggage, and over a box of vacuum bags. In the kitchen, every cabinet door was open, even the oven, microwave, refrigerator, and freezer were standing open. A film of water covered the floor in front of the refrigerator. It was still running, but the freezer side couldn't keep up with the warmer air. Kate slammed the refrigerator and freezer doors shut. She had no idea if it would help, but she had to do something. The kitchen was a mess, overturned from top to bottom.

She staggered to the door leading to the dining room and the front foyer, turning on lights as she went. The dining room was as torn up as the kitchen. The glass front of the china closet was unbroken, but the drawers were open with linens tossed about. Even the foyer coat closet was open. In a daze, she went to Henry's office. The desk drawers were out; the cushions to the armchairs were on the floor, the stuffing hanging from them. Even the pictures on the walls hung askew. Nothing had been left untouched. She picked up a square pillow, and hugging it to her, she sat on an armchair. With no seat cushion or one for the back, Kate sat near the floor. Her stomach churned, nausea rose in her throat, and she shook. She buried her face in the pillow, screamed, and began to wail. The sound was more a fierce howling than sobbing. If she had been angry over the situation before, it was nothing to compare with this rage. Panting, she sat up, threw her head back, and tried to gain control of the consuming emotions. After a minute, she looked around the room. Even in the jumble, all the furniture seemed to be there; if anything were missing, it would be something small. The bookcase on the wall opposite the fireplace was half-empty, but even with books scattered on the floor, it didn't seem any of them were gone. Yet, it was hard to tell amid the clutter.

Still holding the pillow, she slowly stood and leaned against the desk wondering what to do. There was no doubt the upstairs would be in the same condition. She hated to think what had happened in the sunroom. Still, she needed to see it all. Kate dropped the pillow and walked on wooden legs into the foyer, past the staircase, and into the sunroom at the back of the house. This was her favorite room. The plants had made it an indoor garden; she had enjoyed sitting on the lounge and reading. When the light came on, it was plain the room had not escaped. Plants were scattered on the tile floor, and the lounge's cushions shared the armchairs' fate. The mundane thought of needing a cleaning service made her laugh. She put a hand over her mouth to stop the nervous reaction. If all she could think about was restoring the house to order, it was clear she wasn't thinking straight.

Kate bent and picked up a small terracotta pot that held an aloe. The spiky light green plant had lost several of its plump leaves. The plant's roots still clung to a clump of dirt hanging to the inside of the pot. She scooped up more of the dirt from the floor and packed it back into the container. It was a useless stalling effort, wasting time before calling the police. She righted an overturned end table and set the pot on it. Dusting her hands, she left the sunroom and climbed the stairs to the bedrooms. The upstairs rooms were no surprise. The bedrooms and baths looked as if an indoor tornado had hit them. In her bedroom, a jewelry box was open, the contents scattered on the top of the dresser. Nothing seemed to be missing. She started to pick up a silver necklace, but stopped. The police might want the scene untouched. Still, she set the bench at the foot of the bed back on its legs and sat on it.

Calling the police was what any homeowner would do. Yet, she wasn't any homeowner. The house was the scene of a murder and evidently an ongoing crime spree. Henry and John had been involved in something Henry had kept hidden from her. Jim Burton's death couldn't count in the mix, but Grace's missing box certainly could. Now, whoever they were they had searched the house. If she had been home when they broke in, they might have killed her, unless they knew she was gone. Kate put her hand to her forehead, closed her eyes, and tried to think. Mrs. Farber knew she was coming to Chicago; Ronda knew she'd be gone, who else knew she was out of town? There was Alisha, but she didn't know until Kate turned up at her house. Yet, she could have phoned someone. John Holden also could have let someone know it would take her hours to get home.

It was no good trying to figure out who had searched the house or when they did it. If it had been one person, it would have taken at least several hours to go through everything. If there had been two or more people, they could have been in and out in a short time. Maybe there would be fingerprints, but she doubted it. It was also plain they were not ordinary thieves, for nothing was missing. She didn't expect the police to catch the burglars. They'd had no success in finding Henry's killer. If the office break-in was to take the box, they must not have found what they were looking for, and came to ransack the house. None of this could be a coincidence.

She left the bedroom and hurried downstairs to the kitchen where she'd dropped her suitcase and purse. The sight of the ravaged house was sickening. Her first thought was to start putting it right, clean up the spilled cereal and flour, and try to erase any signs of the intruders. Whatever they were looking for must be small, or they wouldn't have gone through everything. She cleared a spot on the kitchen table and set up an overturned chair. She put her purse on the table and took out her cell phone along with John Holden's business card. She was shaking; it wasn't from fright, she was past that, and she clenched her jaw in anger. John knew what was going on. She was certain he could explain this break-in better than the police could. She placed the card on the table and jabbed the numbers into the cell phone. It was late, he might not answer, and if he didn't, she would not leave a message… there was too much to explain.

However, he did answer and her grip on the phone tightened.

"Mr. Holden, or should I say John, since we know each other. This is Kate. The one you threw out of your office. I'm home now."

"Yes?"

"I came home to a house completely torn apart. Do you know what they are looking for?"

The pause made her think he did know.

"I have no idea what you're talking about. What's happened to your house?"

Kate snorted. "You don't know? I think you do. I'm giving you a chance to tell the truth before I call the police. You did tell me to call them, but I think you are bluffing."

"Look, Miss Shore—"

"You can drop the Miss. You called me Kate when you stayed here. I don't care what identification you have. When I tell the police who you are, you'll be accounting for every minute of those two days. Do you think you can? I doubt it."

"I assure you, I can account for my time. When was I supposedly at your home?"

"Forget it. You know those dates. I'm sure you have already made up some excuse. How silly of me to think you wouldn't have." Kate sighed. "But I'll still tell the police. I had hoped you would help me."

"My best advice is for you to call the police."

"Did you advise Henry to call them? Is that why he said, I can't do that? You must tell me."

"I'm sure your brother had his reasons for whatever he did. You seemed to have had a good relationship with him. Maybe he was trying to protect you."

"Protect me from what?"

"Please, Miss Shore, it is best you tell the police whatever you think you know. I'm sorry for your troubles. The sooner you let the police handle things, the sooner you'll find some peace."

"I would be overjoyed to do it." Her voice rose with each word. "But I'm in danger. Someone stole a box from our attorney's office... it belonged to me, and the house is broken into. You tell me how to get out of this. Do you think the police can stop something else from happening?"

When he didn't reply, despair settled over her and she slumped in the kitchen chair.

"Okay," she said. "Never mind. I'll figure it out for myself. My brother cared about me. Maybe he was right to keep the police out of whatever it is."

Kate hung up, and seconds later when the phone rang, she let it go to voice mail. It was John again, urging her to call the police and ask for protection. She put the cell phone back into her purse and remained sitting. For the minute, she didn't feel threatened. Either the crooks had found what they wanted and would leave her alone, or they had not. If they thought she knew where it was, they wouldn't kill her before finding it. Not a cheerful thought, but probably the truth.

Her bag was still packed; she could pick up a few more clothes and take off, this time going straight to Aunt Iris. It was hard to believe Henry had done anything wrong, but it seemed he hadn't wanted to involve the police. If as John suggested it was to protect her, it wasn't working. Weariness, tension, and worry kept her from being afraid; she didn't have room for more emotions. The crooks had gotten into the house without setting off the alarm. That meant they had the code or knew how to get around it. She might as well have left the house unlocked, for all the good locking it did. The same for reporting the break-in; there was nothing the police could do. Still, she would have to report it. There was always the chance they might catch the burglars. With the decision made, Kate dialed the Greenfield police.

While she waited for them to arrive, she took her suitcase upstairs. In the bedroom, she began putting things back into their places. Even the bathroom was in disarray. The thought of strangers touching her belongings was repugnant. If there happened to be fingerprints, there should be enough downstairs. Fifteen minutes later, two uniformed policemen arrived. When she let them in the front door, the shorter one looked around.

"They really tore it up," he said.

The other older man frowned at him.

Kate was past caring about their comments; she wanted them to do whatever they needed and leave. The older patrolman said, "Are you alone in the house?"

"Yes. When I came home, I found it this way, and no one is here."

While he spoke with her, the younger one began a search of the rooms. He either didn't believe her, or perhaps needed to survey the damage.

"Do you have any idea who could have done this?" he asked.

"No, but if you'll talk with Detective Simpson this could be in connection with my brother's death."

"The Shore case, that's right. I thought the address was familiar. Do you have some place you can go?"

She thought about Ronda but was too tired to talk with her. "Not really. I'd like to stay here, if it is all right."

The younger man came into the living room. "There is no one on the premises."

As if double-checking, both men made a tour of the house, the older one snapping pictures with his cell phone. In the kitchen, Kate sat waiting for them. When they came back, they took a more formal statement from her, and she signed it.

"Detective Simpson will be out to see you in the morning," the older patrolman informed her. "Are you sure you want to stay here?"

"Yes, very sure. Thank you for coming."

It was nearly two o'clock when the patrolmen left. Kate was almost too tired to lock up behind them. She climbed the stairs to her bedroom, where she undressed and fell into bed. She was asleep in seconds.

~ * ~

Morning light poured through the sheers hanging in Kate's bedroom windows. She had not drawn the drapes and she awoke with a start. Her bedroom was on the backside of the house, and the trees on the property line gave some privacy, but she always closed the drapes. She sat up and grabbed the robe at the foot of the bed. The clock read six; she'd slept less than four hours. Her head throbbed and her body felt stiff, as if the muscles had never relaxed. The past two days hung over her like a thundercloud. Sitting on the edge of the bed, she looked around the room. The closet door was open and several items of clothing lay on the floor. One tennis shoe was by the corner of the dresser. She remembered trying to straighten the room, but she hadn't done a good job. She felt a chill and drew the robe closer around her neck. The heating was on and a soft rush of warm air flowed from a vent. The house wasn't cold; it was her reaction to stress. She stood and resolved to stay strong.

She wondered when Detective Simpson would show up, and wished he could solve the growing list of crimes, but she didn't have much faith in the authorities. It wasn't their fault; they would do all they could, and she was determined to keep investigating on her own. She grabbed some underwear and went into the bathroom. She took a long shower, washed her hair, and standing before the foggy mirror, dried it. Back in the bedroom, she dug out a pair of jeans, a sweatshirt, and a pair of socks. When she found the hidden tennis shoe, she finished dressing.

Downstairs, the messy kitchen was disheartening. Maybe a call to some cleaning service would be in order, but first she needed to eat. With no appetite, she forced down cereal and coffee. After eating, she put on a jacket and went out the front door. She sat on the steps waiting for the detective, and watching the neighborhood awaken. Next door, Mr. Shelden backed his car down the drive to the street. When not playing golf, he joined a group at a local restaurant for breakfast. Before the murder, his wife, Alice, had told Kate he went to the meeting once a week. Since it was early morning, maybe it was where he was going. As she watched Mr. Shelden leave, she heard Alice call to her.

"Kate? My, you are out early."

Alice was still in her robe, but she came to the waist-high picket fence on the property line. Her short hair not yet combed, and absent makeup, her face seemed as gray as her hair. Kate stood and went to meet her. She was surprised at the greeting; Mrs. Shelden had been standoffish after Henry's death, making it plain that murder harmed the property values.

"How are you, Mrs. Shelden?"

"Please, it's Alice. I'm fine. How are you?"

Kate smiled. "I'm fine, too. The mister off to his group breakfast?"

"Yes. A nice break for me, his having breakfast out." She leaned forward. "Not to be nosy, but are you moving?" The note of hope in Alice's voice was unmistakable.

"No. Not right now, anyway. Why?"

"Well, I saw the van yesterday afternoon...just thought we might be losing you."

Van, Kate thought, what van?

"You saw a van at my house?"

"I'm sure I did."

"What time? You said afternoon, early afternoon or late? What did it look like?"

Mrs. Shelden took a step back. "I guess it was late, maybe around five. It was a medium-sized truck, white, with a big moving sign on the side."

"Do you remember the name of the company?"

"No, I think it just said 'Movers.' I do know it was in big black letters. On the side facing my yard. Probably on the other side, too. But of course, I didn't go around there." She folded her hands across her stomach, a satisfied look brightening her face.

"Did you see the mover himself? Could you describe him?"

"I don't believe so. Besides, there were two of them. Both in dark blue coveralls, you know those things movers wear. Say, if you aren't moving, what were they doing? Were you getting an estimate? I didn't think that was it, because those moving companies usually send out a man in a suit to do the estimate and make the arrangements. I supposed you'd already done it. You really aren't moving?"

"If I am, no one told me. Do you have any idea how long they were here? Did you see them go inside?"

"Well, I wasn't watching everything they did! All I know is I let Snookums out around seven and the truck was gone."

Snookums was the Shelden's big gray Persian cat. One day last summer it had attacked a bird's nest in a tree in Kate's backyard. After that, she had never cared for the cat.

"Listen, Alice. Would you be willing to tell the police all you know about those men and the moving van?"

Alice turned a lighter shade of gray. Her eyes widened, and she moved a little distance back from the fence. "What? Why would I?"

"They may have broken into my house. You can describe all you saw. It would be a big help."

"No, no. I don't think so. I've had quite enough to do with the police asking all those questions, after, well, after your brother."

"Please, I'm sure they would appreciate it. I know I would."

Mrs. Shelden gathered the skirt of her robe higher and started a retreat to her front porch. Kate called after her. "I'm sorry to bother you, Alice. I'll have to tell the police what you have told me. They will want to talk with you. It shouldn't take long."

A black Ford turned off the street and pulled into Kate's driveway. As Mrs. Shelden hurried across the porch, she gave a startled look behind her, and entered her house. The sound of the door slamming carried in the crisp morning air. Kate left the fence and went to greet the two men who were getting out of their car. The taller one was Charles Simpson; he had come after Henry's death. He was slender, had thinning brown hair above a lightly tanned face, which seldom held a smile. Still, she remembered a soothing air about him, and he had told her to call him Chuck.

Detective Simpson held out his hand. "Hello, Miss Shore. What's the trouble? Something about a break-in?"

Kate shook his offered hand. "I'm afraid so. I called last night. They couldn't do anything. Whoever did it was gone."

The other man, a bit shorter and with a body-builder's physique, stood waiting for an introduction. A wide smile on his brown face, and a sparkle in his black eyes. Detective Simpson pointed toward him.

"This is Andrew Johnson. Came to us from Berryville. Andy, this is Miss Katherine Shore."

Kate put out her hand and Andy shook it.

"Glad to meet you," she said.

Andy had stopped smiling. "I've studied the file. Wish we had something to tell you. We're still working on it."

Kate gestured toward the house. "Let's go in. I did change some things, but I don't think it will matter."

Inside the house, Simpson asked Kate to give an account of her actions for the past two days. Andy recorded the conversation on a handheld device. The three stood in the kitchen for a while until Kate picked up two more chairs and told them to sit down.

Detective Simpson shrugged. "Might as well be comfortable," he said. "We'll get someone over to search for evidence, but from what you've said, I don't have much hope."

"You'll want to talk to Mrs. Shelden, too. She saw a moving van here yesterday evening."

Simpson looked at Andy and raised an eyebrow. "Maybe I'll give you the pleasure," he said with a half-smile.

It took Kate over thirty minutes to tell them everything she knew. She spent most of the time explaining how certain she was John Holden was the man who had visited Henry. She told of her meeting with him, how he denied everything and had identification to prove who he was.

"We'll double check him. Since you spoke with him, did he sound anything like the man on the threatening call?"

She hadn't thought of that. "Not unless he disguised his voice. All I can say is he didn't sound Southern."

"Can you think of anything else?" he asked.

"No. I don't think I've forgotten anything."

The three of them stood, and Chuck Simpson looked around the kitchen.

"Big mess. I hope they found what they were looking for."

Andy looked surprised. "Oh, yeah?"

"Yeah. Then they can let this poor lady alone."

Kate appreciated the show of sympathy. She ached all over, as if her body had taken a beating. Andy and Simpson started toward the living room. Simpson held out his hand and stepped aside, waving Kate forward.

"Okay, give us the nickel tour."

Kate took them throughout the house, pointing to the more disturbed areas. In her bedroom, she described how it had been before her straightening efforts.

"You really didn't find anything missing?" asked Andy.

"Not so far," she answered. "Not anything big, anyway. Maybe I'll miss something later. When can I start cleaning? I might hire a professional company."

"We'll try to be out of here by this evening," Chuck told her as he turned to his partner.

"Andy, call the forensic team, and visit next door to see what Mrs. Shelden has to say."

Andy nodded and hurried from the bedroom. Chuck stepped back and motioned Kate to exit the room. As they walked to the staircase, he stopped her at the top landing.

"Look, Kate. I know what's going on here is probably bigger than our small-town police department is equipped to handle, but I want you to know we'll do our best.

"I know you will and I appreciate it."

"About the phone call, I'll put in for your phone records and see what comes up. May take a while to get them. I wish we could have an officer here on the property."

Kate held up her hand. "I get it. You don't have many officers, right?"

"That's about it. Do you own a gun?"

"A gun? No. I've never even held a gun of any kind. I wouldn't know what to do with it."

Simpson narrowed his eyes. "Probably not a good idea you get one now."

"Probably not."

Kate started down the stairs ahead of him. A gun, she thought. Here again, just in different words, was *take care of yourself*. If she bought a gun, took lessons, learned how to use it, could she kill someone with it? For an instant the 'yes' that flashed startled her. It was a jolt of self-realization. She *would* fight to protect herself, maybe even kill. At the foot of the stairs, Kate turned to the detective.

"What does it take to get a handgun?"

He looked surprised. "You have to apply for a license. There's a seventy-two hour wait after purchase. You'd need to take a sixteen-hour course."

Kate shrugged her shoulders and laughed. "Good gracious. A little late for me to start that form of protection. How long does it take a criminal to get a gun?"

When Kate continued to laugh, Simpson's jaw tightened.

"Sorry I mentioned it," he said.

Shortly after the detectives left, a two-person team arrived to collect what evidence they could from the torn-up house. Still wearing her jacket, Kate took her purse and backed the Acura out of the garage. She would leave them to it. If Ronda were home, she'd camp there until the house was hers again.

<h1 style="text-align:center">Five</h1>

When Kate pulled into Ronda's driveway, Ronda was standing on the front porch. As Kate got out of her car, Ronda waved to her.

"You're back," she called. "How was the trip? You didn't stay long."

Kate crossed the lawn and started up the steps. "No, not long, but a lot happened."

Ronda opened the front door, motioning Kate forward. "What, what? Tell me everything."

The house was the same age as Kate's, except it was smaller. There was no second floor, and the foyer opened directly into the living room. An archway on the left led through the dining room and to the kitchen. Ronda started into the living room, but changed directions, leading Kate toward the dining room.

"Let's sit in the kitchen. I'll make some tea."

Newspapers and a couple of magazines covered the granite-topped island. Ronda hurriedly gathered them and stuffed the papers into a corner basket. She motioned Kate to one of the high-backed stools.

"Sit, sit," she urged. "I'll put the kettle on. Now tell me about your trip."

Kate removed her jacket and hung it on the back of a chair. She took a seat at the island and sat with an elbow propped on the counter, wondering how much to tell Ronda. She hadn't told her about the threatening phone call, but she *had* told her she was going to pick up the box at Jim Burton's office. Ronda didn't act as if she knew about the break-in...still three blocks away and not even on the same street, she wouldn't have noticed.

Ronda was opening a cabinet and taking out cups and saucers. She looked over her shoulder.

"Well, don't just sit there. Something interesting must have happened."

"Oh. I'm sorry. I don't know where to begin. Did you go past my house yesterday?"

Ronda set the cups on the island and threw her arms up, her eyes wide. "What am I thinking? Your mail. I picked it up yesterday."

Ronda hurried from the kitchen into the utility room. "I put it out here. So when I went to the car I wouldn't forget to bring it to you."

In a minute, Ronda came back and plopped a box and several envelopes, along with a flyer for the local auto dealership on the counter in front of Kate.

"There. A lot of mail for one day. Well, wouldn't be so much if it weren't for this package."

Kate picked up the envelopes, all the while looking at the box wrapped in brown paper. Ronda tapped Kate's arm, and pointed to it.

"Open the package. Did you buy something on line? I love getting packages, what is it?"

Kate put the envelopes down and drew the box toward her. It was about twelve inches square, tied with string, and addressed to her. There was no return address. Kate carefully picked it up and set it on another stool at the island. Ronda's face flushed a shade lighter than her red lipstick.

"Aren't you going to open it? I can't wait to open packages I get. How do you know they sent the right stuff?"

"I don't know. I haven't ordered anything."

Ronda batted her eyelashes. "Well, I'd be even more curious."

Before Kate could answer, Ronda's lips formed a plump red oval, a look of inquiry on her round face.

"Say, did you get the box you went to the lawyer's office to collect?

The question startled Kate. She had come to Ronda's house to find a refuge until the forensic team finished. She had been hesitant to tell Ronda about her trip and the break-in because the past two days were nearly overwhelming. She didn't want to confide in anyone until she understood what was happening.

The teakettle whistled and Kate jumped. Ronda clicked her tongue in exasperation and turned to take the kettle off the burner. "You don't have to tell me if you don't want to," she called. "Isn't any of my business, anyway."

Kate put her hand to her forehead and exhaled heavily enough to puff her lips. Ronda probably had a right to know what was going on, but Kate couldn't think straight enough to decide what to reveal. It might be all right to tell Ronda everything; still she hadn't known her long.

Ronda poured the tea and set the sugar bowl and a small pitcher of cream on the island. She kept her lips in a tight line and her chin held high. Clearly, she was unhappy with Kate's silence. Kate tried to smile.

"I'm sorry, Ronda. I shouldn't burden you with my problems."

Instantly Ronda's round face brightened. She scooted her high-backed stool closer to Kate.

"Don't be silly. You can tell me anything. Who am I going to tell? I don't know anyone around here. Your secrets are safe with me." Ronda poured some cream into her tea and gave Kate a conspiratorial smile. "So tell me, what did happen in Chicago. Why did you come back this soon?"

"It isn't what happened in Chicago that should interest you, Ronda. Seems we aren't as safe in this small town as we thought."

Ronda's eyes widened and she leaned forward. "What do you mean?"

"My house was broken into."

"When?"

"My neighbor said she saw a moving van parked in front of the garage maybe between two and five yesterday afternoon. When did you pick up my mail?"

Ronda pressed a be-ringed hand to her plump chest. "Kate! How awful. When did you get home?"

"After midnight."

"Did you call the police?"

"Yes. Were you home all day yesterday?"

"All day. Except when I jogged over to your house to get the mail."

"When was that?"

Ronda shrugged. "Gee, I don't know, maybe a bit after lunch."

"And you didn't see a big white moving van anywhere in the neighborhood?"

"No. I didn't see anything."

"Where was the package? It's too large to have fit in the mailbox."

"Oh, yes, well, you being away, I thought I should check on the house. You know, make sure everything was okay. The package was at the front door. I picked it up because it wouldn't have been safe to just leave it there."

Kate took a sip of the tea. If Ronda was at the house around twelve-thirty or one, she wouldn't have seen the van. She set the cup back on its saucer, her shaky hand making the china clatter.

"It is a good thing you didn't run into the robbers when you picked up the mail."

"Robbers? How do you know there was more than one?"

"Alice Shelden, my neighbor, saw two men."

Ronda leaned forward, her eyes a penetrating blue. "Tell me everything."

Kate shrugged. "Not much to tell."

Kate told Ronda what had happened after she arrived home the night before. While she spoke, Ronda refilled their teacups and put out a small plate of sugar cookies. When Kate finished, Ronda heaved a heavy sigh.

"I can't believe it. After what you've been through. Do the police have any idea who did this? Do they think it has anything to do with Henry's death? Oh, I'm sorry to bring it up, but isn't it possible? Can you think of anything to make both things happen? Sounds like they were looking for something."

Kate gave a harsh laugh. "Oh, they were looking for something all right."

"What do you think it is?" Ronda breathlessly asked.

"I don't know."

Ronda frowned, the furrows on her forehead deepened beneath the makeup. "Oh Kate, surely you know something. You can't have lived in the same house with your brother and have no idea what got him killed. Now a robbery. Think, girl. You must have some suspicions. Maybe Henry was up to something."

"Up to something? Like what?"

Ronda shrugged and waved her hand. "Oh, I don't know. He ran that big business for years. You hear of shady deals going on all the time. Men get in over their heads."

"Stop right there, Ronda. I know my brother. He would never have done anything illegal." Kate had growing doubts about Henry's activities, but resented Ronda's implication.

"Sorry. I thought he was a good guy, too. I'm only trying to help."

Kate stood and reached for her jacket. "It's okay. I wish I did know something."

Ronda picked up the package and the letters. "Here don't forget these. Don't you want to open the box and see what it is?"

"Not right now. It can't be anything important. I need to go home and see if I can start the cleanup."

Ronda walked with Kate to the front door. When Kate stepped out onto the porch, Ronda stood with her hand on the doorframe. "Guess this is your time for getting surprise presents."

Kate turned toward her. "What do you mean?"

"Well, you didn't say what happened with the package you make the trip for. Did you get it?"

"Oh, that. No, but I suspect it will turn up."

Ronda narrowed her eyes, but Kate hurried away. Once in the Acura, she started the car, waved at Ronda, and headed home. She hated to think of the work waiting there. Along with cleaning the house, she'd need to reset the code on the alarm system, and call a locksmith.

She glanced at the package on the passenger seat. She was certain that beneath the brown paper was the box Henry had left with Jim Burton. There was no postage on the package; clearly, someone had put it on the doorstep. If the two movers left it, they must have been at the house earlier, or Ronda was mistaken about the time she found it. If the burglary at the Burton law office was to take the package, someone had to know it was there, and the only reason for returning it to her was that someone didn't understand the contents. It wasn't out of compassion or kindness. The people behind this expected her to know the meaning of what Grace had left for her. They would probably contact her to find out what, if anything, the contents of the box meant.

The forensic van stood in the driveway. Kate pulled in beside it and got out of the car. When she stepped up onto the porch, a young man in a gray police uniform and a similarly clad young woman came through the front door. They were carrying a couple of navy-blue cases.

"Are you finished?" Kate asked.

The dark-haired young woman nodded. "Yes. It's all yours now. Sorry about the mess."

"It can't be helped. Do you know a locksmith I can call?"

"No problem there," the man said. "Lewis Locks is the only one in the book."

They seemed in a hurry and both walked swiftly to the police van. Kate watched as they backed out and headed down the street. She stood on the porch for a bit, looking at the peaceful neighborhood. There was a faint whiff of wood smoke in the air, someone burning yard debris or the early use of a fireplace. Before Henry died, they had discussed having some wood delivered. Henry had pointed out a place beside the garage to stack it. She wouldn't bother with wood now. She wasn't even certain about staying in the house. Kate left the porch and put the car into the garage. She took the mail and package into the kitchen and dropped them on the table.

The torn-up kitchen was discouraging. She pulled a chair to the table and sat, her shoulders slumped, and tears stung her eyes. Defeat descended upon her; not one optimistic thought presented itself. She couldn't stay here. The house would never sell in this condition; it would need repair and cleaning. Moreover, there was no guarantee it would sell, and if it did, she wasn't sure where to go. Kate bowed her head, closed her eyes, and fought to summon strength enough to take the next step. The constant emotional pain made it difficult to make decisions. Adjusting to Henry's death was hard. If he'd died of a heart attack, it would surely be easier to accept. Although, maybe not. The death of any family member was painful. Sorrow was a burden it took time to overcome. She still missed her parents, but the sadness had grown easier to bear. The same would be true for Henry's death, if it were not for the mystery.

She lifted her head and looked at the package. There was no doubt it was the one stolen from the law office, only now it had a new outside wrapping. The sight of it brought a flurry of conflict: gladness at having it, but anger over someone intercepting and examining it. Perhaps even removing some items. The thought of an evil person handling things from her mother was sickening. It was tempting to throw the box into the trash without opening it. No matter how painful, facing the facts was the only way to work through this nightmare.

She left the package setting on the counter for later.

The urge to run away was close to overwhelming. It was definitely an option. Although running wouldn't solve anything. Feeling nauseous, Kate stood, removed her jacket, and took it and her purse upstairs to the bedroom. The bedroom didn't look too bad because of the straightening done before.

Back downstairs, she made a call to Lewis Locks and found he could come that afternoon. The small bit of good news lifted her spirit. It encouraged her to start cleaning the kitchen, and upon consideration, it wasn't necessary to call in a cleaning crew. Drawers were easy to put back into cabinets, broken dishes swept up and dumped in a trash bag. The refrigerator, with the door closed, had stabilized its temperature. Yet, in disgust, she removed all the food and threw it away. After sweeping and mopping the floor, the kitchen looked as empty as it had on the day they had moved in. It was ready for inspection by a new buyer. She'd call a realtor and put the house up for sale. Before the break-in, she might have stayed, but not now. Moving was a form of running away, but she would not hide. Wherever she went, she would make sure Henry's killer could find her, because the desire for justice was stronger than her fear.

As she finished cleaning the kitchen, the man from Lewis Locks arrived, and watching him gave her a break from her own work. Even though she hoped to be leaving soon, the new locks were a comfort.

Cleaning the house helped relieve her tight muscles and drain what felt like poison running through her veins. In the living room and office, the cleaning and repairs went faster. It didn't take long to set up overturned tables, collect broken vases, and lamps. The slashed cushions, torn on only one side, went back onto chairs and sofas with their good sides showing. When a buyer came along, it would be time enough to call a used furniture dealer. She wouldn't take the furniture. Picture albums and other personal belongings could fit in a large trunk; there was one in the attic. Henry had brought it from the house in Chicago. It was big enough to hold anything she'd want to keep. Movers provided wardrobes for clothes and her suitcases could hold the rest. Subconsciously Kate was cutting her life down to the essentials. A smaller yet far harder version. One person didn't need a large house; it should be easy to find a suitable apartment. The challenge was in making emotional and character changes to her personality. It wasn't easy to change lifetime habits. As Kate cleaned the rose-colored carpet, her resolve grew with each forward and backward sweep of the vacuum.

The sun was setting by the time she finished with the bathrooms. They were clean and sparkling. This time, when cleaning Henry's bathroom, she threw away the personal grooming items. Before, it was too hard to get rid of his every trace. Now, his clothes closet was empty, too. A large black plastic bag sat at the top of the stairs. The local Goodwill was in for a windfall. Kate inspected the cleaned rooms, turned off lights, and carried the cleaning supplies along with Henry's clothes to the kitchen. She left the bag for Goodwill in the utility room to remind her to take it away, although it was unlikely she'd forget. After starting a fresh pot of coffee, Kate took a pair of scissors from a kitchen drawer and sat at the table with the package before her.

Cutting the string and removing the outer paper revealed Grace's gift. It was as Mrs. Farber had described: a package with clear packing tape holding the wrapping together and Grace's cursive writing on top, *For Katherine*. Kate would have recognized her mother's handwriting anywhere. However, it was plain the box had been unwrapped and rewrapped. The tape stuck in only enough places to hold the paper, much of it creased, making wrinkles in Grace's words. Kate laid the scissors aside and went to the kitchen counter to pour a cup of coffee. Sitting back at the table, taking a sip of coffee, she tried to imagine why the thief had returned the box. Certainly not out of goodness. It was possible they had gone through the box and removed what they wanted. If so, they wouldn't have returned the rest to her...she rejected any considerate motive; she was not dealing with kind people. They gave it back because they didn't understand the contents. They returned the box hoping she would find a message from Grace.

Kate set the coffee cup on the table and removed the paper from the box. Immediately, she recognized the white box with pink, blue, and yellow wildflowers printed on the lid and four sides. Long ago, it had held a blue and white Delft vase, a gift to Grace. Kate couldn't remember who gave the gift or what had happened to the vase. She only remembered that when she was a little girl, Grace had given Kate the box in which to keep doll clothes. As she outgrew dolls, she forgot the pretty box, never thinking what might have happened to it. Seeing it now brought a flood of memories. Two caring parents, an okay brother, if you overlooked his youthful pranks. In retrospect, even Henry's teasing took on a soft lavender haze. Snapping back to reality, Kate lifted the lid and set it aside.

The first thing she removed was a Steiff Bear, the fur on the tops of its ears worn thin. She knew this bear; her father had given it to her one birthday. She had called it Teddy, not original but it had seemed right. The next item was a small storybook; the cover had the faded print of distant hills with a castle nestled among them. She had read the stories many times. Fairytales. Most of the stories contained a lesson, like a parable, the make-believe situations revealing a deeper meaning. Kate hadn't thought about those childhood tales for years. *Red Riding Hood* proved things were not always what they seemed. *Beauty and the Beast* made the point even stronger. A situation could seem bad, but not be bad, good but not be good. Kate thought of the saying, 'a wolf in sheep's clothing.'

She flipped through the yellowed pages. There were *Hansel and Gretel*, taken in by the tasty house made of candy, but it was only a trap to lure them. Again, a story in which something wasn't what it seemed. She could completely sympathize with *Alice in Wonderland* because after Henry's death she was lost in a strange world, too. She was off balance, questioning everything, weighing appearances against reality. She closed the book and reached for a small jewelry box. The little silver box had a heart etched on the lid that opened to reveal a red velvet interior. There was only one item inside, a gold ring. She lifted the ring out, and slipped it onto her smallest finger. The ring was familiar. A little ring, a child's ring. Turning the ring round and round, she struggled to remember what the ring meant. It was probably hers.

Green felt, the color of a girl scout's uniform, lined the bottom of the box. Fastened to the felt was a silver oval about the size of a quarter. The small pin had a sprig of flowers engraved upon it. Again, the item stirred long forgotten memories. She lifted the piece of felt and unhooked the clasp holding the pin in place. She vaguely remembered wearing the little brooch on a nice dress. Her mother had fastened it to the white collar of a blue dress. Kate closed her eyes and tried to remember. She had been dressed up, maybe they were going somewhere. She had been eight or nine years old. No, they weren't going anywhere...someone was coming to visit. Aunt Iris, of course, that was it. The pin had been a gift from Iris.

"Why do I have to be dressed up?" Kate had complained. *"It's only Aunt Iris and Uncle Bert. Besides, I don't like this pin."*

Grace had frowned. "You must not say that," her voice stern. "You will wear it and act as if you like it. Be polite when someone is kind enough to give you a gift. You owe them that much."

"But what if I don't want it?"

"Katherine, you must learn what you want doesn't matter. Doing your duty is the important thing."

When Iris and Bert had arrived, Grace stood behind Kate and gave her a little push forward.

"Tell Aunt Iris how much you like the beautiful brooch," Grace urged.

Kate had smiled, but found it hard to find something to say. Finally, after a frown from Grace, she managed, "Thank you, Aunt Iris. It was nice of you to give me this."

Grace took up the slack. She hugged her sister and gushed, "It is a beautiful pin. Katherine will wear it always. Doesn't it look good on her dress?"

Iris had beamed and patted Kate's cheek. "I knew it would look good on you."

The afternoon visit went well; Kate remembered the high point for her was the strawberry tarts, almond cookies, and lemonade. The adults had tea or coffee. As always, Grace kept everyone smiling, never allowing any unpleasantness to darken the conversations. However, when Iris and Bert had gone, Grace called Kate to her.

"You could have been a bit more enthusiastic."

"I thanked her for it."

"Make sure you wear it when Iris is around. Otherwise, do as you please."

Kate had smiled. "She isn't here much, and I'm not usually dressed up."

Afterward, the pin stayed in the bottom of her jewelry box and until now, she'd lost track of it. Grace had never again insisted she wear it. To Kate's adolescent mind, there seemed something not quite right about the situation. She had tried to make sense of it. If she had told the truth, it would have hurt Iris. She didn't want to do that. Yet, to make a big show of liking it seemed false. However, time passed and other things became more important.

Kate pinned the brooch back onto the piece of felt and again picked up the storybook. As she paged through it, a small envelope the size of a thank you note dropped onto the table. A bit of scotch tape had been holding it to the inside back cover. The pale lavender ink in Grace's handwriting spelled out Kate's name. At last, here must be the reason for the box. It was so like Grace to use an embossed gift card even for a small note to her daughter. She read it twice, savoring words from her mother even when they didn't have much meaning. *You must be alone in the world, Katherine, or you wouldn't be reading this, or maybe not. Things don't always turn out as we plan. If you are, this is to remind you we loved you. This one thing is true. Be the strong girl I know you are. Mother.*

Kate placed the note back into its envelope. Unlikely as it seemed, Grace's message did give her strength. However, the items Grace included in the box were a mystery. It would take some thought. Unless they were merely sentimental childhood tokens. How disappointed the thieves must have been if they expected the box to hold the information they wanted. She smiled as she put things back into the box. Grace had been right to arrange this. If Kate had married, or if Henry were still alive, the message would have been a lovely gift. She would have treasured it, but now it was an encouragement. Grace had taught her to be strong and loyal to her family, and she would.

She started to put the flowered lid back onto the box, but remembered the gold ring on her little finger. She opened the silver box and twisted the ring to remove it from her finger. A faint green tinge marked where the ring had been. A memory rushed back. This time she did laugh. She had found the ring on a trip to the Lincoln Park zoo. She was five years old, not yet in school. When she had seen the glint of gold on a dirt pathway, it had made her squeal with joy. She'd grabbed the gold ring, brushed off the dirt, and put it on her finger. No amount of persuading from Grace or even Henry could make her remove it. She had insisted it was a treasure. Later, when it left a green mark, Grace had explained that not all that glitters is gold.

Kate slowly put the ring into the silver box and a cloud-like wisp of an idea began to form. Perhaps there was a connection between the items. As a child, she had loved the Steiff bear and Grace had told her how much her father wished he could be there on her birthday. He missed other birthdays, and in his absence sent other expensive presents. Grace had insisted Kate understand that her father loved her; he just didn't have time for her. For a moment, a pain pricked her, like Teddy, it too brought back a memory...the sadness she'd felt upon hearing her father didn't have time for her. Still, she could not have disappointed her mother by complaining. In the same way, she was required to keep from hurting Aunt Iris by acting as if she liked the brooch, when in reality she did not. It was like being pushed in one direction and pulled in another.

She put the lid back on the box and gave a rueful laugh. The entire contents of the box seemed false. The book of fairytales...on the surface stories to entertain, but each harboring a dark secret, an underlying meaning. The little yellow ring that wasn't gold. The message of Grace's gift was obviously to remind Kate of a happy childhood. To give her strength to face life alone. Unless there was a different message. Each item had in some way pointed out that appearances are one thing and reality is another. Maybe Grace was trying to soften some ugly truth Kate might discover. She had always believed certain things about her life. Until doubts and questions began lurking at the fringes of her mind, making her wonder if she'd ever know the truth about her family.

Abruptly she stood and picked up the box. She carried it to Henry's office where she turned on the light and put the box in the deep bottom drawer of the desk. Before leaving the room, she looked around and saw it looked presentable enough to show a prospective buyer. Tomorrow she would call a real estate agent. The question of where to move didn't trouble her; it could take a while for the house to sell. When she hit the light switch and the room darkened, light from the foyer making a gray haze a few feet into the den, Kate wilted with weariness. She put her hand against the doorframe, standing still until the sensation passed. She hadn't eaten anything except the tea with Ronda and the cup of coffee after cleaning the house. With the house in acceptable condition, there was nothing left to do this evening. A nourishing meal might help her relax and with luck get a good night's rest. There was little to make a dinner from after the thorough kitchen cleaning. Besides, she was far too tired. Her head ached and she doubted she had the strength to cook.

Kate took her purse and jacket and headed toward the garage. She threw the large black plastic bag containing Henry's clothes into the car's back seat. There was a Goodwill drop-off in a small strip mall near a MacDonald's. She went through the fast food's drive-in lane where nothing on the menu looked appetizing, but she had to eat something. After making a choice, she headed home with a bag of hot, greasy food, the chocolate malt the only part of the meal with any appeal.

When she drove past Ronda's house, the porch light was on and there was a car in the driveway. Ronda had company, and it killed any idea of stopping there. It was probably for the best since Kate was far too tired for conversation. Ronda would ask about the contents of the box. At times, she was too pushy. It was an uncharitable thought and Kate chided herself for it. Ronda had been kind and provided friendship when Kate had no one else.

At home, she pulled into the driveway. When the garage door rolled up, she shivered and sat for a moment to prepare. It was an involuntary reaction to the house's condition the day before. Now the house was back in order; it had taken hours but it was worth it. The main thing was to get inside, eat, take a shower, and try to sleep for eight hours.

When she entered the kitchen and set the food on the table, she couldn't stop looking around the room. Instead of dropping her purse and jacket in the kitchen, she headed for the foyer. Stepping to the dining room door, she removed her jacket while moving on to look into the office, and the sunroom. While unnecessarily taking the purse and jacket upstairs to the bedroom, she was inspecting each room.

There was no one in the house, but she was still nervous. The stress of the past months had weakened her. It was hard to admit how much because it cast doubt on her ability to continue. Yet, in a way, the fear strengthened her determination to continue the fight.

With the confirmation of being alone in the house, Kate returned to the kitchen and sat at the table. The contents of the fast food bag had cooled and became more unappealing. Still, she choked it down. In the morning, a trip to the grocery store would provide better meals in the future. If there were a future. The memory of the telephone call refused to stay suppressed. Each time it surfaced, the urge to run grew stronger. Maybe she should leave, let the house sit empty; it might sell faster. With the house ready for immediate occupancy, a buyer eager to move in would find it suitable. Kate stopped the rambling thoughts. There was no way to know the best course of action. She cleared the table and put the paper bag into the trash.

As she turned off the kitchen light, she felt better; the food had helped. A shower and sleep might do even more to restore her. As she passed the doorway to Henry's office, the phone rang. The sound echoed through the house as if the rooms were empty. Startled, Kate stood still. With the third or fourth ring, she shook off the shock and turned on the office light, quickly going to the desk to pick up the receiver. Maybe it was Ronda.

"Miss Shore? Kate?"

It sounded like John. Her throat turned dry, making it hard to speak.

"Yes," she whispered.

"Are you all right?"

She was certain it was John...still she asked, "Who is this?"

"John Holden. I need to speak with you."

The Greenfield detective, Charles Simpson, must have called him. She had told the detective about John, and hoped it was the right thing. She didn't know who John really was. Maybe she was in greater danger now. She moved to the back of the desk and sat in the office chair.

"Kate, answer me. We need to talk."

Kate's jaw trembled. "So talk."

"Not over the phone. We need to talk in person."

"You could have talked with me when I came to your office."

"The situation has changed. When can I see you?"

Kate tried to think what to say. Detective Simpson knew everything she knew. If John had something helpful, he should tell Simpson, too.

"We could meet at the Greenfield police station. Did Detective Simpson call you? I told him everything."

"Yes, he called me this morning."

Kate waited. When John didn't say more, she knew he'd not agree to meeting at the police station.

"Did you convince him you have never been to Greenfield?"

"Kate, please. Yes. Of course, he believed me. I used a false name because Henry insisted."

"Sure, blame it on Henry. So I'm the only one who knows you by that name. The only one alive, I mean."

"Henry was protecting you. He didn't know he was going to die. We would handle the situation and you'd never have known anything was wrong."

"What *is* wrong?"

She heard a heavy sigh. "All I can do is try to help now that you are involved. I can't do it over the phone. I must see you alone. And it is better if the police don't know we are in contact."

"That's crazy, I told them you'd been to this house, and I went to your office. They already know we've talked."

"I contradicted your story. I claimed to have never seen you until you came to the office. It would be strange if we should suddenly become friends."

"Yes, it would be *very* strange."

"This is no time for sarcasm. I can understand how frustrated you are, but try to trust me. It is asking a lot, but I do care what happens to you. I feel a little responsible."

"A little? Then tell the police the truth and let them do their job. Last time we talked you told me to tell the police, and I did. What are you hiding?"

"If you will meet me, I'll explain. But it must be alone."

"I can't think right now. I'll call you in the morning."

"Do you promise?"

"Yes, yes."

"You can pick the meeting place, but it must be someplace private. Okay?"

Kate slowly returned the receiver to the telephone's cradle. She bent forward, leaning across the top of the desk with her hands supporting her throbbing head. Why couldn't John have said what he wanted over the phone? She had tried to deny it, but Henry had been keeping secrets. John said it was to protect her. If Henry had lived, he certainly would have taken care of the problem, whatever it was, and she would never have known.

She suddenly became aware of lying on the desk and bolted upright. Henry had been in nearly the same position when she found him. Kate jumped up and ran from the room, into the foyer, and up the stairs. She didn't stop until she reached her bedroom and fell across the bed. When her breathing had returned to normal, she stood and headed for the bathroom. In the medicine cabinet, she found a bottle of Tylenol and took two, washing them down with a full glass of water from the bathroom tap.

When she looked in the mirror, the image there was shocking. It wasn't her uncombed hair, the lack of lipstick, or gray pallor...it was the dreadful expression in her eyes. The lavender circles beneath the dark green eyes gave them a wild stormy look as if they were observing an approaching catastrophe. Kate turned away and closed her eyes for a second. The room seemed to spin, and she put a hand on the sink to keep from falling. After a minute, she left the bathroom and gathered a pair of pajamas and a robe. Before John's telephone call, she had planned the evening. There was no good reason to abandon the plan.

As the shower pelted her body with warm water and steam filled the room, her headache began to fade. She lathered her hair with shampoo and a pine scent arose, providing a kind of aromatherapy.

By the time she was in bed, her muscles were relaxed. It helped her to make a few decisions. She was going to sell the house. There was nothing to keep her in Greenfield, and many reasons for leaving. She would meet with John and let him tell his story; afterward she might know what to do. If she learned who had killed Henry and why, it would end the threat to her. She needed to bury the past along with her family. Wanting to forget them seemed callous and unlike her, but as John had said, the situation had changed. Hers certainly had; they could agree upon that.

Six

Katherine lay in bed, relaxed from the shower. After making the decision to call John and meet with him, she speculated what he might say. He could explain what was going on between him and Henry. He probably knew who was threatening her, perhaps even what it was they wanted. Maybe he held the answer to the entire horrible situation. The longer she thought, the more restless she became. Detective Simpson had believed John's story, so it was her word against his, and John had identification to back his claim. Maybe she shouldn't meet with him. It seemed every decision she made she ended doubting.

She turned one way and another, pulling the bed sheets into twisted ropes. The comforter seemed too heavy and hot; she sat up and threw it to the foot of the bed. When she fell back onto the pillow, she stared at the ceiling where moonlight put faint blue stripes on the white paint. Outside, wind blew brown leaves off the trees, and caused the semi bare branches to rattle against the windowpane. In the fields, weeds had withered; late October was the dying season. Before long, snow would fall, covering winter's destruction in pristine white. A cycle of death, burying, and rebirth. Kate tossed about on the rumpled bed and wondered if she would endure long enough to reach a springtime of her own.

Pictures like a movie reel played before her closed eyes, each frame bringing the past to life. No matter how she wished to sleep, the room was too alive with faces and voices, making her wonder if there might be an answer among them. Something had brought her to this situation; nothing happened in a vacuum. The threat of self-pity had stalked her from the day of Henry's death. It was a new sensation. She had never been sorry for herself. Quite the reverse. She had seen her life as one of privilege. Kate put the back of her arm across her forehead and wondered what had gone wrong. On the surface, the Henry Shore family was above reproach. Yet, doubts and fears concerning them plagued her.

The warm shower and the pills had lost their effect. Unable to sleep, Kate searched her memory for clues to the truth about her family. She had excused faults in those she loved. No one was perfect; you didn't love them because of how good they were. Love which didn't overlook those failings was a weak love. You loved despite those imperfections. She had never questioned or demanded answers. She didn't complain when she felt shut out of family discussions. She had accepted it when told, '*you wouldn't understand.*' She recalled times when there was tension in the Shore home and Grace's talents burned the brightest then. There had been an incident just before her father's death.

~ * ~

One morning upon awakening, Kate had looked from her upstairs bedroom window and seen a strange SUV parked in front of the garages. Thinking perhaps there were guests who needed attention, she quickly dressed. She hurried downstairs to the kitchen to see if cook had been informed. When she came through the swinging door, she stopped in surprise. A stout looking man sat at the center island drinking coffee. He looked up and said, "Hello, Miss. You must be Katherine."

"Yes. And you are?"

He stood and smiled. "I'm Jason, with Ace Security. You'll see a couple of the guys outside. Don't mind us; just go about your business. You'll be safe twenty-four seven."

Startled, she had left the kitchen and gone upstairs to Grace's bedroom. Grace was at her dressing table applying makeup. "What is it, Katherine? Don't frown so, those wrinkles may become permanent."

"There is a man from some security company; he's in the kitchen drinking coffee."

Grace sighed. "You don't begrudge the poor man a coffee break, do you?"

"Of course not, but what is he doing here? He said there are two more men outside."

"Yes, it's your father's idea. There have been too many robberies in the neighborhood. Don't worry about it, we will be fine."

"Oh," Kate said and turned to leave, but Grace had stopped her.

"Katherine, wait. Did you remember my bridge club this afternoon?"

"Yes, the refreshments will be ready. Should I tell the security men we are expecting guests?"

"What a good idea! Tell security to check identifications at the door," Grace laughed. "The girls will be impressed."

~ * ~

In the gray darkness of her bedroom, recalling the incident, Kate frowned. She hadn't been aware of any burglaries, but she had accepted Grace's explanation. Clearly, something had been wrong, and it probably centered in Shore Import/Export, not the neighborhood. As she examined the past, a burden settled upon her. She had lived in a dream world. Even the last years with Henry, she should have made him include her. There was no excuse for such ignorance. It was painful to realize she had allowed them to keep secrets. Whatever had been wrong, she could have helped, or at least shared a deeper relationship with those she loved. Looking at it now, the perfect life seemed false and shallow. She'd lived with people she didn't really know.

All her life, she had been silent as a post, and just as dumb.

Her thoughts turned darker as she blamed herself for her position in the family. Yet, it couldn't all be her fault; her parents should have included her. Perhaps no one was to blame. Kate sighed, and tried a more comfortable spot in the bed. At this point, analyzing the past seemed useless. She had to decide how to deal with John. There was no problem in putting blame on him. For all she knew, he *had* killed Henry. He had provided an acceptable alibi to the police, but she wasn't ready to believe him, not until there was proof. She *would* call John in the morning. In addition, she would stick with him until she found out the truth—about the family business, about Henry's death, and maybe even the truth about herself. Remaking the decision brought a short, troubled sleep.

With the morning light came a sharp wind out of the north. The sunlight was too thin to bring much warmth. Katherine dressed and took a three-quarter length coat downstairs and put it along with her purse in the utility room. It was near ten o'clock, and before she could change her mind, she called John at his office.

"John, it's Kate. Meet me at the Wayfare Inn's restaurant. It's at the interstate's Greenfield exit. Can you be there by three o'clock?"

"Yes. No one should recognize us there."

"Do you know where it is? No, wait, of course you know. You had to pass there when you came to Greenfield." She couldn't stop the scorn in her voice.

"I'll be there. Make sure you are and come alone."

"Detective Simpson isn't welcome, then."

"Don't be cute, Kate. You're in more trouble than you know."

"I doubt it. Goodbye."

Kate ended the call before he could say more. It would take John three hours to reach their meeting place. She could make it in a bit over an hour. There were a couple of filling stations on either side of the exit off ramp along with the Wayfare Inn and restaurant. The location was far from Chicago and not too close to Greenfield. Thinking of what he'd said, she couldn't imagine being in more trouble than she already was. He must have been trying to scare her into keeping the appointment. He didn't need to worry; she wanted information enough to risk most anything. Maybe at this meeting she'd find out why he had denied knowing her. Too late, she considered some device to record their conversation. If she called Simpson, he might still be able to arrange something. She didn't know police procedure, but felt sure Simpson wouldn't do it without some valid reason. There was no sense in thinking too far ahead...by this evening she'd know how to proceed.

She needed to fill the time before leaving to meet John. A call to Sunshine Realtors could do that. She picked the agency because the name sounded cheerful. No matter how things turned out with John, the house was going on the market. Surprisingly, Myron Gilbert, a broker at the agency said he'd come to her house at twelve-thirty.

"Oh, I didn't expect you so soon."

"I see, how about tomorrow?"

Kate hesitated. There was no reason to wait, for she didn't know what tomorrow might bring. "I can give you an hour. Is that enough time?"

"Yes. We'll see you shortly, Miss Shore."

While waiting for the realtors, Kate returned to the kitchen where she made coffee and ate a bowl of oatmeal loaded with raisins and walnuts. The meal would hold her until she was back from the meeting with John. She tried to keep from speculating as to why he wanted to see her. He hadn't wanted anything to do with her before. He'd said something about how the situation had changed. Not for her it hadn't. She was no better or worse than she had been. Her stomach had trouble letting the oatmeal settle so she drank a small glass of milk that seemed to help, although her jangled nerves might be more to blame than her stomach. As time for Mr. Gilbert to arrive neared, Kate tried to relax. She'd never sold a house, or entered into any contract. However, she would not back out; there couldn't be much to it. She would rely upon the real estate agents.

Kate looked at her watch; the realtors were a little late. Normally, it wouldn't matter, but today she had a more important engagement. Maybe it wouldn't take long to finish with them. She hoped this wasn't an indication of their efficiency. When the doorbell rang, Kate hurried to the front door.

The two agents, a man, and a woman, stood on the porch. The man looked to be in his fifties, with thinning hair and an expanding waistline. The woman looked much the same, except for a fuller head of hair, and she was carrying a slim briefcase. They reminded Kate of a set of salt and pepper shakers. Not too tall, and a bit round. A solid no nonsense looking pair, she hoped they would live up to their looks.

The man held out his hand. "I'm Myron Gilbert. This is Rosa."

Kate shook his hand and held the door open wider for them to enter. "Come in. Shall I show you around, or do you want to explore on your own?"

They stood in the foyer peering up the stairs and into doorways. Rosa began making notes on a clipboard she carried. Myron used his cell phone to snap pictures. With the entryway well documented, Myron said, "We'll take a tour on our own, if you don't mind."

"Certainly, that's fine. I'll wait in the kitchen."

Kate could hear them going upstairs. When they came down, Rosa smiled at her as they checked out the utility room and garage. At last, they returned to the kitchen. She was sure the house was in good shape, but she waited for the verdict. Myron and Rosa sat at the table with her, Rosa producing a legal looking paper from her briefcase.

"You have a beautiful home, Miss Shore," Myron said.

"Please, call me Kate. Now, how do I go about selling?"

"Have you decided on a price?"

"I'm hoping you'll know what it is worth."

Myron looked at Rosa, the communication between them making Kate wonder if she'd made a mistake of some kind.

"What would you say to two hundred fifty thousand? Just the asking price, mind you."

"Fine. How soon do you think it will sell?"

"We'll do our best, but there is the time of year to consider. Spring and summer are usually better...more people moving, you know," Myron said while Rosa was busy filling out a long form.

"I understand. I am anxious to leave, though."

With the price agreed upon, Rosa scooted her chair closer to Kate and began explaining the listing contract, and showing her where to sign. She should probably ask more questions, but if Myron and Rosa sold the house for anything near the listed price, she'd be satisfied. As Kate signed the last page, she thought of Alice Shelden next door. When the house sold, she'd probably be satisfied, too. As long as the buyers met with her approval.

As she ushered Myron and Rosa out the front door, her expectations were not great, but she had done her part. She'd leave the house empty if she had to. She felt a bit bad about Ronda, but Ronda could make other friends. She should have by then, anyway. Ronda seemed to need friends. Kate could do without them, and she had for a long time.

With the realtors gone, Kate took the time between one-thirty and one-forty-five to practice some muscle relaxing techniques. At fifteen minutes until two, Kate backed the Acura out of the garage. She should reach the Greenfield exit at three o'clock.

As she sped along, there wasn't much traffic on the county highway. The wind had shifted, coming out of the west and the afternoon sun grew stronger. Kate pulled to the side of the road and quickly shrugged out of her coat. She threw it into the back seat and climbed into the car. If the earlier tension-reducing exercise had helped, it hadn't lasted. She wasn't afraid of John. Although he did make her nervous, he couldn't do anything in a public place like the Wayfare's restaurant. She felt sure he'd be there, unless it was a setup, sending her right into the clutches of Henry's killer.

She struggled to put aside such thoughts. There was no reason to be afraid, she could stay in the car until she was sure John, and only John, was there. Maybe it was crazy to have agreed to meet him alone, anything could happen; she should have brought Ronda. As soon as the thought came, she dismissed it. If she had asked anyone, it should have been Detective Simpson. Still, if John saw someone with her, he'd probably leave.

When Kate arrived at the on-ramp intersection, she pulled into the Wayfare's parking lot. She slowly drove past John's black Lincoln, pulled around the corner of the restaurant, and parked. She sat still, her hands on the steering wheel. Finally, she took the key out of the ignition and put it into her purse. She got out of the car and walked swiftly to the restaurant door.

Inside, she waited a second, letting her eyes adjust to the dim interior before stepping into the dining room. John was in a booth near the front window. He must have seen her arrive, for he stood and came toward her. She met him halfway. He took her arm, seated her in the booth, and took a seat across from her.

"Thank you for coming," he said.

"What else could I do?"

A waitress hurried to them and asked for their orders. The dim room was nearly void of customers. A family of four, parents and two young children occupied a table near the back. A man and a woman, clearly not together, sat one at either end of the counter. Three in the afternoon was a slack time, too late for lunch, too early for dinner. Kate had picked three because it suited each of their travel times, and no one should recognize them there. John already had a cup of coffee on the table in front of him; he must have left early to arrive ahead of her. He asked if Kate would like something to eat. She inwardly cringed; food was the last thing her stomach needed. John order more coffee and she asked for tea. When the drinks arrived, Kate sat silently waiting for him to speak.

John moved the coffee cup to one side and leaned forward, studying her.

"Henry didn't want you involved; that's why I used a different name. We met at your house because we couldn't risk anyone seeing us together. Henry and I didn't know each other before the sale of the business."

"Henry said you did." Kate stirred some sugar into her tea. "So another lie."

"Okay, yes. I won't lie to you from now on. You must believe me."

"We'll see. Why did you want to meet me? You said something about the situation changing. Since I didn't know what the *situation* was to begin with, why don't you tell me?"

John took a long drink of coffee. No doubt stalling. However, he'd had more than enough time to prepare his story. Kate tried to be patient.

John smiled, probably a salesman's technique, but the smile slipped and disappeared. "It is hard to explain in a short time," he said.

Kate leaned back and crossed her arms. "I have plenty of time. I can sit here all night. Especially if I learn something to set my life straight."

"All right. I'll start where it began for me. Jared Roth and I played at the same golf course. He was a casual acquaintance until he approached me with the purchase of Shore. We talked about it for several months. It sounded like a solid opportunity. I was recently divorced...I have two children, and there are heavy expenses."

Kate held up her hand. "Wait. You have a family?"

"Yes. Well, more or less."

"You told me you had no one at all. I see. Another lie."

"How could I tell you anything about myself when Henry insisted we keep my meeting him secret?"

Kate half smiled. "Go on. I won't interrupt. I'll assume everything I thought I knew is wrong."

"You're angry. I'm sorry."

"Forget it. You went in with Jared to buy Shore. It must have been okay with everyone because it went through."

"Yes. It seemed fine. Until I started working there. Your sister-in-law, Alisha, is something else again. She was the one who got Jared interested in Shore. How much did you know about Henry's divorce?"

"They both agreed to it. Alisha grew bored with Henry; he was always working. There were no children to consider, so he didn't stop her when she wanted to leave him."

"There was a bit more to it than that. Alisha didn't like the direction Henry wanted to take the company. There were business associates Henry wanted to drop. It would mean a big cut in the profits. They fought over it, and Alisha left because he wouldn't do things her way. Still, she didn't give up. She met Jared and got him interested in the business. He was her way back into the company, but Jared needed a partner. He asked me. We made Henry an offer and he was glad to sell. He planned to take the money from the sale and live on investments."

"What went wrong?"

"For one thing, I found out where the real profits came from. You won't want to hear this, and I swear it is the truth, at least the truth as I know it."

"Go ahead."

"Your father had a good business going. But it didn't make a fortune. Then some men approached him with a smuggling scheme."

"Smuggling!"

"Yes. The ideal setup. They were extremely careful. Shipments came in and out, forms filled out, and cargo inspected all proper. They were good at what they did. This went on for years. While she was married to Henry, Alisha made it her business to learn about it. When Henry took over, he wanted to cut back. Ease out. He thought it was too dangerous. It was why he was eager to sell. He knew Jared and Alisha would carry on, but didn't care."

"Something went wrong, didn't it?"

"Yes. Part of it was Henry's fault. Because he knew Alisha, and how risky the business was, he took some insurance with him. A packet of jewels. I don't know how many or what they are. He hid them. The smugglers think you know where they are."

"I do not. I can't tell them anything. I wish I did know. I'd give them back in a flash. You can tell them this."

"I can't tell them anything. I don't know their identity. Alisha and Jared handle that end of things."

"I guess Henry wouldn't tell them either and they killed him. Pretty stupid because now no one knows. So, why are you here?"

"I'm not here for that. I don't think you know. Henry wouldn't give back the jewels, and he knew who the contacts were and if he had told, people could go to jail. Maybe even me."

"Do you know who killed him?"

"No. Absolutely not." John's forehead wrinkled; a puzzled look flickered in his eyes. "I don't understand. If Alisha or Jared knew I was in communication with Henry, they haven't done a thing about it. They act as if they don't know."

"Maybe they don't."

John nodded. "Maybe, because I was sure I wasn't followed. I had scheduled a trip out of the country on the pretense of looking at some Peruvian pottery. When I got back, I said it wasn't worth buying, it wouldn't sell in our markets. They seemed to believe me. I think after I left Henry, someone else came. We must have passed each other. All I can say is how sorry I am."

"Sounds as if Shore is in a mess, but I don't know why I should care. I have more reason than ever to tell the police."

"You can't threaten them. They want secrecy even more than the jewels. They'd give up finding them to keep you quiet. Henry stealing the shipment put a real crimp in the business. Others backed off, believing the operation wasn't safe. At least not with a list of names floating around. Alisha and Jared are losing customers."

"Good. Maybe it will put them out of business."

"It might, but they have a backup plan. I am sure they don't want to use it, but if they do, you and I will lose a lot of money. It will be a disaster for me. I'll lose all I put into Shore."

"That is too bad. I suppose I'm sorry for you, but it shouldn't affect me."

"It will stop all payments to you. Henry thought they might try to shut down and sell off the equipment, inventory, and anything with value. It's an old trick. A buyer spots a business with valuable assets, buys it with owner financing, but instead of running the business, they sell everything and run with the money, leaving the previous owner holding an empty bag. The jewels were Henry's insurance; even if they sold off everything, he'd have enough money."

"If they did, what would I have left?"

"The down payment, the house, and the few payments they have already made. I suspect I'd be cut out altogether."

Kate looked at the cup of cold tea; a bluish sheen floated on the surface. She was numb, a coldness settled over her. Money, it was only money. She had never earned any, but she'd find a way. From deep in her memory, something Aunt Iris always said came to her.

"Man does not live by bread alone," she mumbled.

John must have heard because he answered, "But without it, man doesn't live at all."

She jerked up her head and stared at him. "I don't know what to do. What if I do nothing? I'm selling the house, I'll go away."

"And look over your shoulder the rest of your life? Never know who killed Henry?"

"What are you going to do, go along with them, keep things the way they are?"

"I don't believe I can. I wanted Henry to give me proof of what was happening and find a way to stop it, make a legitimate business of it. Henry didn't want to...it would be too risky to be involved. When I left him, we hadn't come to any conclusion. Henry felt safe; no one could prove he'd taken the jewels. If the business shut down, he'd still be all right. It didn't leave me much choice. All I could do was hope Henry didn't tell, hang on, and act as if I didn't know."

"You can still do it."

"No, I can't. I know too much. If I continue with an illegal operation, I risk jail, and if I fight Jared, I could endanger my children. These are not nice people. For now, my protection is to act ignorant and keep quiet. However, I can't forever."

"What do you expect from me?"

John slumped in the booth and stared out the window. Long shadows were stretching under the trees surrounding the parking lot. The sunlight seemed thinner, the sky a faint blue, nearly white. They had been in the restaurant over an hour. There were several more cars parked near the building, and the waitress was looking at them expectantly. John turned to Kate and narrowed his eyes.

"I don't know exactly. I've had some ideas, but they probably won't work. Maybe you don't care about some financial loss, or even finding out who killed Henry. You could try to cut all ties and hope they forget about you."

"Do you think the people who lost the jewels would forget me?"

"I don't know, maybe, but the real danger is they think you know about the list of names and information Henry kept. Henry might have hidden them together. If you find the list, the jewels might be there, too."

"I didn't know any of this until you told me. Alisha could tell them I never knew a thing."

"Do you want to put your safety in her hands?"

Kate closed her eyes against a building headache. She needed time to think. Alisha had never seemed a threat, but she'd not been a friend. If it came to money or a friend, Kate knew which Alisha would choose. There would not be any help there. John sat quietly; she knew he was waiting for an answer.

"I spoke without thinking. The only way Alisha would admit my innocence was if it were to her advantage. So what are these ideas you have?"

"I could walk away, maybe try to sell my interest, but what excuse could I give? They'd probably think I know more than I do. They couldn't let me go. I worry about my children. I could keep still and hope for the best, but I'd risk jail. The only possible way seems to get solid proof, take it to the police, and hope they believe I'm not involved."

"Those are *your* options...what about me?"

"Basically, the same. Keep still and hope for the best. Maybe in time, they will give up. I don't know how long they'd keep looking for the jewels. Or work from inside the company to find the list of names."

"What did you mean, 'work from the inside'?"

"I can't gather the needed information. I could arouse suspicion. I asked Henry to tell me where to look; he knew how they made contact. Using what he'd tell me I could put together enough to bring in the police. That should prove my innocence."

"And Henry didn't want to?"

"No, revealing all he knew would show his past involvement. If you were working at Shore, in the business office, you'd have an opportunity to learn things. Maybe find what I need."

Kate laughed. "Why would they hire me?'

"To keep an eye on you. You could tell Alisha you need a job, something to keep you busy, with Henry gone you feel too alone."

Several people came into the restaurant and the waitress seated them in surrounding booths. She stopped beside John to ask pointedly if they wanted anything else. John said no, and she gave him the bill. Kate scooted to the edge of the seat and stood in the aisle as John stood and placed a tip under a saucer. They quickly walked to the counter where John paid for their drinks. When John opened the door, a cold wind swept in and Kate remembered leaving her coat in the car. John took her arm and led her to his Lincoln where he opened the door for her. She got in, thankful to be out of the wind. John got in the driver's side and sat behind the wheel. The interior of the car had a leathery smell and the cushioned seat was comfortable. Kate held her purse on her lap and wondered what she was doing in his car. She should have left the restaurant when he started talking about 'some plan' of his. She turned to him.

"I should go. I doubt I could help you."

"You'd be helping yourself, too. If we find a way to put an end to this illegal operation, we can run Shore properly. It might not make a fortune, but it is a good business. You would receive the payments due you. To say nothing of being safe from the crooks who are looking for their jewels. If they weren't arrested with the others, it would certainly scare them away from you."

"Tell me again why we can't go to the police right now."

"We don't have any proof. We don't know who the different contacts are, where the items come from, where they go, or even what they are. We have nothing to tell the police."

"If they thought the police were looking into things, it might be enough to make them stop."

"They wouldn't stop; greed is too strong. They'd be more careful, and you and I would probably have some unfortunate accidents."

Kate shivered, and not from being cold. John was right. Although he might not be right about what *she* should do. There was too much to decide. In the first place, she wasn't sure she believed him.

"I must go, John. I will think about what you've said. I listed the house this morning. If it sells, I might move back to Chicago. I'll talk with you later."

John nodded, but his dark eyes seemed to waver between hope and doubt.

"Okay. It's a lot for you to consider. One thing, very important. You and I do not know each other. The only way I know of you is I knew Henry had a sister named Katherine. I've seen you one time. When you came to my office. As far as I know, neither Jared nor Alisha knows you were there. I don't think they know about the detective's call to me. We have to be careful. Don't slip. No more talk of my visit with Henry. If you decide to help, you and I are complete strangers. Understood?"

"Yes. When you left Alisha's house, I told her I thought I knew you. But she brushed it off because I used the wrong name."

John put his hand on her arm, applying a bit of pressure.

"Henry was right to be cautious. My false name has kept our connection secret. We have to keep it that way. I'll call you in a couple of days to see what you have decided. It's safer for me to contact you. Don't call me."

Kate agreed, opened the car door, and stepped out. The wind had calmed, but the early evening was growing cooler and the sun was low behind a bank of dark clouds. As she turned to walk around the corner of the restaurant, she saw John watching, and he was still watching when she slowly drove past him and headed toward the street. When she reached the county highway, her rearview mirror showed the Lincoln under the interstate's overpass, heading for the west on-ramp. It was past four-thirty and dusk came early in the gray day, so she turned on the Acura's headlights. It could be dark by the time she reached Greenfield. There should be some bright, golden days left in late fall before winter set in, but her world had turned as gray as the slacks she was wearing. Nothing in her life seemed bright; there was too much doubt and confusion.

Traffic was light on the country road, and when several vehicles passed her, Kate drove faster. Other drivers were hurrying home from work, or to some known destination, while she drifted. No one was waiting for her and there was nothing to do when she got home. Her only interest was in sorting out the things John had told her. If she could believe him, Henry Sr. had engaged in smuggling. Her brother knew about it and even took part. His only redeeming act was in selling to get out of such a business. Kate hated to admit it, but Grace had probably known if her husband was engaged in something illegal. She had loved her husband and helped him in all ways. Kate had never heard her mother speak one word against Henry Sr. She praised him for being a fine husband and father. Kate squeezed the steering wheel tighter and blinked her eyes.

If John were right, Kate's entire life was a fantasy. Nothing was as it had seemed. Grace must have feared the ugly truth might come out. If it did, and Kate was alone, the box was Grace's way of salvaging a few good memories. Kate tried to remember where she had put the flowered box. Yes, it was in Henry's desk, the deep file drawer. She wouldn't leave it there; she'd make sure it was safe, and made the trip with her when she moved. It would be one of the first things to go into the huge trunk in the attic. She mentally sorted through things she'd want to keep. All her clothes, jewelry, and other personal items, of course. There was one figurine, a Dresden shepherdess wearing a blue gown, and holding a staff and with a lamb at her feet. It was small, less than seven inches tall. There was silverware and a set of good china...Kate pressed her lips together and stopped the wandering thoughts. She did not need any of it. Things, nothing but things. Expensive items purchased with ill-gotten gains. A sick feeling settled in her stomach and her throat was dry. She might keep the figurine, but not much else.

Nearing Greenfield, she stopped at the Conoco station to top off the gas tank. It was over half full, but in the circumstances, it was wise to have a full tank. She got out of the car, put on her coat, and pulled the collar up as she pumped the gasoline. All the thinking about moving and what to take was a maneuver to keep from deciding what she should do.

She must face the truth, or at least find out if it *was* the truth. If the family had kept secrets to protect her, maybe she had never wanted to know. She easily accepted their decisions, even about her social life. Kate got back into the car and slammed the door, a rueful half smile on her lips. Social life...she didn't dare use the words 'love life.' She acknowledged she was no beauty, tall with a strong face, rather than a pretty one, and piercing green eyes, but her looks hadn't been the problem. Character and personality had played a part. She should have stood up to Henry or her father when they discouraged those relationships.

Driving the last few miles in the gloom, and thinking of her appearance, Kate laughed. The truth was she preferred to be strong and healthy. When people did like her, it was for herself, not some physical attraction. She had easily accepted the fact; if her family had told her the truth, she could have accepted it, too. She was sure of it. A slow anger simmered beneath the surface, a familiar feeling she had learned to suppress. From years of practice, she was skilled at keeping emotions hidden. Kate had always smiled a lot. It was unpleasant to insist upon doing things that displeased others. A friendly, people-pleaser. That was what Grace had taught her to be. Before Henry died, Kate had never spoken to anyone the way she had to John. She had occasionally expressed a dislike, or an opinion to Grace, but Grace had discouraged it. *You can catch more flies with sugar than vinegar,* she would say. Kate had always complied and kept silent the reply she wished to make.

All the things John had said took hold in her mind like a spreading poisonous plant. He'd made terrible accusations against her family. Worse, she hadn't defended them. The old Kate would have left immediately. It couldn't be true. Henry was not a thief. Yet, he was dead. When the truth came out, she'd have to accept it, no matter who was at fault.

It was six, and dark, when she pulled into the driveway, raised the garage door, and drove inside. She slowly went into the utility room. When the kitchen light came on, the brightness hurt her eyes. She was unreasonably tired; nothing in the day should have made her this weary. She shuffled through the kitchen and into the foyer, removing her coat as she went. Her stomach rumbled; she needed to eat. She quickened her steps, ran upstairs to change clothes, and hurried back to the kitchen. A bowl of vegetable soup, a glass of milk, some crackers, and she might feel human again. Heating the soup and setting the table kept her from thinking about the day. She would have to make a decision, but it didn't have to be this minute. She ladled the hot soup into a large white bowl. She sat and slowly began to eat. The warmth and flavor of the soup and the cold richness of the milk began to restore her strength.

As she cleared the table and put the dishes into the sink, she felt better. She started to set the kettle on to heat, expecting to have a cup of tea before going to bed. When the front doorbell rang, she jumped, a bit of water sloshed and sizzled on the stovetop. Her calm was broken and the weariness returned. When she reached the front door, Ronda was peering through the etched glass. Kate turned on the porch light and opened the door. Ronda came in shivering and bracelets jangling.

"Brrrr, it's getting cold out there," she said.

Kate took her to the kitchen where Ronda put her coat on the back of a chair and sat.

"I just put the kettle on; do you want a cup of tea?"

"Sure, unless you have something stronger. I nearly froze walking here. I should have called first. I'm glad you're home."

Kate smiled. "What made you walk?"

"Oh, I don't know. Just a whim. Say, where have you been all day? I did call earlier and when you didn't answer, I drove by. Is everything all right?"

The kettle boiled and Kate turned off the burner, and set out two cups. When she didn't answer Ronda said, "Where you went, is it a secret?"

"No, I just went out for a while."

"I see Sunshine Realty didn't waste any time in putting up the for-sale sign."

Kate hesitated in pouring the hot water over the tea bags. She hadn't noticed the sign when she arrived home. Too busy with other thoughts, she'd have to pay more attention. It was easy to be distracted with what was on her mind.

"Yes," Kate said. "I called them this morning."

Ronda looked around the kitchen. "You sure you were robbed? The place looks fine to me. Did you tell the real estate people about the robbery? It might put some buyers off; make them think it was a bad neighborhood."

After Kate put the cups on the table, she put out cream and sugar along with two napkins. "Sorry I don't have any cake or cookies. I threw them out because of the robbery, so yes, I'm sure it happened. I don't remember if I told the realtors about the robbery."

Ronda took a sip of tea, and cocked her head to one side studying Kate, the overhead light making Ronda's pale orange hair glisten.

"Know something? You are a mystery. Where will you go if this place sells?"

"Probably back to Chicago."

"Why there?"

Kate shrugged, stirring sugar into the tea. There was no possible way to explain the situation to Ronda without telling her everything. John's warning came back to her, and keeping their relationship silent seemed wise.

"It is easier to go there. I know the city; I can find a small apartment. I can't stay in this house. It's too big, too many bad memories."

"Well, can't argue that. Greenfield isn't exactly the hot spot I thought it would be. I might just up and move myself. Say, we could go in together on a place. Maybe one of those high-rise buildings, a good view of the lake. Sharing the rent, we could afford a snazzy place."

"I thought you liked it here. Besides, it may take years to sell. It would be odd if both houses sold near the same time."

"I don't have to sell." Ronda laughed, her eyes sparkling. "I'm renting. I had a six-month lease just to see how I'd like it here. The lease is up; I can stall about signing another. I doubt they'd put me out. I pay the rent on time." Ronda raised her teacup to her plump red lips.

Kate smiled but struggled for something to say. Ronda was all right for a neighbor, but anything more was unthinkable. The impulse to run rose like a fever. People and circumstances seemed a trap she couldn't escape. She'd never want Ronda for a roommate, and there was no polite way to say so. She stood and turned to the stove, reaching for the teakettle.

"Would you like another cup?" Kate asked over her shoulder.

"What? Oh no, this is fine. I can't stay long."

"Would you like me to drive you home, it is dark."

Ronda reached into her pants pocket and took out a cell phone. "I'll call Arne, he can pick me up. Did I tell you about him?"

Kate went back to the table and sat. "No, I don't think so."

Ronda leaned forward. "I've known him for a long time. He was a friend of my late hubby. Well, he looked me up a couple of months ago and we've been going around a bit."

"Anything serious?" Kate asked.

Ronda smirked. "Naugh, he's just for fun. Not like a girlfriend you can share secrets with. Oh, that reminds me, did the box you went to Chicago for show up? You said it would."

"I'm surprised you remembered."

Ronda rolled her eyes, a sly proud look on her face. "I have a good memory and not much gets past me. 'Course, I'm not nosy. If it is something personal you don't have to say."

Kate didn't want to lie, or refuse to tell about the box. It was an uncomfortable position. Yes, it was personal. No one had a right to know, even though the contents and Grace's note were innocent enough. Kate put her hands under the table, clenching her fists. Whoever sent the box knew what was in it; it must have meant nothing to them. It would mean nothing to Ronda.

"Strangely enough, it did show up."

Ronda raised her thin, penciled eyebrows. "And?"

Kate shrugged. "And what?"

Ronda laughed. "Some old family secrets, I bet."

Kate joined in the laughter, weariness making her laugh all the harder. "I wish it did hold some great secret. Better yet, I wish there were *no* secrets."

As Kate's laughter died, she used a napkin to wipe her eyes and Ronda sat silently watching. Kate straightened in the chair and lifted her chin, blinking away a final tear.

"I'm sorry, Ronda. I'm so very tired. Are you sure I can't drive you home?"

Ronda raised her cell phone and pushed a number. "No, Arne will be here in a jiffy. Are you okay?"

"Yes. A night's sleep and I'll be fine."

Ronda put on her coat and started for the front door, Kate walking behind her. The porch light was still on and they stood looking out the front door window. The street was dark except for the corner streetlight. Cold moonlight turned the lawn pale blue. In minutes, a dark sedan pulled into Kate's driveway.

"There he is," Ronda said. "Now you get a good rest. Maybe we can do something fun tomorrow. Give me a call, okay?"

Kate opened the door and Ronda stepped out onto the front porch and waved at the car in the driveway. "Don't want to keep him waiting, you know." Ronda giggled, hurried down the steps and along the walk to the driveway.

Kate closed the door, watching through the window as Ronda and her friend drove away. Inside the house, the furnace clicked on and the foyer grew warmer. Her shoulders slumped in weariness; she went through the house turning off lights on the way upstairs. When she climbed into bed and drew the comforter up to her chin, Kate closed her eyes and her mind shut down. It was too overloaded to do anything but fall asleep.

Seven

The next morning when Kate awoke, she felt rested; *everything was as it should be. Henry was probably already up; he was an early riser. This was a nice house and even though their parents were gone, with Henry in charge not much had changed. Perhaps he'd like a nice roast for dinner*—in a flash, her mind cleared. Panic washed over her and she trembled. Henry was gone. She was alone. She sat straight up in bed. Reality was worse than a nightmare. Henry's killer was still out there, and he'd called her. Worse, because of what John had said, she suspected several people were in on the scheme. John had claimed Jared and Alisha had bought Shore because of the illegal profits. Now things were not going the way they planned because Henry had taken a shipment of jewels. This couldn't be true. Kate put her cold hand to her hot forehead and tried to understand. She knew nothing about how to live in this new world.

The first thing was to get out of bed, put her feet on the floor, stand, and get dressed for the day. What the day might bring was a complete mystery. As the shower steamed the bathroom mirror, Kate stepped into the warm spray and tried to relax. One day at a time...she could handle one day at a time. Maybe the real estate people would bring someone to look at the house. She should keep the place tidy and in good order.

After dressing, she made the bed and straightened the room. Downstairs in the kitchen she put bran flakes in a bowl and threw in a few raisins. Thoughts raced through her mind as she ate. After two cups of coffee, she cleaned the kitchen, and went into Henry's office. It amazed her that she was able to sit at the desk where Henry had died. Still, she wasn't the person she had been; she'd become a stranger. A stranger who was still changing. She wondered who and what she might be when this was over. Bright sunlight filtered through the cracks in the closed drapes. Kate sat in the gloom and tried to make some decisions. Remembering the box Grace had left for her, she pulled open the file drawer. She set the box on the desktop and stared at it. There was no sense going through the items again; there was no hidden meaning in them. If there were, she'd missed it. The house was silent, filled with furniture it still felt empty. Not even her presence made any difference. It was as if there were nothing alive under this roof.

If she didn't move, Kate felt she might become an inanimate object, like a piece of furniture, or simply melt away into some thin vapor. Most probably, she was losing her mind. There were too many things coming from all directions, no one to help or give advice. No one she trusted. John had said what he wanted from her. It couldn't work. Even if Alisha bought the story about Kate needing something to occupy her time, she couldn't be a spy. Pretend she didn't know John, dig around in company records, and get fellow workers to confide in her. It was insane. She didn't care about finding smugglers. Maybe she would tell the police anyway. If the company folded, it was what they deserved. John had said if that happened, there would be no more payments. Maybe she'd need to get a job, but she couldn't imagine what kind of work. There was no use worrying about it now. She stood and picked up the flowered box. If the house sold, it would be among the things she wanted to keep.

The trunk in the attic was going with her for sure; it was the place for the box. Kate went to the upstairs hallway where she pulled down the attic steps. Holding the box in one arm, she climbed up and stood peering into the dimly lit attic. At the far end, a small slatted window let in air and some light. There was a cord dangling from the ceiling and Kate tugged on it, hoping the bulb was still good. The yellow light brightened the area and she stepped into the dusty room. There wasn't much there. Some boxes, old records Henry had kept. A beach chair… she never knew why they kept it. The closed trunk's metal top was nearly as big as a desk. The trunk had been with the family as long as she could remember. She thought her parents had used it once on a long trip to Europe. It looked large enough to hold clothes for several months. She set the box on the floor, wiped dust from the trunk's top, and lifted the lid.

Inside were removable compartments made of heavy cardboard covered in dark green cloth, and a partitioned area at one end to hang clothes. She removed one of the top drawers revealing the open center area. She took out an armful of old curtains and put them on the floor. Those could stay in the attic for the next owner. There were a few other things in the trunk: a pair of gym shorts, a hairbrush, and some ancient magazines. Nothing she wanted to keep. She removed the contents of the trunk and stacked them in a corner. She wasn't sure what to do with the boxes of papers Henry had kept. She'd need to go through them. There might be something to disprove what John had said, although, if Henry were guilty, she doubted he'd keep an open record of it. She'd do it later when the house sold. For now, it was enough to put the flowered box in a safe place. She settled it in the center of the trunk and replaced the green drawer above it. When the time came, she had no idea how she'd get the trunk down from the attic. Still, the Mayflower movers had put it up there…they could get it down again.

Leaving the attic, Kate wondered what she would do for furniture if the place she rented was unfurnished. The attic access springs drew the door up and closed it with a thud, and she started downstairs. Most everything was too big for smaller rooms. Although it might be wise to keep the bedroom set; she did like it. It had been hers for years. When she reached the bottom of the stairs, she sat on the next to the last step and stared into the foyer. With her legs drawn up, she wrapped her arms around them and rested her chin on her knees.

She couldn't even decide about the furniture. Yesterday, none of it was worth keeping, too many memories attached. Today, leaving it felt like abandoning an old friend. Her eyes filled with tears and a sob clogged her throat. She struggled to control the self-pity. She wasn't sure where to go or what to do. She changed her mind constantly and the conflicting emotions left her weak. She had never needed to make important decisions, When the realization hit, it was demoralizing. A woman of her years, as helpless as a teenager. It was disgraceful.

Kate quickly stood and headed for the kitchen. She had no reason to go there, but she could not sit on the stairs until cobwebs covered her. Maybe the house would sell right away. That would force her to act. To keep busy because she could not stand having nothing to do, she put the kettle on for a cup of tea. Part of the time anger at her family flared up like a blowtorch. They should not have kept such secrets. They must have thought she wasn't smart enough or strong enough to share them. Although her doubt and self-incrimination washed away the blame. It was probably her fault. Maybe she didn't *want* to know. She paced the kitchen while the kettle boiled. If this back and forth went on, she *would* go crazy! That was then; this was now. She must do something. Yet, knowing that brought more conflict. Either she could do what John asked, or try to hide.

The house seemed to close around her, silent and stifling. She couldn't stay inside. She turned off the burner under the teakettle and ran to the foyer closet to get a car coat. On the porch, she closed the front door, locked it, and put the key into her pocket. The day was sunny but crisp, the wind stung her cheeks, and she raised the coat's hood. The neighborhood was on the edge of town; beyond it, open fields stretched to a distant tree line. Kate headed for the road. When she reached the paved, two-lane road with ditches and hedgerows on either side, she began walking, taking long strides, her hands in the coat's pockets. Fields filled with golden stubble lay beneath an eye-piercing blue sky. Cold brightness filled the day making it brittle, ready to shatter with the softest blow. It mirrored Kate's vulnerability, and she didn't like the feeling. She'd find a way to stay in one piece rather than break.

It was late afternoon before she stopped walking, turned on her heel, and headed back. She was tired and thirsty. The wind had died, the coat became too warm, and sweat dampened her hairline. The walk had cleared her mind, emptied it of the confusing thoughts. Although there were no answers, the questions seemed less important. She couldn't do anything about other people; their actions were their own responsibility, just as hers would be. She walked slowly but steadily toward home. When she heard the rattle of a vehicle on the road behind, she moved to the verge and stood in the dead weeds. An old tan pickup pulled even with her and stopped. The driver leaning out the window looked many decades older than the truck. With his white hair poking from under a straw hat, he smiled at her.

"Need a ride, young lady?"

"I believe I do," she said.

He reached across the bench seat and opened the door. "Climb in. I'm headed for the hardware store, where can I drop you."

Kate stepped up into the truck, sat beside the old man, and pulled the door closed. He put the truck in gear and they chugged toward town. The pickup made a bouncy ride but a welcome one. There wasn't much conversation, but when Kate heard it was another three miles to town; she realized how far she'd walked. She was entitled to be tired. They reached the edge of Kate's neighborhood and the farmer offered to drive her to the house.

"No, it's only a couple of blocks. But I thank you for the ride. I wonder if I'd have made it back before evening."

Kate stood on the sidewalk and watched the man drive away. He reminded her of the nice people in the world. It was encouraging. She could make her way among those sorts of people. Trudging along the sidewalk the last two blocks home, she thought of Aunt Iris. Iris was the same type person as the old man. Solid, ready to help when needed. Somewhat pushy, but she could probably overlook it.

The idea of stepping into Iris' world didn't seem as threatening as before. Maybe not stay there forever, but long enough to find out who Katherine Shore really was.

To keep busy, Kate went throughout the house picking out things to take when she moved. Things such as the figurine which she put into a box to carry to the attic. There was an excess of towels and sheets, but they were of good quality and she decided to keep the linen. When the box was full, she lugged it to the attic. The trunk didn't hold as much as she had expected. However, doing it now would save time with the final packing.

The kitchen presented a problem; there were too many dishes for one person. In the dining room, she made a stack of the best dishes, bone china with a silver rim, a set never used since Grace had been gone. It was expensive china, but of no use to her. She did not see dinner parties in her future. Maybe Iris would like to have them. With china and silver cluttering the dining table, Kate dropped down onto a chair and covered her face with her hands. In her current circumstances, moving and starting a new life hardly seemed worth the effort. It wouldn't bring Henry back or keep her safe.

The sun was sinking below the horizon, leaving purple shadows outside and a dusky gloom inside the house. Kate turned on lights and set about putting dishes back into the china cabinet. It was near time to make dinner. She wasn't hungry, but she would eat if for no other reason than to have something to do. She was tense, muscles tight, the back of her neck stiff. She rolled her shoulders trying to relax; she doubted the robbers would return. There was no reason to be nervous, except that John had not called, and she wondered why. He must want to know if she would join him in his scheme. If he had decided against it, he should have called to tell her. Perhaps no call was a good sign. The uncertainty was maddening. She could end it by ignoring the problem or telling the police what she suspected, but she might never know who killed Henry. Kate stopped pacing the foyer and looked out the window.

The For-Sale sign in the yard cast a lavender shadow behind it. Selling the house was another worry; it could drag on for months, a kind of trap. It should have gone on the market the day after Henry's funeral, but decisions then were no easier to make than now. Kate opened the front door and started down the walkway to the mailbox. There probably wasn't anything important, maybe a utility bill, and some advertisements. On the way back, she stooped to pick up the newspaper off the porch. Perhaps Sunshine Realtors had put an ad in it about the house. That would be encouraging; maybe it would sell quickly after all. Inside, she locked the door and set the security system.

She took the mail and the newspaper to the kitchen and put them on the table. The *Daily News* wouldn't have any earth-shaking news but maybe something interesting was happening at the community center. Kate settled in a chair, a cup of tea before her, and opened a white envelope. A key fell out onto the table, making a sharp clinking against the wood. The single sheet of paper, typewritten, read like a ransom note. *You know what we want. Put it in the Greenfield post office box. The number is on the key. If you don't, we'll make sure you join your brother.* She read the note twice and picked up the metal key that had a number taped to it. This was crazy; these people would not see reason. She was puzzled more than afraid. If they meant to frighten her, they had made a serious mistake; the letter was energizing rather than scary. Sending this note, they had given physical evidence of their threat. Here was something the police could work with, even the small Greenfield force. She'd call Detective Simpson tonight and make sure he'd be at the station tomorrow.

The rest of the mail was uninteresting. She laughed. Nothing like a threat on your life to make you feel alive. John had said not to call him, but he'd surely want to know about this letter. Still, she'd agreed to let him make the next contact and she would. Even her appetite had returned. As she broiled a hamburger patty and steamed some peas and carrots, she felt better. Waiting for danger was far more stressful than facing it. She was almost glad they had sent the letter; the police might have doubted her before, now she had proof. Kate poured a glass of milk and sat down to eat. The letter and the key lay in the center of the table. It demanded an answer, and she would give it one.

After cleaning the kitchen, she went to Henry's office, turned on the small desk lamp and took out a note pad with Henry's name printed across the top. Seeing Henry's name might give them a jolt. The blackmailers, thieves, smugglers—she didn't know exactly what to call them—would find a surprise when they opened the post office box tomorrow. Taking up a pen, she began to write. *I know nothing about stolen jewels or lists. I am giving your threatening letter to the police. Do not contact me again. Katherine Shore.* There. Nice and concise. This should put an end to one of her problems, and if the police found Henry's killer, that would eliminate another. And if John never called, it wouldn't matter, she'd not need him. Rereading her reply, she paused. They hadn't mentioned jewels and lists in the note or in the telephone call. It could confirm their belief Henry *had* told her where they were.

She started to reach for the sheet of paper to crumble it and toss it away. It was a silly idea; they wouldn't believe it anyway. In the morning, she'd take the threatening letter to Detective Simpson and forget it. That should be easy; she'd had years of practice 'looking the other way.' If Henry were alive, she'd still be living in a 'make believe' world.

The room was dim except for the circle of light from the lamp; the note lay on the desktop. Her heartbeat quickened. In the silence, she could almost hear the thump of it. An envelope lay beside the note. With one quick motion, she grabbed the note, folded it into thirds, and stuffed it into the envelope. Her mouth turned dry and her chest heaved as if she had been running. She was actually going to acknowledge these criminals by communicating with them.

Confronting John in Chicago and meeting with him had been easy enough, she wasn't afraid of John. Yet, standing up to him, not immediately agreeing, was new. As was quickly listing the house for sale. In the years before, she nearly always agreed with what others said or wanted. She stared at the envelope. If she put it in the post office box, it would be the most defiant thing she had ever done. Kate stood, picked up the envelope, snapped off the lamp, and marched toward the foyer. After putting on her coat, and fishing the car keys from her purse, Kate headed for the garage, the envelope in her hand. The Acura rolled out into the early night. She was determined to reach the Greenfield post office before she could change her mind.

The post office was one block off the town square. Not many stores were open, only a Quick Trip and a Chinese restaurant; the rest were dark. Streetlights and neon signs kept the downtown area bright. Kate pulled into the diagonal parking in front of the post office and turned off the car. She sat staring at the two large plate glass windows; behind them was the closed half of the post office, while the lobby and the section with rows of boxes remained open. The key in her pocket still had the paper tag attached. This was it. Either put the note into the box or drive away. Mentioning the jewels didn't matter; let them wonder how much she knew. If they were in some way connected to John, they'd know what he'd told her. The important thing was to strike back; this was something she could do. She stepped out of the car onto the asphalt street. The chilly night breeze sent a piece of paper and several dead leaves scuttling along in the gutter. Kate hurried across the sidewalk. In a few strides, she was opening the glass door.

Inside, the lobby was dim despite the overhead floodlights, but bright enough to see the metal box numbers. The empty building was a silent dead zone, the silver-colored boxes like little caskets in a funerary wall. She looked at the key and up at the first row of boxes. The numbers were too low. She moved to the next aisle where the numbers were closer to the one on the key. When she found the correct number, she hesitated. Maybe this was stupid; putting an answer in the box might seem a challenge, causing them to take some drastic action. As long as they thought they could get what they wanted, they wouldn't kill her. Her reply might remove their reason to keep her alive, but they'd gain nothing by killing her. Maybe they'd do it for revenge. She closed her eyes and struggled for a moment of clear thinking, which did not come.

She put the key into the lock and turned it, the small oblong door opened, she quickly put the envelope into the box and shut the door. She hesitated for a few seconds before relocking the mailbox. She put her head down and started toward the lobby. The outside door opened and a gust of wind came inside with a man who was wearing an overcoat. Acting as if he were alone, he went straight to a box in the first row. Kate hurried past him on the way out and he kept his head lowered. Maybe this was post office etiquette. A private place, at least during the night.

Harboring doubts over her action, Kate backed away from the curb and started home. Not home really, only a place of shelter until she could find a true home. She was adrift, her thoughts and emotions confused. On the plus side, acknowledging her condition had given a firm starting point. There was nowhere to go but on to something better. She had dropped the box key into the cup holder; it lay there, proof of what she had done. She took up the key and peeled off a paper number she would never forget. Once past the business district, she lowered the driver's side window and flung the key far across the road, hoping it would land in a weed-choked ditch. If not, traffic would flatten it into a shapeless scrap of metal which was even better.

When the car rolled into the garage, the door clanging section-by-section lower behind it, Kate slumped over the steering wheel making vague plans for tomorrow. It probably wouldn't help, but she intended to give Detective Simpson the letter, perhaps continue packing, and check with Sunshine Realty. Summoning the last of her energy, Kate made it into the house. After turning off lights and checking the security system, she went to bed. Soon as her head hit the pillow, her eyes refused to close. Blue/gray shapes danced across the white ceiling, the shadows of tree limbs wavering in the wind. It seemed like hours before she was settled enough to sleep, but with it came nightmares.

She was in a large, closed shopping mall. It was dark except for soft lights in the shuttered shops. She could not find the exit to reach the parking lot. Every turn led to more closed shops. In the wide tile concourse, the echo of her footsteps was the only sound in the mall. Lost and alone, she tossed in her sleep, frantic to find a way out.

Morning found Kate tired, but determined to repair her life. She called the police station and set a time to meet with Detective Simpson. "I'll explain when I see you," she had said. She ate breakfast and dressed. She put the envelope containing the letter into her purse and reached the Greenfield police station at one-thirty sharp. Simpson's Ford stood parked next to the station. Inside, a policewoman manning the front desk pointed Kate to an office down the hallway. Simpson stood, moved around the corner of his desk, and held a chair for her. Kate sat holding her purse on her lap. Sitting behind his desk, Detective Simpson gave her one of his half-hearted smiles and asked the purpose of her visit.

While she explained, he fiddled with a pencil, and once smoothed a few strands of his pale brown hair. Earlier she had told him of talking with John Holden in Chicago, and he'd reported on his investigation of Holden. It was about what she'd expected. Holden was convincing and he wasn't exactly in Greenfield's jurisdiction. She thought Simpson was growing weary of her pressing for help he couldn't give.

She took the envelope from her purse, leaned forward, and placed it on his desk. He picked it up, examined the front, and removed the sheet of paper. She gave him time to read it.

"Well? What do you think?" she asked.

"There is no return address and no stamp."

Kate fidgeted, clutching her purse. "I know. Someone put it into my mailbox."

"And you say there was a mailbox key with it."

"Yes."

A sudden chill make Kate tremble. She had thrown away the key, a terribly stupid thing to do. She shouldn't have done that. Must be out of her mind, certainly not able to think straight. She swallowed, trying to keep from dissolving in tears.

"I threw it away. After I put my answer in their box. I can tell you the box number, three-four-six. I'll never forget it. You can check on that box, can't you?"

He wrote something on a note pad as he said, "We'll see. Tell me what you said in your letter."

Kate hesitated. If she told him what she'd said about jewels and lists, she'd have to tell him about meeting John a second time.

She didn't trust John, but before telling Simpson what might be slanderous lies, she had to know more.

"I told them I had no idea what they wanted. That Henry had never confided in me. Can't you find out who rented that box?"

She leaned toward the desk, studying Detective Simpson's narrow face. He twisted his thin lips to one side, and his grayish eyes seemed to regard her with sympathy. Maybe he was beginning to believe her. He must, he had the letter in his hand. He laid it on the desk and smiled as if it were painful to do so.

"Don't worry, Miss Shore. I'll look into this. You've had a lot of trouble lately. I don't blame you for being upset. I'm sorry we haven't had more progress in your brother's case. We haven't stopped looking. And about the break-in, since nothing was taken, we can't run down the stolen items in pawnshops, places like that."

In an attempt to engage him further she said, "Are you satisfied with what Mr. Holden told you? Do you believe he's never been to Greenfield?"

"As I told you, what he said checked out. He had proof of where he was on those dates you provided."

"So you think he is telling the truth?"

"One thing I've learned, Miss Shore, is bad guys lie, it is what they do. That is why we depend on proof."

"And right now you don't have any proof, only a crime. Is there *any* hope of finding Henry's killer?"

"There is always hope. People usually kill for a reason. It can be love, hate, money, or maybe in self-defense."

Kate abruptly stood and held out her hand. Detective Simpson stood also and quickly went to stand at her side, taking her outstretched hand.

"You can always come to me," he said. "Call if anything else worries you. I will look into the post office matter. I know it all moves too slowly."

Kate thanked him and stepped toward the door. He followed closely.

"You keep the house security system set, don't you? I'm sure you do!"

She stood in the hallway and nodded. He gave a small smile. "Well, that's good. You should be safe there. But don't hesitate to call if something scares you."

Kate assured him she would and hurried out the door. Tears blurred her vision; she wanted to scream out in frustration. He *didn't* believe her. Maybe he thought she had written the letter. Something to bring forward to keep them interested in Henry's case. She climbed into her car and choked back a sob. Being weak and helpless was unacceptable. The family had always depended upon her strength to keep the house running smoothly. She had taken care of the troublesome details of everyday life. It gave them the freedom to go about their duties. Many times, Grace had said Kate was a calming influence.

Trying to live up to Grace's assessment of her, she wiped the tears away and started the car. She should have been forceful with Simpson, or maybe not; they already suspected there was something wrong with her. She could stop at Ronda's and visit for a while; it might take her mind off Detective Simpson. He was nice enough, and was probably doing all he could, but she wished he were more concerned. He acted as if they'd given up on the break-in. Since the crooks hadn't taken anything, the crime wasn't so important. As Simpson had said, they needed proof. Looking at the situation from his point of view, there wasn't much proof. Only Henry was dead and the house broken into. She wondered if Simpson considered the telephone call, Holden looking like Leland, and now the letter as proof of anything. Those all depended upon her word. The more she thought about what he'd said, the less help she expected from him.

When she drew near to Ronda's house, she saw a dark gray sedan parked in the driveway. It was disappointing, as it meant she couldn't stop. It looked like the car that had picked Ronda up from her house the other night. Ronda had said his name was Arne. Other people did have a life, couldn't expect them to be available at her whim. Probably best anyway, she was too tired for much talk. Besides, she didn't want to tell Ronda about the 'mailbox incident,' as she now thought of it.

Best thing was to go straight home, curl up in a ball, and hope to go to sleep. Yet remembering the nightmares sleep brought, the idea lost its appeal.

At home, Kate left the garage door open and walked to the mailbox before going into the house. She wished there'd be a reply to the letter she'd put in the post office box. If the crooks answered, they might reveal something that would trap them. She wondered what her pen pals had made of the letter she'd sent. The only thing in her mailbox was the electric bill. The small envelope was welcome; she was comfortable paying household bills. As she walked back toward the open garage, a car horn sounded and she turned around. The gray car she'd seen at Ronda's house was pulling into her driveway. Ronda was waving to her from the passenger's window.

"Hey," she called. "Where have you been? I thought I saw you drive past a few minutes ago."

As Kate neared the car, Ronda opened her door and stepped out. She pulled down the tail of her sweatshirt, tightening it over her ample chest. Kate tried to smile. She'd thought of visiting with Ronda, but now that she was home, tired and let down from the trip to the police station, she wished Ronda weren't there. Ronda met her and took her arm, pulling her toward the car's window. Inside, a dark-haired man with a square face leaned across the seat. He looked heavy but in a muscular way, no fat on him. His brown eyes sparkled almost as much as the rings on his fingers. He smiled, revealing white teeth.

"Kate, this is Arne. I told you about him."

Kate smiled. "Hello, Arne. How are you?"

Arne looked up at her, suddenly sober. "Glad to meet you. Ronda told me you've been having some troubles around here."

Kate wanted nothing more than for Ronda to get back into the car, and Arne to drive away to wherever they pleased. To let her go inside to hide, and not have to talk. Ronda had probably told this stranger everything she knew. Kate hoped they didn't expect her to invite them in for coffee.

Ronda tilted her head. "You look pale. Aren't you feeling well?"

"I'm fine." Kate shook the electric bill. "Just picking up the mail."

"Where were you before? I called around one o'clock. We're going to The Pig Stand for barbeque. How about coming with us."

Arne smiled up at Kate. "Yeah. Take your mind off your troubles. They got the best barbecued pork in the state."

The thought of greasy, spiced pork made Kate's stomach clench.

"I don't think so. I'm tired; I have things to do. Thanks for the invitation. You two go and have a good time."

She started to back away, but Ronda followed her.

"What have you got to do? You're alone too much...come have some fun."

"Maybe another time."

"Say, you haven't gotten another threatening phone call, have you?"

"No, nothing like that. It is the thought of moving, I didn't realize how much work was involved. Deciding what to take to a smaller place," Kate gave a short laugh. "It really is tiring."

Ronda patted Kate's shoulder. "I guess I understand. We'll leave you in peace. I've heard grieving takes a lot out of a person. You sure you'd be up to moving so soon?"

Relieved they weren't going inside, Kate relaxed enough to smile. "I'm going to call Sunshine Realty and see if there is the chance of a sale. I might be around longer than you think."

As Kate backed toward the garage, Ronda nodded and walked to Arne's car where she opened the door.

"You have my number, if you want company," she called over the top of the open door.

As he started the car, Arne smiled and waved. Ronda stuck her arm out of the window, several bracelets jangling, as she yelled, "Goodbye."

Kate watched until they were halfway down the block. She stepped into the garage and stopped to take her purse out of the car before reaching the kitchen door. She pushed the button to close the garage door and listened as it clattered down. Most of the time she was tense and tired. It was like being in a giant maze where every turn ended back at the same place. There was no progress in finding

Henry's killer, or in stopping the threats to her. Simpson had the same as told her they'd not be able to run down the men who broke into the house. He seemed in doubt about tracing the telephone call, too.

That night as she crawled into bed, she thought about John, wishing he would call. It was one more unsettled situation. Thinking of telephone calls, she didn't believe she'd told Ronda about the threatening call. Still, maybe she had. It was hard to remember. She squeezed her eyes shut and prayed for sleep. She hadn't accomplished anything, not even the call to the realtor.

Eight

Two weeks later on a Sunday, Sunshine Realty staged an open house. Kate did what she could to help, leaving a tray of freshly baked chocolate chip cookies on the kitchen counter. During the three hours when the house was open to the public, Kate stopped at Dairy Queen for a strawberry sundae which she didn't finish, and spent the remainder of the time in the Greenfield Library. It was disturbing to have strangers wandering through her private space, although she had hidden most of the personal things she hadn't already packed.

She had learned the realtors, Rosa and Myron Gilbert, were married. This made her first impression of them correct. They had look like a short, round matched set. When the showing was over, Myron informed Kate that fourteen people had toured the house. They considered it a good number for this time of year.

During the next three weeks, the Gilberts showed the house twice, and an agent from another company showed it once. The Gilberts assured her this meant there was interest. The days passed slowly, and she hated the waiting. Waiting for a buyer, waiting for a call from

John Holden, waiting for the Greenfield Police to catch the criminals who had destroyed her life.

Most days Ronda stopped by or called. Almost as if Ronda were keeping track of her, always asking what was going on in her life. Many times, Kate had wanted to ask Ronda how she knew about the threatening phone call. She doubted she had told her about it. She held back because of the slight chance she *had* told her. It was becoming increasingly difficult to know what she had told people. Detective Simpson had called one time to assure her, just to set her mind at ease, he had given John Holden another hard look and Holden had checked out. Simpson thought she'd like to know. She wanted to laugh; John had fooled him completely. Instead, she had thanked him and hung up the receiver. By the end of November, she felt certain John would never call. He had been so positive his plan would work, that it was the right thing for both of them.

She speculated that perhaps John had thrown in with Jared and Alisha. She imagined the three of them enlarging the smuggling part of the operation, somehow having smoothed over the loss of the jewels John said Henry had taken. Since she hadn't received any further threats, perhaps she was safe. No one was asking her to hand over the jewels, which she doubted Henry had taken. Why John told her he had was a mystery. For that matter, she didn't know *anything* Holden said was true. Each day brought more doubts. Several times, she started to call him, but each time backed away. Let well enough alone, she thought. Still, her situation was not well enough; it wasn't close to being well.

By Christmas, Henry had been gone four months. There were no more letters or calls. Perhaps the crooks had accepted the fact she was of no help. Her personal mail consisted of Christmas cards from Aunt Iris, Ronda, and surprisingly from Alisha. Several business connections sent holiday greetings, the bank, Sunshine Realty, and even the dentist she'd seen once. Snow came and went, making her wish she had bought firewood. Some days were bright, the snow glaringly white, others gray with wind and ice. Changes in the weather were the only changes in Kate's life. She spent days choosing and packing household items she wanted to keep. When she made no effort to decorate, or celebrate Christmas, Ronda had demanded she attend a New Year's party she was giving.

Kate did not want to go. What she wanted was to sell the house and find some place to hide for the rest of her life. However, because Ronda would not give up, Kate did attend the party. Arne picked her up and kept telling her what a swell time they would have. The gathering was everything she expected. Strangers, except for Ronda and Arne, laughing, drinking too much, talking too loud, and music that made her head pound. Ronda didn't seem surprised when Kate left shortly after midnight. Arne, a slight slur to his words, insisted upon driving her home, but Kate convinced them the walk would help clear her head.

The night air was crisp…a full moon turned the spiky frozen lawns a pale blue, and the homes she walked past were still wearing their colored Christmas lights. Haloes surrounded each streetlight at the top of their poles. Kate pulled the collar of her coat up against the icy air. After the noise of the party, the neighborhood seemed as silent as the inside of a snow globe. The sidewalks were clear of snow and ice, but she still placed each step of her flat-heeled slippers carefully. She'd worn a silk full-length green sheath with silver beading at the neck. Trying to be festive, she'd put her hair up with a silver clip in the front. She walked briskly, shivering a bit even with the heavy satin lining in the coat. When she cleaned the soles of her shoes on the doormat and entered the foyer of her house, the only thing she wanted was a warm bed.

~ * ~

The next day, Kate walked through the house searching for items to add to the trunk or the boxes she'd stored in the third bedroom. She was more than ready for a buyer. The Gilberts swore they were on the job and after the holidays, they felt the house would sell. Unable to find anything else to pack, she gave up and turned on the television in the living room.

A day later, when the telephone rang, a small spark of hope ignited. Perhaps the Gilberts were right and they wanted to show the house.

"Hello," she said.

"Kate?"

"Yes,"

"This is John."

She knew it was. His voice hadn't changed even though she hadn't heard it for weeks.

"Are you there, Kate? I know I said I'd call after our meeting, but I can explain."

"I hope so, because if you'd changed your mind about the plan, you could have let me know."

"This is a tricky situation. I thought I could find what I needed without you. But I can't, and if the police get involved, you and I will be losers. Are you ready to help?"

Kate had despaired of the police finding Henry's killer and waiting for the house to sell was torture. She wanted to shout yes, anything to break her emotional 'log jam.' Still, she'd always been cautious, and hasty decisions were not her nature.

"Let me think,"

"You've had time to think."

"I know, but you didn't call."

"What were you going to say if I had called?"

"I don't know."

A heavy, long sigh rolled through the receiver. John sounded exasperated. No wonder, but she still couldn't decide.

"I'm sorry, John. Give me two days. You have waited this long."

"Okay, but no longer. Either you come in with me on this, or we can lose a lot of money. I don't know about you, but it would badly hurt me. I need information about the smugglers. It could lead to where Henry hid the jewels. I'll call in two days."

Kate slowly hung up and spent the rest of the day trying to make an intelligent decision. The risk of financial loss wasn't reason enough to do what John asked. Finding proof of illegal activity didn't interest her, unless it led to information about Henry's killer, who might have some connection with the company. If she asked Alisha for work, it would be to find proof for Detective Simpson. She was certain the police would never find the answers in Greenfield.

Trying to decide to help John kept her mind off the worry of selling the house. The morning before he was to call for an answer, the front doorbell rang and Kate hurried to answer it. She hadn't heard a car in the driveway, but there on the porch stood Aunt Iris and Uncle Bert. Kate blinked as her mouth dropped open.

Aunt Iris was wearing a stocking cap on her short gray curls. Her cheeks were rosy from the cold, and her eyes were a sparkling blue. Behind her, Uncle Bert was holding a wicker basket and stomping his boots. Before Kate could speak, Iris pushed past her.

"Gracious, girl, don't stand there keeping the door open, you'll let out the heat."

Kate stepped aside and ushered them toward the kitchen.

"Bert," Iris ordered. "Put the basket on the counter."

As they bustled around removing hats and coats, Iris explained, "I would have called before coming, but you're usually home."

Kate nodded as she gathered their garments and carried them to the hall closet. Iris followed Kate, while Bert remained in the kitchen.

"Mind if I pour myself a cup of coffee?" he called.

"No, go ahead," Kate said over her shoulder.

With the coats hung, Iris began a tour of the house. Kate walked behind her, letting Iris inspect the housekeeping. With so many pictures and other decorative items already in boxes, the house was neat as a furniture showroom. At the foot of the stairs, Iris stopped and turned to Kate.

"I suppose the upstairs is about as empty?" she asked.

"I'm trying to be ready for a sale. The buyers might want to move right in."

Iris pursed her lips, and when she tilted her head, her violet blue eyes caught a spark of light. Grace's eyes had been the same beautiful color. Looking past the plumper cheeks and rounder figure, Kate could see how alike the sisters were. At least physically.

"I wonder if it is wise for you to leave here," Iris said, her hand on the staircase newel post.

"I don't know if it is wise, but I really can't stay."

Iris raised an eyebrow. "Well. When you do sell, I have just the thing for you." Iris started walking through the foyer toward the kitchen, and looking back at Kate, said, "That is the reason we are here."

Kate hurried to keep up with her.

"It's nice of you to think of me, but I might go back to Chicago."

In the kitchen, Bert was sitting at the table reading the Greenfield newspaper, a mug of coffee beside him. As Iris and Kate came into the room, he looked up and smiled. Bert didn't speak much; he seemed happy to leave the job to Iris. He was retired from the postal service and for a second Kate wondered if he could tell her how to find out who rented a certain mailbox. Quickly rejecting the idea, she instead turned to Iris.

"What's in the hamper? Something good, I bet."

Iris went to the counter, opened the basket, and began removing plastic containers.

"I didn't want to drop in uninvited and have you make dinner."

"Oh, I wouldn't have minded. Although I must admit, I don't keep as much on hand as I once did. Here let me help." Kate reached for a container with a snap on lid. It felt cool. "Should this go in the refrigerator?"

Iris nodded as she set out a round bowl covered in clear wrap. "Yes, for a bit. It's a meatloaf; I thought we'd make sandwiches of it. Along with this cold vegetable salad."

As Iris continued removing items from the basket, the counter was soon crowded with food. Homemade sliced bread, the salad of pickled carrots, broccoli, green beans, and beets, and a flatter box of oatmeal cookies. The last thing out of the basket was a small chocolate cake. Iris removed its cover with a flourish.

"Bert always likes sweets after a meal." She looked around expectantly. "I didn't bring anything to drink. I'm sure you have coffee and tea enough."

"Of course, whatever you'd like."

With all Iris had brought, Kate didn't want to let down her end of the meal. As it was not yet noon, she wondered if the food was for lunch *and* dinner, and if they were expecting to stay the night. If they were, she could quickly put clean sheets on the bed in Henry's room. The guest room had boxes cluttering it. She wanted to ask how long they planned to stay, but it could sound impolite. However, there was John's call to think of, *if* he did call this time. She couldn't talk to him with Iris listening, and explaining everything to Iris was out of the question. It was hard enough without another opinion.

"Now, sit down, Kate. We'll talk for a bit before having lunch. Bert, move over and put the paper away. You'll need to tell some of this to Kate."

Bert obeyed, and puzzled, Kate took a seat at the table.

Iris filled two more cups with coffee and put one in front of Kate. When Iris had given them spoons, napkins, and put out cream and sugar, she sat at the table. Family made Kate compliant. Iris was a 'take charge' person, so Kate let her. Grace had been near helpless. Therefore, Kate had always taken over for her. She didn't mind. Whatever suited them suited her.

"You probably wonder why we are here."

Kate nodded.

"We are on the way to Bert's sister. Greenfield wasn't more than twenty minutes out of the way. I intended to come see you anyway, but this seemed convenient. We have something for you, don't we, Bert?"

Bert smiled and nodded.

Kate took a sip of coffee, closely watching Iris. Whatever it was, she wondered how to tell Iris *no, thank you.* She began steeling herself to refuse.

"This isn't right now," Iris began. "Bert, you tell her, because you know Cory better than I do."

Bert folded his hands on the table in preparation for his speech.

"There is this fellow, Cory Landers. A nice young guy, a real worker. He was doing social services work. He goes to our church, likes to fish. I've been doing my share of fishing since I retired and we started fishing together. He told me about a plan he has. About starting a home for boys. A place for them permanently, or for a while if that's all they need. He's already bought a place just outside of town. The farm has a big old house, several stories, room for fifteen or twenty boys. He's good at raising money. Going around doing that now. So what do you think?"

"I think this Mr. Landers is doing admirable work. I wish him well."

Iris turned to her husband and smacked her lips.

"Oh, Bert. You didn't put in Kate's part."

"Gosh, guess I didn't," Bert said with a laugh. "See, Cory can't do this all by himself. He needs someone to run the house. Make it like a home. Take care of the food buying, cleaning, things like that. Except when it gets up and running, he's hoping they can grow most of the food."

Iris leaned forward. "I've been out to the farm. The house is huge, a silver stone monstrosity, reminds me of your parents' place. Not near as nice, but even bigger. You could manage it. I expect Cory will hire a counselor for the boys. As you know, running a big house isn't as easy as some might think. I believe it's a perfect job for you. Bert told Cory all about you and he'd like to talk with you."

Kate was stunned, torn between how nice it was they would think of her, and how impudent of them to be planning her future.

"I don't know."

"Of course you don't, not right off. There is time," Iris said. "You can come stay with us and talk with Cory about it. Get to know each other. I think you'd work very well together." Iris turned to her husband. "Don't you, Bert?"

Bert smiled and nodded enthusiastically.

"It sounds like a worthy cause, but I haven't sold this house and if I do, I was thinking of going back to Chicago."

Iris stood and began collecting the empty coffee mugs.

"Huh. What could you do in Chicago? You don't know anyone there besides that ex-sister-in-law. No. The place for you is in some worthwhile service."

Resentment arose in Kate. Yes, she knew how to run a home and take care of others. It was suitable work for an unattractive old maid. She shut her eyes and swallowed the bitterness in her mouth. If Iris knew what John had said about the Shore family, she might not be eager to put her in a position of caring for children. Iris would never understand Kate considering a hunt for Henry's killer.

Bert pushed away from the table and stood. "How soon are you planning on feeding us, Iris? Time for me to take a short walk?"

"Plenty of time, Bert. Be sure to button up. Be back in about thirty minutes, now."

Bert left the kitchen, nodding and hitching his suspenders up over his shoulders. Iris started setting the table.

"Aunt Iris," Kate said. "I'll help set the food out, but first come with me."

Iris looked surprised, but followed Kate into the dining room. There Kate opened the tall china closet. She took out one of the silver-rimmed china plates.

"Would you like this set of china? It is a big set: soup bowls, saucers, salad plates, the works."

Iris looked bewildered. "Why, don't you want to keep it?"

"I don't know what I'd do with it. It's too good for every day. Couldn't you use it, maybe for church dinners?"

Iris took the plate, tracing the rim with her finger. She smiled. "How Grace loved her fine things."

"Yes, she did. She'd like you to have them. There is a set of silver that goes with it."

Iris replaced the plate into the cabinet; Kate could feel her processing the possibilities.

"It is a large set," she said. "If you helped Cory, the dishes are much too good for a bunch of rowdy boys. Maybe the church hall could use some refinement." She turned to Kate, her violet eyes sparkling. "What do you think?"

"I think any use you'd put them to would be suitable. I have packing boxes and bubble wrap, so you could take them with you."

Iris put a hand to her plump bosom. "My, I never expected such beautiful bounty. I only came to get you."

Bert returned to find them in the dining room packing dishes and silverware. Iris pointed out the boxes which were ready to be loaded into their SUV. When they finished, it was time for the meal Iris had provided.

By mid-afternoon, the kitchen was clean and leftovers placed in the refrigerator. Iris insisted Kate keep them, except for the oatmeal cookies Bert held onto for an afternoon snack.

As Iris pulled on her stocking cap, she turned to Kate, a stern look on her face.

"Now, think about the job at the boys' home. You won't find anything you're better suited to do. Promise me you won't forget."

"No, Aunt Iris, I won't."

Kate didn't know how she could forget. It was a perfect way out, if she could put Henry's brutal murder aside and let a killer walk free. Although she doubted she could because Henry deserved better, and maybe she did too.

"We won't stop to see you on the way home," Iris explained. "It's out of the way and after a few days Bert will be in a hurry to get home." Iris rolled her eyes, but Kate could see it was in a good-natured way.

She stood on the front porch waving as Iris and Bert drove away. Walking back into the silent house, Kate missed them. Iris reminded her of Grace. In the kitchen, Kate put a cover over the rest of the chocolate cake...maybe a piece of it and milk would do for dinner. The visit from her aunt and uncle had been a surprise, as was the job they proposed. She could handle the work, but getting along with some stranger, like Cory Landers, was a different matter. Besides, it felt like giving up on justice. It was hard to imagine working in an office as an undercover spy for John, but if that was what it took, maybe she could do it. The two positions were poles apart.

That evening, sitting in the glassed-in sunroom watching the light fade from the sky, Kate's mind wandered, searching for a clear path. She thought of a poem, something about two roads diverged in a wood and which one to take. In her case, safety or an uncertain maybe dangerous way. Before the last five, nearly six months, her life had been safe, secure, and easy. Such a life was something like living in a velvet box, barely living at all. The word 'velvet' sparked the thought of another poem, one by Elinor Wylie. If she remembered right, the poem described her previous life. In the silent sunroom, she softly spoke it aloud.

If you would keep your soul
From spotted sight or sound,
Live like the velvet mole:
Go burrow underground.

Maybe it was time to come out into the sunlight where the brighter the light, the darker the shadows. She gave a harsh laugh. She was already in those shadows. Circumstances had forced her into something she'd never have been brave enough to choose. What Aunt Iris offered was tempting. It would not be the same as having the protection of her family, yet it would surely be safer than going after Henry's killer. It was a frightening thing to consider, yet she *was* considering it. The first hurdle was to convince Alisha she needed a job. She couldn't claim it was for the money; maybe offering to work for a smaller than usual salary would help. Alisha must never suspect it was to search for evidence of smuggling, or some connection to Henry's killer. The longer she thought of how to go about infiltrating the company, the more confident she became. If Alisha refused, there would have to be another way. One step at a time was the present plan.

John couldn't know her true purpose in going along with him. She'd look for the proof he wanted, but at the same time, she'd search for a killer. She didn't believe Henry's killer was a stranger who stumbled into the house. The killing had a reason and it had something to do with Shore. John had given his version, making Henry out to be a thief, and while she couldn't discount it, there could well be something else. She would have to fool Alisha and Jared about one thing, and John about another. No one could know the truth, not even Detective Simpson, at least until she found some proof for him. The move to Chicago would seem logical; there was no reason to stay in Greenfield.

The decision energized Kate. It could fail, but she would have tried and that meant a great deal. "Henry," she whispered, "I won't let you down. I can be as secretive as you were." It was an ironic thought: she'd be carrying on a family habit. Never tell anyone what he or she doesn't need to know.

~ * ~

When John called, she was ready with her answer.

"I'll move to Chicago as soon as possible."

"Good, but remember, you don't know me. After you have worked here a while, it will be natural for us to become friends."

"Don't worry, I can keep a secret."

"Glad to hear it. We won't talk again until you have some news for me."

John had sounded a little nervous; it made her wonder if something had changed. If it had, he should tell her. However, she'd decided to go through with it. It was an uncertain future, a strange sensation yet exciting. She had found a goal.

Later, to speed things along, Kate called Sunshine Realty.

"Mr. Gilbert, this is Kate Shore."

"Yes, Miss Shore, what can I do for you?"

"I'm hoping for a quick sale. Do you think lowering the price might help?"

"Why, yes it would," he said.

They settled on reducing the price by five thousand and Gilbert sounded as if she'd made him the happiest salesman in Greenfield. It might be foolish to agree to a lower price because a buyer wouldn't offer full price anyway, but she was eager to move. Since she had a plan in place, she made another call, this time to a moving company. They could pick up everything she was taking with her, and put it in storage. It could be delivered when she'd found an apartment. By the end of the day, Kate had a feeling of accomplishment.

A week later, the day the movers came, Gilbert of Sunshine Realty called.

"Miss Shore, I have a couple who would like to see the house."

"Yes, of course. Bring them right over."

When Kate hung up, the movers were carrying the last box to the truck. She hurried to make the house presentable and just as she finished, the realtor pulled into the driveway. Gilbert and a young couple got out and came to the front door. When Kate opened the door, the three entered the foyer.

"This is Mr. and Mrs. Wesley," Gilbert said. "They are buying a small bakery here in Greenfield."

Kate stayed in the kitchen as they toured the house, letting them feel free to examine it. In a short time, Gilbert ushered the couple to the back yard, around the side of the house and to the front porch. He left them there and rang the bell. Kate hurried to let him in. He wore a wide smile as he stepped inside.

"It seems you have sold your house, Miss Shore."

"Really? Are they sure?"

"Oh yes. They like it very much, and you'll get your new price. They want a quick closing."

"I'm amazed."

"That is the way it usually is," Gilbert said. "We can close in a month, if it is agreeable with everyone."

"Yes, that is fine. I can be back in town whenever you call."

"Oh, and something else. Their last home burned and they lost most everything."

"I'm sorry. No wonder they need something this fast."

"Well, they wanted me to ask you about the furniture. Is there any of it you want to sell?"

Kate thought for a second...things were happening too fast, but she didn't want to miss an opportunity. "I'm sure we can work it out. My bedroom furniture is all I want."

"Don't worry about a thing," Gilbert told her. "Rosa will bring the contract for you to sign, and before you know it will be time to close the deal."

When the realtor left, Kate sat in the kitchen, wondering what had happened. Her life was becoming a series of shocks of one kind or another. Although this was a good shock, she didn't have anywhere to go. It meant finding another place to live almost immediately. Maybe she could move into the storage bin where the movers had taken her belongings. Kate started an online search for a rental. Over the next two weeks, she drove to Chicago twice looking for a townhouse. Between trips to the city, Ronda either called or came to the house.

One day Ronda brought sandwiches for lunch. As she put potato chips into a bowl, looking exasperated she scowled, "I don't know why you insist on moving back to a big place where you don't know a soul. Why do it?"

"I know several people there. When I find a job, I'll make friends."

Ronda sat at the table munching a celery stick. "I didn't think you'd be leaving so soon. I'm hurt, you know. I thought we were friends."

Kate poured Seven-Up into glasses filled with ice. "You are a friend. But like the old song, the best of friends must part."

"We don't have to. I'll come visit. I may even move there. Arne has an apartment and he's offered me to stay with him."

"Arne lives in Chicago? He must like you a lot to drive such a distance."

Ronda smirked. "Well, he does stay with me when he comes. Not like he's driving back and forth every day."

"I'll give you my address, and you have my phone number. We'll stay in touch."

"Oh yes, we will, but why are you looking for work? I thought you were okay in the money department."

Kate took a bite of the tuna sandwich and chewed slowly, delaying an answer. If she were going to be any good at deceiving people, she'd need to think faster. Her financial situation wasn't Ronda's business. Ronda and Arne had become harder to get rid of than gum on the bottom of a shoe. She could be abrupt and end it right now, leaving a trail of hurt feelings in the wake. However, Grace's admonishment about 'sugar and flies' kept lurking around.

"Don't worry, I won't ask you for a loan," Kate covered her mouth and laughed.

"Glad to hear it," Ronda chuckled. "I thought you might change your mind about leaving since you didn't get any more threats."

"How did you know about that?"

Ronda raised her thin eyebrows above shocked eyes. "I don't remember, you must have told me. You were so nervous about it."

"I don't think I did."

"You must have. Oh wait, you probably told the detective, what's his name, Simpson? This is a small town, things get around. When the police questioned that old lady next door, he might have told her, and you know, from there it would spread."

"You mean Alice Shelden? She might gossip, but I doubt she'd want scandal in her neighborhood. She'd be more likely to hide it."

Ronda stood, picked up her plate and napkin, and hurried to the sink. "Well, however it got around, I expect it is all over town."

Kate hadn't thought about the telephone call or the letter for some time. The reply she had put in the post office box had seemed to end it. The idea of Greenfield's gossip chain feasting on her misfortune made her sick. She couldn't wait to leave. When Ronda came to the table and took her plate, Kate looked at her.

"Don't you think being the sister of a murdered man and receiving threats is enough to make me move?"

Ronda set the plate down and hugged Kate. "I'm sorry. I don't think." She sat across the table from Kate. "What will you do if the threats follow you? Can't you think of any way to stop them? Give them what they want?"

Kate stood, carried her dishes to the sink, and turned to Ronda. "I'd be glad to, but I don't know what they want." Lying or evading the truth was coming easier, especially when it felt justified. She wasn't about to let Ronda know what John had told her.

"Maybe it is something Henry left for you. Have you been through all his things?"

"Everything." And even if she had found something, she was sure she wouldn't tell Ronda.

~ * ~

It had taken Kate three weeks before she found a suitable townhouse. It had a garage, which helped with the parking situation. It was a risk going to the city before securing a position with the company; still Alisha might be more inclined to help if Kate were already there. She spent the week before closing on the house in Greenfield by moving into the townhome. The day of the closing, Kate left Marks Title Company and found Ronda and Arne parked in front of the building. She walked to Arne's car.

"I didn't expect a sendoff," she said.

Ronda leaned across Arne to look out the driver's side window. "We couldn't let you go without telling you the good news."

Kate shaded her eyes against the glare of the winter sun. "What news?"

"We got married. Arne and me!"

"Congratulations. I hope you'll be very happy."

"The best part? We'll be living in Arne's apartment. We'll still be neighbors, well, sort of."

Kate blinked. "I don't know what to say."

Arne started his car and smiled at Kate. "We'll look you up when everyone gets settled. You take care, now."

Ronda held up her left hand and wiggled her ring finger, the diamond sparkling. "See you! I'm Mrs. Mertina now!" she called.

As they sped away, Kate slowly walked to the Acura. Instead of leaving Ronda behind, it seemed she'd gained Arne. They probably meant well, might think Kate, being alone, may need friends. Although she expected to be far too busy to socialize. Normally, Kate would not have formed a friendship with Ronda, or to be honest, most anyone else...her family had been enough. When she had been set adrift by Henry's death Ronda had seemed a safe haven. Although, after a few months, she came out of shock, and didn't feel the need of Ronda's friendship. Perhaps it was unkind, but she didn't completely trust her.

That night she made up the bed in the new townhouse. The bedroom was the only furnished room, and she was glad she'd kept her old bedroom suite. The other two bedrooms contained boxes, suitcases, and the trunk. She planned to use one bedroom for an office and the other as a spare bedroom. She hesitated to call it a guest room, because she didn't expect guests. The living room was small and wouldn't need much furniture: a sofa, a chair, and a television. One part of the kitchen counter formed a bar dividing the kitchen from a little dining area. Once unpacked, she'd finish furnishing, but for now the place would serve her purpose.

After a couple of days of ordering new furniture and straightening the rooms, Kate gathered her courage and placed a telephone call to Alisha.

"Kate!" Alisha exclaimed. "How are you?"

Holding her cell phone, Kate's hand shook and she used the other hand to steady it.

"I'm fine," she said. "Listen, I wanted to let you know I have moved to Chicago."

"This is a surprise. I didn't know you were serious."

"I think it will be better for me. I couldn't stay in that house."

"No, of course not. I understand. Now you are here we'll have to do lunch someday."

"Actually, that is the other reason I'm calling. I want to take you to lunch. You can pick the day and the place."

Alisha was quiet for a bit and Kate waited. Then Alisha laughed.

"Sure, why not? We always got along together. How about Wednesday, eleven-thirty? There is a Russian tea room called Roman's...do you know it?"

"Yes, Mother took me there. Are you sure this isn't an inconvenience?"

"Of course not. So welcome back, Kate. See you Wednesday at Roman's."

Kate was trembling as she closed the cell phone. She couldn't believe it; she'd completed the first step of the plan. She thought about calling John, but decided against it. He didn't need to know anything until she'd secured a job at Shore Import/Export. He could wait; he'd kept her waiting long enough.

Yet maybe it was better because he'd found out he *did* need her. He had tried to dig up the information and failed. The best place in the company to find this was probably in the accounting department. If Jared kept money from the smuggling operation mixed in with other funds, there'd have to be a way to identify them. Unless he conducted those transactions on the outside. If so, there wouldn't be any chance of finding the proof John wanted. It didn't matter because she still needed to be at Shore to find a connection to Henry's death. She didn't know what to look for, but hoped she'd know when she saw it.

She filled the days before the luncheon by finishing the townhouse and stocking the small kitchen with a few essentials. There was a park nearby and when the sun was out and the day not too cold, she took long walks. She stopped questioning the task she'd undertaken, and instead she had started a journal. A notebook with lists of things to accomplish, along with space to make entries when she found something important. Perhaps the planning was unnecessary when she wasn't sure of getting the job. However, on Wednesday she'd try her best to become a Shore employee.

When she arrived at the tearoom, it was as she remembered. It was located in a two-story building with a small parking area beside it. There was a large glass window with the name *Roman's* forming an arch above the picture of a decorative china tea set. Inside, Kate saw Alisha sitting at a downstairs table. Alisha waved and Kate made her way past several tables. Kate removed her coat and hung it on a nearby coat tree. She wore a tailored dress, hoping it suggested a sort of business attire. Her pearl jewelry was conservative. Alisha, in contrast, was all in silver, bracelets, long earrings, and a thin silver chain that hung at the neck of her dress. Kate smiled as she pulled out a chair and sat.

<h1 style="text-align:center">Nine</h1>

Kate waited until they had finished eating to approach the purpose of the luncheon. The waiter cleared the dishes and brought more tea along with a plate of small spice cookies. When he left, Kate blotted her lips with the flowered napkin.

"Alisha, this has been nice. Thanks for coming, my treat, you remember."

Alisha smiled. "Well, if you insist."

"I do, because I have an ulterior motive."

Alisha raised a delicate blonde eyebrow. "Really. Now what could it be? You want me to introduce you at the club, get you started in a good social circle, right? Say no more. I'm thrilled to help. It is high time you came out of your shell. I have a hairdresser who will do wonders with your hair. It is already a nice color, and if you'd wear the right makeup—"

Kate raised her hand. "No. Wait. Thank you for your interest, but what I want, what I need, is a job."

Alisha's lips formed a perfect O. Her long eyelashes fluttered and she clicked her tongue. "I can't believe it. You are a relatively young woman, free of any entanglements. I'm sure you don't need the money...what is wrong with you? Why do you want a job, and why ask me?"

"Because I want to work at Shore," she confessed.

If her announcement of wanting a job had surprised Alisha, she looked stunned over where Kate wanted to work. "Why?"

Fearing she'd ruined her chances, Kate tried to focus. She'd forgotten the reasons she had intended to use. She reached across the table and covered Alisha's hand with her own.

"Yes, it sounds crazy, but you know I'm not much fun in a social setting. Work is the only thing I'm comfortable doing. Don't you see? I only want to work, maybe in accounting. I kept all the household books, paid all the bills. Put me in a corner of the office and treat me as any employee."

A look of pity darkened Alisha's eyes. Kate had to swallow the humiliation it caused. Still, she'd put herself in this situation, made herself an object of pity, it was to be expected. If it got her entry into the company, it was worth the price.

Alisha lifted her hand from Kate's and found a tissue in her purse. She blotted a spot beneath one eye, and wiped her lips. With order restored, emotions controlled, she took out a lipstick and small mirror. After she reapplied the lipstick, she returned everything to her purse. She straightened her shoulders and smiled.

"Kate, you never change. I thought you made this move to start a new life."

"It's hard to change. Maybe I'd find some friends of my own at work. Would it be so wrong for me to work there? I'll change my name if it's a concern."

"Don't be silly. Changing a name isn't going to help you."

"I'm asking you for work because I doubt I could get a job anywhere else."

"That's probably true. No outside experience at your age. Oh, Kate."

"Will you put in a good word for me? I hope I'm not asking too much."

Alisha chuckled. "We don't have a human resources department. Shore isn't that large. Most everyone has been there for years. When we do need someone, we call an employment agency. Let me think about it." Alisha stood and opened her purse, taking out car keys. "I wish you'd try having fun once in a while. You're almost family, and I don't like feeling responsible for you. I'll talk to Jared."

Kate paid the luncheon bill and hurried out onto the sidewalk. She caught up with Alisha as she neared her car.

"I am sorry to burden you," she said. "I know you're right, but it really is hard to be something you aren't. Will you let me know?"

Alisha unlocked her car and gave a weary smile. "Of course. I'll call soon as I know something. I can't think of anything duller than keeping books. You poor thing."

Kate watched Alisha drive away and turn the corner. When she was gone, Kate wilted. She was as tired as if she'd run for miles. Yet on the drive back to the townhouse, a tiny flash of pride brightened her spirit. She had done it, maybe not well, but she had taken the first step. Alisha hadn't seemed totally against it, so maybe she could influence her husband. If Jared agreed to hire her, that could be the easiest part of the plan. Jared might consult John before deciding. If he did, John would surely agree. Unless John had had another change of mind. So far, he hadn't seemed reliable and was prone to switching plans without telling her. It was John's idea to get her into Shore to find the information he wanted, but she had reasons of her own to pursue.

After arriving home, Kate changed into jeans and a sweatshirt and tried to relax; there was nothing to do but wait. There was still some unpacking that could help keep her mind occupied. All the furniture Kate had bought had arrived. A small square table and chairs for the dining area and two stools for the kitchen bar. The living room had a sofa, a recliner, a wall television, and a bookcase. Her bedroom was the most completely furnished because of what she'd brought with her. In the bedroom she used as an office, the old trunk stood beneath a window and a new desk and chair along with a file cabinet completed the room. While Kate waited for Alisha's call, she started going through the boxes of Henry's papers. Most of it was bills, the deed, and sales contract on the big house in Chicago, six years of income tax, and other personal records. She used the trunk top as a sorting table. There was a stack for personal bills and records, and another stack of documents from Shore.

A thick folder held the Shore sales contract and a bunch of other pages Kate didn't understand. At the bottom of the folder was a small address book. She set the office records aside to read later when she wasn't so distracted. She started on personal family bills by placing them in order of their dates. Henry had kept far more than she considered necessary. Repair bills on the roof of the Chicago house, along with credit card charges long since paid. It was clear whatever else her brother had been, he was a meticulous packrat. What she did *not* find was a packet of jewels or a map to where they were. She chuckled at the thought. It was difficult to believe John's story of stolen jewels...it was easier to believe Henry might have been in some shady dealings. Henry hadn't been a coward, but it was doubtful he'd do something as risky as taking jewels from a smuggler. It was still painful to think of his death. No one had the right to take his life. As the anger grew, she knew she would do whatever possible to find and punish the killer.

Her thoughts buzzed like bees, *who* and *why* swirled around in a painful swarm. Every time she thought of the way Henry had died, it made it impossible to continue living without an answer. John said he didn't know, yet had suggested someone doing business with Shore was to blame, even casting doubt on Jared and Alisha because he suspected they continued dealing with the smugglers. How Jared Roth did business didn't concern her, but if Kate found proof he'd killed Henry or hired it done, nothing could save him. It would be too bad if Alisha were involved, because the only thing that mattered was justice for Henry. As Kate continued sorting old records, she set up a file on her laptop. Henry had been a 'belt and suspenders' sort of guy. He had computer workbooks in Excel for every household expense, spreadsheets with formulas Kate could transfer to future purchases. She had thought it excessive, because a checkbook and her own memory could handle most everything. However, at tax time she had to admit the volume of receipts was a help.

She imagined some computer in Shore's accounting department had much the same information as the old business records in the boxes she'd taken from the attic. If Henry kept both paper and computer files for personal expenses, he must have done the same when he ran Shore. Being cautious, she decided to keep all the old business records. If, and it was a big if, she started work at Shore, she'd compare what their computer files showed with the ones Henry had kept at home. What use these files might be was a mystery. Yet when starting with nothing, it was worth considering everything, even things that seem unimportant. She had transferred Henry's computer files to the laptop, making it easy to use them. Before moving from Greenfield, she had destroyed the hard drive on Henry's desktop computer, installed a new drive, and donated the set along with copier and printer to the Greenfield Senior Center. With the laptop and cell phone, she was truly mobile.

In the laptop's new file, she used Excel to set up a worksheet for a purpose other than financial. It was to be a question and fact sheet, one column for questions, another for facts, and upon thought a third for random information. It wasn't clear what might fall into the third section, but she'd know when she heard it. After a couple of days fiddling with the setup to use if she got inside Shore, she stopped. There wasn't anything else to add. The sheet on the computer was a copy of what constantly ran through her mind, an endless cycle of questions.

Not being able to decide which household records to throw away, Kate put them in the file cabinet and turned to preparation for being a working girl. Well, not so much *girl*, as Alisha had pointed out, but still she'd need to look the part. The goal was to fit in, become an accepted employee, someone who could check purchases and sales without suspicion. More importantly, someone whom the others would feel comfortable with in sharing gossip. She wondered if her last name would be a help or hindrance gaining fellow employees' confidence. In an effort to fit in, Kate went shopping for clothes that she considered appropriate office attire.

After a long week of preparing for what might not happen, Kate was sitting in her small living room when Alisha called with the news.

"Yes," Alisha said, "Jared decided to be generous."

"What exactly did he say? Are you sure he means for me to start work at Shore?"

"His exact words? 'Why the hell not, especially if she'll work for minimum wage.' If I remember right, those were his exact words." Alisha softly laughed. "Jared thinks you'll soon get tired and quit anyway."

Kate could scarcely breathe, as excitement and fear fought for dominance. "So, when should I start?"

"It's up to you. There's a girl in accounting, I think her name is Sharron, she's so pregnant she's about to pop. They were going to get a temp while she's out, Jared thinks you'll be ready to quit by the time Sharron comes back, if she does. Whatever, it gives you a chance to play office for a while."

"Do you think I could start Monday?

"He said it was up to you. Do what you want. Anything else?"

Kate could feel Alisha's shrug; she was clearly tired of the subject. Before Alisha could end the conversation, Kate said, "One more thing. Who should I report to on Monday?"

Alisha sighed. "I don't know. I still wonder why you want to do this. Oh, I suppose see Gladys, she handles things."

Kate thanked Alisha and let her hurry off to some spa, or perhaps to an interior decorator. She imagined this was the last she'd hear from Alisha, unless Alisha needed her for something, although she couldn't think what it might be. Kate stayed for a while on the sofa holding the phone in her lap. It had happened. She had the job. It was Friday; there were two days to prepare. She wondered if John knew, maybe a call to him was in order, or maybe not. Since they weren't supposed to know each other, a call could seem strange. Maybe a call to Gladys was appropriate. Yet, from the way Alisha sounded, Gladys probably didn't know anything about a new employee taking Sharron's place.

She didn't know how long a maternity leave was, but hoped it was long enough to find a killer. The weekend loomed ahead, an empty stretch of time to endure.

~ * ~

By Monday, Kate was nearly too tense to function, like an over-wound clock. It was a struggle to move at a proper speed, or move at all. She left home by seven-thirty, dressed in a tan suit which she hoped suitable for the office. On the way to Cooper Industrial Park, she wondered if the employees had assigned parking spaces, then the morning traffic took all her attention. A slight fog hung over the lake and surrounding area, making headlights necessary. Knowing the area helped, but the amount of people hurrying to work was distracting. Inside the industrial park, the driving was easier. Reaching the fenced-in compound of Shore brought even more relief, especially when Ralph Myers stepped out of the narrow guardhouse. As she drew near and stopped, she lowered the window.

Ralph seemed surprised to see her again. No doubt, he didn't know she'd be coming to work there. He tipped his ball cap, a few strands of gray hair falling over his ear.

"Miss Shore, visiting again, are you?"

"No, Ralph. I'll be working here."

Ralph's gray eyebrows rose above his black-rimmed glasses. "For good? Is there another change of some kind?"

She'd need to squash his suspicions before they became a rumor. She laughed.

"No, Ralph. Certainly not. No changes at all. Mr. Roth has kindly agreed to let me work for a while. I needed something to occupy my days. Being alone can be lonely."

A flicker of pity passed through his faded eyes. She hated people feeling sorry for her and hated even worse deceiving them. Venturing out into the wider world was making a fraud of her. Ralph nodded and smiled at her.

"Well, that's nice of him. Don't let them work you too hard, now."

"I won't."

Kate slowly drove through the gate and across the asphalt lot to the office. There were parking spaces directly in front of the building and a row on the other side of the driveway. She picked a spot in the far row, hoping it was out of the way. Several other cars were there, and a couple of pickups. The dockworkers usually parked behind the building in the area facing the warehouse and the open shed-type building. There was paving between the office building and the dock area. A gravel road curved around the back end of the main building to reach the unpaved side near the railroad tracks. The office building was Kate's main interest; the warehouse or dock wouldn't hold the information she needed. Records and office gossip were surely the place to find where money came from and went to. Who were the suppliers and customers, and if any of them had something against Henry.

Kate pushed through the glass doors and stepped into the small lobby area. A receptionist desk stood centered on the back wall. A staircase with a brass handrail was to the left of the desk. There were two doors near each back corner. One led to a hallway with a break room and the restroom. The door to the left opened to a short hall with two offices. A young red-haired woman sat behind the reception desk, the same desk that had been there for years. Evidently, Alisha had recognized the value of the lustrous walnut which would cost a fortune to replace. However, the tile flooring, wall pictures in narrow metal frames, and modernistic light fixtures were new. The pictures were different views of the lake, each at a different time of day, and they were a good blend with the dove gray walls. She had to admit Alisha put a good face on the business. Henry wouldn't have cared about décor. There wasn't a lot of walk-in business. Still, maybe Jared brought customers in on occasion. The young woman at the desk, dressed in jeans and a sweater, was busy answering the telephone and directing calls. When she finished she smiled at Kate.

"May I help you?"

"Yes. I'm starting work today. I believe I'm to see Gladys Tindel."

She looked Kate up and down, her surprise evident, but she recovered quickly and smiled, revealing two deep dimples.

"Yes, Gladys in accounting. Do you want me to call her, or did she tell you to go right in?"

Kate immediately knew two things: she was very over-dressed, and if Gladys knew she was coming, she was the only one. Kate smiled and held out her hand.

"I'm Kate. I think I'm to replace Sharron while she is on maternity leave."

The young lady reached across the desk to shake Kate's hand.

"Glad to meet you. I'm Polly Carter. You won't see much of me, except maybe in the break room. It is on this floor." Polly stood and stepped to the side of the desk. "Would you like me to show you where it is? The restroom is on this floor, too."

Kate wanted to hug Polly; her willingness to put a new person at ease was wonderful. Still, it presented a problem. If she allowed Polly to show her around and the girl learned Kate knew the layout of the building it could be awkward. There was already far too much deception around her coming to Shore, best to keep it at a minimum.

"Thank you, Polly. Your offer makes me feel so welcome, but I must tell you I know this building. My name is Kate Shore, but I have nothing at all to do with the company. Other than Mr. Roth giving me a chance for a job."

Polly nodded, her short red curls bouncing. "So are you the Shore who used to own the business? The Shore who got killed—" Polly stopped short, her face turning red as her hair. "I'm so sorry," she began.

Kate smiled. "Please, don't be embarrassed. I didn't want to cause a problem coming here to work. I didn't have references to find another job, and Mr. Roth was kind enough to let me try here."

"Oh. I understand. Lots easier to get a job where you know people. I must have answered a dozen ads before I found this."

"How long have you been here, Polly?"

"Henry hired me about two years after Senior passed away." As if quickly realizing Kate's connection to both men, she reached to touch Kate's arm. "Gee, I'm sorry. Your dad and brother both."

"Thank you. I'm glad to meet people who knew Henry. So you've been here, what, eight years?"

Polly nodded. "Going on nine this coming September."

"You must like it."

"Well, hope you don't mind me saying, but when the sale happened we were all pretty uncertain."

"Oh, I understand. But it seems to be working out."

Polly smiled both dimples on display. "Yes, Mr. Roth and Mr. Holden have been good about leaving things mostly the same. Except..." Polly waved her hand around indicating the room. "... Mrs. Roth spruced the place up."

"Yes, it looks nice.' Kate looked at her watch. "I guess I should find Gladys, or should I call her Mrs. Tindel?"

Polly giggled. "No. Gladys will do. You probably know her."

"I know of her. But I wasn't around the office much."

As the phone began to ring, Polly went to her seat behind the desk. She answered the call, directed it to Mr. Roth's line, and turned to Kate.

"Good luck. Let me know if I can help. Maybe I'll see you in the break room."

Kate thanked her and headed for the door on the left side of the lobby. The first meeting with Shore employees had gone well. Ralph seemed glad to see her, Polly was friendly, and could possibly be a source of information. Kate stepped into the short hallway and wondered if they used the offices in the same way as before. The smaller one was for the account manager, Gladys; the much bigger room had three desks and the computer equipment. Kate stepped to the first door and knocked. These offices also had access from the loading docks at the back of the building. Since no one had entered through the lobby, they must have come in the back way, or weren't there yet. Kate knocked again.

The door was swiftly jerked open. Gladys Tindel's eyes blinked behind her rimless glasses. She was holding a stack of papers.

"Oh, I thought you were Tuttle. He wants these printouts."

Kate took a step back. "I'm Kate Shore. Did Mr. Roth tell you about me?"

Gladys looked puzzled for a second, but brightened. "Yes. Kate Shore. You're here to help while Sharron has her baby. You're a little early; she isn't leaving until this Friday. Never mind, she can show you what she does. What computer programs do you know?"

Gladys started down the hallway toward the other office. "Never mind, Sharron can get you started. Tuttle will help if you have questions after Sharron is gone. Follow me."

Kate kept silent and did as Gladys instructed. When they entered the larger office, Gladys took the papers to the desk in the right-hand corner of the room. She dropped them on the desktop. "Here you are." She stepped aside and pointed to Kate. "Sam, this is Kate Shore. She'll be helping out while Sharron is gone."

Sam Tuttle stood; he was near Kate's height. A shirt hung loose over his jeans, both seemed too big for his thin frame. He brushed back his thin hair, helping it cover the bald spot. He gave a quick nod and held out his hand.

"Good to meet you."

Kate extended her own hand. "Nice to meet you, too. Hope I won't be too much trouble as I learn my way around the office."

Sam's narrow lips twitched a bit and he seemed on the verge of taking his seat, yet remained standing. Kate wanted to put him at ease but didn't think it was her place. She looked at Gladys who patted Sam's shoulder.

"We'll let you get back to work. Sharron will tell Kate what she needs to know."

Sam bobbed his head, returned to his swivel chair, and picked up the papers Gladys had left. Gladys took Kate's elbow and steered her toward the far left corner of the room. They passed an empty desk. Gladys pointed to it.

"That is Bill's desk. Bill Greer is our outside sales guy in the states. He is on the road most of the time, but when he is in town he needs a desk."

"How long has he worked for Shore?"

"Your dad hired him. Bill was just out of jail..." Gladys shook her head. "...for some reason Henry thought he could make a salesman out of him."

"Did he?"

Gladys laughed, while the young woman Kate took to be Sharron, joined in a quiet chuckle.

"Did he, Sharron?" Gladys asked as she reached Sharron's desk.

Sharron didn't get up. Alisha was right; Sharron was extremely close to becoming a mother.

"He sure did," she answered. "For one man, Bill covers a lot of territory."

Sharron was in a blue maternity top with a large yellow daisy print. Her black hair was in a high ponytail tied with a yellow ribbon. When she smiled, her white teeth all but sparkled. Kate didn't think she'd ever seen a healthier looking person. Gladys walked to the wall and unfolded a chair she brought to Sharron's desk.

"There, I'll leave you to it. Sharron, in case you didn't hear, this is Kate Shore. Fill her in on what she's to do."

As Gladys walked away, Sharron smiled and motioned to the chair. "Sit down and we can get acquainted. You can put your purse in one of those drawers if you want to." She pointed to a three-drawer file cabinet near her desk. Kate did as she suggested and sat on the folding chair beside Sharron's desk. Sharron let her computer screen go to a screen saver and turned to Kate.

"Kate Shore. What does this mean for the company? Will there be more changes?"

Doubts about the wisdom of trying to work in her family's old company clouded her mind. Maybe this wasn't such a good idea. Hopes of finding something to explain Henry's death faded. The shock of losing Henry was still strong; it probably caused her to make stupid decisions. She tried to smile at Sharron.

"No changes, Sharron. None at all. Mr. Roth and Mr. Holden are in charge of everything. You know I lost Henry; I'm a bit at loose ends. Mr. Roth was kind enough to let me work here. I'll do my best."

Sharron's dark eyes softened as she reached out to pat Kate's arm. "Don't worry, you'll do fine. I only asked because we are just settling down since the sale."

"So many changes for everyone. Just tell me what I should know and I'll try to follow."

Sharron gave Kate's tan suit a long look.

"First of all, wear what you are most comfortable in. Gladys always says, be neat but comfortable. You'll spend most of the day sitting here entering orders into the computer. Keeping track of sales and shipments. Bill will send a fax, email, or phone in his orders. Or if he picks up a supplier, he'll give the information on it." She nodded toward Sam's desk. "Sam does most of the customs forms and arranging shipping on overseas orders. My job isn't hard. Sometimes boring, but you can get up and take a break. When there is a lot of data to enter, the time can go pretty fast."

Sharron stopped, arched her back, and put her hand to rub her side.

"Maybe it is time for a break now, okay?"

Kate quickly stood and moved the folding chair to the side, while Sharron made it to her feet.

"There now. Let's go."

Sam didn't seem to notice them leaving. In the short hallway, Sharron turned to the left and they followed the hallway behind the lobby. Sharron pointed Kate to the break room while she stopped at the restroom.

"Not room for this baby and my bladder too," she laughed.

Kate drew a paper cup of water from the large glass water cooler. Her mouth was dry and she tried to take in what Sharron had told her. She didn't immediately see any opportunity to find the information John wanted. If Jared did business with people who were smuggling items into the country, there was no way she'd know if a shipment contained something illegal. Short of having all the invoices in her hand while opening and sorting each crate, box, and package, it seemed impossible. Sam handled the forms needed for customs, and arranged shipping. Even he couldn't swear to the contents without examining each shipment. As she sat at a long table waiting for Sharron, she couldn't see how being in the office would help. However, there was nothing else to do, so she might as well be working, and maybe Jared was right. By the time Sharron came back, Kate would be ready to quit.

Sharron returned to the break room looking much relieved. She took a small bottle of orange juice from the refrigerator and sat at the table with Kate.

"When is your due date?" Kate asked.

"Supposed to be in two weeks."

"How long is your maternity leave?"

"Three months. Gladys said depending upon how things are going, I could take longer."

"I guess you'll know when you're ready to come back."

Sharron nodded. "Maybe. I might not come back, but don't tell anyone. My husband, Rory, works for Rosen Auto Supply, and there could be an opening in Texas for a district manager."

Kate took another drink of water. Things in the business world moved so quickly, she felt a jolt of panic. What if Sharron didn't come back! It took a second to realize Sharron's plans couldn't affect her. If Sharron didn't return, and Kate wanted to quit, she would. Gladys could easily find someone for the job.

After finishing her juice, Sharron scooted her chair back and stood. "Might as well see what I can teach you."

Kate agreed and they returned to Sharron's desk. They spent the hours until lunch with Sharron doing regular work and explaining each entry as she went. The office computers shared a network, also the printer and copier. A couple of the accounting records were password protected. Sharron said those were where Gladys collected data and kept the company's financial records. Sharron, Sam, Bill and even Jared and John fed information to Gladys so she could bring it all together. Gladys also managed payroll.

"How many work here?" Kate asked.

Sharron began silently counting on her fingers. "Ten, I think. The guys in the warehouse change, usually at least two, sometimes more."

By five o'clock Kate was ready to go home. She knew one thing for sure: tomorrow she would wear tennis shoes, no hose, and a loose shirt with slacks. It was amazing how tiring sitting at a desk was... muscles grew stiff, and her eyes burned from staring at the computer screen. Something else was clear. She needed to take notes. Four more days and Sharron wouldn't be around to help.

The after-work traffic was as heavy as the morning commute. Lines of vehicles rushing in their own pattern. If the roads were dirt, there'd be well-worn pathways. Even the Acura seemed to head toward home with little effort from Kate. Busy thinking about the past eight hours, she barely noticed the traffic. At times during the day of learning, her true purpose in being at Shore had slipped from her mind. Although it wasn't a worry because once settled in, there should be time to start digging.

After a quick dinner, Kate spent several hours relaxing. It was still surprising she'd managed to get the job. The day in the office didn't seem real. Amazingly, the other employees accepted her; they carried on as if nothing were different. The sister of their murdered ex-boss had dropped into their midst and it hadn't caused a ripple. Unless there was something under the surface. Maybe some common feeling an outsider wouldn't notice. They might have been too friendly and welcoming. Her last name had to set off some speculation. Still, she had the job, and if there were undercurrents and they didn't interfere with her agenda, it didn't matter.

The next day, wearing comfortable clothes, she parked behind the office building as Sharron had instructed. She locked the Acura and started toward the back stairs. Behind her, a car door slammed, Sam Tuttle was getting out of a small gray car. She stopped on the loading platform waiting for him. He was nearly Kate's own height, and possibly weighed less than she did. As he walked up the stairs, he kept his head down. Perhaps he was extremely shy...he hadn't said more than 'hello' yesterday. Kate held open the back door waiting for him. As he came near she said, "Good morning, Sam. Are we the first to arrive?"

He looked startled, but nodded and reached to take the door from her. He nodded again, indicating she was to enter before him. Kate smiled and went into the back hallway. As Sam went inside, she tried again. "Nice morning, isn't it? Looks as if we could have an early spring this year."

Sam bobbed his head and walked faster, moving ahead of her. At least he wordlessly agreed about the weather. Since Sharron was leaving, the chance of getting information from an employee was fading. Kate doubted she had nerve enough to question Gladys. That left the receptionist, Polly. She would know about calls in and out of the company, and who might visit in person and why. Meager information, at best. Still, it was only the second day. No point in becoming discouraged so soon.

Gladys arrived just before Sharron. She stuck her head in to say 'hello' and went to her office. Sharron came in, stowed her purse in the file cabinet, and held up a small canvas bag.

"Be right back, got to put this in the frig. You can sit in my chair; I'll take the folding chair today."

Kate almost panicked. She couldn't remember a thing Sharron had told her yesterday. Sitting behind the desk, the dead computer before her, carrying on with her plan seemed impossible. Did people go through this every time they started a new job? Respect for working people grew. Sharron returned, her pale green maternity dress flaring around her knees as she walked. Evidently, Sharron too felt an early spring season coming. Time was quickly passing, almost seven months since Henry's death. Kate had given Detective Simpson in Greenfield her new address and he had her phone number, but she had given up on hearing from him. There was no blame or anger; she understood how little evidence he had to go on. Really no evidence at all. If anyone here knew something about Henry's death, he or she would have told the police. If they were innocent. Kate had never had a suspicious nature; trust was her natural mind set. In the past months, her nature had changed.

All morning, Sharron sat beside Kate, guiding her step by step as Kate made computer entries. Sharron explained who the suppliers were, both domestic and foreign, and who old steady customers were.

"When Bill comes into the office, you'll see why he is good at his job. Bill never met a stranger." Sharron laughed. "He claims to know every novelty distributor in the country."

"What do Mr. Roth and Mr. Holden do?" It was a leading question, but Kate couldn't resist...she well knew what their jobs were.

Sharron hesitated for a second. "Well, we don't see much of either one. They travel a lot. Mostly Gladys deals with them. Giving them all the reports, getting their approval of different things. Usually one of them stays here while the other travels. They have offices upstairs, 'course you probably know that."

Kate leaned back in the desk chair, resting her wrist for a bit. "Yes, I know those offices. I guess they deal with big accounts, overseas companies."

Sharron nodded. "Yeah. They find a company in some country that is making something that would sell well here. Sometimes they convince some other company we can sell them something they want cheaper. It is really a very big twisted and complex arrangement."

Perhaps it was, from Sharron's point of view, but for years, Kate had seen Shore as a trading operation. Her father put buyers and sellers together, dealt with the complex customs and shipping arrangements, sometimes taking a chance on buying goods to hold in his own warehouse, if it seemed more profitable. He often described it as a huge gambling game, only using actual goods instead of cards and chips. Now, because of what had happened to Henry, and John's suspicions, she wondered if this game was rigged. Maybe it always had been. If so, she desperately needed to find the truth. Her doubts were strong enough to push her into this new life. If she found what she suspected, her illusions about her family would completely shatter. It wouldn't destroy her love for them, but it would make her see their lives in a different way. If the process changed her, perhaps for the worse, it was a risk worth taking.

The rest of the week progressed smoothly. Sam Tuttle managed to start saying 'good morning' when they met at the loading dock door. Gladys bustled in and out with occasional directions. On Friday, near the end of the day, they met in the break room to share a cake and give Sharron a few gifts. Mostly things for the baby. Polly gave Sharron a dangling mobile to hang over the crib.

"It helps them develop their attention span," she explained. "Gives them something to watch."

Neither Jared nor John participated, but Gladys gave Sharron a small bonus check which she said was from them. There were hugs all around, everyone telling Sharron to let them know when the baby was born. Afterward, Sharron left an hour early, part of her going away gift. When she was gone, the office seemed unusually quiet. Polly went back to her position and Sam to his. Kate returned to Sharron's desk, sat behind it, and realized it was her desk now.

She had a responsibility to do the job the best she could. Her salary was less than Sharron's had been, but there was a good reason. Besides, she expected to gain information that was, for her, more valuable than money. A little before five o'clock, Gladys made the rounds giving out paychecks. When Gladys reached Kate, she handed her a check and smiled.

"Before you go home, please come to my office. We can talk there."

Kate barely had time to say "Of course," and Gladys was gone.

Gladys had control over the office accounting department, even to a lesser degree the outside employees. Although Ralph and the night guard didn't need instruction. Kate wondered if Gladys intended to fire her, and after only one week. If so, Alisha couldn't help her. Perhaps she could prevail upon John. Thus far, they hadn't spoken. Would he want her in place enough to overrule Gladys? Kate quickly shut down the computer and tidied the workspace. She took her purse and headed to find out what Gladys wanted.

Gladys sat behind a large wooden desk. An armchair stood before the desk. Family pictures sat on the desk and on top of the bookcase. The room seemed well lived in, like a home away from home. It was no wonder, because Gladys had used it for more years than Kate could remember.

Gladys waved toward the armchair. "Sit down, Kate."

Kate sat, her shoulders tense. Gladys seemed to study her. At last she spoke.

"I know why you are here," she said.

Ten

The office seemed to darken; the light from the window behind Gladys put a spotlight on her silvery hair. Kate first flushed hot, and then chilled. She swallowed but her throat was dry; it almost closed, making a reply impossible. She shouldn't be here, she had never shown an interest in the business, and Gladys knew it. She knew Kate's position in the family. Grace's little helper. The one who did what they told her, and didn't question. Stupid little Kate, grown into a dull adult who wouldn't say boo to a bug. Kate opened her mouth to speak, but wondered what to say. Gladys saved her the trouble.

"You want to know more about your family, don't you?"

Kate nodded.

"I can understand," Gladys said. "You didn't have much of a relationship with your father, did you?"

"No, not really." It hurt to say it, but Gladys seemed to know already.

"Now they are gone. You must feel lost being this alone."

Kate finally realized her secret was safe; Gladys had no real idea why she was there. Kate smiled.

"I do feel alone. I hope you won't mind putting up with me for a while."

"Of course not. If you forget Sharron's instructions, just ask me. Maybe learning the business your family owned for most of your life will make you feel closer to them. You will see what it was that occupied your father, and your brother. When someone is devoted to their work, it is like living two lives. One at home and one at work."

"You've been here at least fifteen years, haven't you?"

Gladys smiled. "Twenty-one. I was thirty-three when Henry hired me."

"I do remember when Father hired you," Kate offered. "I was around fourteen."

Gladys reminded Kate of Mrs. Farber, Jim Burton's secretary. Women essential to the businesses they worked in, as Gladys said, it was like living two different lives. She realized she didn't know anything about Gladys' private life.

"I'm embarrassed to ask, but do you have a family, Gladys?"

A warm smile brightened the older woman's face. "A loving husband, Roger, and my twin boys. Not children any longer. They are twenty-nine. One is married. They don't need me now."

"I'm amazed. You raised a family and I'm sure my father couldn't have done all he did without you."

"I don't know. If it hadn't been me, some other woman would have taken the job."

"Why have you stayed this long?"

'It's a good job. I owe your family a lot. If I can help you adjust to your new life, I'll be glad. Your father spoke of you often. He was proud of how capable you were at an early age. Of course, he was harder on Henry Junior. Expected so much of him. Still, fathers do."

Kate wanted to ask Gladys a dozen questions about the business. She leaned forward.

"I hope you won't take this amiss, but was my father ever moving illegal goods in or out of the country?

Gladys frowned. "Who told you? Maybe your Uncle Bryon?"

"No. I haven't seen him or Aunt Elaine since Henry's funeral. Why would you suspect him?"

"Because he and Henry started this business together. Bryon wasn't at all suited to the work. Henry bought him out and grew the company alone. When it became successful, Bryon was bitter. He started hurtful rumors."

"I knew something had happened between them. In what way wasn't Bryon suited to this business?"

"He isn't a people person, not a good salesman, and definitely not detailed oriented. He was full of ideas, but no notion of how to carry them out."

"So he tried to ruin the company's reputation?"

"It didn't work. Henry followed the rules and regulations to the letter. Sam Tuttle has been here almost as long as I have and he makes sure we are within the law." Gladys looked at her watch. "Oh, dear. I'm supposed to meet Roger at six. We have a dinner date."

Kate quickly stood. "I'm sorry. Please don't let me keep you."

Gladys took a jacket from the closet and started putting it on as she picked up her purse. "Don't worry about it. I'll lock the office, but Mr. Holden is still here. He stays very late some nights. Makes overseas calls, the time difference you know."

Gladys went through the office turning out lights, stepped into the hallway, and locked the door behind her. Kate followed her through the warehouse entrance. Gladys hurried to her car and waved goodbye, calling out, "I'll see you Monday."

Kate stood on the back platform while security lights came on at either end of the yard and under the overhanging roof. To the left at the entrance gate, two men were standing beside the guardhouse, Ralph leaving, and the night man starting his shift. The early evening turned misty blue and a cool breeze came from the lake. Across the paved yard, the shed warehouse looked closed for the night. If there were lights on in John's office, they weren't visible from the platform. Kate had nothing to look forward to at home other than a lonely meal and perhaps a TV movie.

She turned around and reentered the building, taking the back stairs to the second floor. If Jared were there, she should stop and thank him. For the entire week, neither Jared nor John had been in the accounting office. They communicated by phone and used the computer network, but none of it in connection with Kate's work. Entering the upper hallway, she saw Jared's closed door. The two long windows beside the door revealed a dim room, lit by the fading daylight coming through the front window.

John's door stood open. The light from the office cast a yellow stain across the hallway's dark green carpet. She hesitated before stepping into the doorway. John was looking at papers on his desk; the overhead light put a gleam to his brown hair. Kate didn't speak, but he jerked his head up, his dark eyes filled with surprise. She came forward, a few steps into the room.

"I'm sorry if I startled you. Should I have called first?"

John straightened the papers before him, moved them aside and stood. "No, it's all right. Has everyone left?"

Kate shrugged. "Far as I know they have. Jared's office is dark."

"Yes. He left at noon. They are entertaining customers this evening."

"Are you going?"

"No."

"Why not?"

John sat and pointed to the armchair near the desk. "You might as well sit, since there is no one to wonder why you are here."

Kate did sit, but didn't remove her coat. "Why am I here, do you suppose?"

A quick light sparked in his eyes, making gold highlights flash. "You've found something. I knew it wouldn't take long. There was a list of 'off the books' customers, right?"

She almost hated to disappoint him. "No. I haven't found anything. The truth is I wouldn't recognize it if there were some irregularity."

John picked up a pen and slung it across the desktop. His lips turned down in either disgust or anger, but he quickly brightened and smiled. "You've only been here a week. I can't expect much this soon."

Kate leaned forward. "John, why don't you talk to Jared about this? Ask him to buy you out. Get your money back and invest in something else."

"If Jared had money, he wouldn't have needed me."

"Maybe he could borrow enough from a bank. Instead of sharing profits with you, make payments to the bank."

"Same answer. He wouldn't have needed me if he could get a loan from a bank."

"I don't know what to say, John. As far as I can tell, the accounting office runs strictly by the book. Mr. Tuttle is a quiet man who Gladys says keeps the shipping and customs rules. Nothing out of line." Kate stopped, remembering what Gladys had said about her father's brother, Bryon.

"What is it?" John asked.

"What makes you think this company does anything illegal...did you hear this from Bryon Shore?"

John leaned forward, and raised his eyebrows. "What does Bryon Shore have to do with this company?"

"Not a thing, that is the point. According to Gladys, a long time ago he spread some nasty rumors about my father. He was mistaken, of course. I thought you got the idea from him."

"Oh. I never heard of the man. Still, maybe he has the answer. Where can we reach him?"

Kate gasped. "Absolutely not. He is my uncle and he has nothing to do with this company."

John raised a restraining hand. "Okay. Don't get upset. He could know something; he might know where Henry hid the gems. Or maybe Jared got information from him."

"What information?"

"The list we are looking for. The names and contact numbers for the people who use Shore for their smuggling operation. People Henry dealt with who could know what he did with the gems."

"You believe Jared is doing business with these men and keeping the profits for himself." It was a statement rather than a question.

John closed his eyes and nodded. "Yes. This is dangerous. If or when the police find out, we are done for. I will lose everything I've put into this. You won't fare any better. If this Bryon knows anything, we need to contact him."

Kate crossed her arms and sat silent, thinking about the situation. Whenever John explained the circumstances, it never seemed right. There had to be a way for the business to continue without the risk of ruining everyone's lives. An investigation might involve Gladys and Sam Tuttle. She looked up to find John watching her.

"Why don't you threaten Jared? Tell him you know what he is doing and if he doesn't stop, you'll report it."

"I've tried. That was what I was doing when I didn't contact you. I thought if I could stop him, I wouldn't need to involve you. He laughed at me, said prove it."

"You want me to find proof."

"Yes. Gladys must know something...she's been here for years. She probably knows more than she admits."

"John, this is insane. I find it hard to believe my family did anything illegal. If Jared is involved, he is doing it on his own."

"You have come this far and they accept you in the office. It might be keeping you safe as well."

"What do you mean?"

"They can keep an eye on you. You haven't been threatened lately."

"No, and I haven't found anything either."

John stared at her. "If you do, for your safety, be sure to tell me first."

It was dark when Kate left the building. She slowly drove to the guardhouse gate. A light inside revealed a man who looked through the window at her, raised the gate bar, and waved as her car rolled by. On the drive home, Kate considered what John had said about the danger to her. After the post office incident, there had been nothing further. Perhaps John was right, or maybe they were convinced she didn't know anything. Either way it made little difference. The next three months were set. While doing Sharron's job, she'd look for the information John wanted. Although her main reason for being at

Shore was to find who killed Henry, and why. There was no one to trust; this was a private, secret search. She had little hope of success, but she had to try.

~ * ~

Saturday Kate went shopping for the few groceries she needed, did some laundry, and cleaned the house. Sunday, she made a quick trip to fill the Acura's gas tank to be ready for Monday. A workweek was new, eight hours a day committed to an activity not under her control. Always before, she did things at leisure whenever needed. However, she could stick to a schedule for three months. In a way, it was too short for her purpose. There was the chance Sharron might not come back if her husband took a promotion to Texas. It was too far ahead to worry about. Life had become like a strange land where she didn't know the language.

Sunday afternoon she wrote a short letter to Aunt Iris and an email to Aunt Elaine and Uncle Bryon in New York. Iris had an email account, but rarely used it. She preferred written correspondence. The New York branch of the Shore family had made use of the internet. The email to them was short, simply letting them know that she had moved back to Chicago. She didn't mention working at Shore; it seemed a bit deceitful but not enough to include that bit of information. If what Gladys had said about Bryon were true, the less they knew the better. Iris was a different matter. Along with the new address, she explained why working with Cory Landers would not be possible, as she had agreed to help at Shore. Sharron needed time off for the baby and it was only for three months. It wasn't an outright lie, but she couldn't tell Iris what she was really doing. Iris wouldn't understand, and might try to stop her.

Monday, she arrived at work a bit early. She was nervous about doing the job without Sharron to correct any mistakes, but at the same time eager to process the information alone. Gladys was her efficient self and Sam Tuttle still quiet but with a friendly smile. At break time, Kate went to the lobby to say hello to Polly. Since Kate had no idea where to look for the information she wanted, it seemed wise to be on chatting terms with everyone. Polly was busy answering the phone and directing calls to the various offices. Kate learned John wasn't there as Polly repeatedly took messages for him. In between calls, Polly explained Mondays were usually busy but she'd see Kate some other time.

At lunchtime, Kate went to the break room and found Polly heating a bowl of soup in the microwave. Sam had taken her place at the front desk to answer the phone while she ate lunch. Kate took a sack containing a sandwich out of the refrigerator and sat at the long table. Polly sat opposite her and pushed back a curly lock of her red hair.

"Sam or Sharron usually relieves me at noon," she said.

Kate stopped unwrapping the sandwich. "Oh dear. No one told me. Should I be out there now?"

Polly laughed, making her dimples deeper. "Don't worry. I think they didn't want to spring it on you all at once. Nothing to it. Say Shore IE. Take names and numbers. There aren't many calls around noon."

It didn't take many people to staff the company, but everyone kept comfortably busy. Gladys had to help with a couple of entries, as Kate had forgotten where they belonged. Otherwise, she considered the day a success. In the late afternoon, Jared came downstairs to the accounting department. He looked as if he spent a great deal of time in the sun. There was hardly a shade's difference between his brown hair and his forehead, all of which made his blue eyes more noticeable. He wasn't very tall. Kate guessed him somewhere around five nine. Gladys was talking to Sam when Jared came in.

"There you are," he called to her.

Gladys turned and smiled at him. "You're back. How was Mexico?

"Great!" His smile was bright against his tan. "I picked up a pottery maker. They will let us handle the shipping and distribution here. Better yet, I may have a wholesaler in Arizona who will take the first batch."

"We can always use a new account. You have all the information?"

Jared handed her some papers. "I think so."

"Come on, we'll go to my office to set it up."

Kate noticed Sam listening to the exchange, probably judging what part he'd play in getting the new products into the country. From what she'd seen, Sam's knowledge was invaluable. About fifteen minutes later, Jared came back into the larger office. He started to the door, but stopped and came to Kate's desk.

"How's it going?" he asked.

"Fine. Anyway, I hope it is. Maybe Gladys could tell you more accurately."

Jared flashed a short smile. "Must be okay, she didn't complain."

He shifted from one foot to the other, looking as if he wanted to leave but thought he should say something more. Kate grew a bit uncomfortable and she suddenly remembered she'd never thanked him for the job.

"Jared, Mr. Roth, I truly want to thank you for this opportunity. It must seem strange having me here. I hope Alisha explained."

"Yes, she did. You don't need to thank me. We needed to find someone because of Sharron's baby. Guess it worked out for both of us."

He smiled once more and quickly turned toward the door. As he left, Gladys came from her office to give Sam some papers, before stopping to speak with Kate.

"Is this the first time you've met Jared?"

"No. I saw him at Henry's funeral. But we didn't talk."

"We'll all become better acquainted as time goes on. I have to say he is a good salesman. Might not think so here in the office, but in this short time, he has brought in several new contracts. He must be doing something right...we can use the business."

Gladys patted Kate's shoulder and went back to her office.

At home that evening, Kate thought about the day. There was nothing different about the day other than Jared's visit. Gladys seemed impressed with his ability to bring in new business. Maybe Alisha had picked her second husband because of this trait. Contacting businesses in other countries and convincing them they could profit from Shore's services wasn't easy. Jared truly must be a good salesman. Either that or he had some help, like knowledge of people eager to find an easy way to transport illegal goods into the country.

John seemed sure it was the secret to their success. Still, how to know if a shipment was concealing something? Sam Tuttle handled shipping arrangements, and filled out the customs forms. It was a tangle of rules and regulations. So far, she had no reason to inspect that area of the business. It seemed John's great idea of getting access and finding names and account numbers would fail.

After the second week without Sharron, a routine fell into place. From there on, time passed swiftly. Kate had started relieving Polly at lunchtime and enjoyed the break from her own work. She tried to arrive early each morning, hoping to find something she could report to John, but with no success. As for her own investigation, there wasn't one person who had a bad word for Henry. Much less a reason to hurt him.

She hadn't met Bill Greer yet, but from the way the others talked, he seemed harmless. Still, he was the only employee who could have secretly been in Greenfield. Outside salesmen could easily cover their tracks...John had. At the end of each day, she was tired and ready to go home. It was surprising how much of the day the work took. Not just the eight hours in the office, but the time spent getting ready in the morning, and the personal chores left to take care of in the evening. She spent weekends cleaning the house, shopping, and preparing for the coming workweek. The schedule renewed her admiration for working women, especially those also raising children.

After two months in the new home, she had rarely entered the third bedroom, so it seldom needed dusting. Henry's files remained unsorted, part of them in the file cabinet and the rest sitting on the big trunk. Each weekend she determined to straighten the room, but there was no rush. It seemed easier to keep the bedroom door shut. Besides, if Sharron decided to reclaim her job, there would be plenty of time to attend to old records.

One Sunday afternoon, Kate considered tackling the task, but instead dropped down onto the sofa and turned on the television. So far, she knew nothing more about Henry's killer, and John was extremely displeased with her efforts to discover illegal activities at Shore. If Jared had made contact with smugglers, the company records she had access to didn't show it. She should have known the move to Chicago and working at Shore was a long shot. However, it did keep her busy and the pain and anger over Henry's death at bay, although the emotions still simmering under the surface kept her from giving up the search. If a killer lurked among Shore's employees, he was as hard to find as one among Shore's customers. Until she found answers, she'd have to suspect everyone.

Since she'd moved to Chicago, no one had threatened her; maybe John was right about her being safe so long as *they* could watch her. Although, she wished whoever it was *would* make contact. Kate pointed the remote at the television and turned it off. She was too restless to watch anything. She stretched out on the sofa and closed her eyes.

When the doorbell chimed, she bolted upright. Sudden noises or unexpected actions still startled her. She was tense and never fully relaxed. The bell sounded again as she quickly stood and adjusted her tee shirt over a pair of jeans. When she opened the door, a tall young man stood there, wearing an expectant look on his face. His hair was the color of ripe wheat, and his eyes a silvery-flecked light brown. His lightweight suit was rumpled and his tie was askew. He leaned forward.

"Are you Katherine Shore?"

Kate held the door only partly open. "Yes. What do you want?"

His smile was a bit lopsided, but it was like the sun breaking from behind the clouds. "I am so glad to find you. I took a chance. I'm Cory Landers."

When she didn't respond, he reached into his breast pocket and took out a wallet.

"Here, this is my identification. Bert and Iris Dunbart said they had told you about me."

Kate glanced at an Illinois driver's license. "Oh, yes. You're the one with the boys' school thing."

"Not a school, a home."

"Oh. What can I do for you, Mr. Landers? If you're looking for donations, I'll see what I can do."

He shook his head; a slight spring breeze ruffled his hair. "I'd like to talk with you. If you have the time?"

He made her feel as if she had a Jehovah's Witness on her doorstep. She didn't want to offend him, but neither did she know what to do with him.

"I won't stay long, I promise," he said.

Kate sighed and held the door open. "Fine. Come in."

He stepped into the small foyer and followed her into the living room. She pointed to the recliner. He nodded and hurried to settle into the chair, as if she might at any minute change her mind. Kate sat on the sofa and folded her hands in her lap.

"I suppose Aunt Iris gave you my address?"

He nodded.

"She also has my phone number. Didn't she give it to you?"

Cory nodded again.

"Well, you could have called."

"I find it more effective to arrive in person," he said.

"I guess I have to agree."

His smile seemed to radiate energy, but the grayish blue hollows beneath his eyes told another story. He was several inches taller than Kate and of medium build. He started to slump a bit but quickly straightened his broad shoulders.

"I know the Dunbarts told you about my project. I've been making the rounds of organizations and some churches looking for sponsors. I was in your area this weekend and decided to find you."

"Well, you found me."

He looked tired, possibly thirsty. Kate stood.

"Would you like something to drink? Tea, lemonade? I have soft drinks, if you prefer."

"Lemonade sounds great."

Kate left the living room, passed through the small dining area and into the kitchen. She had made lemonade earlier in the day and took the pitcher from the refrigerator. She turned to take glasses out of the cabinet and it gave her a shock to find Cory sitting at the dining table. She hadn't heard a sound. He noticed her alarm and grimaced.

"I'm sorry. Should I have stayed in the living room? I thought it would save you steps if I were at the table. Besides…" He shrugged. "…I didn't want to spill on the chair."

"No, this is fine."

Kate set coasters on the table, put the two glasses on them, and poured the cold lemonade. Cory took a long drink and sighed.

"That hits the spot," he said. "I haven't stopped all day."

Kate sat opposite him and took a small drink as she studied him. He was nice looking in a wholesome way. Not handsome, still most certainly attractive. Nevertheless, she didn't know what to do with him. If he wanted money, it would be easy. His project was noble and he was obviously a hard worker. Darn Uncle Bert anyway. Probably more to the point, Aunt Iris. They could have let her know they'd given him her contact information.

Cory finished his drink and when Kate suggested more, he nodded. Perhaps he was hungry. It was late in the day. If he were on a mission of collecting donations, maybe he hadn't stopped to eat, or didn't have the price of a meal. Her shoulders slumped. She couldn't turn him out, conscience wouldn't allow it.

"Would you like a sandwich? I have ham and cheese."

Cory's smile brightened. "Would I? You bet. I counted on some kind soul at the last church asking me to dinner. But it didn't happen."

Kate made three sandwiches, but noticing how Cory was watching, she made a fourth, and put a dish of celery sticks and black olives on the table. While Kate prepared the meal, Cory took off his suit jacket and hung it on the back of the chair. As she took plates and silverware from the cabinet, Cory quickly finished a celery stick and said, "Can I help you?"

"No, thanks." Kate held up two tall glasses. "What would you like to drink?"

Perhaps out of politeness he said, "Whatever you are having will be fine."

Since the lemonade was running low, Kate filled the glasses with ice and tea. Cory smiled when she set a glass of tea before him. He seemed easy to please, an agreeable person, but she wasn't sure why it made any difference to her. Cory was almost a stranger, yet sitting at the table with him could pass for normal. Maybe she was as starved for company as Cory seemed to be for food. He finished two sandwiches, had a refill of tea, and had eaten most of the celery sticks.

"I hate to ask," he said. "Do you want the last sandwich? I'll split it with you."

"No, you can have it. I couldn't eat more than one."

Cory reached for the last sandwich. "Probably the reason you keep a nice figure," he said around a mouthful of ham and cheese.

Kate hardly knew what to say. *Thank you* didn't seem appropriate. He wasn't supposed to be noticing her figure. Maybe she had sent the wrong signal by making a meal for him. Still, she hadn't known what else to do. He obviously needed something to eat.

Cory stopped smiling and his eyes darkened. "Oh, I'm sorry. I hope I didn't offend you. I do things like that all the time. You have been nice to me and I take it for instant friendship."

"You meant it as a compliment. It's all right."

As Kate cleared the table, she turned on the kitchen light. The window in the dining area revealed lavender shadows stretching across a side lawn. Cory asked if he could help, but Kate had everything put away and the dishes in the washer within minutes. Cory put on his suit jacket and tried to smooth some of its wrinkles.

'If you see Aunt Iris, wish her well for me," Kate said as she dried her hands on a kitchen towel.

"Yes, yes. I will," he said, standing beside the table.

Kate smiled and stepped into the living room, intending to guide Cory to the front door. However, he didn't budge. She turned and raised her eyebrows. "It's a long drive back to Pinecrest. Or aren't you going there?"

Cory nodded. "I'm going back tonight. I have a nine o'clock meeting about zoning in the morning. You have been very kind. I feel refreshed and ready for the drive home. Before I go, please talk with me about my project.”

Here it comes, Kate suspected. If only he would ask for money. She'd willingly make a large contribution. Yet, from his expression, she wasn't going to get off easy. She sighed and said, “Sit down, but make it short. I have to go to work tomorrow.”

“You are so like Iris described you,” Cory said with a smile.

“And how was that?”

“Competent. Helpful. And obviously very resourceful, having survived such family losses. Now moving and starting a different life.”

Kate noticed he said nothing about beauty or feminine charm. In a way, the lack of flattery was comforting. Whatever Cory Landers wanted, it was surely something well within her capabilities. She waited for him to continue.

“I know Iris and Bert told you about the boys' home. I have the land and I've been making repairs on the house. It is a costly project. I have met most of the legal requirements, but the time will come when I can't do this alone. I'll need a staff. When I worked for Social Services, there were so many young boys who needed refuge.”

“What about the girls? Aren't there many who need the same help?”

“Certainly, but I don't believe I could manage a mixed group. See, I have this idea that if there are boys who can become strong men, as a result it will help more girls. Did you know a majority of the women in prison arrived there because of some man? Men are losing their place in society. Oh, I'm not blaming it all on the feminist movement, but for some reason men are not insisting upon their rightful place.”

“And what is their place?” Kate didn't know if she agreed with Cory, or thought he was some wild-eyed fanatic.

“Men are intended to be protectors; it is in their DNA. If society is to be stable and successful, it needs men who are morally and physically strong. They must head families who feel safe in their care.”

"So you believe the *little woman* should stay at home and tend the children."

Cory gasped. "Of course not! Their role is equally important. It is for each family to find their best solution. A father and a mother working together to produce intelligent and morally fit children. If you hadn't noticed, men and women are different." Cory chuckled as if trying to lighten his declaration.

"I've noticed," Kate answered. Her life was an example of the different roles. Her father never made any effort to draw her into the family business. Still, if she had been a different type, maybe he would have. Knowing whom to blame for the adult she had become was a mystery better left unsolved.

Cory straightened his tie and squared his shoulders. "I'm afraid I've put you off. Be assured I have a great respect for women. My mother is a woman."

He said it with such a serious face and solemn tone that Kate laughed out loud. When Cory stood, so did Kate.

"I've outstayed my welcome," he said. "You know the reason I came. You would be a great help in managing the home. I believe you would find it rewarding, once you get a look at these little guys. They are eager for affection and stability. I'm telling you, what they give back makes my life worthwhile. I have to say, if you come, I couldn't afford to pay more than room and board for a while."

His offer was interesting, but she had a project. There was no way forward without putting the past to rest. It was good Cory had stopped by. His ambition was refreshing. She wished him great success. It was a noble cause. She walked with him to the door. As he stood on the doorstep, he took her hand.

"Give it some thought, won't you? It was hard to believe what Iris said, but I see how right she is. You'd be perfect for this work."

"I think your project is admirable, and I'll be happy to make a contribution—"

Cory held up his hand. "I'm sure you would, but it isn't money I need. What else can I say? I need you. Just think about it."

After he said goodbye, Kate watched as Cory strode along the sidewalk to his pickup. She didn't know much about automobiles, but the truck looked new, with large tires and shiny chrome. For a second she narrowed her eyes with suspicion.

Kate wondered how someone out begging for donations could be driving an expensive-looking truck. She closed the door and dismissed the uncharitable thought. After all, he had been working and received a salary; he could probably afford any type of vehicle he wanted. Walking slowly back to the sofa, she realized how little she really knew about Cory. Although he was unmarried, he had definite ideas on the subject. He could be divorced; maybe it was what had formed his opinion. He liked to fish, Uncle Bert had provided that information. Iris and Bert thought he was reputable.

Cory seemed to be an energetic young man, and one of those people who grew more attractive the longer you knew them. His crooked smile gave him a boyish grin...it inspired trust, a huge help in fund raising. In her present circumstance, where nearly every one she knew was suspect, it was hard to trust a stranger. He hadn't asked for money, but Iris would have let him know her financial situation. Maybe he was smart enough to entice her into the job and when the need for more money arose, as it surely would, there she'd be. A built-in provider. The suspicions were discouraging. It was sad to live without trusting anyone.

Kate finally turned to thoughts of the coming week and hopes of learning the who and why of Henry's death. She had no interest in anything else.

Eleven

Spring was in full swing. Crocus in purple and white appeared first, and some plum trees were in bloom and in a week or two, the daffodils would bring a burst of cheer. As the weather improved, Kate's early morning commute to work was a pleasant way to start the day. Sharron had had her baby. When she had phoned to give the office the news, her voice rang with wonder as she described the little girl. She didn't sound the least bit interested in returning to work, even if she stayed in the area. Gladys hadn't pressed her on the issue, and Kate decided to ignore it, too. The busy workdays also caused Cory's visit to slip from mind. Gladys asked for copies of all expense records. She could pull them up on her own computer, but she wanted a double check and printouts to discuss with Jared or John. It would soon be tax time, and Gladys wanted everything in good order.

Kate had taken over all of Polly's relief breaks, leaving Sam to his work. He had given Kate a rare smile when she had offered to do it. It was a little deceptive on her part, as she enjoyed getting away from her own desk. She found directing phone calls and taking messages was more interesting than making computer entries. John rarely came into accounting, but he had stopped by the receptionist's desk several times. It became increasingly unpleasant and Kate would have liked to avoid him. She had nothing to report and his frustration became evident. His impatience was understandable; there was no progress on her project either.

When John stood in front of the reception desk, carrying a briefcase, and wearing a scowl, Kate didn't smile either.

"I'll be out of town for the next week. You can reach me on my cell with personal messages." He raised one eyebrow, indicating what he meant by *personal messages*. "Gladys has my itinerary."

She scarcely had time to answer before he was striding across the lobby and out to his car. John's being away was a relief; he wouldn't be hanging over her shoulder. He didn't actually press her, but it seemed as if he did by simply being in the building.

Her attitude toward him had changed; it was nothing like she had felt when he came to visit Henry. Thinking of those two days was like remembering strangers. Henry might have had a hidden side, but it was hard to believe he had indulged in illegal business dealings. Surely, Gladys would have known, but when questioned she had claimed it was only a rumor started by a jealous brother. Everyone had a different story.

At first, John had been kind and charming. She remembered how nice he had seemed when he met with Henry. Then he disappeared and she didn't know what to think. Perhaps John had now revealed his true nature. She had never spent time in introspection, about herself or others, apparently a great failing for which she was now paying. The danger was in tipping too far in the other direction and becoming suspicious of everyone.

She'd even sheltered doubts about Grace's love. The box she'd left created more questions than answers. Grace must have felt a strong need to remind Kate of her love. Maybe Grace had harbored a guilty conscience, fearing Kate would learn of the tales told by Uncle Bryon. The safer, happier way was to not question. Yet, it was like drawing a veil over all she had been told. She couldn't go back to such simple trust; Henry's death had made it impossible. If all the parts of her former life were false, she must accept it, even if it changed her.

Sitting at the reception desk while Polly had lunch, Kate thought of the past and chuckled. She wasn't in danger of changing; it had already happened. There was a firmer set to her jaw, her eyes were quick to narrow, and it didn't take much to make her frown. It was difficult getting to know this new Kate. However, there were advantages. In the years past, she was extremely capable of taking care of others; now she wouldn't hesitate to take care of herself. It was a good trait for a woman alone, but it was hard to relax. Her back and neck muscles were always tight. If she found Henry's killer, the tension should disappear, Henry's spirit could rest easy, and so could she. She hadn't heard from Detective Simpson and knew it meant he hadn't found anything new. It was hard to blame him, although she did wonder about the post office box. Maybe it wouldn't hurt to give him a call.

When Polly returned, Kate stood and stepped to the side of the reception desk. Polly had a paper cup of water that she carefully tipped to refill the flowers' vase. She tilted her head as she admired them.

"Pretty, aren't they? Spring is my favorite time of year."

"Yes, very pretty. Did you have to eat alone, or was Gladys there?"

Polly wrinkled her nose. "Gladys went out. Sam kept me company. Not much conversation, if you know what I mean."

"Yes, Sam is a quiet one. But he is friendly, certainly never causes any trouble."

Polly picked up a small stack of pink message slips and ruffled through them. "Not much new here."

"There aren't many calls during lunchtime. Makes it easy on me."

"Did Mr. Holden come in?"

"No, actually he went out."

"I can't keep track of that man! He was out this morning, so I took several calls for him. I intended to give them to him when he came in."

"I'm sorry, I should have checked and dealt with that."

Polly waved the messages. "Don't worry about it. He must have come in and turned right around to go out again. He isn't crazy about taking calls when he is out of the office. I hope none of these are urgent." Polly pursed her lips. "Maybe I'll let Gladys look at them. She'll know if they are important enough to risk calling him."

"I can take them to her, if you'd like."

"Good, because she parks out back and I won't see her come in. Let her have a look, she'll know what I should do."

Kate put the messages in her pants pocket and went to the break room for a lunch of strawberry yogurt and a granola bar. When she reached her desk, Gladys was still not back. After a bit, she asked Sam if Gladys mentioned anything about being out for the afternoon.

Sam shrugged. "Nope. Not to me."

Kate spread the messages on her desktop. She reasoned if Gladys didn't return soon, she'd take the four messages back to Polly. The messages had come only that morning, so there still wasn't a great delay in their being answered. Kate worried about the proper protocol to follow if they were time sensitive. Maybe Jared should have a look at them. However, it was Polly's decision.

The reception's job obviously required more than just answering phones. As Kate restacked the pink message slips, the top one caused her to take a second look. A Mr. Arnold Mertina had left a message for John to call him. The phone number looked familiar; there was even something about the name. Kate stared at the slip of paper. Arnold Mertina, where had she heard that name. She didn't know an Arnold. Maybe she had made an entry in the ledger, a buyer, or seller using Shore's services. It didn't seem likely one name would stand out. Mostly the records were unremarkable.

The name nagged her; even the phone number disturbed her. It was maddening to have something just out of reach. She wished Gladys would hurry back...she'd probably know in a second. She should take the messages back to Polly and forget it; she had work of her own to do. Except she couldn't forget. Before giving up, Kate opened a file on the computer and began a search. The search would find him fast enough. When nothing came using both names, she tried the first and the last names alone. Still no hits, until the one in her mind. Arne, not Arnold.

Kate sagged in the desk chair. She wondered what this meant, if anything. She wasn't positive, but thought Ronda had said Mertina was her husband's name. She hadn't paid much attention when Ronda had made the announcement and flashed the ring. This was crazy. Surely not. What possible business could Ronda's Arne have with John Holden? The questions swirled like a whirlpool, making her mind spin. She stared at the phone number. With a sick feeling, Kate opened the desk drawer and reached for her purse to take out her cell phone. In seconds, she scrolled the contacts to Ronda's name, and compared the message slip and Ronda's number. The sick feeling turned to a dull sort of anger. It was disappointing to have her suspicion confirmed. To make sure, Kate wrote Ronda's number beside the one on the slip, and tried to relax. She shouldn't have become this upset; there must be a reasonable explanation. Maybe Arne was looking for a job. That was probably it. She tried to think back to what she had told Ronda about Shore. She bent forward in concentration, but it was useless, she couldn't remember.

"What are you so deep in thought about, Kate?"

Kate jerked up her head. She hadn't heard Gladys enter the office.

"Oh, you're back." Kate stood and handed Gladys the four messages. "I missed giving these to Mr. Holden. Polly said he doesn't like to be disturbed when on the road. She thought you'd know if any are truly important."

Gladys tucked her purse under her arm and took the slips. She quickly looked through them. "I don't see anything urgent in these names."

"How about Mr. Mertina? Do you know him?"

"No, but that doesn't mean much. Jared and John meet a lot of people. Some turn into clients, some don't. Even Bill probably has a lot of prospects who never reach this office."

"John seemed in a hurry. Do you have any idea where he was headed in such a rush?"

"He has a customer in Canada who needs some handholding. We've dealt with them for a long time, but all of a sudden, they think prices are too high. The change in ownership has rattled a few cages, but we're managing."

"Oh, I hope it turns out okay."

Kate took the slips and Gladys went to her own office. As Kate went back to the lobby, her curiosity refused to subside. She wondered if John were really going to Canada. He'd managed to fool everyone about his location the day of Henry's death. When she returned to the lobby, she handed Polly the messages.

"Gladys said these can wait. Do you remember the call from Mr. Mertina?"

Polly stuck out her lower lip. "Nope. Wait, that's not true, of course I remember getting the call. Why?"

"Sorry, I asked the wrong question. What I meant to ask was did he say what he wanted?"

"No, his secretary just left the message for Mr. Holden to call."

"His secretary?"

Polly nodded and the telephone rang, she answered it. "Shore Import Export, may I help you?"

Kate motioned that she'd leave Polly to her work, and left the lobby with her mind churning out one scenario after another. It seemed Ronda was posing as a secretary. Maybe Ronda and Arne were in some business and wanted Shore to help with distribution, or importing goods from overseas. Ronda might think knowing Kate would give them an entrance. Still, Shore was always looking for clients. No one needed a reference. Without more information, knowledge of the call to John was useless. She sat silently at her desk until Sam gave her a questioning look. She smiled and hurried to get on with her work. The rest of the day sped by and when Kate left for home, she was unusually tired. The possibility of a connection between John and Arne left her weak, but the uncertainty of the reason for it was more unsettling. If a small piece of information did this, maybe she wasn't strong enough to face larger revelations.

Wondering what to do kept her up most of the night. She could call Ronda on the pretense of simply asking how she was getting along. Ronda had said she wanted to keep in touch. If she did, should she mention knowing about the call to Shore? She could wait until John was back and confront him with the message. Neither plan seemed right. John could deny knowing Arne and say he had no idea why he called. Ronda might admit making the call, but give some believable reason for it. Kate had no way of knowing the truth. She might be looking too hard for connections. Morning brought the conclusion that it was unwise to contact John or Ronda about the call. It could give them reason to suspect what she was really doing at Shore. If John and Arne were connected, John hadn't told Arne Kate was working at Shore. If Arne or Ronda did know, they risked calling anyway. She might be over-thinking things, but it was hard to let it go.

Several days later, Kate was too impatient for things go on in the same way. If Jared and Alisha were letting smugglers use Shore, someone needed to stop them. At the same time, putting an end to the illegal activity might shake loose a killer. John would not confront Jared. She had asked him to do this several times. John's objections were strictly financial; it would bring down the company. It was a serious consideration. There were the employees to think of. Gladys, Sam, Polly, even Sharron if she wanted to come back. There was also Bill Greer, the salesman her father had hired years ago. If Shore closed, it would harm them. She didn't have a right to threaten their livelihood. Yet, justice for Henry seemed more important, and she couldn't be responsible for the fall-out. From what she'd seen in the past weeks, Shore was a thriving business. It didn't need illegal income, and if they were all innocent, the investigation wouldn't harm anyone.

Although Alisha was another matter. Perhaps there was never enough money to suit her. She probably had a big influence on Jared. She had convinced him to let Kate work in the office. Kate laughed to herself. Alisha had no fear over Kate being in the office. Poor simple Kate wouldn't discover anything. Up to this point, Alisha was right, and that was the reason Kate had to do something. Talking to John was a dead end, she couldn't trust him. Jared was an unknown. It would have to be Alisha. Kate thought it over carefully. She would confront Alisha with the accusation. Working at it from the smuggling angle might not be the way to find Henry's killer, but there was nowhere else to start.

Uncle Bryon had said her father had made his fortune illegally; John had accused her brother of thievery, and Jared of carrying on the racket. She had a right to the truth, and she intended to wring it out of Alisha, one way or the other. By the time Kate called Alisha and asked to see her, Kate had reconsidered her method of attack. She would not demand police involvement, only that the activities cease. Holding a threat over Jared and Alisha could make them stop and at the same time save employee jobs. The first time Kate called, she had to leave a message, and Alisha didn't return the call. The second time, Alisha put off a meeting as she was far too busy. The third time, Kate had insisted.

"Please, Alisha. If you don't agree to a time, I'll park in your driveway and catch you."

"Oh, all right! I'll come to your place. How about Thursday evening around seven?"

Kate would have agreed to meeting in a boat on the lake, anywhere, as long as she could confront Alisha, and get a straight answer. She suspected Alisha had chosen to meet at the townhouse so she could leave when she wanted. It would be easier and more polite than trying to dislodge her from her own house. Alisha had asked what Kate wanted, but Kate hadn't told her and suspected curiosity made Alisha finally agree. The meeting was three days away and it gave Kate time to prepare. If things went the way she hoped, Alisha would find Kate much changed.

After work Thursday, Kate hurried home. She changed into jeans and a tee shirt, ate a cheese sandwich, and eagerly awaited Alisha's arrival. The doorbell chimed at exactly five minutes to seven. Even the double ring of the bell projected Alisha's impatience. She would want this visit to be short, and Kate agreed. When she opened the door, Alisha immediately stepped over the threshold and brushed past her. Alisha was wearing a tight lavender dress, a silk shawl around her shoulders, and long gold earrings with several matching bracelets.

"As you can see, I don't have all night," Alisha said as she stood in the middle of the living room.

Obviously, Alisha was on her way to some social gathering. Kate pointed to the sofa. "Please sit. This won't take long."

Alisha raised a golden eyebrow, but took the offered seat and put her evening bag down beside her. Kate sat in the recliner.

"First, thank you for helping me get the job at Shore."

Alisha waved her hand in dismissal.

"No, I mean it, what I'm going to ask now won't change that. I'll always be grateful."

Alisha sighed and rolled her eyes. "Fine. Now get on with it. What do you want?"

"I want a straight answer about items being smuggled in and out of the country through shipments done by Shore. Did my father have contact with people who paid him to use our company?"

"Yes, yes, of course he did. How do you think he could have built the company as fast as he did?"

If Kate had been standing, she would have staggered backwards. Alisha's admission was a shock. It took a second to remember her goal. She had asked for the truth; she needed to be strong enough to face it. If it was indeed the truth.

"Why should I believe you?"

Alisha shrugged, the silk shawl slipping off one shoulder. "Don't. I don't care. Why do you want to dig up ancient history?"

Kate quickly gathered her thoughts. She hadn't expected an admission, and she'd been prepared to worm it out of Alisha.

"Maybe it isn't ancient history. Are you and Jared still engaged in this?"

"What? Are you crazy? It's far too risky. I told Jared about Shore's past and he promised to keep us on the right side of things." Alisha narrowed her eyes. "Is there something going on now, because if there is I want to know. Do you realize people go to jail over something like this? We would lose the company."

Kate leaned back and studied the anxiety in Alisha's eyes, and the frown wrinkling her normally smooth brow. Either she was telling the truth or she was a very good actress.

"Don't be upset, Alisha. I only want to know what you know about this. I promise, what you tell me goes no further. I would never inform the police. I don't want the company to go out of business. I simply want the truth."

"Fine. When you lived at home, you must have suspected…" She stopped, a small smile rippling her crimson lips. "…no maybe you didn't. Henry Senior kept accounts outside the regular business. After he died, your brother picked up where Senior left off. I told him it was crazy. The business was doing okay and we didn't need to risk it all."

Kate raised her hand to stop Alisha. "Don't tell me my brother was involved."

"Oh please, Henry was no different than his father. Well, maybe a little different. When we argued over it, he agreed to stop."

"Is that what the divorce was about?"

"No. It's as I said, we grew apart. Henry worked all the time, I wanted to do things, take trips. I got tired of doing it by myself. Besides, Henry cut out all that before we divorced, but it didn't make him pay any more attention to me."

"Did Gladys know? She and a salesman named Bill Greer were with my dad from the beginning."

Alisha shrugged. "Maybe. Probably. It isn't something people talk about. They had jobs to protect, didn't they?

"So what you are saying is my father and brother dealt with smugglers."

"That is what I said, isn't it?"

"When did Henry stop?"

"Around a year after Senior died. It really wasn't Henry's cup of tea."

"Didn't the crooks get upset?"

"Maybe, but I doubt it. I would have known. What could they do? I suspect they found someone willing to accommodate them. Money talks, you know."

"Do you think one of them might have killed Henry?"

"Why would they? It was too long ago. Besides, Henry didn't own the company any longer."

"Could Henry have had something they wanted and when he didn't give it to them, they killed him?"

Alisha picked up her bag and stood.

"I'm sorry, Kate. I just don't see any connection. No one was upset enough to kill Henry. These guys are almost white-collar criminals. They are sneaky, not violent. Henry's death has put a strain on you. Maybe taking a job at Shore wasn't a good thing. Brings it all back. Listen, I have a great therapist. I can get you an appointment, if you want."

Kate stood, and stepped closer to Alisha.

"Are you sure Jared hasn't engaged in anything illegal? And Henry stopped when you say he did?"

Alisha put her hand on Kate's arm. "I'm positive. Jared is a great businessman. He doesn't need any help. I don't want to speak ill of the dead, but Henry wasn't that brave. He wanted out and used my objections as an excuse to drop it. Then he could go on believing he was as strong as his dad was, but did it only for me. Is there anything else? I have to go."

Alisha stood at the door and Kate opened it for her.

"Can I talk to you about this another time?" Kate asked, hoping Alisha would agree.

"Of course, but I promise you I've told you all I know. Are you sure you don't want to see my therapist guy? He really is good."

"No, but thanks," Kate said.

Alisha stepped out into the spring evening and Kate watched as she hurried down the walkway to her car. When she pulled away from the curb, Kate closed the door and, going to the sofa, dropped down onto it and put her head in her hands. She needed to organize her thoughts, put in order what people had told her. She remembered the journal she had started before getting the job at Shore. It was a notebook where she'd entered her goals, and what information she had to start the search for Henry's killer. This business of illegal activity was only important if it had bearing upon his death. It must have some connection, because she couldn't believe a stranger killed him. There was no other reason for the killing. She quickly stood and went to the kitchen to pour a glass of red wine. She took the drink to the den, set it on the desk, and began searching through the drawers for the notebook.

When she found it, the first few pages were lists of things she'd set out to do. Notes about looking for the townhouse, information about turning on utilities, and meeting with Alisha at Roman's. There were also the things John had told her. She'd numbered them. Not in order of importance, but more of when she had learned them. There were no entries after starting to work. She hadn't learned anything new. Now there *was* something to add. Arne Mertina had tried to contact John, but what it meant was unclear. The conversation with Alisha was easy to enter. It was opposite to what John had said. The only thing everyone agreed upon was that Henry Sr. engaged in illegal activities. His brother Bryon accused him, Gladys acknowledged it, but denied it. Of course she would. She must have liked Henry Sr. and even Junior to have stayed on this long. Perhaps she suspected, but didn't ask questions in order to keep the peace. Illegal activity at Shore was hard to accept, and if not for Henry's death, she would have never believed it.

Kate put a big question mark beside the facts as Alisha had stated them. Alisha liked money, but probably not enough to risk everything. Kate scratched out the question mark; she tended to believe Alisha's story. She had meant to ask Alisha about the possibility of Henry taking some jewels, but hearing what Alisha had said made her forget. Knowing how goods moved made it harder to believe John's story. Henry would have needed to know the exact shipment, find a way to get into it, and do all that in secret. Alisha had dismissed the idea of Henry having anything the smugglers would want. It seemed to make sense. Kate put a rough timeline on the notebook's next page. Alisha said Henry stopped dealing with smugglers the year after Henry Sr. died. If it were true, the activity was ten years in the past. Ancient history, indeed. If Henry had taken anything from them, they would have tried to collect long before this.

Staring at the entries in the notebook, Kate felt frustrated. The answer was there, it had to be. A harsh laugh escaped her lips. The next step wasn't clear, but one thing was. She couldn't trust anyone. However, Alisha did seem to have more credibility than John. Her estimation of Henry rang true. Henry was cautious, always had been. Even to the keeping of paper copies of records, when the company had a good backup system. If the computers went down, nothing was lost, but still Henry kept records in a file cabinet. Perhaps she should have thrown them out when she moved, but evidently, caution was a family trait. She couldn't destroy the old records until she'd examined them. Kate lifted the glass of wine and drank the last bit.

It was growing late with a workday ahead. She should get ready for bed, but the wine had made her hungry. The cheese sandwich had been no substitute for a proper meal. In the kitchen, she put a frozen dinner into the microwave. Usually she cooked, but like Henry, she kept a backup, an emergency ration. As she sat at the table eating the orange chicken, her mind was on the notebook in the bedroom/den. There wasn't any way to pull John's story apart, and no one who could confirm Alisha's version. Arne Mertina's name had one sentence behind it. He had, rather Ronda had, made a call to John, and he was newly married. Kate quickly finished the frozen dinner and straightened the kitchen before hurrying back to the den. She opened the laptop and brought up a search engine. It took over an hour to work through all the sites and find the proper records, but when she did, there was more information to put into the notebook.

Arne and Ronda had been married for eight years. Kate stared at the screen, started the search over, and it came up the same. Writing the date in the notebook made it solid and real. Except it raised dozens of questions. Ronda claimed to be a widow, the first lie. Maybe because Arne couldn't be seen by Henry. Henry might have known him. Ronda's reason for moving to Greenfield, certainly another lie. She was in place before Kate and Henry moved to Greenfield, perhaps in order to watch them. Kate put the pen down on the notebook page, the orange chicken in her stomach threatening to turn sour. Arne and Ronda were keeping watch over Henry. They watched, and when John came, Henry did not throw him out; he talked with him. Kate wrote Henry's words in the notebook, *'I can't do that,'* were what she'd heard. They killed Henry because he wouldn't do something. She was certain enough to take up the pen and put it in writing.

Kate quickly dropped down a line and began making entries about the threats she'd received, and the search of the Greenfield house. She didn't know how the ones who had broken into the house fit in, they weren't robbers, they took nothing, but they were still crooks. Yet it seemed too mild a name for them. Whoever they were, and whatever they wanted, they were her enemies. She wrote the word at the head of a column, and with a bitter smile put the names Ronda and Arne under the heading. Such deceit was unforgiveable and when she learned the names of the two who had posed as movers, she'd write their names there, too. Exhausted, Kate closed the notebook, turned off the laptop, and left the den. After a shower, it was past midnight when she crawled into bed. As sleep refused to come, Kate stared at the ceiling and remembered her time in Greenfield and Ronda's fake friendship. In the future, she wouldn't be as trusting.

Things began to fall into place. Ronda knew when she was going to Chicago, and about how long she'd be gone. Kate had even asked her to pick up the mail. An open invitation. Ronda even knew the reason she was going. In a roundabout way, she had asked where Jim Burton's office was. A phone call made the break-in to steal Grace's box possible. When the Enemy couldn't make anything of the box's contents, they searched the house. All easily arranged by Ronda Mertina.

Kate had never questioned Henry about the house in Greenfield being part of the sale of the business. He'd said it was to some tax advantage, perhaps it was. Still, she wondered whose idea it was. If Jared wanted Henry where he could watch him, it meant one thing. If John insisted upon it, another. However, it could be exactly as Henry stated, maybe he suggested it. Yet if there was a strong connection between John and Arne, it put John in a very bad light. When Kate finally went to sleep, she dreamed of a faceless man chasing her down a long dark tunnel, and no matter how fast she ran, the light remained too far away.

The only thing different about the next day at work was meeting Bill Greer, the salesman her father had hired years ago. Kate had finished relieving Polly at the reception desk and stopped in the break room for her own lunch. She was sitting at the table with her usual strawberry yogurt when Bill came in. He wore a wide smile that revealed a gold eyetooth. His round face held sparkling blue eyes and was topped by obviously dyed black hair. Everything about him spoke of a man in his late fifties striving to look thirty. As he came toward the table, he held out his hand. She had no choice but to reach up and shake it.

"Hi, I'm Bill Greer. Gladys told me I'd find you here. I've been out of the office for some time, but you know that." His laugh was as round as his cheerful face. "I have been wanting to meet you. You won't remember me, but I remember you. Your dad picked me up, dusted me off, and taught me everything I know about selling. I saw you from a distance several times all those years ago, and I saw plenty of pictures."

Bill pulled out a chair and sat across from Kate. She had stopped eating to watch this rolling example of salesmanship. He was clearly using the first rule in sales, sell yourself, and he was doing a good job because Kate was immediately interested. She also needed to find out where he fit into the case she was trying to build. Although he didn't look like a criminal, neither did anyone else she knew.

"I do remember hearing your name. My father thought girls were of more use at home. I'm sure you knew my brother much better."

Bill tightened his lips, and sadness drifted across his eyes. "I can't tell you how sorry I am about Henry. It is hardly believable. Who'd want to hurt that boy?"

Bill seemed to think of Henry as a boy, although at forty years of age he was hardly that. Still, if Kate had Bill's age right, he was fifteen or twenty years older, so when Henry came to work at Shore, Bill would have seen him as a boy.

"Yes," she said. "Who indeed. Did Henry make enemies when he was running the company?"

"No. None I knew of. He carried on just as his dad had. There weren't any big changes. Still, I wasn't surprised when he decided to sell." Bill chuckled. "Especially when the opportunity came so easy."

"I was a little surprised because he hadn't *tried* to sell."

Bill laughed, his gold tooth on display. "That Alisha is something. She could have run the company herself, but it wouldn't have left her time for the social things."

"You think Alisha arranged the sale?"

"You bet. She found her super sales guy, Jared Roth, and made sure he got the right company. Henry never had the love for the business your dad did. You ask me, it turned out good for all concerned."

"What do you think about Mr. Holden?"

Bill's smile disappeared, and his eyes shifted slightly. "I don't know him very well. He gets along with Jared and lets me carry on as I've always done. I'd say I know Jared better."

Kate wanted to say it *hadn't* turned out well for all concerned. Certainly not for Henry. She wanted to bring the conversation back to anyone who had reason to harm Henry. Bill should know if Shore ever conducted illegal activities. She had talked to Gladys and Alisha about it; he might have a different view.

"Bill, you knew my father well, didn't you?"

The big smile broke out again. "Sure I did. To this day, I miss him. If it hadn't been for him, I might have never had a chance in life."

"I've heard stories about how he built this company, how he took money from people bringing things into the country illegally. Tell me the truth. It can't hurt him now. Please."

"All I will ever say is whatever he did, it gave some of us secure jobs. He never did anything to put us in trouble with the law. He never asked me to do anything illegal. You can ask Gladys or Sam."

"What if some of the hidden activity spilled over and caused my brother trouble?"

"Now there is something I can answer straight. Henry was a far better bookkeeper than he was a salesman. He made sure nothing came in under the table. He wasn't one to ask for trouble."

Kate smiled. Alisha and Bill agreed upon Henry's character. It wasn't flattering, but it described the Henry she knew.

"What about Alisha and Jared, would they pick up where my dad left off?"

Bill pushed out his lower lip and frowned. "I doubt it. The company is rolling along fine, no need for that. No one here would risk it. Now, what about you, young lady, what brought you back to us?"

Kate stood and went to the sink to rinse the yogurt container before throwing it into the trash.

"Gladys says I'm lonesome, looking for a family connection."

"Do you think you'll stay?"

"I may not have an option if Sharron comes back."

"There should be a place for you here. Say, if Sharron does come back, you can come out with me. I'll teach you to be the best saleslady going. How about it? Sort of payback for what your dad did for me."

Kate brightened with surprise; it was a strangely pleasing idea. Bill looked as if he meant it. Henry might not have had the talent, but maybe she did.

"Do you really mean it?" she asked.

"Sure I do. Most of my accounts are solid, don't need a lot of attention. It could be exciting to start you out."

"I'm not too old?"

Bill laughed. "You don't look a day over twenty. Twenty-five at the outside."

They left the break room with her arm in his and when they entered the office, Gladys turned aside from talking to Sam and said, "I see you've met Bill."

Even Sam rolled his eyes, ducked his head, and chuckled softly. For a minute, Kate felt she had found a part of her family. If Bill were serious about his offer to teach her, it opened up a vista she'd never thought of. There would be travel, meeting new people, and her efforts, if successful, would help the company. She liked the idea of generating business and producing money to support fellow employees.

As Bill joined Gladys in her office, Kate looked at Sam and said, "He really is a good salesman, isn't he?"

Sam nodded and turned back to his computer screen. Anyone who doubted Bill's ability needed only to spend a short time with him. He could probably sell ice cubes to Eskimos; Kate was almost ready to sign up for his training course. She sighed and got on with the afternoon's work. A bit before five o'clock Gladys came out of her office carrying her purse, and waved her hand at Kate and Sam.

"Shut it down. Let's get an early start on the weekend."

Sam immediately began turning off his equipment and straightening his desk. He'd never mentioned a family, but whatever his private life he seemed eager to get to it. Kate did the same, although with some reluctance. Doing the company's work kept personal thoughts away. The weekend ahead meant too much time to think.

On the drive home, she resolved to remain positive and put the free time to good use. There was the notebook to update. She needed to enter Bill's comments about her father. Yet, even good intentions were not enough to bring about any work on Friday night. She spent the evening fighting depression and the feeling there would never be justice for Henry. It was like being lost at sea with no help on the horizon, gray white-capped waves stretching endlessly under a gray cloud-streaked sky.

Saturday morning dawned without a cloud in the sky; sunlight streamed into the bedroom windows. Kate awoke surprisingly refreshed and eager to tackle putting the pieces of scant information together. After a light breakfast, she brought the notebook into the living room, settled on the sofa, and started making entries. Painful as it was, she started in Greenfield. It was certain Ronda had been in place to keep an eye on the Shore household. When Henry was gone, she continued to watch Kate. Ronda's claim of being a widow made it easier to attach herself to Henry and Kate. This was the first big lie. As Kate's feelings for Ronda turned to disgust, she remembered what Detective Simpson had said about crooks. They lie, it is what they do. Because they lie, Simpson demanded proof.

Kate made a note stating the date of Ronda and Arne's marriage, proof of lie number one. Despite her dislike for Ronda, maybe she should call her. She could pretend they were still friends and find out exactly what part the Mertinas played. The next entry in the notebook was John and Arne. If they knew each other when Henry was alive, it brought up more questions. The message for John to call Arne wasn't exactly proof of a relationship between the two, but it was something to explore. Maybe Ronda innocently thought Arne could get a job at Shore, but asking for John seemed strange. Ronda knew a man named Leland had been at the house in Greenfield, maybe she knew that man also went by John. Sitting on the sofa, legs crossed, the notebook on her lap, Kate harkened back to something else Detective Simpson had said. In his experience, people killed for love, hate, money, or to protect themselves. She examined each of the reasons in relationship to Henry. The first one that came close to sounding right was 'money,' or maybe 'self-protection' and both led straight back to Shore Import/ Export.

Twelve

Kate jumped up from the sofa, found her cell phone, and placed a call to Ronda. As the number rang, her doubts grew. She hadn't thought this through; it would be smart to hang up. As Kate wavered, Ronda answered.

"Kate! How are you? I've been meaning to call."

"I'm fine. How is married life?"

"Oh, wonderful. You should try it. Any interesting guys in your new life? Chicago is a big town."

"No. I haven't met anyone." Cory Landers slipped across her mind, but quickly faded.

"We'll have to fix that, honey. Can't have you all alone in a big city. What about the ex-sister-in-law? Won't she help?"

"She would if I let her."

"Then why not?" The sound of jewelry rattling mingled with Ronda's words. She was probably wearing long, dangling earrings.

"Maybe I will, sometime. What are you and Arne doing? Where does he work?"

A sharp, short silence let Kate know she'd touched a soft spot. Ronda laughed.

"He's doing the same thing he always has. Some kind of sales work. He doesn't ask me what I do with my time and I don't bother him." She laughed again. "It's the secret of a happy marriage."

"Did he ever do any work for Henry's old company?" Kate's stomach tightened.

"I don't know. What makes you think he did?"

"Did John Holden ever call him back? I thought maybe Arne was looking for a job with Shore."

"Good gosh, Kate. I have no idea. Maybe he did want a job there. He didn't say anything to me."

Kate's closed her eyes. She'd given a perfect excuse for the call instead of making Ronda come up with her own. When Kate didn't answer, Ronda said, "How do you know he called John, Mr. Holden?"

Kate felt the flush rise from her neck to her cheeks. "Because I'm working there now."

"Oh. Well, I guess it's a natural place for you to work. How do you like it?"

"It is fine. I should go now, Ronda. I called to say hello and see how you are getting along."

"We're okay. Listen, we need to get together sometime. Have one of our girl talks. With you working, I'll let you set the time. Be sure to call me. I'm free any time."

"You're right, Ronda, I don't have much free time. Tell Arne hello for me. Bye now."

The call ended as Ronda said goodbye.

Kate stood in the middle of the living room clutching the phone. She'd made a perfect mess of the call. It was stupid. She wasn't good at lying or trying to get people to reveal things. Still, she had learned something; she picked up the notebook and began to write. Ronda had lied about the call. She knew Arne was trying to contact John because *she* made the call. It was amazing how many people lied and with such ease. Polly was a witness to this lie. Kate could prove Arne didn't have a real secretary, unless she used Ronda's cell phone.

She worried about having revealed her job at Shore. Still, if Arne and John did work together, or if they were strangers, it didn't matter. She needed to find some connection between them, other than the call. If there were a tie between John and Arne, it had to be the company. Kate's shoulders tightened; the tension made her back ache. She stood and stretched. The day was about gone, spent in speculation. The call to Ronda a failure, but it did reveal her deep deceit. It also strengthened Kate's resolve to find the proof that would help Detective Simpson catch a killer.

In the bedroom office, Kate sat at the desk wondering what next to write in the notebook. When nothing occurred to her, she turned to the big old trunk. She had put Henry's work files and the household files into the new file cabinet. She lifted the lid of the trunk and looked down at the box Grace had left for her, the reason no longer a mystery. Grace had known of her husband's shady business. If Kate were ever alone, she might discover the family's past. All Grace could do was leave reminders of their love with the hope it would indeed cover many sins. Kate was satisfied she had discovered her mother's purpose, because if Henry were living, he would have protected her from the truth. Kate closed the trunk's lid and slumped in the desk chair. If it were not for the burning in her chest, she might be able to close the door on her past. Forget what her father had done. Move on and find a life. Maybe even take Bill's offer of becoming a super saleswoman. However, the pain, like a burning lump of coal lodged under her ribs, wouldn't let her. The only thing that would cool the fiery pain was justice for Henry, and then the healing could start. It would leave a scar, but she'd live with it.

She picked up the notebook and started with the first page. Somewhere in there were answers, if she could make the connections. She had listed everything John had said. Kate picked up a pen and put a question mark near the claim Henry had taken jewels as protection. There was only John's word for it; no one else mentioned stolen gems. She again reviewed Detective Simpson's reasons for murder. If John told the truth about jewels, money could be a reason. John had also said Henry had information that could put people in jail. So, the forth reason of self-protection might apply. Yet, he would not have wanted to bring down the company. Henry would not have gone to the police, and that made money the more likely motive.

As the day faded, the room grew dim. Kate clicked on the lamp. A yellow glow spread across the open notebook and shadows from the ceiling light filled the corners of the room. She sighed and closed the notebook. Another wasted day. Her throat tightened and tears burned her eyes. She tried to stop but a great sadness welled up and a strangled cry broke the silence. She put her head down on her folded arms, and sobbed. Gone, everything was gone. If she could have her family back she would forgive them anything; she *did* forgive them. They could have trusted her. Henry could have trusted her, but now it was too late. The only thing left was revenge. The thought jolted her and stopped the tears. Revenge seemed an ugly word; one should pursue justice.

She sat up straight and wiped the tears from her cheeks. No, revenge was the right word. As the thought grew and formed into a solid possibility, she narrowed her damp eyes. She had lost everything, but as soon as she found Henry's killer she would have revenge. Seeking justice had seemed noble and proper; hunger for revenge had a hard edge to it, and it brought a satisfaction simple justice had never produced. Perhaps she was more a Shore than anyone would have suspected. She hadn't known her father well. He had never done her harm, only his distance hurt. A lingering resentment or pain over the lack of a closer relationship caused her chin to quiver, but she quickly steadied it. Lingering over the past was useless, and it was weak. The only way forward was to gain control of the debilitating emotions. The confusion over family love and loyalty mixed with a lost lonesome feeling made a powerful foe. Tossed about by grief, fear, and shock, she was tired, both physically and emotionally.

Everything depended upon finding Henry's killer. She could deal with the disillusionment over her father's past, the sorrow of her mother's death, and even the loss of her brother. The wounds would heal, but not without the balm of revenge.

Kate stood, snapped off the desk lamp, and started for the den doorway, but she stopped in mid-room. She was tired, but it wasn't late. There were still the records in the file cabinet to sort. It was an unpleasant job, yet since working five days a week, there was little time or energy left except on weekends. She went back to the desk, turned on the light, and pulled open a cabinet drawer. She took out a stack of file folders marked household; earlier she had sorted them by date. There were old utility bills, tax records, and even bank statements from years past. Henry had kept everything, and it probably said a lot about *his* personal demons. Maybe he'd been insecure. If only they had talked, perhaps shared feelings about the family dynamic, it could have helped them both. Too late, too late, too late echoed through the emptiness of her heart. She made a pile of papers to destroy.

When she put the household folder back into the cabinet, it was much thinner; she should have destroyed the useless records before. The notebook was the only thing on the desktop and she picked it up to review the notes there. She had started a file on her laptop, too. A rueful smile lifted her lips; she was as bad as Henry with written records and computer files. She'd left the laptop in the living room so taking the notebook, she exited the den. After turning on lights in the living and dining room, she set up the computer along with the notebook on the dining room table. The Excel file she'd started with the columns for each question or fact made it easy to enter items from the notebook to the laptop. It was surprising how clear answers to questions became, only to be discouraged when so many questions had no answers.

The sudden chime of her cell phone broke her concentration. She stood and retrieved the phone from the arm of the sofa. She did not recognize the calling number and hesitated to answer.

"Miss Shore?"

"Yes."

"Hi, this is Detective Simpson in Greenfield."

He didn't need to add Greenfield, his name was exciting enough. "Detective, how good to hear from you. Do you have some information, what have you found?"

"Now don't get your hopes up. I'm just touching base to let you know we haven't forgotten your brother's case."

"Oh."

"But we have found something. It hasn't taken us very far, but it's still something. We have a copy of the application used to rent the box."

Kate sank onto the sofa and held the phone with both hands to steady it.

"The name used on the form is Leland Webern. He had a driver's license and auto insurance with an address as proofs of identification. He paid in advance. We ran down every address and we came to a stop. The parts that did check out were either old addresses with no forwarding, or bogus to begin."

"The photo identification, the picture. Surely, it can help. Please, get it to me. I can recognize him. How about fingerprints on the application? I can get something of John Holden's for comparison."

"See, the thing is, there isn't a copy of the photo ID."

"Why not?"

"They don't make copies. The customer shows the identification when they pick up the keys. Far as prints go, too many people have handled the paper."

Kate slumped back on the sofa. Simpson didn't sound encouraging. "Go on," she said.

"I spoke with a clerk who slightly, I mean very slightly, remembers taking the application. The best she could recall the man was tall, but not overly tall. The thing she noticed most was his mustache. Blond, she thinks, like his hair."

"I see. What will you do next?"

"Keep digging. I thought you'd like to know, not that we didn't believe you in the first place, but now we have proof someone used that name. Or, the person exists and we just can't find him."

Kate sighed. "Maybe you can't find him because he is going by the name of John Holden now."

"Anything is possible. Sorry I haven't called before, but procedures for access to records take some time. We even checked the surveillance cameras, but the clerk couldn't positively identify Webern from them."

"I'm sure you are doing all you can, Detective."

"Well, just wanted to let you know we're still on it."

"Thank you."

When the call ended, Kate sat on the sofa and discouragement grew stronger than it had been before. Detective Simpson's information proved John might be too smart to catch. No one else would use the name Leland Webern. Blond, indeed. It didn't take much to use a wig and false mustache, and put a phony picture on an ID. It was maddening to think John was guilty, or that he knew who was, and not have the proof. He had to have slipped up somewhere.

Kate jolted upright. Why hadn't she told Detective Simpson about Arne Mertina? She quickly redialed the detective's number. When he answered, she couldn't get the words out fast enough.

"Miss Shore, please slow down."

"I'm sorry, I was going to tell you something I'd discovered, but I forgot to."

"Go ahead."

"You remember Ronda, my neighbor. She had a boyfriend named Arne Mertina. When I sold my house, she and Arne were married and moved to his apartment here in Chicago. This past week, Ronda called Shore, leaving a message for John Holden to call Arne."

"And what do you think this means?"

Kate tried to sound convincing. "There is some connection between those two. I asked Ronda why Arne would call John and she said she didn't know a thing about it. But she's the one who left the message."

"How did you know about the call?"

"Oh, I guess I didn't tell you. I'm working at Shore."

"Look, I understand how eager you are, but it really isn't safe to go poking around. Anyone who has killed once usually doesn't hesitate to do it again."

"I'm careful."

"Doesn't sound like it. Okay, tell me what you think it means."

Kate gave him all her suspicions about Ronda being in Greenfield, and the fact Ronda and Arne had been married for a long time.

"Why would they lie about that?" he sounded puzzled.

"I think it was because they thought Ronda as a widow could gain my trust. A married woman is busy with her own household. Or maybe Arne didn't want Henry to know he was around."

"There's an idea. Go ahead."

They spoke for over ten minutes as Kate told him everything she suspected. He seemed receptive and halted her a couple of times as he made notes.

"Thank you for the information. I'm not sure what to make of it right now, but with enough parts something usually comes together."

"I'll call you if I think of something else," Kate said.

"Don't do anything on your own. It could be dangerous, or you might accidently destroy some solid proof. I've seen criminals slip away for lack of it."

"I understand. I'll be careful."

After the telephone call, she was too tense to think about dinner. For a bit, she paced the living room, trying to think of ways to trap John. What Simpson had said made John seem guilty. Especially with Arne in the picture. She picked up the laptop and notebook and returned to the den. There was nothing more to enter in the Excel file and, to stop the unending spin of speculation, she decided to tackle Henry's old office records. She plopped the two files onto the desktop, sighed, and began sorting. It took several minutes for her mind to settle on the paperwork. Some of the records went back to before the sale. They were much the same as the current records she entered every day into the files at work. Maybe she'd ask Gladys to look through them and see if there was anything worth keeping.

The sale documents were in the second folder, and as she read them, she discovered another of John's lies. Henry had not financed any part of the sale. John had told her Alisha and Jared, if threatened, might liquidate everything. This would stop the payments to her. However, even if the business went bankrupt, it wouldn't harm her. Henry had received payment in full and their income was from the investments he had made. When John had said it, she had supposed payments went straight to the brokerage. She should have questioned the details of the sale and known there were no additional payments. With each uncovered lie, she felt more ashamed. She picked up the notebook and put a line through one more thing John had said.

She put the papers concerning the sale into the file folder and settled it back in the cabinet's drawer. She kept the other folder with office records out to take to work on Monday. They belonged to the company, and had nothing to do with her. Gladys would probably throw them away. She picked the file up, intending to secure it with a large rubber band when a small black notebook fell onto the desktop. She'd seen it before; it was probably Henry's old address book. She picked it up and put it to one side. It was too private to return with the office records. She left the den with the file and laid it on the small table near the front door, making sure she wouldn't forget to take it. There was nothing more to do except try to rest and get ready for the next week. John's many lies made it hard to expose him. He seemed covered from every angle.

Back in the den, she picked up the address book and sat down to scan the pages. There were familiar names, and a weary smile touched her lips. Names from a past life. She should probably throw it away, yet it had belonged to her brother. She could get rid of it later when she was ready to let go completely. Near the back, the pages meant for notes caught her interest. The first page held several blocks of numbers and names. It listed the name, what appeared to be a date, or in some cases, two dates, and below that strings of numbers. Some were the right length for phone numbers, but others were not. The back of Kate's neck began to tingle, her hand shook, and a certain knowledge settled over her. She had no idea what the names and numbers meant, only that they were important. Possibly the protection Henry had taken with him. The information to send people to jail.

Alisha had sworn the illegal activity had stopped a year after Henry Sr. had died. She had wanted no part of it, and neither had Henry Jr. It might have taken a year to drop those associations gracefully. Kate sat holding the little book and tried to imagine what that year might have been like. Henry must have convinced the smugglers the information was safe with him. They would have believed him, because to reveal it would have destroyed Shore, too. She wondered if there was a statute of limitations on smuggling activities. To prosecute the company there would have to be evidence it had happened. With nothing going on now, the police couldn't prove anything. Besides, individuals were the guilty parties, and to her knowledge, they were all dead. Of course, there was only Alisha's word for this.

She looked down at the book and counted three names above lines of numbers on the first page. Henry had written tiny block letters and numbers in black ink. Turning the page, she saw three more sets of names and numbers. She recognized one of them and her throat tightened enough to choke her. Leland Webern. She closed her eyes for a second. It was time for careful thinking, and not doing anything stupid. If she were right, these were names, dates, and perhaps order numbers indicating which shipments held illegal items. She doubted the entire shipments were illegal. The smuggled items were probably deep inside legitimate goods. However, those transactions were long past. No one would care about it now. Henry could have revealed this information at any time, but he didn't.

Henry would not have done anything to shut down Shore. People he cared about would lose their jobs. Alisha had admitted knowing what went on years ago and said it would never take place while she and Jared were owners. She had probably told Jared, and he must have thought it safe enough to buy into the company. Kate felt sure Henry, Alisha, nor would Jared do anything to harm Shore. So if Shore was safe, why kill Henry? Was John afraid Henry would change his mind? Henry's words flashed before her: *I can't do that.*

Maybe John wanted Henry to turn in the incriminating information. Kate raised an eyebrow. He might have wanted to because Jared *was* running illegal goods through Shore. It would mean Alisha had lied. For some reason, Kate believed Alisha more than she did John. A deep weariness settled over her and she carefully closed the little book and held it to her breast. Perhaps it didn't hold all the answers, but it was something Henry thought worth keeping. Tucked away in the attic of the Greenfield house where the robbers had failed to look, Henry's record had been safe. It was a small victory but it gave Kate hope. It was surely this and not jewels Henry had taken to secure their safety. It was hers now and she'd do her best to use it wisely. Unless something happened to change her mind, she too would protect Shore and its employees. It was inconceivable that Gladys, Sam, and Bill were part of anything illegal. Yet, based on her past judgment, even of family members, she could be wrong.

It was late; there was no sense in more speculation. Kate looked around the room wondering where to hide the book, but decided it was a waste to worry. It had been in with the other records; it might as well remain there, for now. However, as soon as she could rent a safe deposit box, it would have a new home. Possibly forever. Before putting the book into the file cabinet, Kate made a copy of the two pages. She would keep the copy and take it to work. Maybe one or more of the names and numbers were in the office records.

It threatened to be a long weekend, even though Saturday was nearly over. After a boring evening of television, Kate climbed into bed and went immediately to sleep. It was Sunday afternoon before she dressed in jeans and a tee shirt. She tried to read or watch a news broadcast, but she was too restless. She'd tucked the copy of names and numbers into her purse, although it was not likely she'd forget to take it to work. With nothing else to do, she stretched out on the sofa, hoping she'd think of some way to prove John was Henry's killer. She was deep in thought when the doorbell chimed. Startled, she jumped to her feet. She had to stop being this nervous, she thought, as she walked to the front door.

Cory Landers stood on the doorstep holding a rather ragged bunch of daisies, the green and gold bow drooping. He smiled proudly and thrust the bouquet toward her. The silver in his light brown eyes made them sparkle.

"I brought you these," he said, his crooked smile widening.

Kate took the flowers and managed an astonished, "Thank you. What are they for?"

"For you."

"Yes, but why?"

Cory held his hands wide in a gesture of exasperation. "Because I thought you might like them. They are a little limp because I bought them yesterday. Although I did keep them in water overnight."

Kate stepped back, motioned him into the living room, and went to the kitchen for a vase. He followed her and watched while she put the daises in a white vase and drew some water. Without asking, he pulled out a dining room chair and sat. Kate put the vase in the center of the table. Cory nodded.

"They look nice there."

"They do. You didn't need to bring them; I haven't changed my mind about the boys' home."

"I'm not here about that. I want to take you to dinner. How about it?"

Kate stood frowning at him. "Do I look like going out to dinner?"

"No, but you will. I'll wait right here while you get dressed. Where would you like to go? I like Italian, but if you want something else, that's great too. I eat almost anything."

She didn't want to get dressed, go somewhere, and have to make conversation. Most probably have to explain why she wasn't interested in his project. Before she answered, Cory said, "Come on now. It won't be bad. You fed me and I owe you. I always pay my debts. I'll feel terrible if you refuse."

He'd obviously made an effort to look nice, and he did. Maybe it was what he said—he felt obligated, although her sandwiches didn't deserve a dinner out in return. She should go; otherwise, she'd spend the rest of the day thinking about the coming week. Kate nodded and smiled.

"Okay, but you choose the place. I too eat anything. I'll go change."

Cory settled on the sofa and picked up the remote to turn on the television. Kate took a quick shower and put on a pale blue dress with a flared skirt. As she combed her hair, she decided on a bit of light make-up, and at the last minute, gold earrings, and a short gold necklace. She looked in the mirror wondering if she'd overdone it. After all, this wasn't a date. He was probably in town on business and had nothing to do on the weekend. Taking her out was better than spending the rest of the day in some hotel room. When she entered the living room, Cory clicked off the television, stood and held out his hand.

"You look great. Ready to go?"

Kate nodded and they stepped out onto the small front porch. Kate locked the door and put the key into her bag. She turned toward the street and they started down the walkway. She looked in both directions but Cory's fancy pickup wasn't in sight. Instead, he led her to a sleek bronze-colored BMW.

"Where is your pickup?" Kate asked.

Cory opened the passenger side door. "I don't take ladies to dinner in the pickup. Well, not until after three or four dates."

He laughed and hurried around to the other side of the car. After adjusting the seatbelt, he started the car, and took off.

"Do you really not care where we go?" he asked.

Kate held her purse in her lap and said, "No, I don't care."

She was still adjusting to the expensive, obviously new car, and Cory's acting as if this were a date. If it were, he would have called first, not dropped in this casually. Still, he'd said before that phone calls were too easy to refuse. She smiled; his showing up in person did get results. The late Sunday afternoon traffic was light, and the shadows of street-side trees painted dark stripes on the sunlit pavement. Cory reached toward the car's radio.

"Would you like some music, or shall we just talk?"

"Just talk, I think. You can tell me about yourself. Do you have a family? Where do you live?"

"I'm not very interesting. Compared to you, my life is dull."

Kate considered what he'd said. Not a tactful comment, but probably true. Not many were in the middle of a murder investigation.

"You must be referring to my brother's death."

Cory glanced at her. "I'm sorry if I upset you. I'm too forward, but I don't believe you gain anything by holding back. If you have an opinion, you should express it. Otherwise, how do you ever get to know anyone? I mean really know them."

She had to agree. She'd spent the last months coming to the same conclusion. Cory's family must be open with one another. She wished hers had been.

"You seem to know a lot about me, probably from Aunt Iris. Tell me about your life; it will be a welcome change for me. I need to think about something other than my situation."

"Okay. I have an older brother and a younger sister. They are both married. My brother is set to take over the family business when Dad retires."

"What business is it?"

"Meat packing. My granddad started with one processing plant. Now there are four. All in different Midwest cities."

"My, sounds like a large enterprise. Why aren't you working in the family business?"

"I don't want to and they don't need me. Jake is the big executive, he loves it."

"So they don't mind you're doing this orphanage thing?"

Cory laughed. "No, they don't mind at all."

"Wouldn't they help support the boys' home?"

"They certainly do give to charities, but not to mine. I don't want them to. What credit is it to me if I'm given it on a silver plate?"

When they reached the southwest side of the city, Cory turned in at an artfully lit wooden sign reading *Edgewood*. The narrow driveway wound through manicured green lawns, and blooming hedges to where tall spreading trees surrounded a low brown stucco building. Cory drove under a porte-cochere where a young man came to open Kate's door. She stepped out as Cory came around the back of the car to hand the keys to the attendant. Two concrete steps stretched the full length of the wide entrance where double doors with brass edged glass insets opened to a spacious lobby. On the right was the reception stand, and behind that a glass door to a small bar.

As Kate stood on the dark maroon carpet amid the rich upholstery and polished wood, she wondered if her dress was appropriate. However, Cory wasn't wearing a tie, and his jeans hadn't suggested a place such as this. He took her arm and they walked to the blonde young lady at the entrance to the dining room. Cory smiled as he approached.

"I'm Cory Landers. Sorry I didn't call in a reservation. I hope you aren't too busy to take us."

"Of course not. Right this way, Mr. Landers."

The dining room was a bit over half full. White tablecloths and a bud vase holding pink carnations adorned each table. Music, so soft it took a minute to recognize it, played from hidden speakers. Kate and Cory followed the hostess to a table at the far side of the room near tall narrow windows overlooking a garden. Once seated, a waiter brought large, leather-backed menus. They both declined a before dinner drink, and the waiter departed.

Cory looked over the top of his menu. "What do you like? I came here because they have everything."

"I'm sure they do," Kate laughed softly. "You must have been here before."

"Yes. When we were all living at home, this is where Dad brought us for Sunday dinner. It is very busy midday, and everyone is dressed up, but not Sunday evenings."

"It is a lovely place."

"Glad you like it. Now, what shall we have?"

Cory settled on poached salmon which suited Kate, too. In the softly lit room, with quiet conversations, and the sound of silverware on china, she began to relax. It was so different from the grief, anger, and fear haunting her. It reminded her of how life had been, before reality descended. Cory ordered a light white wine to go with their fish.

Cory laughed and rolled his eyes. "I don't think a small glass will impair my driving, do you?"

"No doubt the food will offset it."

"Wait until you see the dessert cart. Anything on it will dilute a small glass of wine."

Over salad Cory asked, "I wonder why you're working at the business your brother sold. Does it feel like some kind of family connection?"

Kate blotted her lips with the white napkin. "Funny, that is what Gladys thought."

Cory raised his eyebrows in question.

"Gladys runs the office. She has for years. My father hired her."

"Is she right?"

Kate took a sip of wine, thinking how much to tell Cory. It was pleasant to stop thinking about the task she'd set. Monday would be soon enough to again start tracking Henry's killer.

When Kate hesitated to answer, Cory said, "Did you work there when your family owned it?"

"I had no interest in it. My contribution was in keeping the home running smoothly."

"What did your mother do?"

"She entertained," Kate said with a smile. "She left the housekeeping to me."

"That must be why you have all the domestic skills Iris bragged about."

"It wasn't all work. I had a good childhood...I was happy."

As the waiter removed the dinner plates, Kate leaned back and tilted her head. "There now, you have my history. Not very exciting, is it?"

"It sounds nice. Certainly didn't prepare you for this last year, did it?"

There it was again. The killing wasn't easy to escape, not even for this evening. Kate pressed her lips together. Cory put his napkin on the table.

"I'm sorry. Let's talk about me. It is a subject I never tire of."

They both laughed and Cory motioned for the waiter to bring the dessert cart. It was a delicious display of tarts, cake, and slices of pie. It was obvious Cory wanted to have something.

"You pick what you want," Kate said. "But make it something large and I'll take a small bite."

Cory took a piece of three-layer black forest chocolate cake and the waiter provided a dessert plate and fork for Kate. Cory put more than a 'small bite' on Kate's plate. She objected but ate it all.

On the ride home, Kate listened while Cory talked about his family.

"They don't actively support my project, but they indirectly do because of my income from the business."

"Do you really need to solicit contributions?"

"Yes, because my personal income is only enough to live on. It really helps, though, because all the contributions can go directly to the project."

"Why did you pick Pinecrest for the location?"

"It's a peaceful place. A solid community, an example for troubled boys. Lets them see that life can be good. There is enough land to grow vegetables for us to use and later sell. It would teach the boys about producing and earning a living."

"Where do you expect to find these boys?"

In the light from the dashboard, Cory turned to glance at her. "It wouldn't be a problem. The problem is there will be too many and not enough room."

It was eight-thirty when Cory parked in front of Kate's townhome. He sighed and said, "Here we are."

"Yes. It was a lovely evening. I enjoyed it."

"Shall we do it again?" He laughed and added, "Not the same place. We don't have to go out to eat. I'm busy, and you are working, but we could make time for a movie, couldn't we?"

Kate clutched the purse in her lap and didn't know how to answer. The desire for revenge didn't leave room for something as normal as a social life. Besides, Cory couldn't possibly be interested in her. He'd paid his debt, over-paid for the few sandwiches she had served him.

"Call me," she said.

Cory laughed. "What? I can't just show up?"

Kate lowered her head and laughed, too. "You can, but I can't say I'll be free as I was this evening."

Cory nodded, opened his door, and walked to the passenger side to open Kate's door. He helped her out, and walked with her to the door. As they stood under the outside light, Kate removed the key from her purse. Cory took it from her, unlocked the door, and handed the key back. They stood for a minute, Cory holding her hand.

"Miss Shore, I've had a nice evening with you. I hope it won't be the last one. Have a good night."

Before she could respond, Cory turned, jogged down the steps, and walked swiftly to his car. Before opening the door, he turned, smiled, and waved. As he drove away, Kate raised her hand and returned the salute.

Inside, Kate went to the bedroom, kicked off her slippers, and put them into the closet, along with her purse. As she changed into jeans and a tee shirt, she thought about Cory. It was puzzling. He hadn't talked about recruiting her for work at the boys' home. He was good looking, obviously well off, he shouldn't have trouble finding female companionship. He could surely do better. In the past, BHD, Before Henry Died, she might have thought he was being polite, doing Aunt Iris a favor by taking out her niece. Kate raised an eyebrow. It had happened before.

She went to the kitchen for a bottle of water. Cory would either call, stop by another time, or he wouldn't. With half a chance, she could be interested in him, but not before there was justice for Henry. She stopped between the living room and the bedroom, and corrected herself. Not justice, revenge. She wondered how far she would go for revenge, and decided she'd go as far as necessary.

Thirteen

When dressing for work on Monday morning, Kate put Henry's small address book into an envelope and tucked it into her purse. She also put the notes copied from it into her billfold. When leaving the townhouse, she picked up the file folder of old records to take to work. The swarm of early morning traffic was heavy, but the Acura seemed to have memorized the familiar route, leaving her mind free to think of the day ahead. She was at her desk a few minutes before Gladys arrived. Kate gave Gladys time to settle at her desk, and then took the file folder to her. She laid it on the desk in front of Gladys.

"What's this?" Gladys asked.

"I just got around to sorting Henry's records. I thought you should look through them as I don't know what to keep."

Gladys opened the folder and leafed through the papers. "I'll go over them, they are probably duplicates."

"Do what you think best. I have no use for them."

Leaving Gladys, Kate went back to her own desk. She had told Gladys the truth, there was no reason for her to keep the file folder, especially when she had the records on her laptop. She'd copied them from Henry's computer. If Gladys confirmed that none of them was important, she'd delete the laptop file.

At noon, Kate sat in for Polly at the receptionist desk. When it came her turn for lunch, she found Gladys in her office and asked for time to run an errand.

"I know we don't take an hour for lunch," Kate said, "I'll probably not be long. I need to run an errand."

"Don't worry, the work will be here when you get back," Gladys joked.

Kate quickly took her purse from the desk drawer and hurried out into the hallway. If traffic wasn't too heavy, it could be fifteen minutes to the bank, fifteen minutes there, and fifteen minutes back, yes, an hour should be plenty of time. And Gladys wouldn't object if it took longer. Getting the little book safely locked away would be a relief. For months, it had been in the house and the files in the townhouse, but since she'd discovered the notes on the last pages, she couldn't get rid of it fast enough.

When she reached the back door onto the loading platform, she rushed through it. John was standing there, about to enter the building. Startled, Kate abruptly stopped.

"Oh, John."

John narrowed his eyes. "Where are you going in such a hurry?"

"Nowhere. Well, not anywhere special."

"In the middle of the day?"

"Gladys approved it."

"I'm sure she did. How is the job working out? Have you found it interesting?"

"You might say that. I need to leave. Gladys is generous, but I am on a lunch break."

Kate started toward the steps down to the parking area, but John took her by the upper arm.

"Listen, you won't be around here forever, Sharron may come back. Haven't you found anything yet?"

Kate jerked her arm away. "No. I told you, I don't have access to all the records. Besides, I do not believe Jared is doing anything illegal!"

John gave a harsh laugh. "You don't? Someone had a reason to kill Henry. What do you suppose the reason to be? Information he had?"

"He certainly didn't steal any jewels. Why did you tell me such a ridiculous story?"

"How do you know he didn't?"

"I've been through everything he left. I would have found them."

"What did you find?"

"Nothing. I have to go. I'll talk to you later."

Kate ran to the steps and hurried down. When she reached the Acura, she unlocked it and quickly opened the door. John stood on the platform watching. She put the car in gear and drove away. She didn't stop trembling until she was past the security gate and out of Cooper Industrial Park. She tried to recall the conversation with John. Wondering if she had said anything to make him suspect she'd found the names and numbers. No, but her nervous manner might have made him suspicious. Still, if she could find a way to prove his connection to Arne, she would confront him about it. She'd need more than the message left for John to call Arne. John could deny knowing him, just as Ronda denied knowing anything about the call. Maybe Detective Simpson could make something of it. The traffic wasn't heavy, but it was busy. By the time she reached a branch of City National Bank, she had relaxed. John couldn't hurt her. He was the one who should worry.

With the address book safely in a deposit box, Kate drove back to work. The questions of what to do next ran through her mind like a never-ending recording. The copy of names and numbers had to be a starting point. She could search office records other than the ones assigned to her; few had passwords, yet if someone noticed, it might be hard to explain. Maybe use the excuse of being nosy, although it probably wouldn't work. It could be better to present the names and numbers to Gladys or Sam and ask if they knew what they meant. Somehow, that didn't seem right. All afternoon, when her thoughts were not on work, she wondered what to do about the list.

Fifteen minutes before quitting time, Gladys stopped by Kate's desk. She was carrying one of the records Kate had left with her that morning. She handed it to Kate.

"This shipment was lost. It happened just before the sale."

Across the room, Sam lifted his head and turned his swivel chair toward them. Gladys smiled. "Yes, Sam, I know you don't like to remember," she called. Kate stood, and looking at the paper, said, "I don't understand. What do you mean lost?"

Sam powered down his computer and came across the room. "Let me see," he said upon reaching them. Kate gave him the paper.

He bobbed his head, showing the thinning hair on top. "Yeah, still a mystery." Sam's look of near anger turned his pale cheeks dark and his olive-colored eyes narrowed. "I take it personally. Still don't know how it happened. Someone must have changed the destination, and once it was on the way, changed the record back. It couldn't have gone missing in our warehouse."

The three of them standing near Kate's desk were a study in mixed expressions. Kate knew she looked surprised, while Gladys appeared resigned, and Sam seemed angry. Gladys sighed and shrugged.

"It was a mess. Took ages for the insurance company to settle. Glad it wasn't a more valuable shipment."

"What was it?" Kate asked.

Sam snorted. "A bunch of stupid stuffed toys. Plush bears, kittens, things like that. The fuss they made you'd thought it was something important." Sam started back to his desk, but turned with a frown.

"Hope it's the last I hear of it," he said.

Kate looked at Gladys and cringed. "Sorry he is upset. Does he think it was his fault?"

"Not really. Although he deeply resents anything going wrong with a shipment."

"Were the records changed, like Sam said?"

"No, I don't think so. The shipment came from Brussels straight to our warehouse. That is probably where the mix-up occurred. Our records show we shipped it, but the buyer never received it."

Kate looked at the date on the shipping order. "This was just before the sale. I bet Henry was upset with so many other things happening."

"He certainly was. Still, we managed to work through it. Mr. Roth wasn't too concerned because the insurance was in place, and the company in Brussels didn't make a fuss. Mr. Holden was the one we had to reassure. For a bit, Sam's job was in question."

"Poor Sam."

"Yes, but he'll get over it in time. I'll keep this slip for a while; we can throw the rest away. We obviously lost the customer, but it was a small account. It was a new one Mr. Holden brought in. That's probably why he was upset." Gladys shrugged as she walked away.

Kate wondered if the lost shipment had any meaning. It certainly wasn't a secret. Of course, Henry hadn't bothered her with his burdens. He should have confided in her, if for no other reason than having someone with whom to commiserate. As Kate straightened her workstation and prepared to leave, she thought about the lost shipment. She could understand Sam's frustration; his was a detailed job, and he was a careful worker. Good it was simply inexpensive toys, letting the insurance company off easy and making it better all around.

On the drive home, Kate continued to think about the lost shipment. Taking the records to Gladys had been the right thing to do; she knew which to keep and which to throw away. Kate hadn't asked Gladys about the names from Henry's little book, but it was becoming clear what the names and numbers were. The numbers looked the same as order numbers. The dates might be shipping dates, and the names either buyers or sellers. If this were true, something made them important enough to keep. When Kate parked in the townhouse garage, she sat in the car for a few minutes, lost in thought. It was doubtful those names and numbers were in Shore's records. Kate took her purse, stepped out of the Acura, and started to the kitchen door. She hardly noticed passing through the kitchen because her mind was ablaze with one thought, *Henry, what did you do?*

Weary from a long tense day, Kate changed clothes and started to make dinner. All the while trying to arrange the new information. The names and numbers were probably what John wanted. His name, maybe his true name, was with the others. It meant they were all involved in the same thing, and it was outside Shore's regular business. As she sat down to a bowl of rice and vegetables, Kate tried to stop thinking…it made her too nervous. She took a minute to relax before taking a first bite, hoping to head off an upset stomach. Stay calm and make wise decisions was the rational way to proceed. She ate slowly and tried to separate emotions from facts.

After cleaning the kitchen, she went to the den and turned on the laptop. When the Excel file opened, she began entering things she had learned. Each item brought forth another question. Henry must have kept the list for protection. Kate shut her eyes and forced the confusion from her mind. Examining her family's past was like looking in fun house mirrors that distorted everything. She fought to see the evidence objectively, not shaped and shaded by her feelings. She had been proud of her family, maybe too proud, because if they were beyond reproach so was she. Her loyalty was not the virtue she'd thought it to be, but a form of protection for her. If Henry had been less than perfect, so was she. Maybe when this was over, she could work on her failings.

Henry had not given John the names and numbers, and neither would she. Certainly not until she knew who had taken Henry's life. At this point, the main suspect was John. As the crime stories say, he had the opportunity and the list was probably the motive. Detective Simpson needed to take a harder look at him. In the meantime, there should be a way to break down his alibi. He might have bought gasoline either the Monday or Tuesday he was in Greenfield. Gas stations sometimes have a security camera. Kate leaned back in the desk chair and slumped in disgust. Surely, Simpson would have thought of that.

She needed to give Simpson proof of some sort. There was the little book with the names. It was additional proof there was a man named Webern. A man the detective was already looking for and could not find. Still, if she gave him the book, it would put Shore Import/Export in danger. So far, there was no reason to believe Gladys, Sam, Bill, or any other employee had taken part in any illegal deal. It was cruel to endanger their jobs.

Kate was tired, it was getting late, and there was work tomorrow. Keeping to an eight to five schedule took discipline. She closed the laptop and prepared for bed. The constant tension took a toll.

The rest of the week passed uneventfully. On Friday, Bill Greer was back in the office and stopped to chat. He'd signed a small Ozark company that made wooden novelties. Bill drew up a chair and sat next to Kate's desk.

"I convinced them I could double their sales. I have several outlets in mind."

Bill looked tired; the blue stain under his eyes and the sag to his jaw line proved he'd worked hard.

"Good for you," Kate said.

Bill nodded and straightened his shoulders. "Yeah, good for me. I've been doing this so long even a new account isn't as exciting as it once was. Say, have you thought about taking on the job yourself? It would be a boost having someone to train."

"I haven't discounted the offer, Bill. It is nice of you. I don't know if it would be right for me. To tell the truth, I'm too unsettled to make decisions."

Bill stood and patted her shoulder. He smiled, the gold tooth flashing. "We all have those kinds of times. Don't forget, the offer still stands."

She watched as he said hello to Sam and went to speak with Gladys. He brought a bit of cheer into the office. With so few employees who had worked together for years, it felt like a family. Kate could see joining them either in the accounting office or maybe on the road with Bill. She didn't need to earn a living, but belonging to something had an appeal. As she straightened the desk, loneliness dropped over her like a heavy garment but she quickly put it aside. Life would not be like this forever. When she avenged Henry's death, she'd be free. Maybe take Bill up on his offer. She might enjoy the travel and meeting new people. Until then, nothing else mattered. The biggest problem was how long it was taking to find the proof so dear to Detective Simpson's heart.

Kate spent the weekend taking care of household tasks, all the while concentrating on John. He hadn't spoken to her since the day she went to the bank. He'd passed through the accounting office several times, but ignored her. Jared Roth was in and out more. He was always friendly and if he was doing anything illegal, he hid it extremely well. He seemed pleased with the way business was progressing; he'd picked up a clothing manufacturing account in India. He had a dozen outlets in the States interested in the chic styles. The increasing profits made Gladys happy. Kate was glad for them all, but she was no closer to her goal.

On Sunday evening, Ronda called. "Just checking to see how you are," she said.

Kate turned down the television and sat on the sofa, the phone to her ear.

"I'm fine. How is married life treating you?" She knew Ronda was no newlywed, but couldn't help throwing out the comment.

Ronda had paused, but quickly jumped back in with, "Just great. Arne is more than I could have hoped for. How is work going?"

"Oh, it's going. Not a lot of excitement. Not like a murder in the family."

"Now, Kate, don't be that way. I thought you were doing better."

"I'll do better when a killer is caught."

"What have you heard from the detective in Greenfield?"

"Not much. He may be at a dead end. No suspects I know of."

"What a shame. Listen, you have my number. Call me, we'll go out sometime."

Kate held the phone tight enough to cramp her hand. She wanted to tell Ronda she knew what part she had played. How she kept watch and told Arne or John every move she made. Still, she kept silent. The enemy should not know they were exposed.

"Maybe. We'll see."

"You sound a little down, Kate. You haven't been getting more of those threats, have you?"

"No. Not a one. I guess they have forgotten me."

"And you never found out what it was they wanted?"

"Nope. They either found it or gave up on me."

"Well, that's good. If something happens, you will call me, won't you? I hate to think of you being all alone. A girl can't be too safe in the city. People break in all the time. I hope you aren't keeping anything valuable there. Arne and me have a safe deposit box at the bank. You should get one. Unless you already have one."

"What a good idea, Ronda. I'll consider it."

"Oh, I thought a smart girl like you would already have one. Your mom did leave you some nice pieces of jewelry, if I remember."

"If you thought I had a box at a bank, why did you suggest one?"

"Just trying to watch out for a friend. You must be tired; I get cross when I'm tired. I'll let you go. But remember, call me, any time."

"I'll remember. Thanks for calling. Goodbye, Ronda."

Kate sat on the sofa holding the cell phone. They were checking on her. Somehow, John knew where she went after he'd stopped her on the platform. She didn't think she'd told Gladys where she was going. It meant someone had followed her. Not John. Maybe Arne. Still, it didn't matter. The book was safe. No one could get it. Yet, maybe it suited John. If he couldn't have the information, the next best thing was her keeping it secret. Perhaps this is the reason he hadn't been pressing her. Still, a long standoff didn't suit her. She had been trying to find a way to trap him into revealing something. It was as if they were at either end of a piece of cloth, each pulling it tight. At some point, the strain would have to tear it apart. Kate didn't plan to fall on her bottom when it happened.

For the next three weeks, she spent evenings devising ways to draw John out of his seemingly secure position. All the while, she sensed he was doing the same thing with her. He made comments that left her wondering what it was he meant to do. Such as one afternoon in the break room. She was there alone having a cup of tea. John came in and sat across the table. He didn't speak for a bit, but seemed to study her. It made her nervous and as she lowered the cup to its saucer, her hand trembled.

"I hear Sharron is coming back soon. What do you plan on doing?" he asked.

"What do you care?"

"Henry took what belongs to me. You are my link. I suspect you have found it and for some reason are keeping it to yourself."

"I am not. I don't know what you mean." Kate felt her cheeks burning. She wasn't a good liar.

John stood and glared at her. "Don't lie to me. I'll know it; others are not as patient as I am."

When he left, Kate relaxed. It was true; Sharron did plan to return to work. In another week, Shore would not need her. She was growing desperate. Once away from the office, she'd lose contact with the records and the ability to watch John. If John believed she'd found the list, he probably knew it was locked away. Ronda's call had given Kate the impression he did. She didn't think he'd feel free to harm her. If she didn't show up at work, someone would check on her, at least for the coming week.

Rather than disturb Detective Simpson on the weekend, Kate waited until Monday. She tried early before leaving for work, but, as she expected, had to leave a message.

"Yes, please have him call Kate Shore. He has my number. Ask him to call me this evening. It's important."

She had decided to bring him up to date, and trust he'd not make trouble for Shore employees. If he couldn't accuse John of anything, she doubted he could implicate Shore with only the list as evidence. Monday evening passed and Simpson did not return her call. The frustration made her pace the living room floor and twist her hands together. With so little to work with, he must have given up, but she hadn't.

In the first months, she had suspected this could happen. The only piece of evidence was the spent bullet they had taken from the den wall. It was probably sitting in a dusty bag in the Greenfield Police Department. She had reported the threats, and at the last contact with Detective Simpson, she'd told him about Arne Mertina's connection to John. So far, none of it helped.

Kate finally dropped onto the sofa, worn out with thinking. She took stock of her accomplishments. She had the list, but didn't know how to use it without tainting the Shore operation. In the end, she'd probably need to turn it over to Simpson and let him make what he would of it. The only unusual thing in the office records was the missing shipment. It was probably lost forever, since the insurance investigators hadn't found it. A load of toys, bears and other plush animals. No wonder no one made much of a fuss over its loss. It wasn't as if they were already some child's precious Teddy Bear. There were no children to cry over losing them. Kate thought of her own Teddy her mother had saved and included in the box of memories. Memories were all Kate had left.

She went to the den, opened the old trunk, and took up the white box covered with colorful flowers. She set it on the desk and sat looking at it. She should let go of the past. Keep the few mementos, but bury the other memories, along with Henry. He wouldn't want her to spend the rest of her life alone searching for answers that didn't exist. It was beyond her ability to find a killer, and the last three months had proved it. The move to Chicago was all right; she couldn't have stayed in the Greenfield house, but taking the job at Shore hadn't helped. A wasted time. She opened the box and lifted out the old bear. His stuffing was still plump and his arms and legs moved, but the ears were ragged.

Kate's eyes grew moist, a sob caught in her throat, and she hugged Teddy to her chest, clutching it tight while tears dampened her cheeks. As the tears stopped, she wondered what Henry had thought about Grace's request. Whatever he thought, he had honored it. She was glad he had. He had probably opened and resealed it; his curiosity would have prompted it. She didn't mind. When Henry sold the business and the Chicago house, he had delivered the box as Grace had instructed. The box was from Henry, too. Henry might have lost a shipment of bears, but he'd saved this one for her. As ordered and careful as Henry had been, he must have felt the loss of the shipment as much as Sam had. He probably worried it would stop the sale, making the operation seem slip shod.

Kate sat stroking the bear and staring across the room at the window, yet only seeing the image of a lost shipment. She pictured it as a square wooden crate. Probably had labels and stamps on it. It could have come by ship all the way from Brussels, Belgium headed for stores in the United States. Perhaps her bear had arrived that way. Since Grace had wanted her to have the old toy, Kate stood, took the bear to her bedroom, and centered him on the bed pillows. There, she thought, I'll keep him in sight as a reminder that once people cared about me. Even Henry, in his way. He'd cared enough to take the box to Mr. Burton's office. She smiled at the bear sitting there, and turned to leave the room.

When the phone chimed, Kate answered quickly, hoping it was the detective. Instead, Cory said, "Hi. Hope I'm not calling too late."

"No. How is the renovation job coming along?"

"Slow, but okay. Because of regulations, it had to have a complete inspection. Of course they found the heat and air are inadequate."

"I'm sorry. Will it cost a great deal?"

Cory sighed. It was late in the evening and she expected he was tired. They hadn't gone out together since the dinner, but he had made regular telephone calls. Because, as he had explained, he wasn't near enough to keep dropping in.

"Probably," Cory answered. "I worry it is becoming a money pit. I do want it just right before having boys move in. How are things going with you?"

"I'll be out of work soon."

"Is that good or bad?"

"I don't know."

"I'll not press you, but there is still an opening here."

"Yes, you've reminded me on several occasions."

"Listen, Kate, I want to see more of you. Distance has been a problem, but if you aren't working there, why not come here? You could stay with your aunt until finding a place of your own. You should know by now I don't want you here just for the work. Don't you want to spend time with me?"

She liked Cory, maybe more than liked him. If she could drop the search for Henry's killer, her feelings for Cory might have a chance.

"I like you, Cory. I admire what you are doing. We are not teenagers; I wonder if we have a future."

"See? That is what being close together would tell us. Give us time to make sure."

Cory seemed to see things clearly; he wasn't afraid to take a chance. She wasn't either, really, it was the unsettled past standing in the way. As they talked, she told him more of what she'd set out to do. He didn't discourage her. He listened and said, "You have to do what you think is right." His saying it was comforting.

~ * ~

Detective Simpson called Kate on the second day Sharron returned to work. Kate had stayed a couple of days to bring Sharron up to date. However, much of the time was spent in everyone admiring the pictures of Carrie June, Sharron's baby girl. When the detective called, Kate went to the deserted break room to talk with him.

"I want you to come to Greenfield," he said. "I have some pictures for you to look at. And I want to talk with you."

Kate's throat tightened. It was surely something important if he wanted her to return to Greenfield. She swallowed and said, "Yes. I can come tomorrow. Can you tell me what it is now?"

"Don't get your hopes up. It isn't much of anything, but I can explain better in person. What time do you think you'll get here?"

"By noon, I believe."

At the end of the workday, Kate said goodbye to the staff: Gladys, Sam, Sharron, and Polly. They seemed sincerely sorry to see her leave, but she promised to visit. As she drove out the gate and waved to Ralph, Bill's offer to teach her the sales trade held more appeal than she thought possible. However, the coming trip to Greenfield occupied all of her attention.

It was difficult getting to sleep, and she was awake early the next morning. She left the townhouse by eight o'clock and traveled at a speed that put her near Greenfield ten minutes before noon. She drove straight to the police station. The building looked quiet. One patrol car stood in the lot; next to it was Simpson's Ford. Kate parked and hurried inside where the officer behind the front desk seemed to be expecting her.

"Detective Simpson is in his office. You know where it is?"

Kate smiled and nodded. She'd been there before, over four months ago. She went along the hallway to the door of Simpson's office. When she entered, he stood behind his desk and pointed to the chair in front of it. He didn't smile, it wasn't his style, but his gray eyes were friendly. When she sat, he lowered his tall, thin frame onto the desk chair and nodded at her.

"You look well," he said. "Hated to drag you down here, but I've some pictures to show you."

"But I didn't see anyone except Leland and later, Arne. I never saw the men who broke into the house."

"Yes, but humor me, I'll explain."

He reached for a brown album with pages that were about eleven inches square. When he opened the book, it took up most of the middle of his desk. He turned it toward her and pushed it to the edge of the desk. Kate scooted her chair closer and peered at the open pages. Under a plastic page protector, there were pictures of men, three rows on each page with two pictures to a row. Kate looked up at Detective Simpson.

"What am I supposed to see?"

"Keep looking, there are a couple more pages."

Kate turned the first page to study the pictures. When she came to the next page, her mouth opened in surprise. She pointed to two pictures.

"Leland and Arne!" she exclaimed. "Have you arrested them?" Realizing Simpson couldn't have as John was still in Chicago, she felt her cheeks flush.

One corner of Simpson's thin lips turned up and he chuckled. "No, sorry to say. I wanted your formal identification of these two. Now we have conformation that this is the Leland Webern you insisted was at your home."

"Can't you see? He looks the same as John Holden?"

He nodded. "Looks like him, yes. To identify him as Webern is another thing. Holden's identification seems solid. After finding this, we'll dig into it more. I didn't stop looking for Webern, and what I found was, you might say, out of my district."

"But you can get the Chicago police to help, can't you?"

"Sure, but he didn't commit the crime in Chicago. Authorities in Antwerp, Belgium would like to speak with Mr. Webern. The end of January, last year, there was a robbery. A diamond merchant lost one hundred million in jewels. They strongly suspect most of it left the country. They caught a couple of the crooks, and recovered a small amount of what they took, but the largest part is still missing."

Kate fell back in her chair. Leland Webern, a jewel thief. The information whirled around in her head. She pointed to Arne's picture.

"Was he involved?"

"We don't think he was. Mr. Mertina is a homegrown mutt. An edge of the mob kind of guy. He has several arrests for petty theft, threatening people, strong-arm stuff. I put his picture in with Webern because you made a connection between them."

Kate raised an eyebrow. "Not much of a connection. Only the phone call, which Ronda denied knowing about."

Simpson took a form and a pen from his desk drawer. He handed them to Kate. She studied the sheet of paper. It stated that she had identified the two men. At the bottom was a place for her to sign and enter the date. She hesitated, but couldn't find a reason to refuse. Kate signed and returned the form to Simpson.

"Thank you," he said. "I doubt this will go anywhere. We'll notify officers in the other country of what we've found. I'm not up on extradition or even if they can reconcile Holden with Webern. It's out of my area."

"What about Arne?"

"We can keep an eye on him."

"If this other country takes Leland, or John, away what about Henry's death? Isn't a murder more important than a theft?"

"You'd think so. But we have to prove it."

"You will keep trying, won't you?"

"Sure, I don't like unsolved crimes. Not one bit." Simpson stood. "It's all I have for now. Thank you for coming." He stepped around the corner of his desk and held out his hand.

Kate stood, shook hands with him, and sighed in disappointment. She had hoped for more. Officials in Antwerp seemed to know who Leland was and maybe had proof he'd committed a crime in their country. However, that didn't help solve her problem. As he walked Kate to the station's front door, Simpson didn't seem any happier than she was.

"We'll keep on it," he said. "Let me know if anything happens in Chicago. Okay?"

Kate nodded and left.

It was early afternoon when Kate started back to Chicago. She didn't hurry, there was no reason to. The job at Shore was over, she didn't need to get up early, so it didn't matter what time she went to bed. She would miss the routine. The familiar trip left her mind free to wander. John might be an alias for Leland, or the other way around. She decided it didn't matter; he had admitted talking with Henry and was now part owner of Shore. She knew he was the same man. No wonder he was careful about leaving fingerprints at the house in Greenfield. When she worked at Shore, she should have taken something with his prints on it; it would be hard to do now. The police probably couldn't demand his prints, not without arresting him for something.

Now, it seemed as if part of what he'd told her was true. There *were* jewels involved, and John thought Henry had taken them. There had to be more people involved other than Henry and Leland. Arne certainly played a part. He and Ronda had watched her, maybe Arne took Henry's car. It would explain how Leland could leave in his own car. Yet, Arne didn't need Henry's car, not with Ronda a few blocks away. Kate tightened her lips and struggled to find answers. The only reason had to be to throw suspicion away from Leland. It proved someone other than Leland was at the house that day. The truth was slowly coming together, but not nearly fast enough.

Kate arrived home and upon entering the townhouse, nearly collapsed with weariness. It was emotional, not physical. Having her mind in constant turmoil sapped her strength. Unable to make sense of what she did know, Kate gave up for the day, had a light dinner, and went to bed.

The next day, she slept late and around one o'clock went into the den. There was nothing to do but enter the new information into her notes. In the evening when the phone rang, Kate answered. It was probably Cory, as he'd been calling around this time of day. However, it wasn't Cory and she didn't recognize the number. Strange telephone calls made her muscles tighten.

"Who is this?"

"John. How are you, Kate?"

When he spoke, she recognized his voice. "What do you want?"

"Is this any way to treat an ex-employer?"

"Why are you calling? I can't spy for you any longer. I didn't find out anything."

"Oh, but I think you did. You know about the missing shipment."

"Which you already knew about when you bought into Shore."

"Now you know I'm not lying about missing jewels."

Kate froze, the cell phone pressed to her ear. The missing shipment was a load of stuffed toys. Nothing to do with jewels, or maybe it did. John was linking the two."

"Kate, are you there?"

"Yes. Again, what do you want?"

"What did you tell Detective Simpson about the lost shipment?"

"I didn't mention it," she told him. *I didn't mention it,* I should have. Still, she hadn't yet made the connection between the shipment and stolen jewels.

"I see," John said. "Why not?"

"I don't know. I didn't think of it."

"Maybe because you didn't want to reveal anything to tarnish Henry's memory. Or you've found it and decided to keep it."

"No, not at all."

"Why did you go to Greenfield to speak with him?"

"He called me; it was nothing. Only to tell me they were still searching for Henry's killer."

Kate pressed her lips together and hoped John believed her. She couldn't let him know she'd identified him as Webern.

He laughed harshly. "I think you did tell him. That is the reason you went, isn't it?"

"Of course not. He isn't interested in Shore. He only knows you are a part owner."

"And that is all?"

"As far as I know, it is." It was okay to lie to a liar, Kate rationalized.

"Let's keep it that way, Kate. Stop trying to link me with the person who talked with Henry. It isn't healthy for you."

"If you are threatening me, I'll report it."

"Kate, you know you're safe, at least until we find what Henry hid. I'll be in touch."

Kate didn't answer, and he broke the connection.

There it was, John as much as admitted the lost shipment contained the stolen jewels. She sat at the dining room table staring out the window. She really didn't know why she hadn't told Simpson about the shipment, except it truly didn't seem relevant. Now it was. John wanted two things: the list, and the shipment. However, she was glad she hadn't told Simpson, it wouldn't help. He'd tell customs, they'd try to tie John to Leland, but without the jewels, there was no proof. John didn't know where the jewels were. If he did, Henry would probably be alive, and there would be no threat to her.

It was another hour before Kate wondered how John knew about her trip to Greenfield. Her slowness was discouraging. If she wasn't sharper than this, she should give up. The only excuse was the trauma of the last months. It was still difficult to realize she was completely alone. Grief and a desire for justice, and the dark longing for revenge, occupied her every thought. Cory was a bright spot, but his proper world was lost to her. Such a world was an illusion. People were never what they seemed, even her family. Although, part was her fault for being oblivious to her surroundings.

Fourteen

The next day Kate did an on-line search for security companies. She wanted the car, the house, and her cell phone checked for tracking devices. Perhaps paranoia was getting the better of her, but she had to know. Somehow, John knew she had gone to Greenfield. He knew about the bank in Chicago, but someone could have followed her there. However, she was sure no one had followed her to Greenfield. She picked an agency who promised quick and thorough service. She described what she wanted done and by afternoon, an older man in a brown uniform knocked on her door. When she opened it, she expected to see a van or truck with the company logo, but there was only a blue SUV at the curb. The man had a toolbox and looked like a plumber there to fix a leak. When Kate said as much, the man laughed.

"I doubt you want to advertise that you are using our service, do you?"

Kate opened the door wider and smiled. "No, of course not. You're right."

While they stood in the middle of the living room, Kate explained. "I think someone is spying on me. I want a complete search."

"Do you want to know who it is?"

"I believe I do know. I want it stopped. I don't care what it costs."

He put his toolbox on the floor, bent over, and took out a piece of equipment. "Show me your car and I'll get started."

Kate took him through the small kitchen to the garage door. She turned on the light and stepped aside. He nodded and moved past her into the garage. She stood in the doorway watching. She knew nothing about the procedure, but he seemed to be doing a careful search. Presently, he came to her.

"I've found it. What do you want done?"

"What do you mean? I want to be rid of it."

"Do you want the one who put it there to know you've found it?"

Kate put her hand to her mouth and took a step backward. She hadn't thought about it.

"Do you think they would try to put another one on it?"

The man pursed his lips and squinted at her. "I doubt it. Not if they think you're wise to them. The thing is, do you want them to know? Because, now you know something they don't."

Kate began to understand what he meant. If she took the device off the car, they might try something else. However, if she left it in place, she could control the information. Let them track her to the grocery store and hair salon. Even to visit Aunt Iris. If she wanted to keep her travels secret, she'd use another car. She could rent one.

"Can you tell how long it has been there?" she asked.

"No, but it isn't very advanced. Easy to put on and remove."

"Show me. In case I do want to remove it."

He took her to the right rear wheel well. She got on her knees and let him guide her hand to the device. When Kate understood how to remove it, she stood and brushed off the knees of her jeans. Now it didn't matter if the tracker stayed on the car. Maybe she could deceive them in some way. The technician was right to give the option. She was pleased with his service.

They went back inside and Kate asked, "Are you sure you found everything on the car?"

He nodded. "I believe so. I'll start on the house now."

"What if it is something turned off? I don't keep my phone on all the time. I want you to find anything that doesn't belong here, even if it is a stray bottle cap."

Alisha had been in the house. She could have planted a bug somewhere. Kate didn't think she did, but she wasn't sure. Having misjudged people and events in the past, she was becoming overly cautious.

The technician took another instrument from his tool kit. "This," he said, "will find even the nails in your walls. Just a joke, but it can pick up everything. Even things not transmitting. Benign objects, so we have to investigate what turns up. I suspect that's what you want. When I finish, you can be sure your home is your private space."

Kate hoped it was true. She stood in the corner of the dining room and let him search the house. *Debug*, she thought. In her former life, that meant the pest control service. In a way this wasn't much different, only these bugs were far more dangerous. John/Leland and Arne thought she was the link to what they wanted from Henry. When the threats first started, she had been willing to give them anything to make them leave her alone. Still, what she did with the list of names and numbers proved she had changed. They may want the information and jewels, but she wanted revenge. She was betting she wanted her goal more than they wanted theirs.

She sat on a dining room chair and waited. It seemed to be taking a long time, but looking at her watch proved her wrong. It was tempting to follow the man, but she really didn't want to watch the search. It was bad enough to have a stranger invade her home. If she didn't see him examining the bedroom and den, it would be easier to forget. The search was probably useless; no one had access to her home, unless he had broken in while she was at work. The idea made her cringe. Privacy was a thing of the past. Along with everything else she'd believed about her life.

"Miss Shore," the technician called from the hallway. "You want to come in here?"

Kate jumped up and ran across the living room and into the hall. "Yes? What is it?" Despite wanting him to search the house, she couldn't believe he'd found anything.

"I checked out some of the things that showed up, but they are normal electronics. Others presented a signal, but are benign objects. What I can't explain is something in your bedroom."

He started walking to the bedroom and Kate followed.

"My bedroom?"

He stood beside her bed and pointed the detector toward the pillows. "See?"

Kate had no idea what she was looking at.

"What does it mean?"

He leaned forward and picked up the stuffed bear. He placed it at the foot of the bed and pointed the detector at it again. "Something inside the bear is creating a signal. Other things I detected I could easily eliminate, but there isn't anything on the outside of this stuffed animal, it must be inside. I'm not going to open it without your approval."

Teddy? Kate stood frozen staring at the old toy. "I don't understand. Could it be wires or some metal material used in constructing the bear?"

"Maybe. I don't know without looking at it. One thing I can say, it isn't transmitting. It could be something metal, or maybe some type of chip. It might be the manufacturer put a card in for tracking purposes."

Kate continued to stare at the bear. "Why would they do that? Spying on customers who purchased the bears?"

He chuckled. "No, nothing like that. It would be something to record a sale when it went through a checkout at a store, maybe. It's strictly a guess. I can't tell you for sure without opening up the bear. What do you want to do?"

Kate pressed her lips together and tried to decide.

"You say it isn't emitting a signal?"

"That's right."

"So no one is tracking where it is, or knows something is in there?"

"Not without doing what I did."

"Okay, I'll decide later. Did you find anything else you can't explain?"

"Not a thing. And if we opened the bear, I could tell you what's in there."

"Are you sure it isn't sending out a signal of some kind?" Kate had no idea what was in Teddy, but suspected it was better to investigate in private.

"Definitely not," he said, handing Kate one of his business cards and a receipt for her payment. "Call us anytime."

"I will, and thanks for the swift service," Kate said as they walked to the front door.

She stood in the open doorway and watched the blue SUV pull away from the curb. The experience left her weak and weary. Finding the tracking device on the car confirmed her suspicions, but it was still a shock. It meant another level in this nightmare situation. She shut the door, bolted it, and returned to the living room to sink down onto the sofa.

It was hard to put her thoughts in order and know what to do next. It seemed right to leave the device on the car, and knowing it was there was an advantage. It was a relief to know the house and her phone were clear. The bear was another problem. She stood and hurried to the bedroom to pick it up and take it back into the living room. Sitting on the sofa, she held the bear around its middle and looked into the fuzzy face. She, Henry, and Grace were the only ones who had had access to the bear, other than the box thief. Of course, there was her father, but it was years ago when he brought the toy home for her. It was highly doubtful he'd put something inside it. The security technician must be right; it probably was a marketing device. An object no one would ever see. Some identification, like the little button in the bear's ear indicating it was an original Steiff Bear.

However, she still had to know what the bear contained. Was it big enough to hold millions in jewels? She pressed the bear's fat tummy, which felt like thick stuffing. If the bear held a secret, the ones who stole Grace's box from the attorney's office hadn't found it. Henry had delivered the box right after the sale of their house and the business. That all had happened about two weeks after the shipment of plush toys went missing. She gave a harsh laugh at the irony. Henry might have known what was in the missing shipment, and hid something in the bear. She held the bear up and stared into its face. "Sorry, Teddy, there is nothing to do but cut," she said. "Don't worry; I'll stitch you up again."

She went into the den and took scissors, needle and thread from the sewing basket. The dining room table served for the operation. It was silly, but as the bear lay on its back with the sheers poised above it, she hesitated. Henry's death had brought a severe change to her life, one that put her sanity in doubt. Maybe everything that had happened wasn't real, an illusion. Still, if a bag of jewels spilled out of the bear's stomach, she didn't know what she'd do. Maybe they would fit into the safe deposit box along with the list of names. An icy breeze seemed to sweep across the back of her neck. If she did find the jewels and gave them to John, he couldn't let her live. She picked Teddy up and slowly turned him over, parting the fur as she went, looking for some previous incision. If someone added something, there should be a sign. She'd hate to cut him open for no reason.

Under one of his arms there was some stitching, a small line about two inches long. Had she not been looking, she'd never have found it, and then only by parting his fur. It looked wide enough to pass a credit card through. She thought about using the site to reopen Teddy, but it looked too small to do much exploring. She couldn't stick her fingers in and feel about. She needed more room, and she didn't have to hide this cut.

Carefully, Kate made a slit in the bear's stomach. At first, there was nothing but stuffing. She widened the cut, and slowly pushed the filling aside. The corner of a small envelope became visible; she carefully pulled it out and put it on the table. It obviously did not hold millions in jewels. She didn't know whether to be disappointed or relieved. With the violated bear in shameful condition, Kate picked up the envelope and opened it. She took out a flat cream-colored plastic card and a key. On the back of the envelope, a note read: this bear *is* special, number thirty-nine. She recognized Henry's handwriting and remembered what Henry had said to Mrs. Farber about the box. That they should 'bear in mind it was special; how like him to do things in the open yet with a hidden meaning. He must have learned from their father. Too bad the family hadn't let her in on the life they really lived. Anger tinged her memory of them. Maybe in the future her emotions would settle into a healthier sentiment. She rearranged the bear's filling and, making neat stitches, put him back together. She left the plastic card and key on the table and took Teddy to the bedroom.

With the bear back on the bed, Kate stood looking out the west-facing bedroom window. Evening was fast approaching and lavender shadows stretched across the lawn. The room around her grew dim and her thoughts turned darker. Henry had put what looked like a gate card and a key inside the bear. His cryptic note with the number was no help as to where to use the two items. Although, given the other circumstances, there was little doubt. Somewhere, there was a gate to open and a lock to turn.

When the room became as dark as her thoughts, Kate closed the blinds and went back to the living room. She sat on the sofa and struggled to form a plan. No one could know about the card and the key, at least not until she knew what they were hiding. Turning them over to Detective Simpson would not help. He might find what they could open more quickly than she could, but if he found the lost shipment, and jewels were in it, Henry's killer would still escape. Somehow, the jewels would lure John into the open. Now she understood his visit to Greenfield. It was hard to admit, but Henry must have taken the jewels that were in the lost shipment. John wanted them back, because they were his. He'd taken them and shipped them through Shore. Henry must have found out and gotten to the shipment before John did. When John demanded their return, Henry had said, "I can't do that."

In a fit of anger, John might have killed Henry. It was possible, but hard to believe, because with Henry gone, so was John's chance to find the jewels. Kate stood and went to the kitchen to make coffee. She wasn't hungry; there was too much to consider. The toasty smell of coffee brewing drew her away from the confusing thoughts. For now, there was nothing to do. Maybe tomorrow would bring fresh ideas. It seemed reasonable that the card and key were to a storage unit. If it were only a key, she'd suspect a bank box. After drinking a cup of coffee, she settled on a plan of sorts. Tomorrow the search could start. A night's sleep made more sense than struggling over questions with no answers.

Early the next morning, Kate dressed, put her hair into a ponytail, and tied it with a scarf. Instead of going to Short's office, she had a new job. Somewhere there was a gate and a lock to open. The first thought she'd had upon waking was there must be a second card and key. The ones inside Teddy were for Kate to find when she received the box. Henry would not have had access to the bear. For that matter, if she hadn't had the house searched, she'd never have found the card or key. As she sat eating breakfast and staring out the window, she wondered how Henry expected to profit from the stolen shipment, if indeed he had taken it. Since she'd found the card and key, it seemed clear Henry had hidden *something*.

Her thoughts went round and round, always coming back to the same spot. It all centered on Henry. He had planned their financial life carefully; the sale of the business and his investments would have supported them nicely. He didn't need the stolen jewels. It made her doubt the previous thought of there being two sets of card and key. Henry might have taken the jewels but meant never to use them, only intending to keep them from someone else.

As Kate rinsed the cereal bowl and wiped the kitchen counter, a new scenario unfolded. Alisha had been convincing when she said Jared would not allow smugglers to use Shore. She had said Henry agreed with her. It came down to deciding which story to believe. After Henry's death, Kate had gone through all his possessions; she was certain there was nothing remotely like what the bear contained. This might prove Henry did not intend to retrieve what he'd stored. In a way, it was comforting. It made her brother something other than a thief. If he had taken the shipment, he did so for a noble purpose. Perhaps as punishment for John using Shore once again for smuggling. John could have tried to restart the practice, and this shipment was the first. Or not. She might never know Henry's true reason for taking it. Kate hung the dishtowel on the rack and sighed. She was still doing it, trying to think better of her family than perhaps they deserved.

Kate put the card and the key into her bag and set it on the small table beside the front door. She was determined to start the search immediately. If only she knew where to start. She ended by dropping onto the sofa and putting her head in her hands. It was certain Henry put the card and key in the bear. If he ever wanted to use them, he'd have needed to access the box in Jim Burton's office. He could not have expected someone would steal the box. They wouldn't have, except she had told Ronda there was a box.

"Henry, Henry, Henry," she muttered, trying to understand what he had done.

Henry, of course, he was the answer. Kate jumped to her feet. He never did anything without recording it. Before driving the city searching for some storage facility, she'd dig through Henry's records, knowing what to look for this time. She hurried to the den and opened the laptop quickly bringing up the past records. For a second, she worried Henry might have paid cash for the storage. Still, he would have required a receipt, proof that he'd paid, but he might not have recorded the expense. She started with the household records a month before they moved from Chicago. The shipment had gone missing two weeks before the sale; however, Henry might have arranged a place in advance.

The Excel spreadsheet with its precise headings filled the screen. For a moment, Kate closed her eyes as if preparing for a leap from a high building. *Please, please,* she thought, *let there be something.* Scrolling slowly, examining each entry, looking for anything unusual.

The room grew warm and her throat tightened. Henry had arranged for the move, hiring a moving company, disconnecting utilities in Chicago and paying connection fees in Greenfield. She scanned the headings looking for something to indicate a rental or purchase. When she sighted an entry under *Utilities*, the new connections in Greenfield, she leaned forward and grabbed a pen to write the name of Greenfield Budget Bin on a Post-It Note. She might have seen the entry before, but it meant nothing. Tucked away with other utilities, it might have passed as trash collection. Her hand shook as she scrolled over the nearby entries. There was electricity, water, sewer, trash pickup, lawn service, even a pest control company. All the necessary services accounted for, Budget Bin the exception.

There were two payments, one in February and the one made the previous August was for a year in advance. Kate copied the amounts onto the note, wishing there were an address as well. Still, Greenfield wasn't a large town. She'd find it. She closed out the application, turned off the laptop, and hurried from the den. It was still early; she'd reach Greenfield before two. She looked around making sure she was taking everything she'd need. She stopped. She was too excited, too eager; it was the way to make mistakes. First, she couldn't use her car. Not unless she removed the tracing bug, and she didn't want them to know she'd found the surveillance. This Budget Bin might not amount to anything. Besides, it was a long drive, depending upon what she found, it might be an overnight stay. Kate hesitated and slowed her whirling thoughts...Budget Bin had held its secret for almost a year and a half; it could wait a bit longer.

As she settled her swarm of thoughts, the payment dates for Budget Bin came into focus. The first one had been in February just before moving to Greenfield in March, the second one in August for a year in advance. With a start, it became clear rent would be due in around a month and a half. Henry had sold Shore close to a year and a half ago; he'd been gone almost a year. If rent on the bin wasn't paid, they might auction off the contents. The winning bidder would have quite a surprise if it contained what Kate expected. According to her estimate, there was enough time to inspect the storage unit and later decide what to do. Maybe she'd pay to keep the unit. Feeling steadier, she went to the bedroom and packed a bag. Next, she checked online for a taxi service. While waiting, she closed the townhouse and made sure to lock the garage. If John or Arne wondered why the car didn't move, one of them might check on her.

When the taxi arrived, Kate directed the driver to the nearest car rental agency. He delivered her to Enterprise, where she rented a Mirage and headed for Greenfield. She soon adjusted to driving the small car and would have preferred her Acura, but the freedom of being surveillance free made up for it. Even so, she kept glancing in the rearview mirror. Since Henry's death, life had become a strange experience. It was surprising she was able to function at all, let alone go in search of a lost jewel shipment. She was determined not to judge what her family had done. She didn't have enough information. With every passing mile, she struggled to make clear her purpose. If she found the jewels, Henry was at fault, but it made no difference. He was beyond reach. Her consuming interest was in bringing his killer to justice, and getting the revenge she wanted. How to achieve it was still unclear, but examining the contents of the rental at Budget Bin seemed the first step.

The afternoon sun caused the pavement to shimmer in the distance. The open land near Greenfield made the town's name an obvious choice. At the edge of town, she drove past a Dairy Queen and remembered she had missed lunch, but food could wait. She should have done an online search for the storage's address, but there were holes in her planning. With no experience, she wondered how she expected to catch a killer. All she had was determination, and it would have to suffice. One step after another had brought her this far, the next should reveal the course ahead. Kate parked the car in front of a convenience store and went inside. The young woman behind the counter, after selling an old man a half-gallon of milk, turned toward Kate.

"Can I help you?" she asked.

"I need directions," Kate said. "Do you know the location of Budget Bin? I think it is a storage facility."

The clerk squinted, tilted her head, then brightened and said, "Yeah. Take Main Street all the way through town. I think it's just past the gas station."

The odor of wieners turning on the spit made Kate think about buying a hotdog, but she was eager to reach Budget Bin. She thanked the clerk and hurried from the store. She took Main Street past the police station, and was soon beyond the center of town. Wal-Mart and

General Dollar, along with a Shell station, put an end to the commercial district. Beside a weed-choked field stood a fenced complex of white metal buildings. Next to the tall iron gate was an office. It had a blue metal roof, as did the three long rows of storage units behind it. The entrance pavement carried on between the rows of storage units.

A tall pole stood to the right of the gate, a second shorter one in front. Kate hesitated, and instead of going through the gate, pulled into a parking place in front of the office. She took the gate card out of her purse and put it on the passenger seat. There was a pedestrian gate in front of the office door. Two large windows revealed a woman sitting behind the counter. The woman put down the book she'd been reading and looked toward Kate's car. Kate wasn't sure how to proceed. She could go inside and ask questions, but Henry might not have used his own name. If this were the right place, the gate card would work. She could ask questions later. When Kate backed away from the front of the office and angled toward the gate, the woman returned to her reading.

Kate put the card near the windshield and waited. When the two sides of the gate slowly parted, she gasped in surprise. It worked. She guided the Mirage through the opening and headed toward the line of units on the right. The units had overhead garage type doors. Near each door was a number. She rolled slowly past unit number one, and at the end of the row, she reached unit number fifteen. While to her left, the units numbered sixteen to thirty. The middle row was a double with units on the backside. She turned to the left and started up the drive between the middle row and the one on the far left, which was now to her right. The first unit on the left was thirty-one. Thirty-nine was about three quarters of the way from the end of the row. When she turned to park in front of the unit thirty-nine, Kate's hands were growing slippery on the steering wheel.

She turned off the car's engine and sat trembling. She slid her purse under the passenger seat and picked up the unit's key. Certain now it would open the lock on the garage door; she climbed out of the car and locked it, putting the car key into her pocket. She took a quick look around the deserted compound. The back of the office had windows facing the storage area, but she didn't see anyone standing behind them. It was mid-afternoon and she was the only one in the facility. It occurred to her how fortunate this was. If others had been accessing their units, she would be even more nervous. The privacy was reassuring. When she stepped away from the car, a mild summer breeze blew her scarf and she brushed it away from her face. She walked between the car's front bumper and the unit's door. The lock was waist-high on the right-hand side of the door's frame. She held the lock in her left hand and inserted the key. When it turned, the padlock opened.

Kate put the lock and key into her pants pocket, and bent down to grasp the handle at the bottom of the door. With a hard jerk, the sweep at the base of the door gave a soft pop and the door rattled upward. She stood peering into the dim interior. It looked empty, with only a long string dangling from a bulb in the ceiling. She stepped forward, reached up, grabbed the light string, and pulled on it. A weak yellow glow brightened the area. The space looked to be about ten by ten feet. A large room for only one item. In the far-left corner stood a large round carton. Kate walked to it to read the shipping label. The container seemed made of heavy plastic, light tan in color. It was too big for her to reach around, and it was a few inches shorter than she was. The lid had a metal band securing it, with a side lever to open the seal.

The largest label gave the shipping, to and from, destinations. As she suspected, the carton had come from Brussels. There were other stamps and stickers, but they meant nothing to her. It was warm in the storage unit and her nerves made it even hotter. She wiped her hands down the sides of her pants to dry the palms, and took hold of the handle on the carton's seal. She tugged, but it didn't budge. With mounting frustration, she tried harder to pull the handle and pop the metal band open. Her arms began to shake and she stopped. Maybe it required a tool of some sort. There was nothing in the storage unit, and she didn't want to ask at the office. They probably didn't loan tools anyway. Maybe she just wasn't strong enough.

To study the situation, she stepped back and looked at the container. It had to be sturdy to withstand the long trip, and the contents were not breakable. Soft plush toys could take a lot of bouncing. She stepped closer and, holding onto the lid, she tipped the carton to its side. It dropped to the concrete floor and gave a short roll before stopping. It had toppled easily and she realized how light the contents were. She could lift the container. It was awkward with little to hold onto, but she could maneuver it. Perhaps drag it to the car and load it into the backseat. It might or might not fit through the car's door. Still, taking it home didn't seem wise. It had been safe here for a year and a half. She put her foot on the side of the carton and pushed it back and forth while trying to decide how to proceed. She could leave it, and return with some cutting tool, maybe cut the thing in half. However, before doing that she would try one more time.

This time, Kate rolled the carton to the wall, placed one foot against it, bent over and took hold of the lever to pop the sealing strip. Using all her strength, she jerked and it gave away, releasing the metal band. She tumbled backward and landed on her backside, her shoes against the container. She sat for a minute staring at the still closed carton, amazed she had managed to break the seal. She used the carton to steady herself as she climbed to her feet. Now the lid was free; she hesitated. The Mirage, parked in front of the unit, gave a measure of privacy, but it wasn't reassuring. She stepped to the door and pulled it down, leaving a couple feet wide gap at the bottom. She didn't expect to remain in the storage unit long enough to be bothered by the heat.

She left the container on its side. If she stood it upright, it would be hard to dig through the contents. It took an effort, but with the band loosened, she managed to remove the lid. This revealed an inner plastic bag, taped shut at the top. Plush toys were visible through the clear wrapping. She wasn't sure which would be better, to pull the entire bag out or open it and remove individual toys. She elected to go slowly and take out one toy at a time. That way she could inspect each one. It was hard to believe there were jewels hidden in this shipment. If so, maybe a jewel was inside each bear or rabbit.

She grimaced as she pulled out the first toy. It was insane to come between an international jewel thief and his treasure. No telling what such a person might do, the person being John alias Leland. However, she didn't expect him to find out. According to Detective Simpson, John took the largest share and shipped it to the company where he'd be in control. Only Henry had beaten him to it. She wondered how Henry knew about this shipment. One thought after another swirled through her mind as she removed the toys.

Soon there was a pile of soft, fuzzy animals, each inside its own clear plastic sack. She was glad the door was only partially open; the mounting heat was better than prying eyes. Halfway through, she stood and wiped the sweat from her forehead. With no sign of any jewels, it was possible this was a wasted effort, but she *had* found the lost shipment. That was something, or it might have been if she'd found it over a year ago, before the insurance settlement. The shipment turning up now would cause more trouble than it was worth. A load of stuffed toys couldn't be worth much. If she went with Bill Greer into arranging shipping and sales, maybe she could give a toy as a gift to a new account. Before she grew giddy from heat and frustration, Kate again dug into the container.

When her hand touched a hard substance, she stopped, and slowly began to withdraw a different type of item. It too was in a plastic bag. Inside the plastic was another bag, a dark material with a drawstring. Kate's heart beat hard enough to shake her chest. The bag was heavy, and larger than the stuffed toys. She licked her lips and, using both hands, brought the sack completely out of the carton. She stood and held the bag up to examine it. A piece of blue tape sealed the top of the outer plastic. Her legs were shaking and she longed to sit, but was afraid to go outside to the car. Instead, she sat on the pile of stuffed toys holding the strange bag on her lap. With mixed emotions, she began to unwrap the package. She put the plastic outer sack to one side and pulled open the dark purple bag, it felt soft as suede. In the throat of the sack was a folded paper. She pulled it out and saw her brother's handwriting. Kate trembled and her vision blurred as she read:

'Kate, if you are reading this, I'm gone, and you got my message about the bear. This is what Leland wanted. I could not let the smuggling start again. This was the best way to stop him. I never intended to benefit from it, but see no reason you can't. As always, Henry.'

Sitting on the floor amid the plush toys, dazed and unable to form a reasonable thought, she simply stared at the note. A single tear dropped and smeared Henry's name. She understood nothing; her family, her life, it was all a jumble. Her lap filled with a treasure; she grew dizzy. Whether from heat or shock she didn't know, only she needed fresh air. Holding the purple bag, she struggled to stand and hurried to the door. When it was raised enough to duck beneath, she stepped outside and got into the car. Once behind the steering wheel, she started the car's engine and the air conditioning cooled her. With the crumpled note in one hand, the bag lay on her lap. It felt heavy with the weight of the jewels, and perhaps with the load of desires, schemes, even death the contents represented. She wanted to shove the bag away, or throw it into a ditch as she had the key to the Greenfield mailbox.

After a few minutes, she grew calm enough to decide what to do. Henry's note made a few things clear. He never had a second key because he didn't intend to use the jewels. Yet, depending upon her to find the key in the bear seemed risky. Maybe Mrs. Farber hadn't remembered all of the message he'd left with their attorney. If Mrs. Farber had gotten it wrong, it was no wonder after Jim Burton's death, and the robbery. Kate stared at the bag. Henry had tried, but events were not as he had planned. Her careful brother. His planning and control certainly did not extend past his death, even with all his efforts. Now it was her problem, but one that could wait until there was time to make a reasonable decision.

She carefully refolded Henry's note and, retrieving her purse from beneath the seat, she tucked the paper into it. Staring at the bag, there was no question as to what it contained. She pulled the neck of the bag wider. Carefully, she removed several small drawstring bags. Each one she opened revealed several diamonds of various sizes or one large colored stone. When struck by the afternoon light, they were dazzling. Along with the little bags were small gold bars in crinkled paper and several velvet boxes containing beautiful rings. With each piece taken out of the bag, Kate's mouth opened wider. It was a large sack and it held many items. The contents of the bag were staggering; the total amount of the treasure was unimaginable. One by one, she took more little bags out of the larger one and laid them on the passenger seat. Soon there was a mound of fifteen bags, plus twelve gold bars and at least ten or more rings, while several diamond bracelets were still in the bag.

The sound of a car engine jerked Kate out of her jewel-induced trance and she quickly looked around. A black pickup had parked at the far end of the middle row of units. Her mouth turned dry and she began putting everything back into the large purple sack. She drew the string tight and tied it in a bow. She leaned forward, clutching the bag as if to hide it. A heavyset man climbed out of the black pickup and walked to a unit door. Kate sat still as a stone, not daring to move. When the man entered the storage unit, she relaxed a bit. The tangled thoughts flooding her mind kept her from moving. Yet, she had to do something and she would, as soon as her mind cleared. Holding the fortune was shock enough, knowing what to do with it was even more paralyzing. She felt as if a train had hit her.

When the man visiting his storage-unit started his truck and drove past Kate's car, she realized how long she'd been sitting there holding a stolen fortune. It was too soon to take any action. What she needed was time and every bit of logic she was able to produce. Once again, she was alone in the storage facility and it gave her courage. She opened the car door, stepped to the storage unit, and scooted under the partially raised door. She placed the bag on the concrete floor and, picking up a few of the stuffed toys, returned them to the carton. She shoved the purple bag in on top of the toys, and filled the container with the remaining stuffed animals. However, with the container on its side, some of the plastic bags kept falling out. Using the wall for leverage, she managed to set the carton upright. She picked up the few remaining toys and dropped them in with the others. Once the lid was in place, she cinched the metal band tight and heard a tiny click. Securing the large barrel type container was useless...anyone could open it, and there was no way to hide it. Still, she maneuvered it back into the far corner, took a last look, and left the unit. Outside she locked the door and put the key into her pocket.

Kate slowly drove out of the secured area and parked in front of the office. She went inside to speak with the clerk.

The middle-aged woman put aside her book and stood to greet Kate. Her rimless reading glasses hung from a chain around her neck. She stepped to the counter and smiled.

"What can I do for you?" she asked.

"I have a unit here, well, my brother did. It is unit thirty-nine."

The clerk moved to one side and began typing on a keyboard below the counter. Kate leaned forward to see the computer that sat on a waist-high shelf. The woman nodded.

"Yes, there it is. Unit thirty-nine. Henry Shore. It's good till the end of August. So, what is it you want? We don't give refunds for unused time. Sorry."

"Oh no, I don't want a refund. You see, Henry is dead. I need to make some arrangement with you if I want to keep the unit for a while longer."

The woman puckered her lips as she consulted the computer record. She looked up.

"You must be Kate Shore."

Kate nodded. "Yes."

"Well, do you want to keep the unit past August?"

"I'm not sure. You say my name is on the rental?'

"Sure is. Says right here, if the rent isn't paid, to send the bill to Kate Shore. There is a Greenfield address and a telephone number for an attorney in Chicago. He said they could reach you. Is that right?"

"I'm afraid the information is out of date. I'll give you a new address for me, and I'm not using that attorney any longer." There was no need to bring up poor Mr. Burton's death.

"Can I see some identification?"

Kate opened her purse to take out her driver's license. She passed it across the counter to the clerk who proceeded to make a copy of it, glancing up at Kate as the copier worked.

"Your brother, Henry Shore, passed away?"

"Yes."

The woman handed the license to Kate, and narrowed her eyes in concentration.

"There was a Shore died here in Greenfield a while back, was that him?"

Kate didn't want to discuss it; her throat tightened. She should have known people in a town the size of Greenfield would have a long memory for gossip.

"Yes. It's a painful subject. Now, how should I pay when the rent comes due?"

The woman seemed to vacillate between sympathy and offense, but settled on acceptance. She once again consulted the computer record.

"Mr. Shore paid in cash. But we'll take a check or credit card."

Kate smiled, hoping to smooth any hard feelings. "I'll be back before the rent is due. I'll know then if I'll need to keep the unit. Okay?"

"Whatever you say. If I don't hear from you, I'll send a notice, but abandoned units can be auctioned off."

The long drive back to Chicago helped settle her thoughts. It was nerve wracking to leave a fortune in an unprotected place. Still, she was certain no one knew about the storage unit. Henry had paid in cash probably to keep from there being either a check or credit card record of the transaction. Yet, on his personal records, he entered the payment, accounting for even cash expenditures. Henry's planning was amazing. He could have told her, but he'd have had to explain his part in the missing shipment. Yes, it was amazing but not surprising. It was one more Shore secret. He'd arranged two ways for Kate to find the unit. If she didn't get the message about the bear from Mrs. Farber, Budget Bin would have sent her a notice when the rent was due. Yet, the plan had a flaw. If she hadn't known about the jewels, she might have donated the stuffed toys to some charity. However, even then, he would have kept the treasure from John. As the sun settled lower in the west and shadows stretched to the east, she tried to decide the next move.

Detective Simpson had said the original theft was over one hundred million. They recovered a small portion of it when they arrested crooks in Belgium. Which meant the sack in the unit must hold many millions' worth of gems. A sobering thought. The diamond merchant in Antwerp would no doubt be thrilled to get them back.

Although, Henry had meant for her to have the treasure. Maybe she could keep it; if she were careful, no one would know. Perhaps she could move abroad, live in secret, and John would stop looking for her. She was too tired to give it more thought. Although, John would not let such a fortune go without extreme measures, and she'd not want to live in hiding the rest of her life. There was nothing to do except the honest, right thing, so long as it included trapping Henry's killer.

It was dark by the time she reached the outskirts of Chicago and the Mirage's headlights brightened the pavement. The traffic took her attention, yet she remembered the shine and glitter of the gems, and a sly smile curved her lips. "Maybe one small ring and bracelet wouldn't be missed," she whispered.

Fifteen

The next morning at six, Kate sat up in bed instantly awake. Arriving home the night before, she'd had a light supper and gone to bed early. There had been no dreams that she recalled, only a solid black stretch of time. The term 'dead to the world' described the night. She blinked the sleep from her eyes, and threw off the covers. The instant her feet touched the carpet, she stood and reached for her robe. Somehow, in the night of deep sleep, a plan had developed. After a quick shower, she dressed. She hardly tasted the breakfast of cereal and grapefruit juice. When the kitchen was straight, she took a cup of coffee to the den.

She sat at the desk and sipped the coffee, deciding whom first to call. She decided upon Detective Simpson. She wanted to finish this today. It wasn't a clever plan, but there didn't seem any alternative. The gems should lure John, and somehow in confrontation, he'd admit he'd killed Henry. Afterward, what the police did to him was up to them. Either try him for murder, or ship him off to face charges for the jewel theft. When they arrested John, his fingerprints would match those of Leland Webern, catching him in one crime, for sure.

If she had known about the Antwerp robbery while working near him, she would have tried to take something with his prints on it. Although she wanted him tried for murder, not theft. If she could get him to admit the jewels were what he and Henry had fought over, it would give Detective Simpson a reason to arrest him.

As Simpson's phone rang, Kate held onto the desktop for support. This call was the first step in what could be an extremely dangerous situation, like lighting a stick of dynamite. It could well blow up in her face. Getting everyone in the same place at the same time was crucial. If, as she believed, John had killed Henry, he'd have no problem doing the same to her!

"Detective Simpson. Glad I caught you. I need your help. Please listen."

As Kate laid out the plan, Simpson's occasional snorts and interruptions plainly said what he thought of it. When she finished, he said, "I can't let you do this."

"You can't stop me. You can't, can you?"

There was a long pause, and a sigh. "No, I can't stop you. But I can be in plain sight at the storage units. That should stop Mr. Holden."

"How will that help?"

"It will keep you safe."

"For how long? When John knows I have what he wants, he'll take it and probably kill me in the process. Please, help me in this. You have nothing against him now; at the least you'll catch an international jewel thief."

After more of Simpson's objection and some conditions of his own, he agreed to her plan. He and several policemen would be at Budget Bin near four o'clock. They would be undercover posing as unit owners.

"Thank you," Kate said. "This may not work. He might not show up. If it falls apart, I'll apologize and stop interfering."

When the call ended, her phone was slippery with sweat. She closed her eyes and took a minute to focus on the next move. One instant she was certain this would work, the next just as certain it would not. It could be either a great success or a total failure, with any number of outcomes in between.

Before making another telephone call, she went to the kitchen and drank half a glass of water. Burning up nervous energy was thirsty work. Sitting on the sofa, she made the next call.

"Hi, Ronda," Kate said. "I'm glad I caught you. I have some news."

"Hey, slow down. You sound really wound up. What's going on?"

"I've found what the burglars were looking for. You remember when the house in Greenfield was broken into? Henry did leave something. I'm going to check it out right now. I just had to tell someone. It is like a treasure hunt."

"What did you find, and where is it?"

"I can't tell you what it is, but it could change my life. Where is it? That's the funny part, it's in Greenfield. I have to go, Ronda. I am too excited to talk longer. I'll tell you about it when I come back. If it is what I think, I'll treat you to a big expensive lunch. Bye now."

She snapped the cell phone shut and fell back onto the sofa. She looked at her watch; she didn't need to leave for a while yet. Besides, Ronda needed time to tell John, or she might tell Arne first and he'd tell John. She was counting on Ronda and Arne still being in John's employ. The tracking device on the Acura would let them know when she pulled out of the garage. Her call to Ronda had given them her destination. Maybe they had too much information and it would make John suspicious. Kate narrowed her eyes; no, John was too greedy. He wouldn't pass up this chance. He'd believe she was trying to keep the gems, and like a foolish woman had blabbed to a friend.

If Ronda couldn't reach John and he didn't show up at the storage facility, there was not another plan. John would eventually know of the call to Ronda. When that happened, Kate might *need* to keep the gems and leave the country, because John would not stop looking for her. Yet, that wasn't an option because Detective Simpson would have the jewels. The only hope was if the treasure were lost to him, John would leave her alone. Unless he went crazy and wanted to make her pay.

She stood and put the cell phone into her purse which she set on the dining room table. She intended to leave before noon, but it was still over an hour away. Kate paced, went to the bathroom twice, and finally settled back on the sofa. She again looked at her watch; time was dragging. She was not hungry, but it never hurt to pack a lunch.

Her mood improved as she made a cheese sandwich and cut a stalk of celery into small lengths. Along with some veggie chips and a bottle of water, she put the sandwich into a zippered cooler and set it beside her purse. With the task done, she locked the front door and drew the drapes over the windows. She expected to come home late or possibly not at all. Unable to find anything more to do, Kate picked up the purse and lunch container and entered the garage. Time to leave, with or without a killer trailing her.

It was hard to keep her mind on driving because it was too full of other things. After today, she'd start a new life. This was the end. If John didn't show up to claim the jewels, she'd stop trying to trap Henry's killer. She'd put the failure aside, knowing she had tried. Henry's death, along with what followed, had changed her. Change might be life's only constant, but now she'd have control of the changes. As she neared the Greenfield exit from the interstate, a new cloud of doubts arose. Simpson might have decided to stop her at the storage gate, or worse, not be there. Glancing in the rearview mirror, she saw another car leave the interstate. It was far behind her, but it appeared to be black or some dark color. A jolt of fear shot through her.

The detective knew she would be entering Greenfield close to four o'clock, and someone could be following her. Maybe the police would be watching. She hoped so, because if not, she was on her own, and that wasn't good. She passed Wayfare Inn and later the Conoco station with a Greenfield police cruiser parked beside it. She stepped on the gas to speed past, not wanting to show interest in the police car. Still, it was encouraging. The officer would note her arrival and if the next car were a black Lincoln, he'd report to Detective Simpson. She debated driving around town instead of going straight to the storage facility. If John were following, it would give the police more time to spot him. It was a thought, but she was far too nervous for any delay. Better to go straight to Budget Bin and have it done.

She drove through Greenfield on Main Street, past the Wal-Mart and General Dollar where she began to slow the car. The storage facility on the other side of the vacant field looked deserted. There were no vehicles she could see, police or otherwise. Kate took a quick look in the rearview mirror; the black car behind her had also slowed, nearly stopping. Her throat tightened and her hands trembled on the steering wheel. The storage facility ahead suddenly felt like a refuge. If she got through the gate and it locked behind her, she would be safe. Instinct took over and she increased the car's speed and swung into Budget Bin's entrance. She displayed the security card and the gate began its slow, slow swing to open. Come on, come on, she urged silently.

When it was barely wide enough for the Acura, she drove through and went straight to the rear of the lot, where, pulling behind the end of the double row, she hid her car from the facility's entrance. Perhaps an advantage, but she could not see if the black car tried to follow through the gate. As her fear diminished, she took note of the surroundings. She had passed a blue pickup parked in front of a unit in the first row, but she hadn't noticed if anyone was in it. She didn't think the overhead door was open. Besides, her unit was on the other side of the double row. If she needed help, the blue pickup owner wouldn't know. She couldn't stay behind the middle row forever. Taking her foot off the brake, she edged the car forward and turned the corner. When she did, the front gate was visible. The black Lincoln stood on the other side of the fence in front of the office.

She slowly moved along the row of units and turned to park in the space before number thirty-nine. There were no other cars in the aisle; she and the blue pickup were the only ones in the facility, unless someone was using a unit on the far side of the last row. As she sat in the silent car, it occurred to her that she'd trapped herself.

She was in the same standoff with John as she had been for the past months. Only now, she'd led him to the storage unit. He couldn't get in, and she was safe only as long as she stayed behind the fence.

Worse yet, she didn't see Detective Simpson. He hadn't liked her plan; maybe he was busy with something else and thought she wouldn't go through with it. A dozen different scenarios scrolled through her mind. Still, staying parked there forever was not an option.

Kate took the unit key from her purse, opened the car door, and stepped to the pavement. She gave a quick look toward the office. The black car was still there, but she couldn't see if anyone was inside. John only had to wait for her. If she left the facility with the jewels, he could quickly take them away from her, and possibly leave her injured or dead. If she left the treasure in the unit, he'd simply run her down, take the card and key, and collect the gems later. In either situation, her safety seemed in grave doubt. It was her fault. She wasn't clever enough to pull off something like this. She really didn't care if John got away with the jewels; the purpose of her plan was to catch him out over Henry's murder. However, it didn't seem likely at this point.

She put the key in the padlock, turned it, and put the lock into her pocket. She reached down, pulled the overhead door up a couple of feet, and ducked under it. There was light enough to find the string hanging from the ceiling. The bulb lit the center of the cement floor, leaving gray shadows in the four corners. The far-left-hand corner was empty. The large tan plastic container was gone! It couldn't be! Kate spun around, looking in every direction. There was nothing to see but a concrete floor, three metal walls, an overhead door, and the light bulb. Kate staggered, pressed her hand to her chest, and could not breathe. For a second she was sure she was going to faint. Bending from the waist, she placed her hands on her knees, and drew in the hot dusty air.

As her head cleared, she stood upright and put her hands on her hips. Clearly, John hadn't taken the container, unless the Lincoln parked by the office wasn't his. Maybe the car was a coincidence. John wasn't the only one with a black Lincoln. If he hadn't followed her today, maybe he had yesterday. Even with the use of the rental car, he somehow knew where she'd gone. He'd found a way to gain entry to the facility and the unit. What a mess she'd made trapping Henry's killer. Nothing had worked out right. Detective Simpson would be happy because she'd keep her word to back out of the investigation. She gave a half laugh...an easy promise to keep because there was nothing else she could do.

When she took a step toward the overhead door, it suddenly folded upward, rattling, and settled open with a thud. She blinked in the brighter light. John and Arne stood between the Acura's front bumper and the threshold of the unit. When they entered the unit, startled, Kate took a step backward.

"What are you doing here?" she said.

John shrugged, his brown eyes glaring. "I could ask you the same thing." He looked around the empty unit. "Why are you here if you've already moved the shipment?"

"I don't know what you're talking about."

Arne twisted a thick gold ring on his right hand. He glanced at John. "You said she'd found it. I don't see nothing here."

John shot him a harsh look. "Keep still."

He moved toward Kate, reaching out as if to grab her. She instinctively ducked and tried to run out the open door. Arne spun toward her and caught the tail of her tee shirt. She jerked away, stumbled out, and slid around the Acura's front bumper trying to reach its door handle. Instantly she knew she should have run toward the office instead of trying to get into her car. John and Arne, one on either side, trapped her against the car. She couldn't move in any direction. John's look was as dark as his eyes.

"Stop this foolishness. You took the shipment already. Tell us where it is and we'll forget about this."

The left side of Arne's sports jacket hung open, revealing a black holster and the butt of a gun. He caught Kate staring at it. He smirked. "Don't worry. I have other ways to get you to talk."

John raised an eyebrow. "See, Kate? Not everyone is as forgiving as I am. I suspected Henry had left you a way to find the jewels. You were just slow finding it. I've been patient, but not now. They aren't worth losing your life. I'll even make you a small present. You've seen the jewelry, haven't you? Will a beautiful ring or bracelet satisfy you?"

Kate felt the heat rise in her cheeks and she knew her eyes betrayed her. John tilted his head and softly laughed. "Beautiful, aren't they? All those gem stones. I'll even throw in a gold bar. There now, tell me where it is." John stopped smiling. "Or would you rather deal with Arne?"

Kate tried to squirm from between them.

"I do not know where it is. Yes, I found the container with the stuffed toys. I don't know where it is now. Why would I come back here if I'd moved it?"

Arne grabbed her face, holding his thumb against one cheek, his fingers against the other side. He squeezed and glared at her. "Get smart, we aren't going to stand around here arguing about it."

He jerked his hand away, causing her head to twist to the side. He grabbed her upper arm and pulled her away from the car while John opened the car door. Arne shoved her into the driver's seat and closed the door, while John ran around to the passenger's side. Before he could get in, a police car rounded the back corner of the row and roared to a stop behind Arne. On the other side, the blue pickup closed in on John. Kate hit the button locking all four of the car's doors. It left John and Arne tugging at door handles. Finally, she'd done something right, and it brought a bit of satisfaction, although she wasn't sure what was happening.

John's car stood in front of a unit across the drive between the two rows. She hadn't noticed it before. She'd been too scared to notice. She wondered how they had gained entry. She hoped they hadn't harmed the clerk. If so, it would be her fault for bring the danger here. Another mistake. She didn't dare move from the car, even when she saw Detective Simpson come from behind the last row of units. A man jumped from the blue pickup and ran toward John. He was in a plain shirt and jeans, but wore a shoulder holster and drawn pistol identified him as police. At the sight of the him, John raised his hands above his head.

On the other side of Kate, two uniformed officers were rushing toward Arne, who ducked and ran for the Lincoln.

"Stop!" an officer yelled.

As Arne kept going, he turned and, drawing his gun, fired at them. Kate screamed and crouched low in the car seat. When she looked around, Arne was on the pavement, one officer securing Arne's hands behind his back while the other stood guard.

The policeman in plain clothes was marching a handcuffed John toward the police car. Kate was trembling and suspected she was in shock. It was hard to understand what had just happened. Obviously, Simpson had taken her seriously and was on the scene. Yet, the jewels were gone. Without the gems, there was no hope of proving John had killed Henry over them.

Detective Simpson gathered with the three other officers around the police car where they held Arne and John. The four men talked and gestured for a couple minutes, then parted. The officer in the plain shirt jogged back to the blue pickup, while the two in uniform climbed in the patrol car and drove out of the storage facility.

Detective Simpson disappeared behind the last row of storage units. Kate sat dazed and wondering what to do. Strangely, one of the first thoughts was she didn't need the storage unit any longer, and they wouldn't give a refund for the unused time. She started to laugh, but stopped, afraid if she did she'd not quit. It was finished and she'd failed. Failure was hard to accept, but it being over was a small comfort. She could do nothing more.

Simpson's Ford rounded the end of the last row of units and came to park beside the Acura. He stepped out of his car and came to where Kate sat behind the locked doors. He tapped on the window. She lowered it and stared at him. He stooped down to face her. His thinning brown hair ruffled by a mild breeze, he reached up to smooth it.

"You okay?" he asked.

"I guess I am."

There seemed some concern in his gray eyes, but since his normal expression was sober, it was hard to be sure. He straightened his lanky frame, clearly uncomfortable in the stooped position. He reached for the car's door handle and tried to open it.

"You intend to stay in there?" he asked.

Kate quickly unlocked the door, but wasn't sure her legs would hold steady if she tried to stand. Instead, she opened the door and turned sideways, planting her feet on the pavement.

Simpson stepped back and with a thin smile said, "We caught your crooks."

"Yes. Not much good, though. What is the charge? Illegally entering Budget Bin?"

Simpson squinted, his eyes looking silver in the sunlight. "Don't worry, we have plenty. Are you going to be all right? Think you can drive home safely?"

"Are you in a hurry to get rid of me?"

He raised his arm and put his hand on the top of the open car door. "No. I'll need you to make a statement. You might even need to testify."

"To what? I can't prove anything. What do you have now you didn't have before?"

"You feel up to following me to the station? I was going let you go home and rest up before finishing. But maybe you'd like to get it over with."

Kate nodded. "I believe I would. I doubt I'll rest until I'm sure it *is* over."

Detective Simpson nodded and went back to his car. Kate started to close the car door, but stopped. The unit's overhead door was still open; the interior like an empty tomb. She got out of the car and lowered the unit's door, even taking the lock from her pocket and putting it back on the hasp. The detective was gone by the time she drove through the gate, but she well knew the way to the police station. Kate parked in front of the Budget Bin's office and went inside. The clerk stood behind the counter smiling.

"Well, that was some excitement, wasn't it?"

Kate was relieved to see she was unharmed. "Yes, it was." Kate put the gate card and the key onto the counter. "I know there are no refunds. I doubt I'll be back, so I want to turn these in now."

"I'll take the gate card, but the lock is yours. We don't provide them."

Kate picked up the key, but put it back onto the counter. "I left the padlock. I don't need it; give the key to the next renter, if you like."

"Okay, but they won't want it. New people want to make sure the lock is their own."

"Well, whatever. Sorry for the disturbance." Kate started to leave, but stopped. "The men in the Lincoln, how did they get into the secure area?"

The clerk brightened, looking eager to tell what had happened.

"The police came by around three-thirty and dropped off our only lady cop. They told me to stay in the back room and keep quiet, but I heard what went on. She acted like she was me. When the crooks came, they first said they wanted to rent a unit. That was their way trying to get in." She laughed aloud. "But Maryann, that's our lady cop, told them they could look around first. Gave them the number of an empty unit, saying they could see if they liked it. They snapped up the offer and we watched as they headed straight for the units across from you."

Kate nodded. "I see. I hadn't thought about it until now."

"You're too shook up, probably." The clerk looked out a window. "I hope they come pick up that crook's car before long. The unit is empty, but I don't like having it around...we can't be responsible for it."

"I'm sure they will. Well, goodbye."

Shortly, Kate arrived at the police station hardly knowing how she got there. The clerk was right. She was totally shaken. When she entered the station's lot and parked next to the building, the shakiness turned into a numb sensation. She felt the same as when she'd stood over Henry's grave. It was probably a natural protection until a person was able to function normally, and to her surprise, she was eager to finish with Detective Simpson. He had been helpful and easy to deal with, but it was time to move on. Her obligation to family was finished.

When she entered the police station, the uniformed man at the desk pointed toward Simpson's office. She nodded and hurried down the hallway. He was behind his desk waiting for her.

"Sit down. This won't take long."

She pulled the folding chair closer to his desk and sat. "First, what happened to the container that was in the storage unit? Did you take it?"

"We did. We locked it up until we find out what to do about it. If Holden's fingerprints match Webern's and the jewels are identified as those taken in Antwerp, I suspect Holden is in for a trip overseas."

"How did you get into the unit? It was locked when I arrived."

"Took the hasp off one side and raised the door."

"Have you looked at the jewels?"

He nodded. His normally serious face now stern. "Yes. More responsibility than I ever wanted. The chief is taking over. He'll contact the customs authorities, find out what to do next. You really handed us a situation. The Greenfield Police will surely remember this case for a long time."

Kate wished she'd taken a souvenir when she had the opportunity. Still, it was better not to have a tangible reminder, she'd never forget anyway. The good news was that time would soften the memory.

"Where are John and Arne?"

"Behind bars, for a long time. Mr. Mertina anyway. If his gun proves to be the one fired in your house, he'll face serious charges."

"You think *he* shot Henry?"

The detective nodded. "It looks that way. Mr. Holden, or Webern, started talking the minute we got him alone. He claims Mertina is the one who did the killing and took Henry's car."

"But why?"

"He probably didn't intend to kill him, just wound him to make him talk. Soon as Mertina fired the gun, Holden ran from the house and drove away, leaving Mertina there; he didn't want anything to do with violence. He says Mertina took the car. He couldn't risk walking to his wife's house; someone might have heard the shot."

Kate slumped in the chair. "Money, it was all for money. Did Arne help steal the jewels?"

"Not according to Holden. When your brother hid the shipment with the jewels, Holden had to keep an eye on him. So he hooked up with Mertina and his wife. When the house in Greenfield was part of the sale deal, he put them in the neighborhood to watch Henry. But Mertina got greedy, wanted more than the payment Holden promised." Simpson chuckled. "He never should have let Mertina know what a treasure was at stake. Mertina knew you were out shopping with his wife, and Holden was talking with your brother. Holden's ways were too soft for him, so he butted in."

"Why did you take the container? When it wasn't there, they could have killed me."

"Not likely. They'd keep you alive until they got what they wanted. Besides, we were watching."

Kate finished making a statement and signed it, and rose to leave. "No offense, Detective, but I hope I don't see you again."

Simpson walked Kate to her car. "Drive safe, now," he said as she started the Acura.

Driving out of Greenfield, she tried to organize the information about the crimes surrounding Henry's death. If Arne's gun proved to be the one that killed Henry, the man was in a great deal of trouble. As the sun settled below the western horizon, Kate found she was strangely void of anger, even at Arne. It was as if Henry had met with a fatal accident, or been killed by a wild animal. It was horrible, but it was in the past, a place where no amount of wishing or manipulation could change events. The revenge she'd wanted was no more satisfying than a mouthful of dust.

She tended to believe John's story, because he was more a thief than a killer. Arne was impatient and seemed the type to use force instead of persuasion. Nearing the city, the heavy late evening-traffic slowed Kate's progress. Neon signs flashed in store windows and streetlights stood like tall electric stalks, their blossoms of light drooping above the freeway. As Kate pulled into the garage at the townhouse, the one person she *was* angry with sprang to mind: Ronda. The supposed friend. She felt foolish for being deceived, but upon thought decided she felt more hurt than foolish. She could not have helped being in such a vulnerable position. After her brother's death, she was lost and lonely, facing a strange new life. Her defenses were down and Ronda had taken advantage. It was cruel. Yet, it was a lesson. Perhaps she should be grateful.

~ * ~

Two days later, after doing nothing but eating, sleeping, and making decisions about her new life, Kate called Cory and invited him for dinner the next Sunday evening. When he arrived, he presented her a beautiful bouquet of twelve yellow roses. As he stepped over the threshold, he smiled his crooked smile and held out the flowers.

"I would have picked out red roses, but they seemed too common. These are beautiful and different, just like you. They even match your dress."

Kate was wearing a soft yellow dress with small ruffles around the scooped neckline. She took the flowers and smiled at him. Cory, looking proud, squared his wide shoulders and headed for the sofa. Kate went to the kitchen to find a vase. Cory sat watching as she arranged the bouquet in the middle of the table that was set for dinner. It was good to see him; they hadn't met for several weeks. He'd been busy with his project, and she with closing her past life. However, their phone calls had made them comfortable with each other. They had shared stories about their families...he had supported her in finding justice for her brother. Cory was smart, too. He was more intelligent than his casual lifestyle would indicate.

When she finished with the flowers, Kate put two glasses and a bottle of chilled champagne on a tray and brought it to the living room. Cory stood to help set the tray on the coffee table, and took over the job of filling their glasses.

"What are we drinking to?" he asked, handing a glass to Kate.

She lifted her glass and said, "To us. Friends forever. I appreciate how kind you have been. I never thought I'd meet so nice a man, and handsome, too."

Cory blushed and lowered his head as he sat down beside her. "Shucks, I'm just doing what any good fellow would do."

They both burst out laughing and, raising their glasses in a toast, took a drink. She watched him over the rim of her glass. He *was* handsome, not like a movie star but in a wholesome, robust way. He reminded her of ripe wheat fields and clear blue skies. He was open and reliable. He finished his drink and set the glass on the tray, and turned his head toward the kitchen.

"What are we having? Whatever it is smells great. I didn't have lunch, so I am hungry."

Kate put her empty glass on the tray and stood. "Honey roasted chicken with potatoes and carrots. A green salad and a chocolate parfait for dessert. Will that do?" she asked, walking toward the kitchen.

Cory picked up the tray and followed her. "I'd say so," he commented.

The whole chicken came out of the oven crisp and browned to perfection. The baked vegetables dish was so hot the oven mitts were almost too thin. Kate quickly set the dish on top of the stove and turned to Cory.

"If you want to help, you can take the salads out of the refrigerator. What do you want to drink? There is iced tea, ginger ale, even milk if you want it."

Cory took the salads out and, stepping to the table, set them on the dinner plates. "What are you having?" he asked.

Kate shrugged. "We can finish the champagne, if you like."

Cory nodded. "Fine with me."

When Kate had the roasted chicken on a platter, she put it in front of Cory's place at the table. With the food arranged, Cory held Kate's chair out for her and they sat to eat. The salad was crisp and cool with a red wine vinegar and oil dressing. Cory carved thick pieces of succulent chicken for each of them. The bubbling wine went well with the meal and they ate in companionable silence. Kate could see years ahead of such comfortable dinners. Cory finished and put his napkin beside his plate.

"That was delicious, Kate. You are a good cook."

She smiled and stood to gather the used dishes from the table. It was satisfying to cook for someone who appreciated it, but she'd done it for a long time and she was tired of it. Cory helped to clear the table and watched while she put the dishes into the dishwasher. With the kitchen straightened, she paused beside the refrigerator.

"Do you want dessert now, or with coffee later?"

Cory's brown eyes darkened the bright flecks dim. "Later, if it's all right with you. I'd like to talk for a while."

Kate hung a dishtowel on the rod on the refrigerator and nodded as they went into the living room. She knew this conversation was coming and she had thought about it for a long time. Cory sat and patted the cushion beside him. Kate sat and he put his arm around her shoulders. "So, are you coming to Pinecrest and establish the boys' home with me?"

It was total Cory, straight to the point. No secrets, and no hidden agenda, nothing like her family. With Cory, there were bumps, disagreements to work out, but she could handle it. If it were the kind of life she wanted.

"Cory, you know how dear you are to me. I love you—"

"But you aren't coming with me, are you?"

She felt his body stiffen, the muscles tense. She pressed her lips together, her back growing rigid. She did not want to hurt him, yet she needed to explain. She couldn't move into a life she didn't want.

"I do care about you, Cory. But maybe I'm not ready for what you want to make your life's work."

"Okay, I get it. My dream isn't yours, at least not right now. It doesn't mean you and I can't go on."

"You're right. You and I can continue seeing each other. I want you in my life. I don't want to lose you. Ever."

"All right. How are we going to do that?"

Kate swallowed and cleared her throat. "Well, I think I want to take a sales job with Shore. Bill Greer, I've told you about him, said he'd teach me."

Cory frowned. "That's a traveling job. You'd be on the road all week, maybe too far away to come home on the weekends. Doesn't he even go into Canada and Mexico sometimes?"

"Yes. I'd get to use the passport I've had for years." She couldn't stop the little lilt of excitement in her voice. Cory scowled at her.

"What are you looking for, Kate?"

"I'm not sure. It's the very reason I have to do this."

"I think you are still unsettled over Henry's death and the threats you endured."

She moved a small distance from Cory, turned sideways, drew one leg under her, and faced him.

"If I went with you and worked at the boys' home, I'd be doing it because it is a good thing. Not because I want to do it. I'd be duty bound. Is it right to do something simply because if you don't, you'll feel guilty?"

"How can you live with guilt, Kate? How can you enjoy any other life if you know you're not doing the right thing?"

Kate abruptly stood, threw her arms out wide and whirled to face him. "That is just it, Cory. If I go to work with you because I'll feel guilty if I don't, and I'm doing it only to keep myself from feeling bad, what good is that? Don't you think the time would come when I'd grow resentful? I need to go, do other things."

Cory stood and took her in his arms. "I don't know what to say. There is so much going on inside your head. How about this, we give it a little time. You'll feel differently when you think about it longer."

She sighed. "Oh, Cory. I have been thinking about it. I've told you how the only life I've had was in doing my duty toward family. I gave it my all. I don't want to step back into the same thing."

Cory pulled away slightly and looked down at her. "And being with me you'd feel trapped, bound to do a good job?"

"Don't put it that way. If we lived together and went in different directions, that wouldn't work. You totally involved with your dream, and I with something else."

Cory stepped away from her, his crooked smile sad rather than cheerful. "If you loved me enough—"

"Do you love me enough to change your life? Drop your dream and do something else?"

"What, what would we do?"

"I don't know. Travel. We have enough money. It wouldn't be lavish, but it could be fun."

Cory bowed his head and chuckled, a harsh gravely sound. She had known this might not end well. Either he'd understand or he wouldn't. She hoped he would, but if not, she was determined to try her own way. Selfish? Maybe so.

Cory faced her and held her shoulders. "Okay, Kate. What do we do now?"

She leaned in and kissed him. "We go on, the best of loving friends, until our ways come together. Until we can go in the same direction and share the same goals. It's all we can do."

Cory leaned toward her. "What do I tell your Aunt Iris and Uncle Bert? They said you are a good worker, a steady, dependable girl."

Kate started laughing and Cory joined in, his eyes sparkling as he said, "They said you'd be perfect to manage the big house, and what do I find? A pretty woman who wants her own life."

"Are you terribly disappointed?"

"No. You are a challenge. I have confidence I'll win you over."

"I wouldn't bet on it." She would have said more, but Cory stopped her with a kiss.

~ * ~

Five weeks later, as Bill Greer and Kate Shore, riding in her Acura, were driving to St. Louis, Bill said, "So are you and Cory getting along okay?"

Kate glanced at him. "We definitely are. I've visited the boys' home, even helped him interview a woman who can run a house better than I can."

"Well, that's good. It wouldn't have worked out for you there, anyway. A person has to be satisfied with their self before they can be a help to anyone else."

Kate raised an eyebrow, wondering if he'd just told her off or not. Upon reflection, she decided to let it drop. If he meant her, he was probably right. Last week, they had attended a trade show in Toronto. Counting travel time and prospecting for customers, it had taken the whole week. They hadn't signed up anyone, but had come away with three possibilities. Bill had said it was good, and with some steady follow-up, they might land one new account.

"So, this trade show we're heading for, what is it like?" she asked.

"Several new startup companies are showing their wares. There should be around one hundred booths. Many of them make unique items. If they are trying to expand, we can introduce them to new markets out of the country. Depending on what materials they use, we can try to find them a cheaper source overseas. We get them coming and going, so to speak."

As I-55 south merged with I-70 west, Bill smoothed his black hair, and straightened his tie. He always made sure of his appearance. It shows respect, he'd told her. People like to talk with someone who shows respect for them, someone who cares enough to look nice for them. He pulled down the sun visor, using the mirror to check his round face. Satisfied, he put it back up and smiled at her.

"It's nice to have a driver. A lady along doesn't hurt either. You remember how smooth things went crossing into Canada last week?"

"Well, we aren't smugglers, after all." She turned to look at Bill; did he catch the comment about smugglers? She wanted to forget smuggling, but her experience made it hard to do.

Bill chuckled and squinted at her. "Has John Holden, or whatever his name is, been *exported* yet?" He was trying to make a joke, so she smiled.

"The last I heard, authorities are still holding him, waiting for someone from Belgium to come."

Bill opened his cell phone and started a search for accommodations. The trip was taking the better part of the day and the trade show didn't start until tomorrow. They would see how things went and if prospects were good, stay over the following night. Kate had adjusted to life on the road and liked it. Maybe not when she was as old as Bill, but for now, it suited her. It put distance between her and the turmoil of the past year.

Detective Simpson had called once to let her know she would not need to testify. Arne Mertina had pled guilty in return for a reduced sentence. John had vouched for Arne's claim that the killing was not premeditated. He'd panicked, lost his head, didn't mean to kill Henry. Kate had mixed feelings about it; Henry was still as dead as if Arne intended to shoot him. John's biggest mistake had been in involving

Arne. Arne was what Detective Simpson had first said he was, a small-time crook. He was responsible for the threatening calls, the break-in, and the mailbox ploy. He'd hired some blond bum to rent the box using Webern's name and phony identification. Arne had been sure threats would work and John had lost control of him.

Bill finished making the reservation for their rooms and put away the cell phone. Kate entered the motel's address into the GPS and grew impatient with the directions.

Bill chuckled. "I didn't have all these gadgets when I started. I had a roadmap and a bunch of quarters for pay phones. Somehow I managed to get where I was going every time."

"Good for you," Kate countered.

"Have you seen the Gateway Arch?"

"No. Well, pictures."

"We have time this afternoon. How about doing the tourist thing?"

The smug voice of the GPS gave Kate more instructions, which she followed by swiftly switching lanes. "Let me get us to the motel and checked in, then we'll see."

Sometimes she thought Bill was treating her training like a sightseeing tour. Every area they drove through had some attraction, and he managed to work them all into their schedule. "It is a big beautiful country," he'd said. Slowly his attitude was soaking into her.

Bill looked at Kate and said, "Holden wasn't so smart after all. Was he?"

"What do you mean?"

"Hiding the jewels in a shipment. Guess he was trying to save money, but look where it got him."

"In jail, I hope. Still, what else could he have done?"

"He could have brought them through customs, declared them, and paid the duty. It would have been high, but far as customs laws are concerned, smuggling simply means bringing something into the country without declaring it. Not exactly a big crime.

"But they were stolen!"

"Not in this country. Only time our officials are concerned is if the smuggled stuff is used in another crime in this country. Even if they caught him, he could have gotten off by agreeing to pay a fine and the duty tax.

"Why do people do it? Smuggle, I mean."

"Drugs, weapons, things that would get them locked up, but if it is a small item like a gem, those get through thousands of times in a year. John should have talked to our Sam Tuttle; Sam could have saved him a lot of trouble."

Kate recalled Sam, Shore's shipping expert. Sam knew all the laws and what forms to file to move merchandise from one country to another. Still, she doubted Sam would have helped John, other than to tell him to declare the gems and pay the duty.

"What do you think will happen to John? I don't want him to go free."

"The diamond merchant in Antwerp will see he doesn't. When they come to get John and the gems, it's their problem from then on." Bill reached across the center console to pat Kate's arm. "You can forget it now. It has been an ordeal, but it's over."

Each passing day put distance between Kate and the pain. Yes, it was over and relief was a soothing balm. In time, it would be a dusty memory hidden under countless new experiences. Such as traveling with an overweight, middle-aged man with dyed black hair and a gold tooth. Who was also cheerful and possibly even wise, and who could teach her many things.

Kate turned to Bill. "Do you think I should have given Simpson the list of smugglers I put in the safe deposit box?"

Bill turned his lips down and wrinkled his forehead. "No, I don't see that being helpful. It's an old list, no sense stirring up trouble. Simpson wouldn't thank you for it. No proof they did anything. Besides, Shore is clean as a whistle now. Say what you want about Alisha, but she's not going to let Jared put her money-maker in danger."

Kate nodded and laughed. Alisha hadn't fooled Bill. It was early afternoon when they arrived at the downtown Days Inn. Kate parked the Acura at the entrance and Bill got out to secure their reservations. She sat in the car's cool air conditioning waiting on Bill, and decided she had a bright future after all.

Meet H. L. Chandler

This author writes in several genre, thrillers, paranormal, adventure, and mysteries. H. L. Chandler has also written stories for children. She has lived across the U.S. and for a short time in Canada.

Other Works From The Pen Of

H. L. Chandler

The Keepers - A story of a family torn apart by an insidious force intent on using each member for its own evil purpose.

Evil Intent - Gary married for money. When the money ran out, it was time to collect Janet's life insurance. Yet, *something* at the mountain cabin where Janet takes refuge has other plans.

Lost in Fear - In childhood, Julie Taylor survived a family massacre. As an educated young woman, she strives to live a normal life. She might succeed if it were not for the evil which plagues her.

Song of the Sparrow - Living with a cruel stepfather, Lugene and Harley grow up fast. But not fast enough to escape the dangers that face them as run-away teens in New Orleans.

Legion's Land - In a post holocaustic world Nora lived a comfortable life. She never questioned the system until it threatened her children. How far will she go to save them?

Hoodoo Murder - A murder and kidnapping put Private Investigator Ladonna Rose in the middle of a case that merges with a tragedy from her past.

Mystery at Sunset Ridge - Is the missing real estate developer a murderer, or a victim? When P. I. Billie Ross gets too close to an answer, she disappears as well.

Murder Bayou - Was Ross Delroque worth more dead than alive? Or was he about to report a toxic waste dump? To arrive at the truth P.I. Ladonna Rose searches for answers among his sadly dysfunctional family.

Sure and Certain Shadows - Ingrid grew up on rough Kansas City streets, proud to have survived. Thrown into an alien world, she fights to stay alive and return to her own planet.

Rest Beyond the River - The story of Micah Hanson's personal tragedy played out against a great natural disaster in the center of the United States.

Letter to Our Readers

Enjoy this book?

You can make a difference

As an independent publisher, Wings ePress, Inc. does not have the financial clout of the large New York Publishers. We can't afford large magazine spreads or subway posters to tell people about our quality books.

But, we do have something much more effective and powerful than ads. We have a large base of loyal readers.

Honest Reviews help bring the attention of new readers to our books.

If you enjoyed this book, we would appreciate it if you would spend a few minutes posting a review on the site where you purchased this book or on the Wings ePress, Inc. webpages at: https://wingsepress.com/

www.ingramcontent.com/pod-product-compliance
Lightning Source LLC
Chambersburg PA
CBHW070627100726
47907CB00007B/1882